Time Goes By

By Margaret Thornton

a&b

Time Goes By

MARGARET THORNTON

First published in Great Britain in 2011 by
Allison & Busby Limited
13 Charlotte Mews
London W1T 4EJ
www.allisonandbusby.com

A CIP catalogue record for this book is available from
the British Library.

10 9 8 7 6 5 4 3 2 1

13-ISBN 978-0-7490-0904-5

Typeset in 13/16 pt Adobe Garamond Pro by
Allison & Busby Ltd.

Paper used in this publication is from sustainably managed sources.
All of the wood used is procured from legal sources and is fully traceable.
The producing mill uses schemes such as ISO 14001
to monitor environmental impact.

Printed and bound in the UK by
CPI Mackays, Chatham ME5 8TD

*This book is dedicated to 'sand grown 'uns' everywhere;
those of us who feel proud to have been born
in the amazing town of Blackpool.*

*And with love to my husband, John, and my thanks
for his ongoing support and encouragement.*

PART ONE

Chapter One

1950

'Please, Miss Roberts . . . what shall I do? I haven't got a mummy, you see.'

Katherine Leigh raised her hand a little timidly as she spoke to her teacher. She felt her cheeks turning a little pink as sometimes happened when she had to explain that she didn't have a mother as had the other children in the class.

It had been all right at Christmas. When they had made cards to take home she had written her card 'To Daddy and Aunty Win'. But it was different now because they were making cards for Mother's Day. She felt sure, though, that Miss Roberts would help her to solve her little problem. She was a lovely teacher and Kathy liked her very much.

Sally Roberts smiled understandingly at the little girl. 'Well, Katherine, dear . . . maybe you could make a card for your aunt instead. Aunty Win, isn't it? Or for your grandma, perhaps?'

Katherine Leigh nodded, a little uncertainly, then she smiled back at her teacher. 'Yes, for Aunty Win, I think. She'll like that. But then . . . I can't write "Happy Mother's Day", can I?'

'Oh, I don't see why not,' said Miss Roberts, 'because that's what it will be on Sunday – Mothering Sunday, although everyone seems to call it Mother's Day now. And you can write "To Aunty Win", inside the card, "With love from Katherine", or "Kathy", if you like.'

'All right, then,' said Katherine.

Poor little mite, thought Sally Roberts, as she went round the tables of her 'top class' infants, giving out the paper required for the making of the Mother's Day cards. She had grown very fond of little Katherine Leigh, who had been in her class since last September. How awful it must be for her not to have a mummy, like all the other boys and girls in the class. Sally knew that Katherine's mother had died when she was a baby, only two years of age, so the little girl had no recollection of her at all. She was well looked after, though, by her father, and his sister whom she called Aunty Win, and Sally felt that she was well loved too.

She was always smartly dressed in a gymslip with a hand-knitted jumper beneath it, or a regulation white blouse in summer. School uniform was not compulsory, although most parents made an effort to conform.

Even in 1950, five years after the war had ended, there were restrictions, and many things were still in short supply. But Mr Leigh and his sister clearly did their very best for the child. Her dark curly hair was always well groomed and shining, tied back from her face in two bunches with red ribbons. Her father and aunt always came along on open evenings and other school functions and were pleased to hear of her good progress. They were, however, quite middle-aged; not old, of course, by any means, but considerably older than the parents of most of the other children, and Sally was sure that Katherine must notice the difference. She guessed that Mr Leigh would be in his late forties, and his sister maybe a few years older.

Katherine was not an outgoing child, but she seemed happy enough and got on well with the other children, especially with her best friend, Shirley, who sat next to her at the table.

There were nine tables in the large classroom, around each of which were four child-sized chairs. A class of thirty-six children – aged six to seven – was really more than enough for any teacher to cope with, but it was the norm in those post-war days, as it had been for many years before. There had been a 'baby boom', with more children than ever being born as a result of fathers returning home from the war, and so classes were expected to become even larger in the next few years. Unless, of course, many more schools were built by the Labour government, elected in 1945 and still holding on to power.

'Now, boys and girls, listen carefully,' said Miss Roberts. 'The first thing we are going to do is write at the top of the card . . .' She wrote on the blackboard, in clear printing, 'Happy Mother's Day'. 'Now, pick up your pencils and copy this. Best writing, mind, because it will be going home . . . No, Graham, don't turn the paper over, or the writing will be on the back, won't it?' There was always one, she reflected.

The children were then instructed to make up their own design of a bowl with flowers in it. In the centre of each table was a selection of gummed paper in bright colours: green, blue, red, yellow, orange, pink and purple; four pairs of scissors with rounded ends; and cardboard templates of bowl shapes, leaf shapes, and various types of flowers – daffodils, tulips and daisy shapes.

It was, in that year of 1950, the beginning of the heyday of 'free activity' in the classroom, when infants, for certain times in each day at least, were free to express themselves in all sorts of ways. Painting easels with jars of brightly coloured poster paints; tables with crayons and drawing paper, plasticine, jigsaws, and creative games; building bricks; a sand tray and a water trough; and a fully equipped Wendy house with a dressing-up box; these were to be found in most infant classrooms. And what chaos was left for the teacher, single-handedly, to clear away after each session! The children, of course, were supposed to do it themselves, but it was more often a case of 'if you want a job doing, do it yourself!'

Sometimes, though, handwork had to be partially directed, and that was the case when cards – for Christmas, Easter, or other festivities – were being made. The children's efforts would vary, helped in some instances by the intervention of the teacher, but parents would be delighted at the finished masterpieces, however messy they might turn out to be.

'Why haven't you got a mum, then?' asked Timothy Fielding, one of the boys who was sitting opposite Katherine.

'Because I haven't, that's why!' she retorted.

'Why? What's happened to her? Has she run away and left you?' he persisted.

'That's quite enough, Timothy,' said Miss Roberts who was passing near to their table. 'Leave Katherine alone, please.'

'Well, that's what my mum says when I don't behave myself,' retorted the irrepressible Timothy. 'She says she'll go away and leave me.'

'I don't suppose for one moment that she really means it,' replied Miss Roberts. 'Now, get on with what you're supposed to be doing, and stop pestering Katherine.' She reflected that some parents did not show a great deal of sense in some of the things they said to their children. Although it was doubtful that Timothy believed his mother either; no doubt it was an idle threat not meant to be taken seriously. Timothy Fielding could certainly be a pest; most likely he drove his mother to distraction sometimes, as he did with Sally if she didn't sit on him hard when he became too troublesome.

'As a matter of fact . . .' Shirley Morris was saying, with a toss of her flaxen plaits as Sally moved away, 'Kathy's mummy died when she was a baby. Didn't she, Kathy? Not that it's any of your business, Timothy Fielding.'

'Yes, she did,' said Kathy, in quite a matter-of-fact manner. 'But I've got a dad, and a very nice aunty who looks after me. Aunty Win; that's who I'm making the card for.'

She didn't feel particularly upset; it was certainly nothing to cry about. She had never known her mother; only sometimes, now and again, in the dim recesses of her memory, she seemed to recall a pretty lady with dark hair and a smiling face holding her in her arms. But she could not be sure whether it was a true recollection or something

13

she was imagining. Only occasionally did she feel the lack of a mother in her life. Times such as now, when they were all making cards for Mummy, or when she was invited to tea at Shirley's house and she realised what a difference it must make to have a mother in the home.

'OK, then,' said Timothy with a shrug of his shoulders, seeming for a brief moment to be a little subdued. But he soon bounced back. 'My mum's all right, I suppose. I'm glad she's there, anyway; I wouldn't want her to be dead. But she isn't half bad-tempered sometimes, much worse than me dad. You should hear her shout!'

'I'm not surprised, with you to put up with!' laughed Stanley, the boy who was sitting next to him, giving him a dig in the ribs.

'Shurrup you!' countered Timothy, shoving him back. A scrap seemed likely to break out until Miss Roberts clapped her hands and demanded silence – or comparative silence, which was all she could hope to get from thirty-six infants – with a threat that those who couldn't behave would have to stay in at playtime.

Peace reigned as they all settled down to creating their cards. Katherine chose blue for the bowl. She painstakingly drew round the template, then cut out the shape, licked the back of the gummed paper and stuck it to the bottom of the card. Then she cut out some yellow daffodils, red tulips and white daisies, and green leaves, and arranged them as though they were growing out of the bowl. Then she coloured in the stalks and the centres of the daisies with wax crayons. Each child had a box of these in their drawer beneath the table. Katherine's were still in quite a good condition as she was a methodical little girl and she always returned them carefully to the container after they had been used. Timothy's, though, were broken and several of the colours were missing.

'Kathy, give us a lend of your green,' he said. 'I've only got this titchy bit left.'

'That's your own fault, then,' Shirley told him. 'Why should she? I know I wouldn't.'

But Kathy uncomplainingly handed over her green crayon. She was amused to see Timothy stick his tongue out at Shirley.

'Well, I wasn't asking you, was I, clever clogs!' he jeered.

Kathy quite liked Timothy really. He could be a bit of a pest, but she knew there was 'no real badness' in him, as her Aunty Win might say. He brightened up the day sometimes and made her laugh, recounting the jokes that his dad had told him. His shock of fairish hair stood up on end like 'Just William's'; in fact, he resembled her favourite fictional character in quite a few ways.

'Ta, Kathy,' he said. 'I've gone and put too much spit on me bowl an' all, an' it won't stick.' He banged his fist on the table, but the red bowl refused to stay put. 'Oh crikey! What shall I do?'

'Cut another one out,' said Kathy. 'Miss Roberts won't mind. I don't suppose you're the only one who's made a mess of it. You have to lick it carefully, you see. Look, I'll stick it on for you when you've cut it out.'

'Gosh! Thanks, Kathy,' he said. 'I'll give you one of my sherbet lemons at playtime.'

Shirley tossed her plaits and looked disdainfully at

Timothy. 'I don't know why you bother with him,' she said. ''Specially when he's been so rude to you.'

'He didn't mean to be,' said Kathy. 'He didn't know, you see . . . about my mother.'

She was pleased with the completed card and so was Miss Roberts. Her teacher told her it was very artistic and that her aunt would like it very much. Kathy wrote on the inside, 'To Aunty Win with love from Kathy'. Then she put it away in her satchel to take home at the end of the afternoon.

Sure enough Timothy was there at playtime, true to his promise. He handed out a cone-shaped paper bag of sherbet lemons. 'Here y'are, Kathy,' he said.

'Ooh, thanks!' she said, popping a bright-yellow sweet into her mouth. 'They're my favourites, them and pear drops.'

'Ta very much for helping me with my card,' he said. 'It looks OK now but it's not as nice as yours. Me dad says I'm all fingers and thumbs when I try to help him, when he's putting up a shelf, like, an' all that.'

'Never mind; it's the thought that counts,' Kathy told him, something that Aunty Win often said. 'And your mum'll like it, won't she?'

''Spect so,' said Timothy. 'I'm gonna buy her a Mars bar an' all. She likes them best.' As an afterthought he held out the bag of sweets to Shirley who was standing at Kathy's side, looking a little disdainful. 'D'you want one, Shirley?' he said.

'No, ta,' said Shirley, although Kathy suspected that she would like one really. She thought it was very generous of Tim to offer her one. Shirley cast him a scornful look as she skipped away.

'Please yerself, then,' said Timothy to her retreating back. 'See if I care! . . . I've got a joke for you, Kathy,' he went on. 'It's a good one; me dad told it me.'

'Go on, then,' she encouraged him.

'What d'you get if you cross a kangaroo with a sheep?' he asked, his grey eyes full of merriment.

Kathy frowned a little, then shook her head. 'I don't know,' she replied. 'What do you get?'

'A wooly jumper!' he cried, falling about laughing. 'D'you get it? You get wool from a sheep, and a kangaroo—'

'A kangaroo jumps – yes I know,' she said. 'You don't need to explain. I get it . . .' Although she was not sure that she did, not entirely, not the bit about crossing the animals. 'It's very funny,' she told him. 'I'll tell it to my Aunty Win.' Perhaps her aunt would be able to explain it.

She glanced across the playground to where Shirley was talking to another friend, Maureen, and at the same time looking a little crossly at Kathy. 'I'd better go and see what's up with Shirley,' she said.

'She doesn't like you talking to me,' said Timothy, 'but I don't care what she thinks. Ta-ra, Kathy . . .' He dashed off to kick a football around with Stanley and some of his other mates.

Shirley was indignant. 'I've told you before, I don't know why you bother with him,' she said to her friend. 'You'd better watch out or else they'll all be shouting out, "Kathy Leigh loves Timothy Fielding!".'

'Don't be so stupid!' retorted Kathy, feeling herself go a little pink. 'He's all right, though, is Tim. Anyway, we're not going to fall out over a silly boy, are we? Here – you can have a lend of my skipping rope. I tell you what; Maureen and me can turn up, and you can be first in if you like, Shirley.'

'All right, then,' said Shirley, somewhat mollified. So whilst the other two girls turned the rope she jumped up and down. They all shouted in chorus, 'Jelly on a plate, jelly on a plate, wibble wobble, wibble wobble, jelly on a plate . . .' taking it in turns to be 'in' until the whistle was blown for the end of playtime. By the end of the afternoon Kathy and Shirley were the best of friends again.

'My mum says you can come to tea on Monday, if you like,' Shirley told her friend. 'And me dad'll see you home afterwards.'

'Gosh, thanks!' said Kathy. 'I'll ask my Aunty Win as soon as I get home.'

Chapter Two

Home for Katherine was a boarding house in the area of Blackpool known as North Shore, not too far from the sea, quite close to the north railway station, and about five minutes' walk from the town centre.

The name of the house was Holmleigh. Her father and Aunty Win liked to describe it as a 'private hotel' rather than a boarding house. There was, in point of fact, very little difference between the two, excepting, perhaps, that the small hotels had names and the boarding houses didn't. Aunty Win had told her that 'Holmleigh' was really just a posh way of spelling the word 'homely'. That was what they hoped their hotel was, a home from home, and it also made quite a clever use of their surname.

Her father, Albert, and his sister, Winifred, ran the hotel between them. Kathy knew that it had been started in the beginning by her grandparents, way back in the early years of the century, which seemed to her to be ages ago. Grandma and Grandad Leigh – Alice and William – who were now well into their seventies, had retired a few years ago, at the end of the war in 1945, and now lived in a little bungalow in Bispham. That was when Albert and Winifred had taken over the responsibility of the boarding house and had given it a name.

Kathy knew that her father was a very good cook – he called himself a chef – and he did most of the cooking when there were visitors staying there. Aunty Win looked after everything else: all the office work and bookkeeping and the organisation of the domestic help. They employed waitresses and chambermaids when it was their busiest time, usually from the middle of May to the end of the 'Illuminations' season – commonly known as the 'Lights' – at the end of October. For the rest of the year they took occasional visitors, usually to oblige their 'regulars', and during the slack period they took the opportunity to catch up with any decorating or odd jobs that needed to be done.

When Kathy arrived home on that Friday afternoon in mid March her father was up a ladder papering the walls of one of the guest bedrooms, whilst her aunt was busy at a trestle table in the centre of the room putting paste onto the next length of paper.

'Hello, dear,' said her aunt when the little girl's head appeared round the door. 'Have you had a nice day at school?' That was what she always asked, and as usual Kathy replied that yes, she had. She had never minded going to school, but it had been especially nice since she had been in Miss Roberts' class.

'Goodness, is it that time already?' said her father. 'I think it's time for a cup of tea, Winnie. You go and put the kettle on, eh? Hello, Kathy love. Go and help your Aunty Win, there's a good girl.'

Her dad was always saying that, and Kathy actually quite enjoyed helping out in the boarding house. When she was a tiny girl, before she started school, she had loved going round with her Aunty Nellie – not a real aunt, just a friend of Aunty Win – who came in once a week to 'do' the bedrooms. There were fifteen bedrooms on three floors, including two attic bedrooms. Kathy used to accompany her aunt with her own little dustpan and brush, and a duster, to help with the dusting and polishing. Aunty Nellie sometimes let her put a tiny amount of polish onto the surface of a dressing table, and then rub hard to make it all shiny and gleaming.

She helped Aunty Win, too, in the kitchen when she was making pies or fruit tarts. She had her own pastry cutters and rolling pin and could already make jam tarts that they were able to eat. She did not help very much, though, when her father was in charge of the kitchen; he was not quite as patient as her aunt. She realised, though, that at the moment she was only playing at helping. But Kathy also understood, with all the wisdom of her six – nearly seven – years, that this would eventually be her job of work. When the time came for her to leave school – a long time in the future – she knew that she would be expected to work in the family boarding house, or whatever they wanted to call it, just as Aunty Win and her father had taken over from her grandparents.

'I'm coming, Aunty Win,' she called. 'I'm just taking my coat off, and I've got something to put away in my drawer. It's a secret, you see.'

On the way home from school she had called in at the local newsagent's shop and bought a small box of Milk Tray for Aunty Win for Mother's Day. She had been saving up from her spending money each week until she had enough. She put the purple box and the card in her drawer underneath her knickers, vests and socks, then went down to the kitchen to join her aunt.

'So what have you been doing at school this afternoon?' Winifred asked her niece. 'You don't do much work on Friday afternoon, do you?'

In Winifred's opinion they didn't do much work at all in the infant classrooms of today. It all seemed to be painting or playing in the house, or messing about with sand and water, from what Katherine told her aunt. Not like it was in her day. She had been born in 1900 and when she started school at four years of age Queen Victoria had been dead for three years. Her photograph had hung in the school hall for many years, so Winifred's parents had told her – they had both attended the same school – and then it had been replaced by one of Edward VII, her corpulent son. Winifred remembered his rather kindly face regarding them as they sang their morning hymns and recited their daily prayers.

She recalled, too, the rows of wooden desks where the children sat in formal rows – 'Straight backs, boys and girls, no slouching'; the chalk and slates on which to write the letters of the alphabet; the map of the world on the classroom wall, with a goodly part of it coloured in red, showing the parts that belonged to the British Empire. She remembered a strict male teacher, too, with a long swishing cane; not that it was often used. The children of yesteryear knew they had to behave themselves; one look was usually enough.

Times had changed, she pondered, and not always for the best, although Kathy seemed to be getting on well since she went into that nice Miss Roberts' class. There didn't seem to be as much messing about, and she could now read very nicely from her book that told of the exploits of Janet and John.

'No . . .' replied Kathy, in answer to her aunt's query. 'Miss Roberts usually lets us do a jigsaw or read a book on Friday afternoon, while she does her register for the week. She has a lot of adding up to do, she says. But today we were making cards for—' She suddenly stopped and put her hand to her mouth. 'Oh dear! It was meant to be a surprise. Pretend I didn't say that, will you, Aunty Win?'

'Of course, dear,' smiled Winifred. 'I didn't actually catch what you said anyway.'

The child had given the game away already, though, talking about hiding something in her drawer. Mother's Day, Winifred had thought to herself. That was one of the times when she felt most sorry for the little girl, not that Kathy ever seemed too worried about occasions such as those.

Winifred poured the tea into three mugs and added milk and sugar. 'Now, Kathy,' she said. 'Do you think you could manage to carry this mug upstairs to your daddy? Be careful, mind, but I've not filled it too full. And there's a custard cream biscuit for him. Pop it into your gymslip pocket, then you've got both hands free. Off you go now.'

Winifred loved the little girl more than she could say. She had tried to make it up to her for not having a mother, and she hoped and prayed that she had succeeded. She felt that she had, to a certain extent, although she realised it could never be quite the same. She had wondered if her brother might marry again, but he had been so distressed at losing his beloved Barbara that he had never, since that time, taken any interest at all in the opposite sex. He was a taciturn sort of man who did not show his feelings. Winifred was sure that he loved his little daughter very much, but he found it difficult to tell her so or even to show her much affection. Any cuddles and hugs, or comfort when she was upset, came from her aunt or grandparents. It was only natural that she should sometimes ask questions about her mother – all her schoolfriends had mothers – and she was always told that her mother had died when she was only a baby, but she must never forget that her mummy had loved her very much.

Albert never spoke of his wife. He had settled into a comfortable little rut. He worked his socks off in the hotel. He was a first-rate cook – or chef, as he liked to call himself – and there was nothing he would not tackle when there were any jobs to be done in the off season. His only means of recreation was to go to the pub two or three evenings a week – he was a member of the darts team – and he was also an ardent supporter of Blackpool's football team. He was there every Saturday during the winter months, in his orange and white scarf, taking his place on Spion Kop. But Winifred could not imagine him ever cheering and yelling encouragement – or even booing! – as many enthusiastic supporters did. She guessed he was as silent there as he was in other aspects of his life. Blackpool was a First Division club and boasted of their most famous player, Stanley Matthews. Albert looked forward to the day when they might – when they would, he was sure – win the FA cup. He filled in his football coupon regularly. Winifred was not sure how much he allowed himself to bet, but he had never, as yet, had a substantial win, only the odd pound or two. They had to be quiet every Saturday evening after the six o'clock news when the football results were read out and Albert checked his coupon.

Winifred was looking forward to the start of the holiday season in a few weeks' time. It would begin slowly, with visitors coming for the Easter weekend and the following week – they were already almost fully booked for that period – but then there would be a lull for several weeks until the Whitsuntide holiday. It was then that the season would start in earnest and would, hopefully, continue until almost the end of October.

Blackpool was beginning to make its name as the foremost resort in the north, maybe in the whole, of England. The town had gained more than it had lost during the Second World War. Many of its competitors on the south and east coasts had been forced to close down for the duration of the war because of the threat of invasion or bombing. Admittedly, the curtailing of the Illuminations in the September of 1939 had affected the income of the Blackpool boarding house keepers and hoteliers. However, following on from that, many of these people were able to make up for their losses by accommodating RAF personnel who were training in the town. Over three-quarters of a million RAF recruits passed through the town during the war. There were also the child evacuees at the start of the conflict, but they did not all stay for very long; in fact, by 1940 the majority of them had returned home.

Later in the war there were American GIs stationed at the nearby bases at Weeton and Warton, and the Blackpool entertainment industry enjoyed a prosperity they had not seen since the end of the First World War.

The war had not deterred holidaymakers from visiting the resort, in spite of the wartime propaganda posters asking 'Is Your Journey Really Necessary?' Many families obviously thought it was still essential to take a holiday, and Blackpool was a relatively safe place in which to stay. The Whitsuntide holidays had been abandoned in 1940 by government decree, but the annual wakes holidays of the textile towns in Lancashire and Yorkshire recommenced in July and from then on Blackpool had never looked back.

The advent of rationing, rather than being a hindrance, had been quite a boon for the hotel keepers, and more especially for the boarding house landladies. They took charge of the visitors' ration books, and this led to the change from the old system of lodging houses to that of full board. Winifred remembered only too well the old days, when visitors brought their own food, which was cooked for them by the boarding house staff. The visitors paid only for their lodgings and for services rendered, such as cooking, laundry, cleaning of shoes, and – in some lodging houses – the 'use of the cruet'.

The system of 'full board' which had begun during the war years was now the norm. It consisted of cooked breakfast, midday dinner, and a 'high tea'. In some residences, as at Holmleigh, supper was also served in the visitors' lounge from nine o'clock in the evening.

In the previous year, 1949, the return of the Illuminations had marked a turning point from post-war austerity. The years of darkness and depression were over, exemplified by the return of the 'Lights'. Blackpool had become the envy of many of its rivals. It was well and truly back in business, catering for a full cross section of the public, from the working classes to those who considered themselves to be the 'elite'.

The hotel had become – almost – Winifred's whole life, the focus of her existence and her ambition. She was proud of what they had achieved since the end of the war. They were coming to be known as one of the best of the small private hotels in Blackpool, with the same visitors returning year after year. She had never done any work outside of the boarding house. It had been taken for granted when she left school at the age of fourteen that she should work in the family business. That was in the year of 1914; the start of the Great War had coincided with the end of Winifred's schooling.

It had been the height of the holiday season in Blackpool, but the initial disruption – when visitors trying to return home found that the trains had been commandeered for the fighting forces – proved to be of short duration. By mid

August it was 'business as usual' in the resort. The holiday industry carried on and thrived throughout the First World War as, twenty years later, it was to do the same in the second conflict. It was an emotive issue, as to whether seaside holidays and leisure times, such as professional sport, should continue when the country was at war. The lists in the daily newspapers of deaths in action were becoming longer and more disturbing. But the 'powers that be' in Blackpool felt that it was good for morale that people should be encouraged to take holidays, as before. It was decided, however, that to continue with the Illuminations would be going too far, and so, despite their initial success, plans to make the Illuminations an annual event had to be cancelled, due to the outbreak of war.

And so the accommodation industry benefited, not only through the holidaymakers, but with the arrival of Belgian refugees, and then by the billeting of British troops. During the winter of 1914 to 1915 there were ten thousand servicemen billeted in the town, along with two thousand refugees.

The Leighs' boarding house played its part in accommodating both the troops and the refugees. Winifred was fascinated and, at first, a little shy of these men who teased her good-humouredly. But as the war went on – with, regrettably, the loss of many of the soldiers they had known – she began to grow in confidence.

It was not until 1917, though, when she was seventeen years old, that she fell in love for the first – and what she believed was to be the last – time. Arthur Makepeace was a Blackpool boy; he was, in fact, almost the 'boy next door', living only a few doors away from the Leigh family. He was three years older than Winifred and had joined up, as soon as he was old enough, in 1915. After a few outings together, when he came home on leave, they had realised that there was a good deal more than friendship between them. They had vowed that, after the war was over, they would get married. Despite their age neither of their families had raised any objections. Many young couples were 'plighting their troth' in those uncertain days.

Arthur was granted leave in the early summer of 1918, then he returned to the battlefields of France. It was universally believed that the war was in its last stages and the young couple were looking forward to the time when they would be together for always.

Then, in the August of that year came the news that Winifred, deep down, had always been dreading. Arthur had been killed in one of the last offensives on the Western Front. It was his parents, of course, who had received the dreaded telegram, and they wept along with the girl who was to have become one of their family.

It was said that time was a great healer, and gradually Winifred picked up the pieces of her life and carried on with her duties in the boarding house. Like thousands of women of her age she had never married, had never even fallen in love again. She had settled down to a life of compromise. But there were compensations to be found: in her local church where she was a keen worker, and in the dramatic society – also attached to the church – where it was discovered that she was, surprisingly, quite a talented actress. And, above all, in her love for her little motherless niece.

Winifred was now fifty years of age and, by and large, she felt that life had not treated her too badly. She had missed out on marriage, though, and children of her own. And she still wondered, despite her quiet contentment with her life, what it would be like to experience the fulfilment of a happy marriage.

Chapter Three

'That's lovely, dear, really beautiful,' said Winifred. She felt a tear come into her eye as Kathy proudly presented her, on Sunday morning, with the card she had made. 'I love the flowers, such pretty colours. And this is your best writing; I can see that you've tried very hard.'

'Miss Roberts said it had to be our very best, 'cause it was going home,' said Kathy. 'It says "Happy Mother's Day", and I know you're not really my mum, but I couldn't put "Happy Aunty's Day", could I? Because it isn't. And Miss Roberts said it would be alright . . . And I've got you these as well, Aunty Win.' She held out the small purple box she had been hiding behind her back.

'Chocolates as well! And Milk Tray – my very favourites!' exclaimed Winifred. She hugged the little girl and kissed her on the cheek. 'Well, aren't I lucky? That's very kind of you, Kathy.'

She didn't say, as she might have done, 'You shouldn't go spending your pocket money on me', because she knew that it must have given the child pleasure to do so. She, Winifred, had always encouraged her to be generous and thoughtful for others; and she knew that Albert, despite his gruff manner, tried to teach her not to be selfish.

'I shall enjoy these tonight while I'm listening to the *Sunday Half Hour* on the wireless,' said Winifred.

'All the class made a card,' Kathy told her. 'But Timothy Fielding made a bit of a mess of his. He licked his bowl too much and it wouldn't stick on, so I helped him to make another one.'

Winifred smiled. That boy's name often cropped up in Katherine's conversations. She gathered that he could be rather a pest in the classroom, but she suspected that Kathy had a soft spot for him.

'He told me a joke,' Kathy went on, 'but I didn't really understand it, Aunty Win, not all of it, though I told him I'd got it.' She told her aunt the joke about the kangaroo and the sheep and the wooly jumper, frowning a little as she did so. 'But a kangaroo and a sheep, they couldn't have a baby one, could they? I didn't know what he meant about crossing them, but I laughed because Tim expected me to.'

Winifred laughed too. 'It's just a joke, love,' she said. 'Quite a funny one actually.' Oh dear! she thought, knowing that it would be her job, when the time came, to explain to her niece about the 'facts of life'. And already, it seemed, she was beginning to question things. 'No; a kangaroo and a sheep wouldn't be able to . . . er . . . mate, to get together,' she began. 'It would have to be two kangaroos, a male and a female, or two sheep, a ram and a ewe, to . . . er . . . to make a baby kangaroo or a baby sheep. Just like you need a father and a mother, a man and a lady, to . . . er . . . produce a baby,' she added tentatively.

But Kathy's mind was already off onto another tack. 'Baby sheep are called lambs,' she said. 'Everybody knows that. But Miss Roberts told us that baby kangaroos are called joeys. That's funny, isn't it? There's a boy in our class called Joey, and everybody laughed when she said it. Did you know that, Aunty Win, that they're called joeys?'

'Yes, I believe so,' replied Winifred, relieved that the subject had been changed. 'Come along now; let's have our breakfast. Bacon and egg this morning because it's Sunday. I'll keep your dad's warm for him and fry him an egg when he comes down. He likes a bit of a lie-in on a Sunday, when he can.'

Albert was usually up with the lark, summer and winter alike. During the summer months, of course, there were the visitors' breakfasts to prepare for eight-thirty. And in the winter, too, he reckoned nothing to lying in bed when there were jobs to be done. On Sunday mornings, however – but only when there were no visitors in – he liked to take his ease for half an hour or so. Winifred took up the *Sunday Express*, if the newspaper boy had delivered it in time, and a cup of tea so that he could enjoy a little lie-in. It was something that the brother and sister had never been allowed to do as children, or even later when they had reached adulthood, and Winifred still did not think of ever allowing herself this little luxury.

Albert came downstairs just as Winifred and Kathy

were finishing their breakfasts. He was washed and dressed – neither had they been encouraged to lounge around in dressing gowns – but not yet shaved, as far as Winifred could tell. She jumped up from the table to make some fresh tea and fry an egg, whilst Albert helped himself to cornflakes.

'I had a lovely surprise this morning, Albert,' she said, after she had placed his cooked breakfast in front of him. 'Look what Kathy has given me.' She showed him the chocolates. 'And a lovely card too, see.'

'Very nice,' he replied. 'So what is this in aid of? I haven't gone and forgotten your birthday, have I?'

'Of course not; don't be silly,' said Winifred. 'You know very well it's not till next month.'

'No, Daddy; it's Mother's Day,' said Kathy. 'Look, it says so on the card. We made them at school, and because I haven't got a mum, Miss Roberts said I should make one for Aunty Win.'

Albert's face took on a morose look. He nodded soberly. 'Oh, well then . . . Yes, I see. But it's no more than you deserve, our Winnie.' Then, suddenly, he smiled at his little daughter and his face looked altogether different. His blue eyes, still as bright as they had been when he was a lad, glowed with a warmth that wasn't often to be seen there. Really, he was quite a good-looking fellow when he smiled, Winifred thought to herself. It was a pity he didn't do it more often.

'That was a very nice thought, Kathy love,' he said. 'Yes, your Aunty Win has been very good to you, and you must never forget it.'

'I won't, Daddy,' replied the little girl.

'Now, when you've finished, Kathy, you'd better go and get ready,' her aunt told her.

'Why? Are you two off somewhere, then?' asked Albert.

'To church,' Winifred told him, although he must have known very well where they were going. 'It's a special service today, with it being Mothering Sunday.'

'Oh, I see,' he replied, looking morose again.

'I'll wash up before we go,' Winifred told him, 'and I'll put the meat in the oven – I've got a shoulder of lamb for today – so you can see to it for me, if you will, please?'

'Don't I always?' he replied a little gruffly. 'I'll do the veg an' all, and knock up a pudding, no trouble. You go off and enjoy yourselves.'

There was a hint of sarcasm in his words, as Winifred knew very well. Albert didn't go to church anymore, so she knew it was no use asking him, not even for special occasions now. He had never entered a church since he had lost Barbara. He didn't understand, he said, how God could have been so cruel to him; in fact, he professed not to believe in him anymore.

Albert and Winifred had been brought up to go to Sunday school and church, as was the norm in those early days of the century. And the tradition was still continuing now, in the early 1950s, Winifred was pleased to see, though not to such a large extent. Winifred and Albert had both been confirmed at their local parish church, Albert and Barbara had been married there and Katherine christened. She, Winifred, still attended the morning service each Sunday, when there were no visitors in the hotel. During the holiday season, of course, it was more difficult and she was not able to attend regularly, but she felt sure that God would understand.

Kathy did not often go on a Sunday morning – she attended Sunday school, which was held for an hour in the afternoon – but today was a special occasion and she was accompanying her aunt there for the Mothering Sunday service. Winifred put on her best coat, made of fine tweed in a moss-green colour, with a fitted bodice and a shawl collar. It was mid-calf length, the style owing a lot to the 'New Look' brought in by Christian Dior a few years previously. She had bought it two years ago at Sally Mae's dress shop. With the matching neat little turban hat and her black patent leather court shoes – the heels a little higher than she normally wore – she felt quite pleased with her appearance. She liked to look nice, although she didn't overdo it; vanity was one of the seven deadly sins, wasn't it? But the weekly visit to church was one occasion on which she dressed up a little more than usual.

'You look nice, Aunty Win,' Kathy told her, and she felt pleased at the compliment.

'Thank you, dear,' she said. 'We must look our best to go to church, mustn't we?' There was no one else to dress up for, she pondered, a little wryly, so she might as well dress up for God; although she was sure he would not care one way or the other. Winifred had kept her slim figure and so the new fitted fashions suited her very well.

'And I like your little hat,' Kathy told her. It was a new one, from the stall in Abingdon Street Market. 'The green matches your eyes, Aunty Win.'

What an observant child, she thought. 'Yes, I suppose

it does,' she agreed, although she considered her eyes to be more hazel than green.

Just a little of her mid-brown hair showed below her close-fitting hat. She wore her hair in a short style which was easy to manage, as she had done for years. She had not, as yet, found any grey hairs, which she thought was quite surprising. Just the slightest dusting of face powder and a smear of coral-pink lipstick added the final touch to her Sunday appearance.

'And you look very smart too,' Winifred told her niece.

Kathy's coat was quite a new one, bought just before Christmas from the Co-op Emporium on Coronation Street. Both Winifred and her mother were keen supporters of the local 'Co-ops'. The 'divi' – the dividend awarded to each shopper on every purchase – came in very useful when it was collected each year, just before Christmas. The little girl had gone with her aunt to choose the coat. It was cherry red with a little black velvet collar, and complemented her dark hair and brown eyes. Her aunt had knitted her Fair Isle beret, fawn, with a pattern of red, green and black. A complicated knitting pattern, but Winifred had been determined to master it. Those woollen hats were quite the fashion amongst the younger girls and she liked Kathy to have whatever her school friends had. She had been delighted when she had received it on Christmas morning as an extra little present. Her black fur-backed gloves had been a Christmas present too, and her patent leather ankle-strap shoes that she wore with white knee socks.

'Now, are we ready? You've got a clean hanky in your coat pocket? Righty-ho then, let's go. We don't want to be late . . . Bye then, Albert,' said Winifred. 'We're going now.'

'Bye-bye, Daddy,' echoed Kathy.

Albert was ensconced in his favourite fireside chair in the family living room at the back of the hotel. He was puffing away at his pipe, engrossed in the sports pages, and he grunted from behind the newspaper. 'Hmm . . . See you later, then. Have a nice time . . .'

It was only five minutes' walk to the parish church, which had been built in the early years of Victoria's reign; greyish-yellow sandstone with a square tower and a clock which now stood at twenty minutes past ten. The organ was playing quietly as they entered and took their places in a pew a few rows from the front. Kathy's friend, Shirley, was in a pew on the opposite side of the aisle with her mother, but not her father, Kathy noticed. The two friends grinned and waved to one another.

At ten-thirty precisely the organist struck up with the opening bars of the first hymn, and the choir processed from the little room called the vestry to the back of the church, and then down the central aisle to the choir stalls. They were led by a man carrying a sort of pole – it was called a staff, said Aunty Win, and he was the churchwarden – and the vicar in his white gown and a black stole edged with green. In the choir were men, women, and boys and girls as well. The boys and girls were a few years older than Kathy. She recognised some of them from the junior school, especially Graham, Shirley's brother, who was ten years old and had joined the choir quite recently. He did not even glance in his sister's direction as they passed by, but kept his eyes glued to the hymn book. No doubt they had been warned not to wave or grin. Kathy reflected that he probably felt a bit of a fool with that ruffle round his neck.

The men and the boys all wore white gowns – called surplices – but it was just the boys who had the ruffled collars. The ladies and the girls wore blue sort of cloak things, and the grown-up ladies had squarish hats on their heads. Kathy liked singing and she hoped that she might be able to join the choir when she was old enough. 'Awake, my soul, and with the sun, Thy daily stage of duty run . . .' sang the choir and the congregation. Kathy tried to join in as well as she could. She could read quite well now and she soon picked up the tune, although she didn't understand all the words. 'Shake off dull sloth and joyful rise, To pay thy morning sacrifice.' What was dull sloth, she wondered? She must remember to ask Aunty Win afterwards.

It was quite a short service, really, although there seemed to be a lot of standing up and sitting down again. Prayers, with the choir singing the amens; a reading from the Bible about Jesus and the little children; another hymn; then some more prayers . . . Kathy's thoughts began to wander a little. She was fascinated by the windows of coloured glass; stained glass, Aunty Win had told her. The morning sunlight was shining through the one nearest to her, making little pools of red, blue, green and yellow on the stone floor. The picture on the window was of Jesus standing up in a boat, talking to some of his disciples: Peter, James and John, she guessed – they were the fishermen. And behind him the Sea of Galilee was as blue as blue could be . . .

Aunty Win nudged her as they all stood up for the next

hymn. It was 'Loving Shepherd of Thy Sheep', and Kathy was able to sing it all as they had learnt that one at school. Then the vicar gave a little talk about families and the love that was to be found there. But he didn't just talk about mothers; he mentioned fathers, sisters and brothers, and aunts and uncles as well. Kathy was glad about that, especially the bit about aunties.

Then the children were invited to go to the front of the church where ladies were handing out bunches of daffodils from big baskets. The children took them and gave them to all the ladies in the congregation, not just the mothers but the aunties and grandmas as well, and some ladies who might not even have been married. They all received a bunch of bright-yellow daffodils. *'Here, Lord, we offer thee all that is fairest, Flowers in their freshness from garden and field . . .'* they all sang, and the organist carried on playing until all the flowers had been presented.

'What a lovely idea,' said Aunty Win, and Kathy thought she could see a tear in the corner of her eye, although she looked very happy.

Shirley dashed across at the end of the service. 'Hello, Kathy . . . Have you asked your aunty if you can come for tea tomorrow?'

'Yes, she has asked me,' said Aunty Win, 'and of course she can go . . . It's very kind of you,' she said to Mrs Morris, Shirley's mother. 'Thank you very much.'

'It's no trouble,' said Mrs Morris. 'We love having Kathy, and my husband will bring her home afterwards.'

They said goodbye and Kathy and her aunt walked home, leaving Mrs Morris and Shirley to wait for Graham.

'It's going to be a busy week, Kathy,' Aunty Win told her. 'You're out for tea tomorrow; it's Brownies on Tuesday; and on Wednesday the drama group is meeting to cast the new play.'

'Are you going to have a big part, Aunty Win?' asked Kathy. She had gone to see the last one with her daddy. Aunty Win had taken the part of the mother and had had a lot of words to remember. Kathy hadn't understood it all, but she knew that her aunt had done it very well.

'I'm not sure,' smiled her aunt. 'I'll just have to wait and see. There are a lot more ladies as well as me.'

'But they're not as good,' said Kathy, loyally.

Aunty Win laughed. 'And then on Thursday it's your open evening at school, isn't it, dear? Your dad and I will be going to see Miss Roberts and find out how you're getting on.'

'Yes, we've been doing all sorts of special things to make a nice display on the walls,' said Kathy.

'Yes, I shall look forward to seeing that. All in all, a very busy week ahead,' said Aunty Win.

Chapter Four

Kathy loved going to tea at Shirley's home. It was a small house, nowhere near as big as the hotel where she lived. It was only a few minutes' walk from Holmleigh in a street of what Shirley told her were called semi-detached houses; that meant that their house was joined on to the one next door.

There was a small garden at the front with a tiny rectangle of grass and flowers growing round it. The garden at the back was not much bigger, but Kathy thought it must be lovely to have a garden at all. At Holmleigh there was just a paved area at the front and a form where the visitors could sit. And at the back it was just a yard with a coal shed, a wash house and an outside lavatory. But they did have three toilets inside the house as well, which were necessary for the visitors.

There was a small bathroom upstairs at Shirley's, and three bedrooms. One of them was very tiny and that was where Shirley's brother, Graham, slept. Shirley said he grumbled because she had a bigger bedroom, but that was because she had to share with her little sister, Brenda, who was three years old. And Mr and Mrs Morris slept in the other one.

Kathy had slept in lots of different bedrooms at her home, depending on whether or not there were visitors staying there. During the winter she had quite a nice-sized bedroom on the first landing, but she liked it best in the summer when she sometimes slept in one of the attic bedrooms. The ceiling sloped right down to the floor at the front and you had to kneel down to look out of the window. It was a lovely view, though, right across everybody else's rooftops. She could see Blackpool Tower, and the tiniest glimpse of the sea, sparkling blue if the sun was shining or a dingy grey if it wasn't.

They had a bathroom now at Holmleigh, but it had only been built last year, onto the kitchen at the back of the house. It was just for the use of the family, but there were washbasins in all the visitors' bedrooms. Aunty Win had told her that those had only been put in a few years ago. Until then the visitors had used big bowls and jugs that her aunt had filled with hot water every morning. There was still a bowl and jug in the attic room that Kathy used in the summer, very pretty ones with pink roses all over. And there was a chamber pot to match as well that went under the bed. Aunty Win called it a 'gazunder'. It was just there for emergencies because there was no toilet up in the attic.

Kathy remembered that until last year, when the bathroom was put in, she used to have her weekly bath – on a Friday

43

night – in a huge zinc bath in front of the fire. The rest of the time the bath had hung on a hook in the wash house. Kathy supposed that her dad and her aunt had used it too, perhaps, on different nights. She still had her bath on a Friday night. The new bath was gleaming white and shiny, but the bathroom was sometimes cold, and she missed the comfort of the fire and the big fluffy bath towel warming on the fireguard.

Shirley's mum made the two girls a drink of orange juice when they arrived home from school on that Monday afternoon, then they played with Shirley's doll's house, which stood in a corner of the living room. They liked rearranging the furniture and putting the tiny dolls on chairs so that they could have a meal. Kathy had a doll's house too. It had been her big Christmas present a few months ago. But this one of Shirley's was a bit different, a more old-fashioned sort of house; Shirley's mum said it was an Edwardian house, whatever that was. It was actually a bit bigger than Kathy's, but not nearly as posh; in fact it was a little bit shabby but Kathy wouldn't dream of saying so. She guessed it might have belonged to Shirley's mum before it was given to Shirley.

'I've called the girl Janet and the boy John, like those children in the reading books,' said Shirley.

'That's nice,' said Kathy. She didn't tell Shirley that she had christened her doll's house children Tim, after her friend, and Tina, because it sounded good with Tim. Shirley would only laugh and tease her about Timothy Fielding and say he was her boyfriend.

'They've had their tea now. Let's put them to bed,' said

44

Shirley, rather bossily. 'Look, they've got a bedroom each, 'cause there's a lot of bedrooms upstairs. Mummy says they used to have a lot of children in Edwardian times, and that's when this house was made.'

Shirley liked to show off sometimes about all the things she knew. She was, actually, one of the cleverest girls in the class and usually came top in the spelling tests, and mental arithmetic – that was when you had to work out sums in your head. Shirley was in the top reading group too, and she, Kathy, was in the second one. Shirley was a bit of a 'clever clogs' – that was what Tim called her – but she was still Kathy's best friend for all that. Kathy knew she was not quite as clever as Shirley, but it didn't worry her. She knew that she always tried her best, and Aunty Win said that that was the most important thing.

'Look, there's a baby in the cradle too,' said Shirley. 'Wrapped in swaddling clothes, like Jesus was. But I'm pretending it's a girl baby. I've called her Jemima, 'cause it goes with Janet and John.'

'Can I play?' shouted Brenda from across the room. She had been playing on the floor, building towers of wooden blocks, but that, suddenly, was getting boring. What the older girls were doing looked much more interesting. She knocked over the pile of bricks and trotted across the room. 'Can I put the baby to bed, Shirley?' she asked.

'No, you can't! She's already in her bed.' Shirley gave her a push, not a hard one, but one that showed she was annoyed with her little sister. 'Go away, Brenda. You're a nuisance! Mummy says you haven't to play with my house. You're only a baby and you'll mess it up.'

Brenda's face crumpled and she looked as though she was going to cry. 'Not a baby!' she protested. 'I only want to help.'

'Oh, go on, let her,' said Kathy. She felt sorry for the little girl. She was such a sweet little thing, with wispy blonde hair the same colour as Shirley's plaits, and big blue eyes that were filling up with tears. 'She can't mess it up if we're here, can she?' Kathy thought how nice it would be to have a little sister like Brenda. Probably she could be a pest at times, but Kathy knew she would love her very much if she were her sister. And she was sure that Shirley did love her, really.

'Oh, all right, then,' said Shirley. 'Stop crying, Brenda. Don't be such a baby! Here, you can hold Jemima.'

That pacified the little girl and they all played happily together, until the next interruption. That was when Graham came into the room followed rapidly by his mother.

'Graham, how many times have I told you to take off your football boots before you come in the house. Just look at the state of you! Now there's mud all over the carpet! Go and get them off at once, and put your football things in the washing basket. Honestly! Whatever am I going to do with you?'

'OK, Mum,' said Graham, quite casually. 'It's only dried mud; it'll brush off. Keep your hair on!'

'And don't be cheeky,' said Mrs Morris, although she was smiling and so was Graham.

'He's a pest,' observed Shirley when he had left the room. 'Mum's always telling him about his football boots and stuff . . . But it goes in one ear and out of the other,' she added, in an old-fashioned way. 'I bet you're glad you've not got a big brother, Kathy. He drives me potty!'

Kathy didn't answer that remark. She was thinking it would be rather nice to have an older brother, just as she had thought, earlier, that she would like to have a little sister, or even a big sister.

Graham came back into the room a few minutes later and flopped into a chair with his *Dandy* comic.

'D'you want to come and play with us, Graham?' invited Brenda. 'I 'spect Shirley'll let you.' But her remark was greeted with scorn.

'Huh! Girls' stuff!' he sneered. 'No thanks! Anyway, shouldn't you be helping Mum to set the table, Shirl?' It was her job, sometimes, to put the cloth on the table and set out the cups and saucers.

'Why should I?' Shirley retorted. 'Why should it always be me? Why can't you do it?'

'Because I'm a boy, that's why,' replied her brother. 'It's women's work, cooking an' cleaning an' washing up an' all that stuff. That's what Dad says. And it's girls that have to help.'

Kathy gathered that Graham didn't reckon much to girls. He hadn't even said hello to her, although he knew she was there. Aunty Win said he was a lovely boy and so nice-looking too. But she had only seen him on a Sunday, dressed in his choir clothes and looking angelic. She didn't know what he was like the rest of the time. Kathy realised, though, that he might be considered handsome, like princes always were in fairy tales. He was dark-haired, not fair like his sisters, and he had brown eyes with a roguish gleam. Like his dad, Kathy realised later when Mr Morris came in from work.

She had seen Shirley's dad before, but at the other times when she had been there for tea, the children and Mrs Morris had had their tea first – a sandwich tea followed by home-made cakes – whilst Mr Morris had had a cooked meal prepared specially for him. Today, though, they all sat down together to a meal of sausages and chips with baked beans. Kathy thought it was delicious. They didn't often have sausages and baked beans at home. Her father, and her aunt as well, were used to cooking rather different meals for the visitors, such as roast meat and two veg, and sausages were usually cooked as 'toad-in-the-hole' which she didn't like very much. Baked beans, too, were frowned upon, except occasionally in an emergency, as Kathy's dad reckoned nothing to 'eating out of tins'. And there was HP sauce, as well. She noticed that Shirley and Graham and Mr Morris put on great dollops of it. Kathy loved it, but was not often allowed it, although it was always put on the visitors' tables for them to have with their bacon and eggs.

'Nice to have you with us, Kathy,' said Mr Morris, giving her a friendly wink which made her feel shy. She smiled back, feeling her cheeks turning pink. 'Special tea an' all because you're here,' he went on. 'Don't tell anyone, but we usually have bread and dripping.'

Kathy knew that was not true and she laughed a little uncertainly. Her own dad didn't often crack jokes or talk very much at all at mealtimes, but Shirley's dad was full of fun. She wondered if he was always like that.

'Take no notice of him, Kathy love,' said Mrs Morris. 'He's a terrible tease. He knows very well he has a cooked meal every night, don't you, Frank? The children and I have ours at dinner time when they come home from school.'

'Yes, I know that, Mrs Morris,' said Kathy quietly. 'I know he's . . . er . . . only joking. I have my dinner at dinner time too. But this is lovely,' she added.

'Aye, take no notice of me, love,' said Mr Morris. 'My missus looks after me real well, don't you, Sadie love?'

'Kathy's dad does the cooking in their house,' chimed in Shirley. 'Doesn't he, Kathy?'

'Well . . . yes,' replied Kathy. 'A lot of the time he does. But that's only because—'

'Aye, it's because they've got a boarding house, isn't that right, Kathy?' said Mr Morris. 'It's Mr Leigh's job; that's why he does the cooking.'

'Yes . . . he's a chef,' said Kathy in a little voice.

'A chef . . . aye, real posh that, isn't it? Like I said, it's his job. You wouldn't catch me in the kitchen. Not on your life!' Mr Morris grinned at his wife. 'Anyroad, my missus enjoys cooking, don't you, Sadie love?'

'I don't suppose I've got much choice,' said Mrs Morris with a sigh. But she was smiling. 'I don't mind a bit of help, though, sometimes.'

'Well, you've got a daughter to help out, haven't you? And soon there'll be two of 'em,' said Mr Morris beckoning towards little Brenda. 'I don't reckon you're so badly off, love.'

Mrs Morris didn't answer. 'Now then, who's for pudding?' she said, a few moments later, getting up to collect the dirty plates.

'Do you need to ask?' replied her husband. 'All of us!'

49

'Yes . . . please,' added Kathy politely.

Pudding was big pear halves – out of a tin, Kathy guessed – with lots of evaporated milk. Once again, it was delicious and a lovely treat.

When they had finished their meal Mrs Morris cleared the table. Kathy noticed that Shirley was helping, and so she did her bit too, carrying her own pots into the kitchen; she was used to helping Aunty Win at home. She noticed that Mr Morris and Graham got up from the table and sat down in the easy chairs, Mr Morris with the evening paper and Graham with his *Dandy*. But then her own dad did that as well. He didn't mind cooking – in fact he enjoyed it – but he wasn't all that keen on washing up.

'Thank you . . .' Mrs Morris smiled at the two little girls. 'A little help is worth a lot of pity.'

'My aunty says that,' Kathy told her.

Mrs Morris laughed. 'Yes, I daresay it's a common saying amongst us womenfolk. Anyway, off you go, you two. I'll soon have this lot cleared away, and then perhaps we can have a game or two – Ludo or Snakes and Ladders – before Kathy goes home. Can you find them, Shirley? They're in the sideboard drawer.'

'Oh, here's the tiddlywinks as well,' said Shirley, rooting in the drawer. 'Goody! Let's have a go at that, shall we, while we're waiting for Mummy to finish washing up.'

Mrs Morris had put a velvety cloth over the table when it had been cleared. There was one just like it at Kathy's home, except that theirs was brown and this one was red.

'We need a flat surface,' said Shirley, 'or the tiddlywinks

won't jump. I know; we'll use the Ludo board . . . Are you going to have a game with us, Graham?'

'What, tiddlywinks?' scoffed her brother. 'No thanks; that's kid's stuff.' He turned back to the doings of Desperate Dan.

'Can I play?' begged Brenda, running in from the kitchen where she had been watching her mother. 'Let me, please let me!'

'All right, then,' agreed Shirley. 'See, kneel up on the chair, then you can reach.'

Kathy thought the little girl was so appealing, shouting out in delight every time one of her tiddlywinks jumped into the pot. There were shouts of 'Shut up!' though, from her brother, and even Mr Morris winced a little at her piercing voice.

'Now then, that's all shipshape again,' said Mrs Morris, coming in from the kitchen. 'We'll have a game or two, shall we, before Kathy goes home. Frank . . . Graham . . . are you going to join us?'

To Kathy's surprise they both agreed that they would.

'There'll be too many of us, though,' said Shirley. 'It makes five and we only need four for Ludo.'

'And then there's Brenda,' said Kathy.

'Oh, she's too little,' said Shirley. 'I tell you what; she can play with you, Kathy, seeing that you seem to have taken to her . . . Let her think she is helping,' she added in a grown-up voice.

'And I'll have a look at the paper while you play,' said Mrs Morris. 'Then we can swap over later.'

Kathy enjoyed the games very much. Mr Morris was such

good fun. Her dad could hardly ever be persuaded to join in games, and it wasn't much good with just herself and Aunty Win, although her aunt had taught her to play draughts and how to do patience, which you could play on your own. It was usually very quiet in the evening at Kathy's home, with her dad listening to the wireless and her aunt knitting or reading. She was enjoying playing immensely now, but she decided that Graham was not a very good loser. He wanted to win at all the games – she guessed that was why he wanted to play, so that he could show off – and he was really cross when Shirley won the first game of Ludo. He won the second one, though, so he cheered up a bit.

Then Mrs Morris joined in instead of her husband, and they played Snakes and Ladders. Graham was very annoyed when his counter had to go down a really long snake. And in the end Kathy won that game.

'It's only a game of chance,' remarked Graham. 'You don't have to be clever to win at Snakes and Ladders, not like you do at Ludo.' Mrs Morris told him off for being impolite to their guest, but Kathy didn't mind. She didn't know what he meant, really. Besides, it had all been such good fun.

When it was time for Kathy to go home Mrs Morris said she would walk back with her. 'I feel that I need a breath of fresh air,' she explained.

'But it's Brenda's bedtime,' said her husband.

'It's all right, Frank,' she replied. 'She can stay up a bit and I'll see to her when I get back. I won't be long. You can perhaps read her a story?'

'OK, then,' said Mr Morris. He didn't seem to mind that.

'Thank you for having me,' Kathy said to him when she had got her coat on, just as her aunt had taught her to do when she went to someone's house.

'That's all right,' he laughed. 'You're a very polite little lady. We've enjoyed having you. Come again, any time.'

'Can I come with you to Kathy's?' asked Shirley.

'No, you stay here,' replied her mother. 'Maybe you could read a story to Brenda as well. She'll like that.'

Shirley nodded. 'I'll read her the one about the three billy goats gruff. It's her favourite.' Shirley was very proud of her prowess at reading and never lost an opportunity to show off a little.

'Ta-ra, Kathy,' she called. 'See you at school tomorrow.'

Dusk was falling as they set off along the street and round the corner to the hotel where Kathy lived. She held Mrs Morris's hand as they crossed the road. She liked Shirley's mum. She was young and pretty, with blonde hair like Shirley's, and she wore bright-pink lipstick. She was nice and friendly too, and never seemed to get bad-tempered, not like some of the mums that Kathy had seen sometimes on the way home from school, shouting at their children.

'I want to have a little chat with your aunty . . . about something,' she told Kathy. 'And I didn't really want Shirley to be listening, not until it's sorted out. She's a bit nosey, is our Shirley; she likes to know what's going on.'

'Little pigs have big ears,' remarked Kathy. 'That's what my aunty says sometimes, when she wants to tell my dad something private. But I don't ever tell tales.'

Mrs Morris laughed. 'No, I'm sure you don't. It's not

really a secret . . . but I was wondering if your aunt might find me a job at the hotel when the season starts . . . You're the only person I've told yet,' she added confidingly. 'But keep it under your hat for the moment. That means—'

'It means I've not to tell Shirley.' Kathy nodded. 'Don't worry, Mrs Morris. It's our secret.'

Shirley's mum laughed. 'You're a little cough drop, aren't you?' That was a funny thing to say. Her aunty said it sometimes when Kathy said something that made her laugh. She guessed it was a nice thing to be.

'We'll go in the back way,' said Kathy when they arrived at Holmleigh. 'The back door's usually open until everyone's in. Come in, Mrs Morris,' she said politely. 'I'll tell my aunty you're here.'

The door opened straight into the kitchen, and that led into the living room. It was the family dining room and sitting room and everything-else room, separate from the rooms at the front which were occupied by the visitors.

'Mrs Morris has brought me home,' called Kathy. 'She wants to ask you something, Aunty Win.'

Aunty Win was knitting and her dad was reading the newspaper and smoking his pipe. He looked up and nodded. 'Hello there. Thanks for having our Kathy.' Then he returned to his paper.

'Come in, come in. Sit yourself down.' Aunty Win jumped up and moved a couple of magazines off an easy chair.

'Thank you . . . I hope I'm not disturbing you,' said Shirley's mum.

'No, not at all . . . Kathy, go and take your coat off, there's a good girl. And then you can read in your bedroom while I talk to Mrs Morris,' said Aunty Win.

'Oh, it's all right; it's nothing private,' said Mrs Morris. 'I've already mentioned it to Kathy, haven't I, dear?' She sat down and paused for a moment before she started to speak. 'Actually . . . I was wondering if you could perhaps find me a job of some sort, Miss Leigh, when the season starts. I could turn my hand to almost anything I'm sure; chambermaid, waitress or . . . whatever you think best.'

'I'm sure I could employ you,' said Winifred. 'We, I should say, as it's my brother's business as well as mine. But he leaves that side of things to me, don't you, Albert?'

'Eh? What?' Albert looked up from his paper.

'Mrs Morris would like to come and work here during the season,' said Winifred. 'We'd be pleased to have her, wouldn't we?'

'Yes, of course,' replied Albert. 'You sort it out, Winnie.'

'Oh . . . do call me Sadie,' said Mrs Morris. 'Most people do, and I prefer it.'

'And I'm Winifred; Win or Winnie for short. But you know that, don't you?'

'Well, yes; Kathy talks a lot about her Aunty Win. In fact, that's how I always think of you, as Aunty Win.'

Winifred smiled. '"What's in a name?" as somebody once said. Christian names it is, then. As you get older some people think it's too familiar to call you by your first name, but I've never minded at all. So . . . Sadie, let's see what we can sort out, shall we?'

Kathy sat at the table, quietly leafing through her *Twinkle* comic, but she was listening as well. She heard Mrs Morris explaining that she hadn't been out to work since before she was married, but that she needed a job to 'make ends meet'.

'My husband, Frank, is quite old-fashioned, you see. I had a good job before we were married. I was a shorthand typist, and I worked for a solicitor in the town. But when we got married Frank made me give it up and stay at home. He thinks it's a man's place to provide, and he does earn quite a good wage; he's a bus driver for the Blackpool Corporation. He says it's a woman's job to stay at home and look after the house. Then the children arrived – Graham and Shirley and Brenda – and so, of course, I've spent all my time looking after them and Frank.'

'And making a very good job of it,' said Winifred.

'Well, yes; I've done my best. But we could do with a bit more coming in, to be quite honest. Graham and Shirley are always needing new things, they grow so fast. And Brenda has to have a lot of 'hand-me-downs' that Shirley has grown out of. I sometimes feel they're shabbily dressed compared with some of the other children – your Kathy, for instance.'

'Well, we've only got Kathy to look after,' replied Winifred. 'And we try to make an extra effort . . . under the circumstances, you see,' she added in a quieter voice. She means it's because I haven't got a mum, thought Kathy . . . 'But I think your children are a credit to you, Sadie.'

'Thank you. Well, I always make sure they're clean and tidy, and I try to see that they don't go short of anything, but it's hard at times. And I'd like to be able to buy a new dress for myself now and again, without having to ask Frank every time.'

Kathy, listening to it all, recalled that Shirley didn't have so many different clothes as she had. And the gymslip her friend was wearing now was too short, but she had never really thought anything about it before.

'I haven't said anything to Frank,' Sadie continued. 'He would only say no, we can manage, and there's Brenda to consider, and all that. I thought if I sorted something out first and then told him later, it would be a question of "fait accompli".'

Kathy didn't understand all that, but she thought how nice it would be to have Shirley's mum working at the hotel. She couldn't leave little Brenda at home, though. Wouldn't it be good if she could bring Brenda with her, then she, Kathy, could look after her? It would be nearly as good as having a little sister of her own.

'Mmm . . .' Aunty Win was nodding solemnly. 'Yes, I see the problem . . . Sadie. You don't want to cause trouble with your husband, do you?'

'Oh, I'm sure it won't come to that,' replied Mrs Morris. 'But he's like all men; he likes to think he's the one in charge.' She glanced cautiously at Kathy's dad, but he didn't seem to be listening.

'You could bring your little girl with you,' said Aunty Win. 'You'd look after her, wouldn't you, Kathy?' She seemed to realise that Kathy had been listening all the time.

'Ooh, yes! I'd like that,' agreed Kathy.

'And Shirley could come as well, if you like,' Aunty Win went on. 'They could amuse themselves, I'm sure, whilst you were busy. And Shirley and Kathy are such good friends, aren't they?'

Kathy pondered that it would have been rather nice to look after Brenda on her own. Shirley was inclined to be bossy and to want to be in charge all the time; like her mum had said that Mr Morris liked to be. Still, it would be good to have somebody to play with during the school holiday. It was often a lonely time with her dad and aunt busy working all the day.

Kathy heard her aunt suggest that Mrs Morris – Sadie – could be a waitress for the midday meals, except for Sunday when she would be at home with her family, and then perhaps she could help with the washing-up. 'It's a mammoth task when we're fully booked,' said Aunty Win. 'At the height of the season we might have as many as thirty guests.'

But Mrs Morris just smiled. 'It's all in a day's work,' she said. 'I've never minded washing up.'

'What I could really do with, though, is some help with the bookkeeping,' said Winifred. 'Albert leaves all that side of things to me, and it's a bit of a headache sometimes. The books have to be kept in order for the taxman, and maths has never been my strong point. We've muddled through so far, more by good luck than good management, but the laws are getting stricter now. I don't suppose you could . . . ?' She looked hopefully at Mrs Morris.

'I'd be delighted,' said Sadie. 'That's a job I could do at home, if it's all right with you. I studied bookkeeping at night school. I've got a typewriter too – I've had it since I was doing my studying – so I could do any letters you want typing.'

'Do you know, this is like an answer to a prayer!' exclaimed

Winifred. 'Except that I'd never have thought of asking God for help with my office work!'

The two ladies settled down to a long chat over a cup of tea. Kathy's bedtime seemed to have been forgotten, so she kept quiet. So had little Brenda's and Shirley's, she thought. She hoped that Mrs Morris wouldn't be in trouble with her husband when she got home.

Chapter Five

Winifred had been a member of the dramatic society ever since it had started, back in 1920. She had felt the need of an interest outside of the home which, in her case, was also her place of work. In some ways it had been a lonely sort of life compared with some of her friends, girls of the same age who had jobs outside of the home; that was until they married, when it was expected that young women would stay at home, caring for their husbands and families. But the recent war had taken its toll, and many young women, bereaved, as Winifred had been, viewed the future as one of inevitable spinsterhood.

The boarding house had been very much a family affair, with her mother, Alice Leigh, at the helm. Alice was just one of a vast army of seaside landladies, veritable matriarchs, who were becoming quite a force to be reckoned with. Blackpool landladies, in particular, were often the butt of music hall jokes and comic postcards, and even more so were their husbands. It was said that these downtrodden little men spent most of their lives in the kitchen, peeling endless amounts of spuds, and tackling great mountains of washing-up. This was not strictly true in all cases. William Leigh, Alice's husband, for instance, had had a job outside of the home. He was a painter and decorator by trade, the job he had been apprenticed to on leaving school and in which he was employed when he met Alice.

Alice's parents had 'not been short of a bob or two', as Lancashire folk were often heard to say. Soon after the marriage of the young couple they had helped Alice and William to buy the North Shore boarding house, and it had proved to be an excellent investment. It had been intended at first that Alice should run the business on her own, with just a little paid help. Later on, however, it had seemed only sensible that William should put his weight behind it as well, taking decorating jobs for other people during the winter months, at the same time doing the painting and decorating that was continually needed at the boarding house.

Now, in 1950, William and Alice were thankfully and happily retired. Albert was more or less in the same position as his father had been. His skills as a painter and decorator had been taught to him by his father. The difference was that Albert had also learnt to cook – in fact he was considered to be an excellent cook – something his father would never have dreamt of doing, and unheard of in the days of the old Blackpool landladies. And the boarding house – now a private hotel – was doing so well that Albert did not need to do jobs for other people. The ongoing work at Holmleigh kept him quite busy enough.

Winifred had never given a great deal of thought as to whether or not she would be able to act, when she had first joined the dramatic group. She had seen it mainly as a way of meeting other young people, and as a means of helping her to recover from the ache in her heart, still there after more than a year, whenever she thought about Arthur. Maybe, at the back of her mind, there had been the thought that she might, sooner or later, meet another young man who could come to mean as much to her as Arthur had done. But the years had gone by and this had not happened. There was, inevitably, a dearth of younger men – as the girls often complained, they were either too young or too old – and the few that joined the dramatic society, in the first instance and then in later years, had somehow never ignited that vital spark of interest in Winifred.

She had, many years ago, struck up a friendship with a friend of her brother. But he, like Albert, was five years younger than herself, not that that would have been of any consequence had they been truly attracted to one another. But after a couple of outings to the cinema and the music hall she had told him that she didn't wish to go out with him again. He had not seemed bothered at all, and she had wondered then if he had only asked her out at the request of her brother who, she knew, sympathised with her predicament.

Then there had been an older man, a solicitor in the town, who had been left a widower in his early thirties. There again, though, Winifred had known that there was no way she would ever want to spend the rest of her life with him, although he had seemed rather keen that she should consider doing so.

Nowadays she did not fret about her lack of a husband. Neither did she envy her married friends. Sometimes, indeed, she felt that she, as a spinster, had the best of it. Some men were so dogmatic and domineering. She was contented – happy, even – in her own quiet way. The dramatic society that she had joined initially to ease her loneliness had proved to be a source of inspiration and motivation to her. To her amazement she had found that she could act and, to her surprise and delight, after a year or two she was playing the female lead in some of the plays they performed.

She was not, by nature, an outgoing sort of person, but she did not find it difficult to take on the guise and the personality of the character she was playing. Neither would she have considered herself to be beautiful; she was certainly not at all like Joan Crawford or Gloria Swanson, the film stars of the time, but she supposed she had a pleasing face and figure, which, with her warm brown hair and greenish eyes, could be used onstage to her best advantage.

Her days of playing the young heroine, alas, were well past. However, she still enjoyed acting the more mature parts, as mothers or unmarried aunts. She had played the mother in J.B. Priestley's *An Inspector Calls*, and one of the middle-aged wives, which called for a certain amount of comedy, in *When We Are Married*, another of Priestley's plays. That one had been their last production. He was one of their favourite playwrights, but this year they were planning to put on a play from the end of the last century.

One of Winifred's best-loved roles, as a young woman, had been that of Gwendolen Fairfax in *The Importance of Being Earnest*. They had performed that way back in 1925 and now the producer – a different one by this time – had decided it was time to bring back Oscar Wilde's most famous play.

Would she be able to cope with the part of Lady Bracknell, she wondered? It was widely expected that it would be given to Winifred, but it was not yet cut and dried. There was to be a preliminary reading of the play at the next meeting. That would be on Wednesday evening.

But before that it was Kathy's Brownie meeting on Tuesday. They met in the church hall at six o' clock. Girls were supposed to be seven years old before they joined the Brownies, but as Kathy would be seven in June she had been allowed to join a couple of months early. This was really a special favour because Brown Owl was a friend of her Aunty Win, and also because Shirley, who had turned seven in January, had pleaded with Brown Owl for her friend to be allowed to join.

This would be her fourth time at Brownies and to Kathy it was one of the special times in the week. She was proud of her brown tunic, the real leather belt and silver buckle, and the yellow tie with a lovely little tiepin shaped like an elf that was fastened to it. Some of the older girls – the eight- or nine-year-olds – had badges sewn on to their sleeves that they had been awarded for passing tests:

homecraft, needlework, artwork, music, swimming and all sorts of other things. Kathy was already learning to tie knots – that was one of the first tests they worked for – and she knew it would be quite easy for her to get her homecraft badge as well. That involved doing simple jobs in the home, like making a cup of tea, setting the table and washing up. She was already used to doing jobs like that.

Shirley was already there when Aunty Win left her at the church hall. Kathy took off her coat and hung it up and went over to join her friend.

'I've got something to tell you,' said Shirley excitedly. 'My mum's going to come and work at your hotel. She's going to be a waitress – I 'spect your aunty will let her be the one in charge, 'cause she says the two she had last summer were just girls helping out in the school holiday – and my mum's going to do the books as well; y'know, sorting out the money an' bills an' all that.'

'Oh . . . that's nice,' replied Kathy. She knew that if she told Shirley that she already knew – or at least had heard something about it – then Shirley would be mad at her and get all huffy like she did sometimes.

'And your aunty says that me and our Brenda can come as well and play with you while my mum's busy working. That'll be good, won't it?'

'Yes, that's very nice.' Kathy nodded. 'Actually . . . Aunty Win did sort of say that you and Brenda might be coming . . . but I didn't know it was all decided. Why didn't you tell me at school today?'

'Because my mum's only just told me, that's why!' said

Shirley, a little impatiently. 'Actually, they had a row – my mum and dad – when she got back from your house last night. It was past Brenda's bedtime, and she'd already had two stories read to her and Mum wasn't there to see to her. So Dad told me to help her to get undressed and have a wash an' all that. And he didn't half shout at my mum for being such a long time. I could hear them from upstairs.'

'Oh dear!' said Kathy. 'I thought he was really nice, your dad. He's good fun, isn't he?' She didn't say that he was not like her own dad who could be grumpy some of the time, because that wouldn't be a very nice thing to say.

'Sometimes he is,' replied Shirley. 'But he can get mad as well. He likes to be the boss, y'see; that's why my brother thinks he can boss me around – he's just trying to be like our dad. Anyway, my mum came upstairs then to see to Brenda and she looked real upset. I thought she was going to cry, but she didn't. She said to me not to worry, 'cause Daddy would get over it, like he always does.'

'So are they all right now?' asked Kathy.

'I think so. They seemed all right when Daddy came home from work. Mummy gave him his tea, then she had to come straight out to bring me here. But she told me and Graham at teatime about coming to work at your hotel. She said that Daddy wasn't too pleased at the idea, but she would work on him. That's when she said me and Brenda could come with her. And I think your aunty said we could have our dinner with you as well.'

'What about Graham?' asked Kathy.

Shirley laughed. 'That's just what he said. "What about me? Who's going to make my dinner?" And Mummy told him he was just like Daddy, always thinking about himself.'

'So what will he do?'

'Oh, he's out most of the time in the holidays playing football. I 'spect he might go to Jimmy's; he's his best friend. My mum certainly won't neglect him,' Shirley added.

Kathy pondered that family life – real family life, with a mother and father and children – must sometimes have arguments and fallings-out as well as fun and happy times. All the same, it must be rather nice, she thought.

Then it was time for the meeting to begin. They all stood round the big toadstool in the centre of the room. They saluted with three fingers and promised to do their best, to do their duty to God and the King, and to help other people every day. Then they went off into their 'sixes'; there were five of these groups. They were called Elves, Fairies, Pixies, Sprites and Gnomes. Kathy was an elf, and so was Shirley. The leader of each six was called the 'sixer'. Kathy knew it would be a long time before she achieved that honour, but for the moment she was enjoying the fun and games and learning the different skills. She could already tie a reef knot and a slip knot, and they were learning to knit – pearl stitch as well as garter stitch. The finished article would, hopefully, make a cover for a doll's bed.

She told her aunt on the way home what Shirley had said about her mum and dad falling out.

'Oh dear!' said Aunty Win. 'I do hope it isn't going to cause trouble. Sadie – Mrs Morris – is only trying to help a little with the money side of things. I'm looking forward to having her. I'm sure she'll be popular with the visitors; she's such a friendly young lady. Never mind, I expect it'll all come out in the wash, as your grandma likes to say.'

Kathy thought again what funny things grown-ups said sometimes.

The play reading was to take place in the same church hall the following evening. The hall was in use every afternoon and evening for groups such as Brownies and Guides, Cubs and Scouts, Mothers' Union and Young Wives, as well as for all the social events that took place in the parish. Winifred was neither a young wife nor a mother, and although both those groups had said she would be welcome to join them she had not done so. She did not want to feel like a fish out of water.

She was, however, a person of some importance now in the drama group. She was always there early in her capacity as registrar to collect the subs and to welcome everyone. She was also vice-chairman of the group and next year it would be her turn to be in the chair.

When the present chairman, Mavis Peacock, arrived she was accompanied by a man that Winifred had not seen before. A new member, she wondered, looking at him with interest – she was careful not to show too keen an interest – although he was what might be called a handsome figure of a man.

'Oh, hello there, Winnie,' said Mavis. She was a woman of Winifred's own age and they had joined the group at more or less the same time. Mavis, though, had always been more interested in the production side of things rather than taking much part in the acting. She was wardrobe mistress and was in charge of the props, and with her brisk efficiency she was an invaluable member of the society.

'This is my brother,' she went on. 'I think I told you, didn't I, that he was coming to live in Blackpool? Well, it happened all of a sudden in the end, and here he is! Jeff, this is Winifred Leigh, a very good friend of mine . . . and one of our leading ladies,' she added with a nod of approval at her friend. 'Winnie, this is Jeffrey Bancroft, usually known as Jeff.'

The two of them shook hands, murmuring the conventional 'How do you do?'. Winifred found herself looking into – and almost mesmerised by – a pair of shrewd grey eyes that seemed to be regarding her with more than the ordinary interest afforded to a stranger that one had only just met. He was not tall, little more than average height, like herself, with hair that she guessed had once been fairish, but was now a greyish blonde, still thick and with the natural waves that many straight-haired women would envy. He smiled at her in a friendly, but by no means a familiar, manner.

'Have you come to join us?' she asked. 'Are we about to welcome a new member?'

'I hope so,' he replied. 'But I've just come along to watch tonight.'

'And to see if you like us?' Winifred enquired.

'Oh, I'm quite sure I shall do that,' he smiled. 'I was a member of a drama group several years ago, but I haven't done much acting just lately. I will be quite content for the moment to act as an ASM if you need one.'

'We certainly do, don't we, Winnie?' replied his sister.

'Our stage manager, Wilfred, is very good, but he's past retiring age now and he's always glad of extra help. Anyway, come along, Jeff, and I'll introduce you to some of the members.'

Winifred decided she would look forward to chatting further with him when they had their cup of tea halfway through the evening; but for now she must get on with the job in hand, collecting the money and welcoming the members.

The play reading began with the casting of the two roguish young bachelors, Jack and Algernon. It was more or less a foregone conclusion that the parts would go to the two youngish men, Dave and Tony, who were both in their mid-thirties. Possibly a little too old for the roles, but there was a shortage of really young men.

There were several young women who were willing and well able to take the parts of the two girls, Gwendolen and Cecily. There was total agreement though, fortunately, when the role of Gwendolen was given to Thelma Bridges, who was Tawny Owl to the Brownie pack. At twenty-three she was a little older, but not all that much so, than the character was supposed to be. The part of Cecily was awarded to Thelma's friend, Isobel, which pleased the pair of them.

When the tea and biscuits were served Winifred, purposely, did not seek out her new acquaintance, but she was not at all displeased, or surprised, when he came to join her.

'Your turn next,' said Jeff Bancroft, pulling up a chair and sitting next to her. 'My sister says you're auditioning for Lady Bracknell?'

'Yes, that's right.'

'Pardon me for saying so, but aren't you too young and . . . er . . . attractive for such a role?' She could see that he was not trying to flirt with her. He was obviously sincere in what he was saying, so she took his words at face value. She smiled.

'Thanks for the compliment! I can assure you I'm quite old enough, although we don't know Lady B's exact age, do we? Yes, I realise I'm not the usual stereotype, but I don't see that that matters. I feel I could put my own interpretation on the role. Does she need to be corpulent and hatchet-faced? I don't really think so. Anyway, she's a character part I've always fancied having a go at. My days of playing the young ingénue have long gone, I'm afraid.'

'Mine too, alas,' he replied. 'But never mind; age has certain compensations.'

Winifred nodded. 'Yes, I suppose so.' She smiled at him questioningly. 'Such as?'

'Well, now you ask me I'm not quite sure, but there must be some.' Jeffrey laughed. She recognised the Yorkshire accent as he spoke, not too pronounced, but typical of the folk from the rugged northern hills, gravelly and issuing from way back in the throat. She remembered Mavis saying that her brother lived in Bradford, the city where Mavis also had been born. 'No, I'm joking,' he went on. 'Of course there are compensations. For a start, we're wiser now, aren't we? Years of experience must have taught us something. We're not so ready to rush into things or make mistakes, or perhaps not quite so many.'

'It's said, isn't it, that the person who never made a mistake never made anything?' answered Winifred thoughtfully. 'I don't think I've ever made any really drastic mistakes . . . but sometimes life takes over, doesn't it, and you haven't much control over what happens to you. You can't always please yourself; sometimes decisions are already made for you.' She realised she was becoming rather introspective. 'Sorry . . .' she smiled. 'I didn't mean to start soliloquising. But don't get the wrong impression. I'm not complaining about my lot. I lead a very contented life.'

'And a very full one, I believe,' answered Jeff. 'My sister has told me about your hotel, and about how you look after your little niece. You've no children of your own?'

'No, I've never been married,' she replied. 'I was one of the very many girls who lost someone in the first war. It's a long time ago, though. Who can tell whether it would have been a good marriage . . . or a mistake? We were very young, but it seemed right at the time. However, it just wasn't to be.' She was finding it very easy to talk to Jeff, but she realised she hardly knew the first thing about him. Mavis had mentioned, casually, that her brother was coming to live in Blackpool when he had managed to sell his house in Yorkshire. And now, here he was, and he did seem to be quite interested in talking to her.

'Yes, it was a dreadful conflict,' he replied. 'Well, both wars were, but I'm afraid I can't speak from any real experience. I was just too young to join up in the first lot, to my parents' great relief. My elder brother was wounded on the Somme. He lost an arm, but at least it meant that he didn't have to go back. And he's still going strong, I'm glad to say. Then I was called up with my age group in the second war, but

I never got any further than the very north of England. I must confess I was relieved. I felt I was rather too old to be a "have-a-go hero", and life was too precious for me to want to throw it away. But at least I did wear the uniform for a while.'

'The same as my brother,' observed Winifred. 'He joined up – he was in the catering corps – but he didn't leave these shores.'

'And then he was widowed, I believe?'

'Yes . . .' answered Winifred. It seemed that Jeffrey Bancroft already knew quite a lot about her family circumstances. 'Albert lost his wife towards the end of the war, but we've both tried to do what we can for our little Katherine – Kathy, we call her.'

'Yes, I was widowed too,' said Jeff, 'three years ago. But my two children were already married with families of their own.' That answered a question that Winifred had been wanting to ask, but had not felt able to. Mavis had not mentioned whether her brother was coming to live here on his own, or whether he had a wife and family. And Winifred, at that time, had not really been curious enough to enquire.

She murmured the conventional, 'I'm so sorry . . . about your wife, I mean.'

He gave a sad smile. 'Yes . . . it's always distressing, but I have to confess that it was not an ideally happy marriage. We were young – too young, as we both came to realise – but we stayed together for the sake of the children. It was a shock, of course, when I lost Beatrice. It was very sudden; an aneurism, and we weren't even aware that she had a weak

73

heart. I grieved for a while, more than I expected to. But then I knew it was time to move on. Both my children have moved away. My son is in Canada, and my daughter's in the south of England, so I don't see them as much as I would like to . . .'

'So you decided to come and live in Blackpool?'

'Yes. Mavis is my only sister and we've always got on well together. I decided to move away from the grime of the mill towns – although it's not so bad as it used to be – and enjoy some of your famous fresh air and Blackpool breezes.'

'And are you enjoying it?'

'Yes . . . but it doesn't half blow here! I was nearly blown off my feet on the lower prom the other day, to say nothing of getting soaked by an enormous wave crashing over the sea wall.'

Winifred laughed. 'Yes, we residents have learnt to beware of the tides. Do you live near the sea?'

'Yes, I have a little bungalow in an avenue near to Gynn Square.'

'And what about your job? You were able to find employment here?' Winifred realised then that she might be seeming rather nosey, but he was so easy to talk to. 'I'm sorry . . .' she said. 'I'm asking too many questions.'

'No, not at all,' he replied easily. 'Actually, it didn't make any difference to my work because I'm self-employed. I'm a freelance artist.'

'My goodness! That sounds very clever.'

Jeff smiled. 'Well, let's say it's one of my very few talents. I'll be able to help you with your scenery . . . I do illustrations for greetings cards and children's books, and for book covers. Anything, really, that I'm asked to do. I suppose you could call me a jobbing artist, but it keeps the wolf from the door.'

'I'm very impressed,' said Winifred. 'Oh . . . I think they're ready to start again. It's been nice talking to you . . . Jeff.'

'The pleasure is all mine . . . Winifred,' he replied. 'And . . . good luck! Or should I say "break a leg"?'

She laughed. 'It doesn't matter. I'm not superstitious.'

Her chat with Jeff Bancroft had enhanced her sense of well-being and had, somehow, imbued her with confidence.

The other lady auditioning for the part was older and plumper, looking altogether more like a typical Lady Bracknell. But there was little doubt when they had both been heard what the outcome would be. The part was awarded to Winifred and the other contender gave way graciously.

'Congratulations!' said Jeff, as they put on their coats ready to depart. 'I knew you'd do it.'

'Thank you,' said Winifred, humbly. 'I must admit . . . I'm rather pleased.'

'Now, may I offer you a lift home?' he said. 'Or do you have your own transport?'

'No, I don't drive,' she replied. She knew it would be churlish to refuse; besides, she had no intention of doing so. 'Thank you,' she said. 'It's very kind of you.'

His car was parked outside, a Ford Popular, about two years old, she assumed, although her knowledge of cars was limited.

'So I'll see you next week,' he said when they pulled up outside Holmleigh. Like the perfect gentleman she had already assumed him to be, he jumped out and opened the passenger door. 'I'm very pleased to have met you, Winifred. Goodnight, my dear. See you soon . . .'

'Goodnight, Jeff,' she said. 'I'm pleased as well.'

She walked to the front door feeling a lightness of spirit that she had not known for ages.

Chapter Six

The spring open evening was one of the most important events in the school year. The children had been in their new classes for almost two terms, by which time the teachers knew them all very well and were able to discuss with the parents their varying strengths and weaknesses.

Each teacher did his, or her, very best to make their classroom as attractive as possible. Sally Roberts, at four o'clock on that Thursday afternoon towards the end of March, looked around her room with a quiet smile of satisfaction. The exercise books had all been marked up-to-date and were arranged in tidy piles on the children's tables, with a printed name card on the top that the parents could easily identify. Sally's own desk had been tidied, and a vase of daffodils and freesias added a spring-like and welcoming touch.

The display on the walls, though, was of the greatest importance. It consisted of the children's paintings and drawings, each one carefully framed and mounted; examples of stories the children had written, and their first attempts at poetry; and a large mural, taking up nearly the whole of one wall, depicting the story of *The Pied Piper of Hamelin*. Sally had read them Browning's poem and they had been fascinated by it. It was very sad, of course, the story of the children being lured away, and just one little crippled boy being left behind. But they had all seemed to take it in their stride, as they had done with Grimms' fairy tales. They certainly were grim, with their instances of wicked witches, cruel stepmothers and terrifying ogres.

Sally had learnt, though, that children liked to be scared at times. They seemed to understand that it was not real, and that they were safe, when the story came to an end, in their own comfortable little world. At least, that was true for the most part. She had reason to believe that one or two of the children in her class were somewhat neglected – and it was usually the case that the parents of this minority were the ones who did not turn up to open evenings or other school events. And there was little the teachers could do, unless the neglect bordered on cruelty or deprivation, when steps would need to be taken. However, this area of North Shore was, by and large, what was considered a good catchment area and there were few real problems.

The mural was the *pièce de résistance* of Sally Roberts' classroom and she looked at it with a feeling of satisfaction. It was largely the children's own work, apart from the large figure of the Pied Piper that she had drawn and the children had coloured in red and yellow. There were rats of all shapes, sizes and colours: orange, brown, fawn, grey, black and white. The houses of Hamelin, likewise, varied in design, mostly with the black beams typical of that part of Germany, standing at crazy angles with steeply sloping roofs and crooked chimneys.

She gave a contented nod, then put on her coat that hung by the door and went out into the corridor, then out of the side door. Phil Grantley was in the car park. This was really a small area of the playground that had been sectioned off for the use of those teachers who had cars, although there were only four of them who felt able to afford one.

'Want a lift, Sally?' called Phil, and she was pleased to accept.

'Thanks, Phil,' she said, scrambling into the passenger seat of his small Morris car. 'Seeing that we have to be back at six, it doesn't give us much time.'

'All done and dusted then?' he asked as they drove off.

'Yes, all ready for the onslaught,' she replied. 'Most of the parents of my class have said they are coming, but it remains to be seen. Do you think this new system will work better?'

It had been decided by the headmaster, and agreed by the rest of the staff, that the parents should be given a five-minute slot, which was all that time would allow, in which to speak to their child's class teacher. It would, hopefully, do away with the queues and the melee that had sometimes occurred in the past.

'It ought to,' replied Phil. 'There was no end of a barney in my room last time, one chap saying that they'd been waiting half an hour and that another couple was barging in. There was very nearly a punch-up till I stepped in.'

'I shouldn't think they'd want to argue with you, Phil,' smiled Sally.

Phil Grantley was a six-footer and well built too. He did a little boxing in his spare time. He was the physical education teacher, as well as teaching one of the fourth-year junior classes, and was often to be seen in his tracksuit, as he was now, because he took most of the classes for games. No doubt he would be more suitably dressed that evening, in a suit and tie. Dress code was carefully observed amongst the staff, it being the view of the headmaster that teachers should set an example in tidiness and suitability of clothing.

'Do you fancy coming for a drink with us tonight, Sally, when we've finished here?' asked Phil. 'I'm hoping it will all be over by half past nine at the latest.'

'Thank you; that would be very nice,' she replied. 'Where are you thinking of going?'

'Oh . . . probably one of the hotels on the prom, the Carlton or the Claremont, maybe. The bars are not too busy out of season and they're not quite so rowdy as some of the town centre pubs. Us lads don't mind, but we must consider the ladies, mustn't we? Some of you prefer a bit more class.'

Sally smiled. 'Why? Who'll be going?'

'Brian and Alan and me, and some of the younger lasses. I don't know about the older contingent or the married women. We can ask them, but they'll probably say no.'

'It's nice of you to include me,' said Sally.

The infant teachers were all women, as was the norm. Sally felt that she fell between two stools; they were either several years younger, or older, than herself. Sally was thirty-four and already felt as though she had been teaching for a lifetime; she had been at the same school for all of the time. Fortunately, though, she loved her job.

Several of Sally's colleagues on the infant staff were young women who were quite new to the profession, aged twenty-one to twenty-five. Some of them were already married and juggling the two jobs of looking after a home and husband, and full-time teaching. It was usual, though, to stay at home when the first child arrived. The other teachers were older, fiftyish and sixtyish, with two approaching retirement age.

Sally felt herself more drawn to the junior teachers, several of whom were of a similar age to herself. She found that the men on the staff – there were five of them, six including the headmaster – added a touch of levity and lightness to the atmosphere. Although all of them, it must be said, were very competent teachers, the men, on the whole, did not take themselves or their profession too seriously, or get as tensed up about it as some of the women did. She got on well with the women, some of them single, as she was, and some of them married with teenage families. She was often included in their outings, usually at Phil's invitation, and she appreciated it.

'We enjoy your company, Sally,' Phil replied, in answer to her remark. He glanced across at her and smiled, causing his craggy face to crease into laughter lines around his mouth and his warm brown eyes that always reminded her of those of her gran's spaniel.

She knew that several of the staff wondered whether the two of them were secretly going out together, but that was not the case. They were, at the moment, just good friends. Sally had discovered that beneath his brawn and his commanding appearance, Phil was really quite shy. He had joined the staff eighteen months ago, but had still not got round to asking her out on her own. Always supposing, of course, that he wanted to do so, and she was not even sure of that. Phil Grantley was something of an enigma. She knew, though, that he was roughly the same age as herself and, as far as she knew, quite unattached.

It was not far to Sally's home, and they did not converse very much on the journey, Phil being a careful driver.

'Cheerio then, Sally,' he said, as she jumped out of the car. 'See you later . . . I shall look forward to our drink together,' he added, almost shyly. Then, 'Shall I pick you up tonight?' he asked, as though he had just thought of it. 'About a quarter to six, is that OK? It'll save you waiting around for a bus.'

'Thanks very much, Phil,' she replied. 'I'd be really glad of that. See you later, then. Quarter to six will be fine.'

Well, that was a step in the right direction, she thought to herself, although she was not altogether sure, really, about the direction she wanted their friendship to take.

'Hello, dear; had a good day?' called her mother as she opened the front door. It was her usual greeting and Sally replied, as she usually did, 'Yes thanks, Mum . . . I haven't got much time,' she added. 'Shall I get ready before tea, or what?'

'Your tea's all ready for you, dear,' replied her mother. 'I remembered you have to be out again for six o'clock. I've made a nice shepherd's pie and it's keeping warm in the oven. Your dad and I will have ours later when he comes in from work. That's the beauty of shepherd's pie; it won't spoil.'

'Thanks, Mum,' said Sally. 'You're a treasure. I'll just wash my hands first, then I'll get ready afterwards.'

'Best bib and tucker tonight, eh?' Her mother beamed at her.

'Yes, that's right, Mum. We must try to impress the parents. Although they'll be looking at the children's work, not at the teachers' clothes.'

Sally knew that her mum, and her dad too, were very proud that she had been to college and had become a teacher. Her mother had told her many times that it was what she would have liked to do, but it had been impossible. She had been one of a large family of children; she had left school at thirteen and had gone to work in a store that sold clothing for both men and women. It was there that she had met her future husband, Bill, and they had married when she was just twenty years of age. She had assured Sally that she had never regretted it, and Sally knew that that was true. She doubted that there could be many couples of her parents' age who were as happy or as satisfied with their lot.

But Millie Roberts had been determined that her children should have all the advantages of higher education that had been denied to her and Bill, should it be possible. Jack, though, their second child and only son, had had other ideas. He had joined the merchant navy as soon as he was old enough and, consequently, he was always away somewhere or other on the high seas. Fortunately he had come through the war unscathed, but it was a great regret to Millie and Bill that they saw him so infrequently.

And it was the same with their eldest child, Freda, who was five years older than Sally. She, too, had shown no aptitude for serious study. She had left school at fifteen and had worked as an office junior for a solicitor in the town. Her parents had been disappointed when, at the age of eighteen, she had told them she was pregnant and was going to marry Clive, the lad she had been going out with ever since she left school. They had supported her, though, rather than regarding it as a shameful event that brought disgrace to the family, as was the attitude of many parents of the time. Freda had made a good marriage; Millie and Bill now had three grandchildren, the eldest of whom, Jennifer, was now almost twenty. But, as it was with Jack, they seldom saw Freda and her family. They had moved several years ago to Birmingham where there was more scope for Clive in his work as a motor mechanic.

So it was that Millie Roberts had come to invest her hopes and dreams in her younger daughter. It had been a great joy to her when, after training for two years at a college in Manchester, Sally had been given a teaching post at a school in Blackpool, one that was practically on the doorstep.

Sally was still contented at home, but she knew that she stayed there now mainly for the sake of her mother. She did not mind her mum's cosseting because it was never too overbearing. Mum never asked too many questions about her private life and she had all the freedom she needed. It was very nice, she had to admit, to have her meals cooked for her and her washing done, although she did pay her way very generously and helped out with the household chores as well.

The sad fact, however, was that Sally should have been married by now with a family of her own. She had met

84

Martin Crossley soon after she had started teaching. He had taught at a secondary school in the town, and they had met at a social gathering of the National Union of Teachers, the organisation she had joined on starting her career. He was the first serious boyfriend she had had. They were soon very much in love but were in no hurry to get married. Sally had felt she must teach for a few years at least as her parents had invested so much in her education; and Martin, too, wanted to save up so that they could have a good start with a home of their own.

But alas, the war intervened. Martin joined the RAF and within a year had become part of a bomber crew. He was the 'tail-end Johnny' which, he informed Sally, was the name for the rear gunner. He was involved, inevitably, in the Battle of Britain, and in the July of 1940 Sally heard the tragic news from Martin's parents that he had been killed in action.

She was overwhelmed by sadness, but it was fortunate that she had the long summer holiday from school in which to try to come to terms with her loss and to pull herself together. During the first couple of weeks, though, as well as the anguish of her loss she was also nearly out of her mind with worry. On his last leave, only a few days before he had been killed, she and Martin had made love together for the first – and the last – time. They had paid no heed as to what the consequences might be, which was most unlike the careful and considerate man she knew Martin to be. In the midst of her tears she prayed frantically that all would be well, although she knew it was rather too late for prayers to make any difference. Fortunately she knew, a fortnight later, that her fears had been groundless.

'Thank you, God, thank you . . .' she had murmured, over and over again. She remembered what had happened to her sister several years before. What a shock and a disappointment it would have been to her parents should it have happened again.

Gradually the pain of her loss eased and the grief became less intense. She had her teaching job to keep her busy. Eventually she found that it brought her contentment, even happiness and, for the most part, fulfilment. She loved the children she taught and she had made good friends amongst the staff. There had not been anyone else, though, who had caused her to feel the way she had felt about Martin.

Sally felt quite satisfied with her appearance as she regarded herself in the full-length mirror. She had decided to wear the dress she had bought just before Christmas and had worn for the family gatherings that had taken place around that time, but she had scarcely worn it since then. It seemed a suitable time now to give it another airing. The dress was a dusky pink colour, made of a fine woollen material, with three-quarter-length sleeves, a full mid-calf-length skirt and a nipped-in waist. She had kept her trim figure – some of her married friends had lost their waistlines after childbearing – and the black patent leather belt accentuated her slimness. With it she wore her black patent leather shoes and a matching handbag. She would take a light coat, although she would probably not need it. Phil was picking her up and would most likely run her home again after their visit to the promenade hotel.

'You look very nice, dear,' said her mother, when Sally appeared in the living room. 'That colour really suits you.'

'Do you think so?' queried Sally. 'I wondered if it was a bit wishy-washy – you know, with me being fair-skinned and my hair and everything.'

Her hair was a silvery blonde and had kept its colour without any artificial aids, and the one or two grey hairs she had found did not show. Her eyes were grey; a nondescript colour really, she thought, but tonight she had highlighted them with a slight touch of mascara and a pale-green eyeshadow. She usually chose pastel colours for her clothes, but she had wondered sometimes if a bright red or blue might make her look more striking.

'No, it's just perfect,' said her mother. 'And you've done your eyes as well.'

Sally laughed. 'Well, I don't often get a chance to dress up, do I? And we're going out for a drink after the meeting, a few of us.'

'You look a real bobby-dazzler,' said her father. He and her mother were sitting at the table, eating their shepherd's pie. Bill Roberts was manager now of one of the gents' outfitters in the town, having stayed in the same line of work ever since he had left school. 'You'll turn a few heads tonight, Sal,' he added.

'That's not really the idea, Dad,' she smiled. 'The parents are concerned with the children's progress, not with what their teacher looks like.'

'All the same . . .' said her dad, nodding approvingly.

'How are you getting to school?' asked her mother. 'Are you going on the bus?' That was her usual form of transport to and from the school, although she occasionally cycled there if the weather was good.

'No . . . Phil's picking me up,' she answered. 'Didn't I say?'

'No, you didn't, actually.' Her mother smiled. 'So that's why you're looking so fetching, is it? Eyeshadow an' all!'

'Give over, Mum!' said Sally. 'You know very well it isn't so. I've told you, Phil and I are—'

'Just good friends!' Her mother finished off the statement. 'Alright, love; I know it's none of my business. But Phil Grantley's a really nice young man; I've always thought so.'

A ring at the doorbell stopped any further comments. Phil was standing on the doorstep looking unusually smart in a grey suit with a dazzlingly white shirt and maroon tie.

'Wow! You look smart,' said Sally.

'Why? Don't I always?' He gave a quizzical grin.

'To be honest, no!' she laughed. 'But you scrub up very well, I must say.'

'And so do you . . .' Phil was looking at her admiringly. 'You look . . . quite amazing, Sally.'

'Thank you, kind sir,' she joked, a little fazed by the intensity of his gaze. 'I can make an effort when it's necessary.'

'Come along, then.' He held her arm in a friendly way as they went down the path, then he helped her into the car. 'We'd best get moving or the parents will be there before us.'

Indeed, a few of the early birds were already there, waiting in the corridor outside the classroom doors.

'See you later,' said Phil with a cheery wink as he went further along the corridor to the junior part of the building.

The business of the evening began at once when Sally had hung up her coat and sat down at her imposing desk.

There were two chairs at the opposite side where the parents could sit. This was one occasion when the children were not invited, so that the teachers could speak to their parents in confidence.

Sally tried to say something encouraging about every child, and never to be too critical or condemning. Some children were exceptionally bright, others average or only mediocre, and some, it must be admitted, were slow to learn, whether through lack of brainpower or through laziness or want of motivation. But they nearly all had some ability in one direction or another, some saving grace, however small it might be. It might be that they could paint or draw very well – some of the less able pupils were surprisingly good at art – or could run fast, or print neatly, or help the teacher with the classroom jobs (such as cleaning the blackboard), or were kind and friendly towards the other children. This was a quality in her pupils that Sally regarded as of great importance.

Shirley Morris's parents were some of the first to be seen. Shirley, in many ways, was a model pupil, at least as far as her schoolwork was concerned.

'Yes, our Shirley takes after my wife,' said Mr Morris with a proud glance at that lady. 'I was never all that good at book learning an' all that sort of thing. But Sadie got her School Certificate, didn't you, love?'

'Yes, Frank,' replied Mrs Morris, giving him a look that quite clearly was asking him to shut up!

'And I'm a bus driver,' he went on.

'Yes . . . so Shirley said,' replied Sally. 'Actually, she wrote all about it in a little story.'

'Did she now?' He looked pleased at that. 'Yes, I've got a good job and I'm proud of what I do. Each to his own, that's what I say. I like to think Shirley takes after me in some ways, though. She's a confident little lass, wouldn't you say so, Miss Roberts?'

'Very much so,' agreed Sally. 'She's very self-assured . . .' Which was a polite way of saying that she was bossy and inclined to be cocky.

'She's bossy, isn't she?' said Mrs Morris, taking the words right out of Sally's mouth, although she would not have put it so bluntly. 'I've noticed her with her little friend, Kathy. She tries to rule the roost and she likes to get all her own way. Of course, that's another way in which she takes after her father.' She cast him a half-joking, half-reproving glance. 'I have told her about it, because I think it's a tendency we must try to discourage.'

'Bright little girls are inclined to be bossy at times,' said Sally, 'more so than boys.' She eyed Mr Morris warily, hoping that any ill feeling between them would not develop any further. It wouldn't be the first time she had had parents sniping at one another when they were supposed to be discussing their children. 'Don't worry about it, Mrs Morris. She'll probably grow out of it, and I don't let her get above herself. Kathy Leigh can hold her own, I assure you. Actually, the two of them are quite good for one another. Kathy's a sensible little girl, and she seems to be able to stop Shirley from getting too big for her boots . . . if you see what I mean.'

Kathy's father and her aunt came about halfway through the evening. Sally had met them both on a couple of previous occasions, but this was the first time she had talked to them at any length.

'She tries hard at everything,' Sally told them when they had looked carefully at Kathy's exercise books: the sums, English, spelling and copy-writing books.

'A few spelling mistakes, though,' observed the woman that Kathy called Aunty Win. 'She's only got ten out of ten once, as far as I can see.'

'Well, I was never much good at spelling,' observed Mr Leigh with a grin. 'But I've got by, haven't I?' Sally reflected that she had heard similar remarks several times already that evening.

'How does she compare with the other children?' asked Miss Leigh. 'With her little friend, Shirley, for instance. Kathy tells me that she's a lot cleverer, in the top reading group and good at sums and everything. Kathy seems to set a lot of store by what Shirley does.'

'We try not to make comparisons, Miss Leigh,' replied Sally. 'There aren't any exams as such until they reach junior school age. Kathy works to the very best of her ability, and that is what is important. She's a trier, and she will do well because she'll have a go at anything, even if she finds it difficult.'

'What would you say she was best at?' asked Mr Leigh.

'Oh . . . composition,' replied Sally. 'Story writing, we call it. As you've noticed, her spelling is not always one hundred per cent, but she expresses herself very clearly. I asked them to write a story about what they wanted to do when they were grown-up.'

'Yes, we've read that one,' replied Miss Leigh, smiling.

'Well, she starts off by saying that she would like to write books, like Enid Blyton . . .'

'Yes, she's just started reading some of them on her own,' said Kathy's aunt. '*Naughty Amelia Jane* and *Mister Meddle's Mischief*, and I've been reading the stories of the Faraway Tree with her, and I'm enjoying them very much myself,' she smiled.

Then, more prosaically, Kathy had gone on to write that until she became a story writer she would work in the hotel, like her dad and her aunty. 'She says she wants to be a good chef, like her daddy, and to look after the visitors and make them welcome, like her aunty does,' Sally told them. 'I was quite touched by that. She obviously admires you both very much. She's a grand little girl, and you must be very proud of her.'

'So we are,' replied Mr Leigh. 'Aren't we, Winnie?'

Kathy's aunt smiled and nodded. 'Yes, indeed we are.'

Sally had had time to appraise them both during their conversation. Mr Leigh she took to be in his mid forties; quite a good-looking fellow, she supposed, with fairish hair and blue eyes, unlike his daughter, who was dark-haired with brown eyes. Kathy must take after her mother who had died when she was a baby, she reflected. She had imagined Mr Leigh to be a taciturn sort of man when she had met him before, but he had seemed much more amenable this evening. He had a nice smile, that she guessed one saw only rarely. Sally was aware that he had smiled at her once or twice and his glance had lingered on her a time or two. Not in too obvious a way, though; just nice and friendly.

Miss Leigh too – Aunty Win – was a very likeable person,

obviously dressed in her best clothes, a smart green coat with a matching hat. It was gratifying when parents took the trouble with their appearance for something as mundane as a school meeting. She had said goodbye to them with a feeling of satisfaction. They had thanked her sincerely for all that she was doing for Kathy. It was good to be appreciated; it was parents such as those who made the job even more worthwhile.

Chapter Seven

'Was it a successful evening, then, Sally?' asked Phil as they set off on the drive to the Carlton Hotel.

There were five of them in the car; Phil's mate, Brian, was on the back seat with Mavis and Eileen, two of the junior teachers. Sally had noticed that Phil had sorted out the seating arrangements, making sure that she had the seat next to him, at least that was how it had seemed to her.

'Yes, very successful,' she replied. 'All satisfied customers, as far as I could tell. How about you? No punch-ups this time?'

'No, it all went very smoothly,' Phil replied. 'The odd query as to why our Jimmy isn't doing as well as Johnny, the boy who lives across the street. It's hard to tell them, isn't it, that Jimmy hasn't got as much upstairs as Johnny has; that he is, in fact, as thick as two short planks!'

Sally laughed. 'Yes, I know what you mean. I try to find

something good to say about every child, but I must admit it's a struggle at times. And I suppose they get more competitive when they go into the juniors, especially in the top year, like you teach.'

'You can say that again,' chimed in Brian from the back seat. He, along with Phil, taught one of the fourth-year classes, the ones who had recently sat for the all-important exam. 'But it's the parents who are far worse than the kids. "Will our Mary pass the scholarship exam? Oh, we do want her to go to the grammar school, don't we, Fred?" It's hard to say that she hasn't a cat in hell's chance!'

'So what do you tell them?' asked Sally.

'Well, I just waffle on about us trying to get as many through as we can. But I try to explain that the secondary schools today are all geared up to what is best for the individual child. And that the secondary modern schools in this area have a very good reputation, and that they're more suited to those who are – what shall we say? – less academically gifted.'

'And do you think they believe you?'

'The more sensible ones do,' Brian replied. 'In some ways, you know, it's very damning to judge a child at the age of eleven. There are so many who turn out to be what we call late developers.'

'They get another chance, though, at thirteen, don't they?' enquired Sally.

'In theory, yes.' It was Phil who answered. 'But many don't take it. They get settled into their school and make new friends, and they possibly don't think it's worth the effort.'

'Do we have to talk shop?' asked Mavis, from the back

seat. 'As far as I'm concerned I've done enough talking about it all for one day. I thought we were going out for a bit of relaxation, to get away from school, to say nothing of a boring husband!'

'Well, you married him!' countered Eileen. 'It's a bit late to say that now, isn't it?'

'What do they say? Marry in haste, repent at leisure?' remarked Mavis. 'Well, I certainly did that.'

'Didn't he mind you coming with us tonight?' asked Eileen.

'He doesn't know, does he? Not that he'd care. So long as he can listen to *Take It From Here* and he's got a good thriller to read, Raymond's not bothered what I get up to.'

Sally was listening with some amusement. The rest of the staff had heard it all before and had learnt to take Mavis's remarks with a pinch of salt. She was a buxom blonde, always ready for a laugh and a joke, a real tonic in the staffroom. She had been married to Raymond for five years, but they had no children. Sally guessed that, in spite of her banter, the couple were quite happily married. And that, contrary to her appearance – she looked more like a barmaid than a teacher – and her seeming nonchalance, Mavis was a surprisingly good teacher. Certainly her class of eight- and nine-year-olds thought the world of her.

It was inevitable, despite Mavis's complaints, that they should talk 'shop'. For the most part it was almost the only thing that they all had in common. They sat in the bar lounge of the Carlton Hotel, the ten of them clustered around two small tables. Sally, who was sitting facing the window, watched the familiar cream and green tramcars, lit up now that darkness had fallen, rattling past on the tramlines on the other side of the wide promenade. And beyond that, the inky blackness of the sea.

They had decided to have a 'kitty', which was the fairest way of paying for the drinks. It would certainly not be right for the men to pay for them all. Brian and Alan were both married, but they joked that their wives had signed their permits for tonight. Sally sipped at her gin and lime and felt contented. Evenings such as this, when she could let her hair down and enjoy herself, had become all too rare. She had settled into rather a rut, although it was one of her own choosing, staying at home in the evenings with her parents, listening to the radio or reading the wide variety of books that she either bought or borrowed from the library. During the winter months she had been attending an evening class for French conversation. She knew the usual schoolgirl French, common to most grammar school pupils, and had decided it would be a good idea to learn to converse in the language. It was questionable, though, whether she would ever get to use the skill. At the moment she was contemplating a trip to Brittany during the long summer holiday, but would it be much fun on her own, she wondered? And would she be brave enough to go alone?

The shop talk had been exhausted and the little group around Sally's table – herself, Phil, Alan and two of the young women from the infant staff – were now discussing Blackpool's football team. They all, it seemed, were keen supporters. Sally went occasionally to the Bloomfield Road ground when her father – quite rarely – was able to get time off from the shop.

'Who are they playing on Saturday?' she asked. 'It's ages since I went to a match.'

'They're playing Preston North End. What you might call a local derby.' Phil leant closer to her. 'Would you like to come along with me?' he asked. He was not exactly whispering, but his voice was low enough for the others not to hear. She wondered, though, why he was being so careful that the remark should not be overheard. 'I shall be going on my own,' he told her. 'I usually go with a friend, but he's away this weekend.'

'Yes, I should love to go. Thanks, Phil,' she replied. 'I'd better dig out my scarf, then I'll look like a real supporter.'

At a quarter to eleven they were all ready to call it a day. Phil dropped Brian off, then Mavis and Eileen, leaving Sally till last. She knew he had gone quite a long way round. He stopped outside her home.

'I'll see you on Saturday, then, Sal,' he said. 'I'll call for you . . . Is half past one OK, then we can get near the front? You'll be all right on the Kop, will you? That's where I usually go.'

'Of course,' she replied. 'That's where I stand when I go with my dad. But I'll see you tomorrow at school, won't I?'

'Yes . . .' he smiled. 'But it's just in case I don't have a chance to talk to you.'

She laughed to herself. 'Yes, I understand, Phil,' she said, still wondering why it needed to be such a big secret. 'Saturday, then. I'll look forward to it.'

'So will I,' he replied. He leant towards her and kissed her lightly on the cheek. 'Goodnight, Sally. It's been great this evening . . . After the meeting, I mean. I've really enjoyed it.'

'So have I, Phil . . . We must do it again sometime, perhaps just you and me,' she said, very daringly. She reached for the door handle, but he jumped up and went round to open it for her.

'See you, Sally . . .' he said, watching her as she went up the path. She turned to wave when she got to the front door; he was still standing by the car.

It's only a football match, she pondered, but at least it was a start. But she would quite like it if it should turn out to be a start to something more.

Winifred was pleased to see that her brother was a good deal more animated than usual after their visit to Kathy's school and their talk to Miss Roberts. She wondered, indeed, if it could be Kathy's teacher who had brought about this change in Albert. She had noticed that he had listened keenly to what the teacher had to say and had talked quite freely to her, unlike the way he often behaved with a young woman he scarcely knew.

'That was a very satisfactory evening,' he remarked, when they arrived home. Kathy was in bed. They had left her in the charge of their next-door neighbour, Mrs Walsh, who was very fond of the little girl and she had seen her into bed at her usual time.

'Will you stay and have a cup of tea with us, Mrs Walsh?' asked Winifred.

'No, thanks all the same,' replied the lady. 'I'll get back if you don't mind. I don't want to miss *Twenty Questions*. Your Kathy's been as good as gold; of course, she always is. What a little treasure she is. I expect you got a good report from her teacher, didn't you?'

'Yes, she's doing nicely, Mrs Walsh,' replied Winifred. 'Thanks very much for looking after her.'

'I'll make the tea just for you and me, then, Winnie,' said Albert, going into the kitchen. Another unusual happening; he normally ensconced himself in an armchair with his pipe and the newspaper whenever he came in from somewhere. She thought she could even hear him humming!

'I'm pleased with our Kathy, aren't you?' he said, when they were settled down with their tea and chocolate digestive biscuits. 'I know she's not exactly the brain of Britain, not quite as clever as some of the kids in the class, but what does it matter? She said herself in that little composition she wrote – well, her teacher called it a story, but they were always compositions when I was at school – she said she'd be working in the hotel when she grew up, so I'm glad she's looking forward to that.'

'Before she becomes a famous authoress!' answered Winifred, with a twinkle in her eye.

'Aye, well, that remains to be seen, doesn't it?' said Albert. 'But she does seem to have a flair for writing, doesn't she? And that painting on the wall that she'd done of the sands and Blackpool Tower, I thought that was really good.'

'She works hard, and that's the important thing,' said Winifred. 'And I don't think she's any trouble in class. Well, we wouldn't expect her to be, would we? And she likes her teacher, which is always a good sign; and I rather think

100

Miss Roberts is quite fond of Kathy too . . . Nice lass, that Miss Roberts, isn't she?' she asked, trying to sound quite nonchalant.

'Yes, a very sensible young woman,' replied Albert. 'Aye, she's got her head screwed on the right way, has that lass. She's a pretty young woman, an' all. I don't remember there being teachers like that when I was at school.' He chuckled. 'Most of 'em were right old battleaxes from what I recall.'

'Yes, they seem to be a different breed now, that's true,' agreed his sister. 'Of course, when we were children everyone over the age of twenty or so looked old to us, didn't they?'

'Yes, maybe you're right . . . How old do you think she might be, that Miss Roberts?' Albert asked casually.

'Oh, not all that young,' answered Winifred. 'Young compared with us, of course. Well, compared with me, I mean. I should imagine she's turned thirty, maybe a bit more. I wonder why she's not married? She's a very attractive young lady. Maybe she lost somebody in the war; she's about that age.'

'Yes, happen so,' said Albert. 'Not that it's anything to do with us.' He remained thoughtful, though, and Winifred could detect a gentleness in his eyes and a trace of a smile on his lips. She didn't dare to hint, though, even jokingly, that he might be smitten with Miss Roberts. If she did he would land on her like a ton of bricks. Besides, she was harbouring secret little thoughts of her own. She was looking forward to the next rehearsal at the drama group more than she had done for ages; and it was not just the challenge of getting to grips with a new play.

They both told Kathy the next morning that they were

very pleased with her progress and that Miss Roberts had said she was doing well. 'She's a very nice young lady,' her father said. 'I reckon you've struck lucky getting into her class, Kathy.'

'Yes, we all like her,' said Kathy. 'She's called Sally. Timothy Fielding saw it on one of her books. It's a nice name, isn't it?'

'Yes, very nice,' agreed Albert, pleased that he could now put a name to the young lady who had impressed him so much. He had thought he was off women for good and all, but now he realised that it might not be so. What the dickens he could do about it, though, he had no idea.

There was almost a capacity crowd at Bloomfield Road on Saturday afternoon. Watching the weekly football match – either the first team or the reserves – was something that Albert liked to do on his own. He was an ardent supporter, but not by any means a shouter. He could feel the excitement inside himself, the suspense whenever the match was nearing an end and it looked as though 'the 'Pool' might lose or draw, and the release of tension when they finally managed to score. He heard the deafening roar of the crowd around him, the cheers, whistles and the raucous noise of the rattles, but Albert greeted each goal in silence; that was his way. Occasionally he had gone with mates of his from the darts team, but he could never bellow out his enthusiasm as they did, and he found that this, somehow, embarrassed him. He wore his orange and white scarf every week, as true supporters did, but not without a feeling of self-consciousness.

He felt the crowd surging around him now on Spion

Kop, pressing against him from the back and sides as he leant against the crush barrier. There had been an accident there a while ago when a crush barrier gave way, but one tried not to think about that. It was turning out to be quite a good match, with Stanley Matthews on top form. Nothing electrifying, though, and the score was one-all at half-time.

The crowd relaxed and began to chat together after the whistle was blown, but it seemed to Albert that he was inconspicuous; nobody tried to engage him in conversation. He looked around him . . . then he felt himself give a start of surprise as he noticed, a few yards to his right, the young woman who had been occupying his thoughts for the last few days. It was Miss Roberts – Sally, as he was allowing himself to think of her – looking most attractive with a little orange bobble hat perched on top of her silvery-blonde hair, and an orange and white scarf wound round her neck. She, too, must be a supporter, then. She was smiling up into the face of the young man who was standing next to her. Albert felt a stab of disappointment and almost anger. He might have known, though, that she would have a boyfriend; she was such a personable young lady. He looked again, more closely; she hadn't noticed him and he didn't think he wanted her to. The fellow looked familiar. Albert had only seen him once or twice before but he knew he was a teacher at the same school. Mr Grantley, he thought he was called, the chap who taught PE and games.

He watched them surreptitiously throughout the interval. It seemed to him that they were good mates, but possibly nothing more than that. They didn't appear to be at all 'lovey-dovey', and he told himself that it was only to be expected that two members of the same staff should attend a football match together.

Blackpool scored again in the second half, making it a win for the home team, the result they had hoped for. Albert hung back, but still kept an eye on the couple as they left the ground. They were not holding hands or linking arms or anything else to show that they were any more than good friends. He was thoughtful as he stood in the long bus queue on Central Drive and remained in a contemplative mood all the way back to North Shore.

'Was it a good match?' asked his sister.

'Yes, not so bad,' he replied. 'We won at any rate, so I suppose you can't ask for more. A bit slow off the mark, though, some of 'em.'

'Well, your tea's ready,' said Winifred. 'I've made a meat and potato pie. I thought you'd be a bit starved, standing outside all afternoon. Come on now, Kathy love. Let's get our meal while it's nice and hot.'

'You'll never guess who I saw at the match this afternoon,' said Albert as they tucked into their meal. He smiled confidingly at his daughter.

'Who, Daddy?' she asked.

'Your teacher, Miss Roberts. She had an orange scarf and hat on as well. I didn't know she supported Blackpool, did you?'

'No, I don't know much about her, really,' answered Kathy. 'Except that I like her. Well, we all like her. I know she's not married, because she's a Miss, isn't she, not a Mrs?'

'Was she on her own?' asked Winifred, watching her brother closely.

'No . . . she was with that fellow that teaches games at Kathy's school. Mr Grantley . . . That's his name, isn't it, Kathy?'

'Yes, we don't see him much 'cause he's a junior teacher. I've seen Miss Roberts get into his car, though, sometimes,' said Kathy. 'Timothy Fielding says that perhaps he's her boyfriend.'

'That Timothy Fielding seems to know an awful lot,' smiled Winifred. 'I expect they're just friends, though, with them teaching at the same school.' She looked reassuringly at her brother as she made the remark.

'Yes . . . that's what I thought,' he replied.

It was later in the evening after Kathy had gone to bed that Winifred decided to broach the subject with her brother, about the thing she knew was on his mind; but she knew she had to be tactful.

'You've taken rather a liking to that teacher of Kathy's, haven't you, Albert?' she began. 'I can tell by the way you talk about her. Well, I can't say I blame you; she seems a lovely lass.'

He did not jump down her throat. She felt that he was pleased she had mentioned it. For his part, he was glad to confide in her, to get it off his chest and talk about this unusual and unsought feeling that had hit him like a bombshell.

'Yes . . . I must confess I'm rather smitten.' He gave a rueful smile. 'Ridiculous, isn't it? You know me, what I'm usually like with women. There's never been anyone since Barbara. I've never wanted anybody else.'

'But time goes by, Albert,' she told him. 'A lot of time has passed since you lost Barbara, and it's all "water under the bridge", as they say.'

'But what on earth have I got to appeal to a nice young woman like that? I'm in my mid-forties, set in my ways. A bit of a grump, I know, at times, and I'm not educated like she is. Anyway, how could I possibly ask her out? I don't even know her, do I, not really?'

'You're still quite a good-looking chap, Albert,' said his sister. 'Don't run yourself down. And it's about time you started looking positively at life, instead of being so negative. Maybe you don't know her very well, but everything has to start somewhere.' She was thinking of how she had met Jeff Bancroft, quite out of the blue. 'And you don't need to speak in a broad accent, you know. I think you put it on at times for effect.'

'Aye, I reckon I do,' he laughed. 'I daresay I could be as posh as the next man if I made the effort.'

'Well, think about it,' said Winifred. 'You never know. Something might turn up. There might well be an opportunity for you to do something about it.'

Sally had enjoyed Phil's company at the football match. They found, as they chatted easily together during the times when they were not watching the game, that they had quite a lot in common, more than she had realised. They liked the same sort of films. Sally was surprised that Phil liked musicals, and he was equally surprised that she enjoyed cowboy films. And they both read detective stories – Ngaio Marsh, Margery Allingham and Conan Doyle, as well as Agatha Christie –

and some of the 'easier to digest' Victorian novelists. She was, therefore, somewhat taken aback and disappointed, too, when Phil brought the car to a halt outside her house and said, 'Cheerio then, Sally. It's been great, hasn't it? See you on Monday, then.'

'Yes . . . great, Phil,' she agreed, trying to sound cheerful. 'Thanks for taking me.' At least he leant across and kissed her cheek, and then opened the door for her. But before she had reached her front door he had driven away with a carefree wave.

So what am I to make of that? she wondered as she took out her key and opened the door. She had expected, at least, that he might have asked her to go out with him that evening, for a drink or to the cinema, or to arrange to see her the following day. Phil Grantley was a mystery and no mistake. She dashed upstairs to her bedroom, unwilling at that moment to face her mother's cross-questioning.

Chapter Eight

Winifred couldn't help smiling to herself. It seemed that she and her brother, somewhat belatedly, were experiencing emotions and feelings that they had assumed were long past and gone. For her part, she had not told Albert about her meeting with Jeffrey Bancroft. Indeed, there was very little to say about it at the moment. He was just a very nice man whom she had enjoyed talking to and whom she believed had shown the same interest in her as she had in him. She tried to warn herself not to read too much into the situation. From the little she already knew of Jeffrey she had gathered he was a friendly man who would find it easy to get on with most people. But she knew she had not felt so attracted to anyone of the opposite sex since she had fallen in love with – and had then lost – Arthur all those years ago. She would be seeing Jeff again on Wednesday. She felt a lift of her spirits when she thought about it. And as she observed her brother she guessed that he would be glad of an opportunity to see again the young woman who had so appealed to him.

And then on Monday Kathy brought home a letter from school that seemed to provide an answer to his dilemma. There was to be a spring fayre on Friday afternoon, commencing at half past three, and this was a letter reminding parents of the event. They had had a similar letter a few weeks back but it had quite slipped Winifred's mind.

'You'll come, won't you, Aunty Win?' begged Kathy. 'And you as well, Daddy. There's going to be stalls selling all sorts of things.' There was a request in the letter for home-made cakes, handmade goods, books, 'bric-a-brac', items for a 'white elephant' stall; anything, in fact, that would be saleable, apart from old clothing (jumble sales were held from time to time as separate events).

'And there'll be games,' Kathy went on excitedly. 'Guessing the name of a doll, and how much a cake weighs, and a bran tub and a tombola – but I'm not sure what that is – and a raffle with lots of prizes. And cups of tea and drinks and things to eat, 'cause it's near teatime.'

'Good gracious! It sounds as though your teachers are going to be very busy,' observed Winifred.

'Some of the mums are going in to help as well,' said Kathy. 'Those that are on the committee of that thingy – you know, the PTFA. D'you think you could come and help, Aunty Win?'

'Oh, I don't know about that, love. I'm not on the committee, am I?' She imagined they would be all much younger than herself, like Sadie Morris. 'But I'll certainly come to the fayre. And I expect your daddy will come as well. You will, won't you, Albert?'

'I don't see any reason why not,' he replied in his usual non-committal way, but Winifred could see that he was not averse to the idea and was even smiling a little. 'There might not be many fathers there, though,' he added. 'Most of 'em'll be working, won't they?'

'The teachers are hoping they'll come later,' said Kathy, 'when they finish work. We're doing a concert, you see; well, just a little one, at half past five. The top class infants – that's us – we're going to sing some songs; well, those that can sing nicely have been chosen, and I'm one of them.'

'Good for you, Kathy,' said her dad.

'And some of the top class juniors are going to do some country dancing. It's going to be really good.'

'I'm sure it is. It all sounds very exciting,' said Winifred. 'We'll look forward to that, won't we Albert?'

'Yes . . . I reckon we will,' he said reflectively.

Winifred had been reading through the script, trying to learn by heart as much as she was able, although they would not need to be word-perfect for a few weeks. It was always easier, though, when your movements were not hampered by a book in your hands and, fortunately, she had been blessed with a good memory that had not let her down yet, despite her advancing years.

Jeff was not there when she arrived, nor had he put in an appearance when they started to rehearse. Snap out of it! she told herself, and concentrate on what you're doing or you're going to look a real fool. You've been given this leading role, so do justice to it.

He turned up about half an hour later and, noticing him from the corner of an eye, she felt a relaxing of her tension. She did not look at him but she was aware that he was watching her.

'Well done!' he said, coming to join her in the interval. 'You're getting to grips with Lady B already, aren't you?'

'I'm trying,' she said. 'It'll be easier when I don't have to rely on the script.'

'When is it being performed?' he asked.

'Oh, not till the end of July. We always give ourselves plenty of time, and make allowances for people going on holiday. We try to arrange our holidays for after the performance, though, if we can. Not that it affects me very much. I can never go away during the summer whilst the visitors are in. We have a break during August, then we meet up again in September . . . You've decided to stay with us, then, have you?' she asked tentatively.

'Oh yes,' he replied. 'I'd already decided after the first meeting.' He smiled at her, his grey eyes looking intently into hers. 'But, as I said, I shall just assist with the stage managing this time and give a hand with the scenery. I'll have a chat with Wilfred after the break and see what he'd like me to do. I don't mind being a "gofer", seeing that I'm the new boy,' he laughed good-humouredly.

Jeff's sister, Mavis Peacock, stood up then to draw their attention to the notices. The main one was that there was to be a coach outing in a few weeks' time to the nearby town of Preston. A well-known amateur dramatic group from that town was also presenting *The Importance of Being Earnest* at one of the smaller theatres there. 'We don't want to pinch any of their ideas, of course,' said Mavis. 'And it's possible that their interpretation will be quite different from ours, but we thought it would make an enjoyable outing. If you're interested in going would you let me know as soon as possible, then I can book the theatre seats.'

'Will you be going?' Jeff asked Winifred.

'Oh yes, I fully intend to go,' she replied. The date chosen was the first Friday evening in May. 'Albert – my brother – sometimes has a darts match on a Friday, but I can always get my next-door neighbour to look after Kathy if necessary.'

'You won't have any visitors in?' asked Jeff.

'No, it's a slack time between Easter and Whitsun. And if we do have a few in we'll be able to sort something out, I'm sure. It's something I don't want to miss . . . What about you, Jeff?' she asked. 'Will you be going?'

'But of course,' he smiled. 'That's why I asked you. I'll put our names down straight away, shall I?'

'Yes please,' said Winifred, very pleased at the way things were progressing.

He was not watching the rehearsal when they started again, but he was there to run her home in his car at the end of the evening.

'Are you doing anything on Saturday?' he asked as he stopped the car outside Holmleigh.

'Not particularly,' she replied. 'Do you mean during the day or in the evening?' Could he possibly be asking her for a 'date', she wondered?

'I was wondering whether you would like to go to the

cinema,' he said. 'I haven't checked what is on, but I'm sure we'll be able to find something that we'll both enjoy.' He laughed. 'I can't get over the number of cinemas that there are in Blackpool.'

'Yes, we're pretty fortunate in that respect,' agreed Winifred. There was the Odeon; the Princess; the Palace Picture Pavilion, as well as the Palace Variety Theatre in the same building; the Winter Gardens cinema; the Tivoli; the Regent; the ABC; and the Imperial, all near the centre of the town, as well as several more in the outlying suburbs. She enjoyed a visit to the cinema but it wasn't much fun going on her own, and Albert never seemed inclined to go with her. She occasionally took Kathy to a matinee on a Saturday afternoon if there was something suitable showing. The little girl loved the singing and dancing in the musicals of Metro-Goldwyn-Mayer and 20th Century Fox, featuring such stars as Betty Grable, Fred Astaire and Ginger Rogers, and of course, she loved the Walt Disney films.

'I'll look in the *Gazette* and see what's on, shall I?' said Jeff. 'That is, if you'd like to go?'

'Yes, I would, very much,' she replied.

'That's great, then.' He grinned at her. 'What sort of films do you like? Have you any preference?'

'Oh, my taste is pretty general,' she told him. 'But I'm not keen on cowboy films, or on gangsters. James Cagney is not one of my favourites,' she smiled.

'Nor mine,' he agreed. 'Laurence Olivier now, or James Mason; they're what I call real actors. But I must confess I'm not averse to something more light-hearted now and again. The

113

'Road' films, for instance. Bing Crosby and Bob Hope . . .'

'And Dorothy Lamour,' added Winifred. 'Yes, I like those too. I took Kathy to see *The Road to Morocco* and she loved it.'

'Will there be any problem regarding your niece?' Jeff asked her. 'Will your brother be able to look after her? He might be going out himself.'

'I very much doubt it,' said Winifred. 'He's usually in on a Saturday. His darts matches are during the week. Don't worry; we'll sort something out, I'm sure.'

'I'll phone you, then, shall I, when we've both looked at the paper?'

'Lovely,' she agreed, smiling at him and feeling like a twenty-year-old going on her first date. He put his hand over hers, then leant across and kissed her gently on the cheek, before getting out of the car and going round to open the door for her.

'Goodnight, Winifred, my dear,' he said. 'Sleep well . . .'

'You too,' she replied. 'And . . . thanks, Jeff. I'll look forward to Saturday.'

'Me too.' He gave a broad smile and a cheery wave as he drove away.

Winifred decided not to tell her brother straight away about her outing with Jeff. He could hardly object, though. She scarcely ever went out, except to church functions or to the drama group. It would be ironic, though, if he should happen to have a date of his own on the same night; two middle-aged people whose life had followed the same routine for so long, and who were now seeking just a little excitement. She forced herself to wake up to reality. She knew – and she knew that Albert would realise, too – that whatever might happen in their personal lives, Katherine had to come first.

Very little work was done on that Friday afternoon at the North Shore school; that is to say very little schoolwork. Lessons were largely abandoned as classes were 'doubled up', releasing half of the teachers to prepare the stalls and games for the spring fayre, helped by the ladies of the committee and their friends who would, later, be in charge of the refreshment room. Several of the older children, those in the fourth-year junior classes, were enlisted to help as well, and they considered themselves to be very important. The rest of the pupils had to contain their excitement all afternoon as they looked forward to what was one of the great social events of the year.

It had been planned to start at three-thirty, which was the finishing time for the infant classes; the juniors did not normally finish until four o'clock, but on this day they were all going home at the same time. It was hoped, though, that very few of them would be going home. It was assumed that mothers – and fathers – meeting their younger children from school would stay for the fayre, and that the older children would have persuaded their parents, grandparents and aunts and uncles to come along as well.

Sally Roberts felt very sad as she watched a few of her pupils, and some from the other classes, put on their coats and then walk dejectedly across the playground. There were only three such in her class, the very ones that she might have known would not be staying to join in the fun; they were the ones whose parents rarely supported the school events or even bothered to turn up on open evenings. Those parents were the ones, however, who would be there, with all guns blazing, should there be a complaint to be made about the teacher or the headmaster.

There was little time to brood, though, as the other children eagerly greeted their parents and guests, leading them proudly around the school. It was not a time for looking at the children's books or talking about their progress, but the teachers had pulled out all the stops to make the school look as attractive as possible. The corridors were decorated with large paintings and friezes made by the various classes. Sally's 'Pied Piper' was there, as well as springtime collages, a depiction of the 'Noah's Ark' story, paintings of Blackpool's attractions – the Tower, the big dipper at the Pleasure Beach, the bright yellow sands and the unusually blue sea, and the tramcars on the busy promenade – and drawings of Mummy and Daddy and 'my house' done by the youngest children, aged four and five.

Sally was in charge of the tombola game. Each person, after paying their sixpence, drew out a raffle ticket and was awarded the corresponding prize. In a true tombola some of the tickets won nothing at all, but it had been agreed that this was too disappointing for the very young children; and so every ticket won a prize, although it might only be a few sweets or a tiny bar of chocolate. The initial outlay was worth it in the end as many were encouraged to have another go.

Kathy Leigh came into the tombola room about ten minutes into the proceedings, with her father and aunt.

'Now, Kathy, are you going to have a turn?' said Sally.

'There are some lovely prizes; you might not win one of the big ones, but you're sure to win something.'

'Yes, we'll all have a go,' said Mr Leigh, feeling in his pocket for some change. 'Here you are, Kathy. You go first.'

The little girl won a brightly coloured pencil and a rubber, with which she seemed highly pleased. Her aunt then won a bottle of Amami shampoo, and her father a bottle of ginger beer.

'It would go very nicely with that whisky,' he remarked, pointing to one of the star prizes.

'Have another go, then, Albert,' said his sister.

'OK. Nothing venture, nothing win,' he said, handing over another sixpence.

They were all astonished when he won the bottle of Black & White whisky.

'Well done!' exclaimed Sally, handing him the bottle. 'I'm very pleased it's going to such a good home! You're not teetotal, then, Mr Leigh?'

'No fear!' he chuckled. 'I'm wondering – Miss Roberts – may we leave these bottles here and collect them later? It'll save us carrying them all round the school. We've a lot to see, haven't we, Kathy?' Kathy nodded, quite pink-cheeked with excitement.

'Certainly,' said Sally. 'I'll put them in the cupboard. Don't forget them, though.'

'There's no chance of that,' said Mr Leigh, smiling warmly at her.

A nice man, she mused as they went away. He had a lovely smile; but she reflected, as she had done before, that he probably did not smile all that often.

117

Kathy was enjoying herself immensely, showing her dad and aunty all the interesting pictures on the walls, and then leading them into the classrooms where the various stalls and games were going on. She chose the name of a doll from a long list of names.

'I think she might be called Sally,' she said, printing her own name carefully on the list. 'It's Miss Roberts' name,' she whispered to her aunt, 'but I don't think many of the others know that.'

It was a lovely baby doll with eyes that closed, dressed in a hand-knitted coat and bonnet. 'You might not win, you know,' her aunt told her. 'It's just luck, really, like the raffle and the tombola.'

'I'm not bothered,' Kathy replied. 'I've got my prize from the tombola and these books, and I'm having a lovely time. Are you enjoying it, Aunty Win?'

'Indeed I am,' Winifred replied. She was pleased to see how delighted Kathy was by everything. She was such a good little girl and so easily pleased. Not like some badly behaved children who were to be seen in Woolworths on a Saturday afternoon, crying blue murder because they couldn't get their own way. Winifred noticed that her brother seemed to be getting into the spirit of things too, in his own quiet way.

In the next room, where there was a home-made cake stall, they met Shirley with her dad. Her mum, who was a member of the committee, was serving on the stall. Shirley had told Kathy that her dad would be able to come because he was on early shift that day and finished at dinner time. Introductions were made whilst Shirley and Kathy smiled at one another.

'I'm pleased to see that most of my fairy cakes have been sold,' said Winifred, 'and the fruit cake that I made.'

'Oh yes, they went very quickly,' said Sadie Morris. 'I didn't know they were yours. You could say they sold like hot cakes,' she laughed, 'whatever that means.'

'Can we go round on our own, me and Kathy?' asked Shirley, after a whispered consultation between the two of them.

'It's all right with me,' said Shirley's mum, 'but you're supposed to be showing your dad round, aren't you?'

'Oh, that's OK,' said Mr Morris, winking at Winifred. 'I think I'll just nip out for a quick smoke in the playground.'

'Behind the bike sheds, eh?' laughed Albert, seeming in a very good mood.

'I don't think there are any bike sheds,' Shirley remarked.

'It's just a joke, love,' said her dad. 'I won't be long, then we could perhaps all have a cup of tea in a little while, before this important concert starts.'

They all agreed that this was a good idea and Frank Morris hurried away, glad to make his escape, thought Winifred.

'Off you go, then, with Shirley,' she said, 'and we'll see you in the tea room in about twenty minutes. You've still got some money to spend, have you?'

'Yes, and I've got a watch on,' said Shirley importantly.

'Well, here's another shilling for each of you,' said Kathy's dad, reaching into his pocket for the two silver coins.

'Thank you, Daddy . . .'

'Gosh! Thank you, Mr Leigh . . .' The two girls beamed with surprise.

My goodness! thought Winifred. Her brother was feeling magnanimous today.

'Come on,' said Shirley. 'I want a go on the bran tub, don't you? And I've seen some hair slides that I like, and now I can afford them.'

Winifred bought some home-made flapjack. She made her own but it would be nice to try someone else's baking for a change.

'Would you like to buy a raffle ticket?' asked one of the older girls in another part of the room. She and her friend were in charge of a small table with books of coloured raffle tickets and a dish of money.

'What's on offer?' asked Albert genially.

'Well, the first prize is a meal for two in a posh restaurant in Blackpool,' the girl replied. 'Then there's this box of fruit, and this big box of chocolates, and this tin of toffees.'

'Go on, then,' said Albert. 'I'll have two tickets, and two for my sister. Not that I ever win anything,' he said as they walked away.

'Don't tell fibs,' said Winifred. 'You won that whisky, didn't you? It might be your lucky day.'

'Oh yes, so I did,' he agreed. 'Remind me to pick it up later, Winnie.'

She didn't think he would need reminding. He had been in remarkable high spirits since his encounter with Sally Roberts.

There was a goodly crowd assembled in the school hall at half past five to watch the display of singing and dancing put on by some of the children. Winifred and Albert had

120

met up again with Sophie and Frank Morris, and after they had all had a cup of tea and a buttered scone they had stayed together. Kathy and Shirley had gone off in great excitement as they were taking part in the musical entertainment.

Before the concert could start, though, it was time for the raffle to be drawn. The prizes were displayed on a table at the front of the hall, and the headmaster, Mr Williams, was asked to draw out the first lucky ticket. Everyone fumbled in their pockets and bags for the pink and green tickets, then waited eagerly to hear the result.

'Pink ticket, number 105,' called out the headmaster. 'First prize – a voucher for two for a meal at the Fishing Net; that's the newly opened seafood restaurant in Blackpool, for those who don't know. Now, who is the lucky winner?'

Winifred nudged her brother. 'Albert, it's yours!' He was sitting there quite unconcerned, like most of the men were, not bothering to check the tickets that his sister had taken out of her purse. 'Yours were the pink ones and I had the green. Didn't I tell you it might be your lucky day? Go on . . .' She gave him a push. 'Go and collect your prize.'

'Do I have to?' he mumbled. 'What do I want with a meal for two? I'd rather have that box of chocolates.'

'Go on with you!' she retorted. 'I don't think you've any choice. It's the first prize.' She waved her hand. 'It's here, Mr Williams. It's my brother's ticket. He's coming . . .'

'Congratulations, sir,' said the headmaster, handing him an envelope. 'Now, would you draw out the next ticket, please?'

Albert did so, and Mr Williams called out the next number. 'Green ticket, number 59, for the voucher to spend at Sweetens bookshop.'

'That might've been better,' Albert murmured to his sister as he returned to his seat. 'I could've given it to our Kathy to spend.'

'Don't look a gift horse in the mouth!' she chided him. 'You miserable so and so!'

'Well, we cook our own meals, don't we?' he persisted. 'Whoever heard of going out for a meal when you can have much better food at home? Especially at Holmleigh.'

'Shut up, Albert!' she told him. 'See, it's time for the entertainment to start now . . .'

Winifred was pleased to see that he did stop muttering, and he watched with interest as the younger children filed in through the door and assembled themselves into three tidy lines, obviously well trained by their teacher – not Miss Roberts – who sat down at the piano.

About forty of the 'best singers', as Kathy had told her aunt, from the third-year infant classes, had been chosen to form a choir. They all looked very smart, the girls in their navy gymslips with the red and blue woven girdle, and the red and blue striped tie that they wore on special occasions. Most of the girls had red ribbons in their hair, Kathy's topping her dark curls and Shirley's tied at the end of her blonde plaits. The two friends were in the centre of the front row, smiling broadly, although Kathy had said they had been told quite firmly that they must not wave to their parents and friends in the audience.

There seemed to be more girls than boys in the choir.

Kathy had told her aunt that the boys were inclined to 'grunt' rather than sing; but that her friend Timothy Fielding was one that had been chosen.

'He sits on the row just behind me,' she said. 'He's got a lot of fair hair that stands up like a hedgehog.'

A good description, thought Winifred, as she looked at the boy she had heard so much about. A shock of blonde hair and a rather cheeky face. He looked as though he might be a handful, but he was very clean and tidy, as were all the boys, dressed in their dazzling white shirts – she guessed they were not usually so clean – and red and blue striped ties.

The teacher played the introductory bars and the children started to sing, 'As I was going to Strawberry Fair . . .' They were surprisingly tuneful and melodious, and the parents and friends listened with obvious delight as the children went through their repertoire of folk songs and old English melodies, the same ones that they had sung at school many years before: 'Early One Morning', 'Dashing Away with the Smoothing Iron', 'The Miller of Dee', and the most poignant song of all, 'The Lark in the Clear Air'.

Winifred was pleased to see that Albert had got over his fit of pique by the time they had finished. He turned to her with a look of tenderness in his eyes. 'They were good, weren't they? I'm proud of our Kathy; she was loving it, wasn't she? By Jove, those songs take me back a bit.'

'Me too,' agreed Winifred.

There was another round of applause as the children and their teacher sat down at the front of the hall to watch the older children do their bit. These boys and girls were ten and eleven years old and they performed very ably the country dances they had been practising for several weeks: 'The Dashing White Sergeant', 'Strip the Willow' and 'Sir Roger de Coverley'.

'I think I'd have felt a bit daft if I were one of the boys,' Albert observed, 'but they didn't seem to mind, did they?'

'I don't suppose it's much different really from ballroom dancing,' said Winifred, 'and you're quite good at that, aren't you? Or . . . you used to be,' she added. She remembered that he had hardly danced at all since the time he had used to dance with Barbara. Maybe she shouldn't have mentioned it.

'That's a thing of the past,' he replied, but he didn't look as morose as he usually did when reminded of the days gone by. 'I've been thinking, Winnie,' he said, as they went to find Kathy, who was waiting outside the hall. 'You can have that voucher for the meal. I daresay you can find somebody to go with you, can't you?'

For a moment she was tempted, but she had a better idea. 'No, Albert,' she said. 'You won it and you must use it.' She wondered if she dared suggest what was in her mind. 'Why don't you invite Kathy's teacher, Miss Roberts, to go with you?' she ventured.

'I wouldn't dare!' he replied. 'How could I do that?' But he looked as though he might well consider it.

'Of course you dare,' she replied. 'You can say it's a way of saying thank you for all she's done for Kathy.'

'But it's free, isn't it? It's not going to cost me anything. Not much of a thank you, is it?'

'You'd be buying drinks, wouldn't you? They wouldn't be free. Oh, go on, Albert,' she coaxed him. I think it would be a lovely idea. We have to see her now to collect your other prize. And what did I hear you say earlier today? Nothing venture, nothing win . . .'

Chapter Nine

The Fishing Net had opened up in the centre of Blackpool some six months previously and was becoming one of the most popular places to dine, or to 'eat out', as people often said. Eating out rather than dining at home was a pastime that was only just starting to be accepted as a popular thing to do. The older generation still regarded it as something strange and unnecessary. Why should anyone want to go out for a meal when you could eat just what you wanted at home and for much less cost?

Food was becoming a little more plentiful in the early Fifties, after the restrictive war years, although food rationing was still continuing. The restaurants, however, such as they were, didn't seem to have much of a problem in putting on a reasonable meal. Venues, though, were somewhat limited. There were hotel dining rooms where outsiders could book a meal, and some department stores had cafés for a quick snack. Lyons Corner Houses were popular in London, but there was nothing of that ilk in the provinces.

And so the Fishing Net was something of an innovation. As its name implied, it served mainly fish dishes. Crabs and lobster, usually served with salad; oysters and mussels for those who wished to be a bit more adventurous and were not too squeamish; and the more usual fish dishes – hake, haddock, halibut or plaice – served with chips or another potato alternative and an accompaniment of vegetables. One could also order gammon or steak, but the majority plumped for fish as the restaurant was best known for its good variety and excellent cooking of this commodity.

It was Sally's first visit to the Fishing Net, although she had often walked past it on her shopping trips to Blackpool and had thought how nice it would be to have a meal there. Which was why she had not hesitated for more than a few seconds – the delay in answering had been due to surprise rather than reluctance – when Mr Leigh had invited her to share in his raffle prize.

'Well . . . yes, of course I will,' she had replied, feeling quite dumbfounded. 'Thank you for asking me, Mr Leigh. How very kind of you . . . Yes, I would love to go.'

The poor fellow had gone quite pink with embarrassment – she guessed he had been plucking up courage to ask her – and she tried to put him at his ease.

'It's . . . it's just a little way of saying thank you . . . er . . . Miss Roberts – for all you have done for our Kathy,' he managed to say, with a little hesitation. 'She's very fond of you, I know. She never stops talking about you. It's Miss Roberts this, and Miss Roberts that, all the time.'

She smiled at him. 'Children are often like that about their teachers in the infant school. Sometimes we're a sort of mother figure, you see. They've had to leave Mummy at home and . . . well . . . I suppose we're the next best thing.' She had stopped then, aware of what she had just said. She could have kicked herself. Little Katherine, of course, didn't have a mother. But to apologise might only make things worse. She had noticed that Mr Leigh had looked a little disturbed; not angry, but the diffident smile had vanished from his face for a moment.

Then he replied, 'Kathy's mother died. She doesn't remember her, but she thinks the world of her Aunty Win. I don't know what I'd have done without Winnie.'

'Yes, I know she does,' Sally replied, a little confusedly. 'She thinks a lot of you as well, Mr Leigh. She often talks about you both . . . I was only speaking generally – about mothers. I didn't mean—'

'That's all right.' He smiled again, then he said, 'Shall we arrange a date, then, for this meal? It doesn't state any particular time.'

They had decided on the following Tuesday. This was an evening that appeared to be free for both of them. Mr Leigh mentioned that his darts match was on Thursday that week, and Sally's only regular engagement was night school on a Monday.

'I don't have a car,' he told her almost apologetically. 'I've never really seen the need for one so far, although it's something I've been considering.'

'Neither have I,' she answered. 'More to the point, neither has my father,' she added, as she could see that Mr Leigh was a little worried about his lack of his own transport. 'Dad works in town; he's the manager of a gents' outfitters, but he says it would be too much trouble to park. Shall we go on the bus, then?'

'Certainly not,' he replied. 'I wouldn't dream of it. No, I shall get a taxi, and if you give me your address I shall come there and pick you up. What time shall we say?'

They decided on six-thirty, then they would be ready to dine at seven o'clock. He didn't think it would be necessary to make a reservation but decided to do so just to make sure.

As Sally watched him leave the classroom with his bottle of whisky – it certainly had been his lucky evening – to meet his daughter and sister who were waiting outside, she started to wonder what she had done. Was it ethical, she asked herself, to accept an invitation such as this from the father of one of her pupils? (She was reminded of the old joke about a woman teacher meeting a man on a crowded bus and exclaiming, 'Don't I know you from somewhere? Oh yes, of course; you're the father of one of my children!') She smiled at the thought, telling herself that it was, as Mr Leigh had said, just his way of saying thank you. But she had noticed a hint of regard in his eyes as he looked at her, not only tonight but at their previous meeting at the open evening. She was not averse to a bit of admiration from a member of the opposite sex. He was quite an attractive man, too, when he smiled, and she guessed he might be altogether different from the aloof and rather stern person that he seemed to be at a first acquaintance.

Should she tell the rest of the staff about it? she pondered. She decided to think about that over the weekend. She had been wondering whether another invitation from Phil Grantley might be forthcoming, to another football match or to something that might be considered more of a proper date. But since their visit to the match last Saturday he had said very little to her. Not that he had deliberately avoided her; he had just spoken to her in the same casual way that he spoke to the other members of the staff. Sally was hurt; she couldn't understand him at all. It really seemed as though there was something on his mind, but if he didn't want to confide in her – which he clearly didn't – then there was nothing she could do about it. She wondered if, unwittingly, she had accepted Mr Leigh's invitation as a way of getting back at him? That could only have some effect, though, if Phil knew about it.

When it came to the crunch she told no one about it except, of course, her parents. She didn't see the point in telling the rest of the staff. School would be breaking up on Wednesday for the Easter holiday and she wouldn't see any of them for the next two weeks. But she had to face something of a cross-examination from her mother.

'What do you know about this man?' she asked. 'I mean, what's his background, and should you really be doing this? Couldn't it be construed as unprofessional conduct, getting involved with one of the parents?'

'I'm not getting involved, Mum,' Sally had replied, rather testily. 'I'm old enough to look after myself and I know what I'm doing. He's a perfectly respectable man. He owns a hotel. He's the chef there, and his wife died several years ago. For heaven's sake, I'm only going out for a meal with him!'

'All right, dear. I'm sorry,' her mother had replied. 'We

just want what is best for you, and what is right for you, your dad and me, that's all.' Sally knew that although her parents were proud of her status as a teacher, they still thought, on the other hand, that she should be married by now with a couple of children.

However, her mother kissed her cheek and said, 'Have a lovely time, dear', when the taxi pulled up at the door. Mr Leigh didn't make any move to come to the house door, which Sally was glad about, nor did her mother remain on the threshold to have a 'nosey', but went inside and closed the door.

Mr Leigh got out and opened the taxi door for her, and she sat on the back seat next to him. He looked very smart in a navy suit with a faint stripe, a pale-blue shirt which, she noticed at once, matched the colour of his eyes, and a maroon tie with a quiet paisley design.

Sally had deliberated about what she should wear. She liked her dusky-pink dress and she knew it suited her; then she remembered she had worn it at the open evening and that Mr Leigh might remember it. If he was anything like her father, though, and like a lot of men, she suspected, he would not have noticed what she was wearing. How many times had she heard her dad say to her mother, 'Is that a new dress, dear? No? I don't remember seeing it before.' Anyway, what the heck did it matter? she told herself. It was just a casual dinner with someone who was little more than an acquaintance. She always liked to look her best, though, and in the end she had decided to wear her moss-green suit with the fashionable wing collar and the accordion-pleated, mid-calf-length skirt, with a pale-green silky blouse underneath in case she took off her jacket.

Mr Leigh smiled as though he was pleased to see her. 'Hello, Miss Roberts,' he began as the taxi drove off. 'I hope you're looking forward to this meal as much as I am.'

'I certainly am, Mr Leigh,' she replied. 'But I wonder if we might be a little less formal tonight? My name is Sally. I feel like a real old school ma'am when you keep calling me Miss Roberts.'

'Certainly,' he replied. 'I was waiting for you to suggest it, actually. I didn't like to, with you being Kathy's teacher an' everything. Anyway, I'm Albert.' He grimaced. 'Not surprising really, is it, that I was reluctant to tell you? I hate it, but that's what my parents called me and unfortunately I don't have another name, so I'm stuck with it.'

'A popular name at the time, I suppose,' she said, thinking to herself that she didn't like it much either. 'Queen Victoria's husband was Albert, wasn't he? I suppose that's why it became popular.'

'I'm not as old as all that!' he retorted, but fortunately he was laughing. She laughed too.

'No . . . sorry . . . I wasn't suggesting that you are. But the next king – Edward VII – he was an Albert as well, wasn't he? Didn't they call him Bertie?' She guessed that Mr Leigh – Albert – would have been born during the reign of that monarch. She, Sally, was born in 1916, during the reign of George V, which made her feel very old when she thought about it; and she guessed that Albert Leigh must be quite a few years older than herself.

'You have a good knowledge of history,' he commented, 'but then you would have, with you being a teacher.'

'It's not terribly relevant to being an infant teacher, though,' she replied. 'But I've always been interested in history, especially modern history, if you know what I mean.'

'Yes, the First World War is being regarded as history now, isn't it?' he said. 'I wasn't old enough to be in that one, but I did my bit in the last one. Anyway – Sally – I'm pleased you agreed to come with me. I hope we'll have a very pleasant evening.'

'I'm sure we will,' she smiled.

The taxi dropped them right outside the Fishing Net and Sally waited whilst he settled up with the driver. There was a welcoming feel to the restaurant even from the outside. The paintwork was sea green and curtains that resembled fishing nets were draped across the windows.

There was a pleasant friendly ambience, too, when they entered the place. Albert gave his name, and a waitress in a smart green dress with a paler green apron and cap showed them to a corner table for two. The tablecloths were of green and white checked cotton, the silver cutlery was bright and gleaming and the table mats depicted seascapes of various resorts and fishing ports of the British Isles.

The same theme was continued on the walls. There were looped fishing nets, lobster pots, and sepia photographs of fishermen and trawlers; stormy seas; herring girls – as the women who used to follow the fishing fleets around the coast of the British Isles were called – engaged on their task of gutting the herrings; and well-known fishing ports of Britain, with Fleetwood, a few miles up the coast, being featured more than once.

The menus were large, both in shape and in content, and

the waitress handed one to each of them, at the same time lighting the candle in a green glass bowl in the centre of the table.

'Hmm . . . We're quite spoilt for choice,' observed Albert. 'Shall we have something to start with? I think the allowance they've given us will run to that . . . But it doesn't matter, of course,' he added hurriedly, as though realising that that might sound rather stingy. 'You choose whatever you want, Sally. We're here to have a good time.'

The list of starters was not quite as extensive as the main menu. Neither of them fancied hors d'oeuvres or soup. 'I'd rather like some shrimps,' said Sally.

'Yes, I'll go for that too,' agreed Albert. 'Morecambe Bay shrimps potted in butter; sounds good. Yes, let's push the boat out, if you'll pardon the pun.'

When the waitress returned in five minutes or so they had both agreed to order scampi with chips – plus vegetables – for the main course, a dish that was becoming very popular. From a separate wine list Albert ordered a bottle of Chardonnay.

'I'm not a connoisseur of wines,' he told her. 'Far from it, but I'm told that Chardonnay is considered to be rather superior to the ordinary Liebfraumilch.'

They all sounded quite glamorous to Sally. Wine drinking was becoming rather more fashionable now because many folk had discovered that pleasure on holidays abroad, but this was something that she had not yet experienced, apart from a short trip to France a couple of years ago with her parents.

'Do you serve drinks at your hotel?' she asked. 'Alcoholic ones, I mean.'

'No, we don't,' he answered. 'We don't have a licence. Very few of the smaller hotels have as yet. It's just the larger ones like the Norbreck and the Imperial, and lots of others, of course. Maybe one of these days . . .'

Conversation lagged a little while they were waiting for their meal. But just as Sally was searching in her mind for an opening remark the wine waiter arrived with the bottle of Chardonnay. He poured a little of the golden liquid into Albert's glass. He tasted it knowingly and when he nodded that it was acceptable the waiter poured out a glassful for each of them.

'Cheers,' said Albert, raising his glass. 'Here's to an enjoyable evening . . . and the start of a friendship?' he added with a slight query in his voice and a quizzical look at her.

She nodded. 'Yes . . . Cheers, Albert,' she replied and they clinked their glasses. 'Mmm . . . very nice,' she commented, after she had taken a good sip of the wine. 'Not too sweet, not too dry; very pleasant.'

'As I say, I'm not an expert,' Albert said, 'but it seems OK to me.' He grinned. 'Well then, Sally, are you going to tell me a little about yourself? For instance, how long have you been teaching?'

She laughed. 'A good way of finding out how old I am, Albert?'

'No . . . no, not at all.' He looked a little confused. 'That wasn't what I meant. Anyway, I don't know how old you were when you started teaching, do I?'

'It's no secret,' she replied. 'Why should it be? I've been teaching for fourteen years, all at the same school. I trained for two years at a college in Manchester and then I was lucky enough to find a post in my hometown, which pleased my parents, of course.'

'And you must have liked it there, at your school, or you wouldn't have stayed?'

'Yes, that's true. There has never been any incentive for me to move elsewhere. I was twenty when I started teaching, so that makes me thirty-four, doesn't it?' she added with a twinkle in her eye.

'All right, cards on the table,' he replied. 'I'm forty-five, and I see no reason to be secretive about it . . .' He hesitated for a moment. 'You're an attractive young woman, Sally. Have you no special boyfriend? Forgive me if you think I'm being personal, but you must have a lot of admirers?'

She laughed. 'If so, then I don't know where they are. No, I don't have a boyfriend.' She was soon to realise why he had asked.

'Actually . . . I noticed you at the football match,' he told her. 'When they played Preston. You were with that young fellow from your school. And . . . well . . . I just wondered.'

'Oh yes, that's Phil Grantley,' she replied. 'I didn't see you there. You're a supporter of Blackpool, then?'

'Of course! You could say I'm one of their greatest fans,' he said with the most enthusiasm she had seen him show so far. 'I never miss a match if I can help it. What about you? Do you often go?'

'Occasionally, when I've someone to go with,' she said. 'I've been with my dad sometimes, when he's not working. And then Phil asked me to go with him, so I did. We're just mates,' she added. 'That's all. Just like I'm mates with most of the other fellows on the staff.' Any regrets that she had felt regarding Phil's lack of interest she was trying to push to one side.

'Actually . . . I was engaged once,' she went on to say, just in case he should think there was something odd about her. 'To another teacher that I met soon after we both started working in Blackpool. But then . . . well . . . the war came along and unfortunately Martin was killed. He had joined up straight away and he was part of a bomber crew. They were shot down during the Battle of Britain.'

'How dreadful for you.' Albert looked most concerned. 'Yes . . . that terrible war caused misery for thousands, in all sorts of ways. As I know from my own experience,' he added. He offered no further explanation and she did not ask. He looked almost angry for a moment, and she assumed that it might be something to do with losing his wife. Then he smiled rather sadly. 'But life has to go on. I expect you have learnt that, haven't you, Sally?'

'Indeed I have,' she replied. 'As I said, I enjoy my job; in fact it's become almost my whole life. Which, I suppose, is not entirely a good thing,' she added thoughtfully.

Their shrimps arrived – tiny pink morsels in butter in little brown earthenware pots, served with triangles of brown bread and butter. They both proclaimed them delicious, and just enough not to take the edge off the appetite.

The scampi dish, too, which soon followed, came up to expectations. The pink shellfish, which were really the tail ends of large lobsters, were moist and flavoursome, encased in crispy breadcrumbs. The chips, too, tasted like the very best home-made ones.

'I must confess I've never had this dish before,' Albert said. 'It's well worth the trying.'

'You don't serve scampi at your hotel, then?' asked Sally.

'No, we never have done. But it's something I may well consider putting on the menu. It would be a nice change for a high tea. I could learn quite a lot from this menu here. I'm pleasantly surprised at the quality of the food and the standard of the cuisine.'

'Yes, it really is excellent,' agreed Sally as she tasted the fresh garden peas and the green beans which complemented the fish.

'Do you know . . . when I won the raffle prize I was not particularly pleased at first,' Albert told her. 'I thought it was a question of "coals to Newcastle", if you see what I mean. I've never been in the habit of dining out. I was conceited enough to think that we put on a better meal at our own hotel, but I know now how mistaken I was. And then . . . well . . . I thought of inviting you along, and I'm so glad that I did. And so pleased that you agreed to come with me.'

'I'm pleased too,' she replied, meeting his eyes for several seconds as he regarded her with obvious admiration. She lowered her gaze, a little discomfited. One 'date' – if you could call it that – was all right, but she was not sure that she would want to go out with him again.

'Now, do you think you could manage a pudding?' he asked, as the waitress arrived to take away their empty plates. They had done justice to the meal, only a few chips remaining on each of their plates.

'I'll leave you a few minutes to decide,' the waitress smiled as she handed out the menus again. 'But I can recommend the lemon meringue pie, one of our chef's specialities.'

'That's good enough for me, then,' said Albert. 'How about you, Sally?'

'Yes, I agree,' she replied. 'It's one of my favourites.'

'We'll both have that, then.' Albert handed the menus back. 'And then two coffees, please.'

'My mother makes lemon meringue,' said Sally. 'But she uses a packet mix; it's really good, though.'

'Yes, it's a very popular sweet at the moment,' said Albert. 'It always goes down well when we put it on. I must confess, though, that I use a ready-made mix as well. Shh . . .' He put a finger to his lips. 'Sometimes we have to consider the time factor and cut a few corners now and then.'

'I'm sure you have a good reputation, though,' said Sally. 'Have you had the hotel a long time?'

'For ever,' he said, smiling. 'At least it seems so.' He explained that the business had been started by his parents in the early 1900s, and it had been taken for granted that he and his sister should work there. When his parents had retired he and Winifred had taken over the boarding house and had tried to make it a little more 'high class'.

'We gave it a name,' he said. '"Holmleigh" – one of my sister's bright ideas – and we refer to it as a private hotel now.'

'And you are expecting that Katherine will work there as well, are you, when she leaves school?' asked Sally. He seemed to pick up on the note of slight censure in her tone.

'Yes, I hope so,' he replied, 'although it's a long time off; Kathy's only six, well, nearly seven. Who knows what might happen in the future? Why? Don't you think it's a good idea?'

'I believe in children being allowed to attain their full potential,' she replied. 'Katherine's a very bright little girl. She may well have other ideas when she grows up. I know she says that's what she wants to do at the moment, but she doesn't really know about much else yet, does she?'

'Well, we'll see,' he replied. 'We got the impression, Winnie and I, that Kathy was just an average sort of scholar. I know she tries hard – you said so – but she's not top of the class or anything like that, is she?'

'No, but children often develop later and surprise us all,' said Sally. 'Anyway, we can't really look so far ahead, can we?'

The lemon meringue pie arrived and they tucked into it with gusto. It was time for a change of direction in the conversation, thought Sally. She had noticed a certain edginess in Albert's remarks. A man who likes his own way? she pondered. But then her married friends told her that most of them did! She had noticed, too, that he never spoke of his wife and she assumed that this must be a 'no-go' area.

'Scrumptious!' he declared, spooning up the last morsel of his lemon meringue. 'That's one of our Kathy's words, and it sums it up very nicely.' His earlier tetchiness seemed to have vanished. He leant across the table, looking more intently at her.

'You were saying earlier, Sally,' he began, 'that teaching seems to have become your whole way of life. And I'm pretty much the same with the hotel; my life revolves around it. Not entirely a good thing, as you also remarked. It seems to me that I need a change, and so do you.' He paused for a moment before saying, 'Would you consider coming out with me again? We get along very nicely, don't we, and . . . well . . . I would like to see you again.'

She did not answer for a moment. She had assumed that this would be an isolated occasion, but maybe she should have guessed that he might have other ideas. It might be churlish to refuse. She didn't need to get too involved with him if she didn't wish to do so. And where could be the harm in accepting? Invitations were pretty thin on the ground at the moment. She liked him, perhaps more than she had thought she might, although his company had kindled no real spark of attraction or excitement in her.

'Yes, why not?' she answered, smiling at him in a friendly way. 'Thank you, Albert. Yes, I'll go out with you again, sometime.' She wanted to make it clear to him that it might not be a regular occurrence, and maybe not just yet either, if that was what he had in mind.

'That's good,' he replied. 'I thought you might say no.'

She could see that he would have been disappointed if she had refused. The relief he was feeling now that she had agreed showed in the more relaxed tone of his voice. She decided she would go along with her decision to see him again with as much enthusiasm as she could muster. It was no use being half-hearted; but at the same time she pondered that she hardly knew the man. It might well turn out that they had very little in common, or that they didn't like one another very much on a further acquaintance.

But he seemed determined to please her. 'What sort of things do you like to do?' he asked. 'The cinema, theatre, dancing . . . or another meal? I don't think you're the sort of young lady who makes a habit of going to pubs, are you?'

She agreed that this was true. 'It's the way I've been brought up,' she told him. 'Like many girls – women, I suppose I should say! – of my age. It wasn't the thing for women to go into pubs on their own, was it, or even with men at one time? Not until the war; I suppose that has changed things to a certain extent. I do have a drink – occasionally – with some of the members of our staff. Yes . . . I enjoy the theatre and cinema, when I go, which isn't very often. I used to enjoy dancing, but I haven't been for ages.' Hardly at all since Martin was killed, she mused. They had spent many happy times dancing at the Tower or the Winter Gardens ballroom. 'The only thing I do regularly – once a week – is my French conversation class.'

'And I have a darts match once a week,' he replied. 'Not always the same night, and occasionally it might be more than one night; but I'm sure it's a problem we can get round. I must admit I go to the pub . . . oh, possibly two or three times a week, but it's mainly for the company. There's just my sister and myself at home, apart from Kathy, of course. We get on quite well, but sometimes I like a change of company and so does Winnie.'

'You'll be getting busy at the hotel very soon, won't you?' Sally enquired.

'Yes, it'll be Easter this weekend, of course, and the first of our visitors will be arriving. After that there's a lull until Whitsuntide, then it's all go until the end of the Lights. At least, we hope it will be. But the boss has to be allowed a night or two of freedom. Bosses, I should say; Winnie and I sort it out between us.' He smiled. 'I'm sure we'll be able to come to some arrangement.'

Sally smiled back, a little hesitantly. It seemed as though he was assuming he would still be seeing her during the summertime. Well, that remained to be seen.

'Actually, I had a bit of a surprise last weekend,' he went on. 'My sister, Winnie, she had a date, of all things! With a man, I mean.'

'And that was unusual, was it?' asked Sally.

'I'll say so! You could've knocked me down with a feather when she told me. Apparently she's met this chap at her drama group. He's only just joined, just come to live in Blackpool, and they seem to have taken quite a shine to one another.'

Sally laughed. 'And why not? Your sister is an attractive-looking woman.' She had been going to say, for her age, but decided not to.

'Well, yes . . . happen she is. But there's never been anyone for Winnie – well, not that I know of – since Arthur was killed. He was her fiancé; at least, I think they were engaged, I'm not sure. I was only a young lad at the time. He was killed right at the end of the first war, not this last one.'

'Good gracious! That's a long time ago,' said Sally.

'Aye . . . er . . . yes, so it is. A lot of women were in the same boat, though. There was a great shortage of men and – like I say – she never seemed to be bothered once she had got over losing Arthur. Then, blow me down! She tells me she's met this Jeff fellow.'

'Have you met him?'

'Yes, just once. He came to call for her last Saturday and they went off to the pictures. He's quite a good-looking chap,

I suppose, and he seems very nice. About Winnie's age, I should say, and he's a widower.'

'So you're thinking it will be more difficult if you both want to go out at the same time, is that it?' asked Sally.

'Aye . . . yes, I reckon it might be. But I'm sure there'll be a way round it. I'll have a chat to her . . . So, what do you think, Sally? You'll risk another outing with me, will you?'

'Yes, of course, Albert. Why not? I've already said so.'

'So shall we say the cinema, then? Not this Saturday – our guests will be settling in. Is the Saturday after all right with you?'

They agreed that they would both consult the *Evening Gazette* and see if they could find a film they would both enjoy; there were cinemas enough to choose from in Blackpool. Albert would ring Sally at her home; fortunately they were on the phone.

'Please don't think I'm in the habit of doing this, Sally,' Albert made a point of assuring her. 'Taking young women out, I mean.'

'I didn't think so.' She laughed. 'Anyway, it's really nothing to do with me, is it, however many lady friends you have had.'

'But I haven't,' he insisted. 'Not since Barbara . . .' He shook his head. 'I've never been interested.'

'Well then, I'm honoured,' she said quietly.

After they had finished their coffee Albert settled the bill and the waitress called a taxi for them. He shook her hand in quite a formal way when the car drew up at her door.

'Thank you for a lovely evening,' she said. 'I'm pleased you invited me.'

'And I'm pleased you came,' he answered. 'Good night, Sally. I'll be in touch with you.' He raised his hand in salute as the taxi drew away.

She was a little dazed with a surfeit of wine; between them they had emptied the bottle. She decided not to give too much thought to what the future might hold until she had had a night's sleep.

Chapter Ten

When Sally returned to school after the Easter holiday she was surprised to find Phil Grantley waiting for her outside her classroom door.

'Hello, Phil . . .' She greeted him cheerfully, as though there was nothing amiss between them. There wasn't, really, as far as she knew, apart from his recent aloofness, which had led her to think that it might be best if she tried to forget her awakening interest in him. 'Have you had a good holiday?' she enquired.

'No . . . not really,' he replied. 'Actually, that's what I want to talk to you about, so I thought I'd have a word with you away from the rest of the staff.'

'Whatever's the matter, Phil?' she asked. He didn't look his normal cheerful self, but then, as she recalled, neither had he seemed so for the last week or so, before the school broke up for Easter. 'You're not ill, are you?' He did, in fact, look rather pale, with dark shadows under his eyes.

'No, I'm not ill,' he replied. 'I've not been sleeping too well; I've had a lot on my mind . . . Look, I can't tell you now. The bell will be going soon, and there isn't really much opportunity to chat at school, is there? There's always someone else around. I'll run you home from school tonight, and then I'll tell you all about everything . . . if that's all right with you?'

'Yes, that's fine, Phil,' she replied, feeling very mystified. 'We'll try and get away on time, shall we?'

He nodded. 'Yes, and . . . er . . . Sally . . .' He was looking at her rather solemnly. 'I'm sorry if I've been a bit offhand with you lately. I realise now that I might have been. I didn't mean it, and I hope you still think of me as a friend?'

'Of course I do, Phil.'

He smiled then, but a little uncertainly. 'OK then; I'll see you later. Back to the grindstone now, eh?' he added, sounding more like his normal self.

Whatever could be the matter? Sally wondered, as she went into her classroom, ready to greet the return of thirty-six eager children. Most of them were keen to get back to school at their age. It was only as they grew older, usually not until they were of secondary school age, that they could be compared with Shakespeare's schoolboy, 'creeping like snail, unwillingly to school'.

The bell sounded a few minutes later and there was a charge of small bodies into the room.

'Hello, Miss Roberts . . .'

'Have you had a nice holiday, Miss Roberts . . . ?'

'We've been away, Miss Roberts. We went to see my aunty in Wigan . . .'

'We went on the sands, but it was a bit cold . . .'

She was greeted on all sides by her enthusiastic pupils. 'Hello, everybody,' she said. 'Come along now and settle down. You can tell me all about your holiday later and what you've all been doing.'

She heard Timothy Fielding, as he passed by her desk, saying in an audible whisper to his friend, Stanley, 'I reckon she'll have us writing about it, don't you?'

She smiled to herself. Spot on, Timothy! she thought. That would be one of the first things on the timetable, to discuss their 'news' and then to write about a day they had enjoyed during their holiday.

Katherine Leigh smiled shyly as she went to her table. Sally wondered if she knew that her father had been out on two 'dates' with her teacher. She and Albert hadn't actually talked about whether he should tell Kathy. It wasn't as if they were courting, she thought to herself, or regarding it as a long-term friendship, although she had agreed to see him again on Saturday. She suspected that Kathy might already know about it. Her smile, to Sally, had seemed to be rather a secretive one. But she hoped that the little girl would keep it to herself and certainly not confide in her friend, Shirley Morris! She was a little busybody, if ever there was one. Sally didn't want it all round the playground that 'Miss Roberts is going out with Kathy Leigh's dad!' Well, she would just have to trust to Kathy's common sense, which she felt the child had in abundance.

Anyway, she had other things on her mind at that moment as well as her friendship with Albert Leigh. What on earth was the matter with Phil Grantley?

The infant classes finished at half past three, half an hour before the junior department. Sally tidied her desk, cleaned the blackboard and sharpened the pencils ready for the next day. Then she put on her coat and went out into the playground to wait for Phil.

She stood by his Morris Minor car and he arrived a couple of minutes later. 'Hi there, Sally; sorry to keep you waiting,' he greeted her.

'You haven't; I've only just arrived,' she told him, clambering into the small blue car.

He got in beside her and soon they were out of the gate and bowling along the road at a fair pace. He turned into a side road where there were no parking restrictions and stopped the car.

'Here we are, then, Sally,' he said. 'Time for us to have a little chat, I think. At least . . . time for me to talk and you to listen, if you will?'

'Of course, Phil,' she answered. 'I've been rather concerned about you.'

He took a deep breath. 'Where can I begin . . . ?' He smiled quizzically at her.

'Well, it's usually best to start at the beginning,' she said.

He nodded, then paused for a few seconds before he began to speak. 'I'm not sure whether you know – probably you don't – that I was engaged to be married before I came to Blackpool.'

'No, I didn't know that . . .'

'Well, it came to an end, quite amicably, but I decided I was ready for a change. So, as you know, I was fortunate to get the post that I applied for here in Blackpool.'

She nodded. She knew that he had come from Yorkshire – a village near Bradford, she believed – and he now lived in a flat somewhere in the North Shore area. He would have been at the school for two years, come September.

'I stayed on good terms with my ex-fiancée, Pamela,' he continued. 'It would have been hard not to do so, really, as her parents and mine had always been close friends. Anyway, about a week before the end of term I had a phone call from my mother, in great distress. Pam had been badly injured in a car crash and she was in hospital.'

'Oh dear! What a shock for you,' said Sally. She recalled that that must have been round about the time that Phil had started to be friendly with her, Sally, and then had so abruptly seemed to go off the idea. 'And . . . is she all right now?' she asked.

He shook his head slowly. 'I realised then that although I was no longer in love with her – I wonder if I ever was, really; we had grown up together, you see, we were sort of childhood sweethearts – I still had feelings for her. I went over to Bradford that weekend, but she was in a bad way. She was still unconscious; she had internal injuries and broken bones and possibly brain damage.' Sally remained silent, not knowing at all what she should say.

'And then – actually it was on Easter Sunday – my mother rang me to say that Pam had died . . .'

Sally gasped. 'Oh . . . how dreadful!'

'Yes, it was . . . dreadful. It was the funeral a few days ago. I only came back last night in time for school; I've been staying with my parents.' He shook his head in a bewildered manner. 'I still can't believe it, can't come to terms with it all. She was so lively and pretty, like you, Sally. Well, no – not just like you – but you know what I mean. She had everything to live for. Life is so very cruel . . .'

'Yes, it can be sometimes,' she agreed. 'Phil, I'm so terribly sorry. And I do understand. I knew there was something wrong, but I didn't like to ask too much.'

'And I didn't want to talk about it,' he replied. 'But I do know that life has to go on. It's a cliché, isn't it, that folk always trot out at times like this?'

Sally nodded. 'Yes, that's very true. I know that from my own experience. I lost my fiancé, during the Battle of Britain. I don't talk about it now; it's quite a long time ago, and lots of other girls lost boyfriends in the war. Another thing that people say is that time heals.' She smiled sorrowfully. 'Well . . . yes . . . it does, but it can take a while. If there's anything I can do, Phil, you know you can think of me as a friend.'

'I know that, Sally. That's why I'm talking to you, rather than to any of the others. Actually, I was wondering . . . would you come out with me tonight? Just for a quiet drink somewhere. I feel that I need to get out. There's no point in sitting on my own, brooding. Like I said, Pam and I were no longer together, but I've been surprised how the fond feelings are still there, and about how upset I've been.'

151

'I'm sure I would feel exactly the same,' Sally replied. 'Yes, I'll go out with you, Phil. I shall look forward to it. Just what we need after the first day back.'

'Good . . .' He smiled at her. 'Let's get moving, then, now, shall we?'

They drove to her home, neither of them saying very much. 'What time, then?' he asked as he stopped the car outside her house.

'Oh, half past seven? Is that OK?' she asked. 'It'll give us a chance to wash off the chalk dust.'

'Yes, that's fine.' He chuckled, seeming rather more cheerful. 'Cheerio then, Sally. See you in a little while.'

Poor Phil! She was quite stunned at his news. It certainly explained his strange mood. She felt no compunction about seeing him tonight. She had agreed to go out with Albert on Saturday. But both of them, Albert and Phil, they were just friends and nothing more . . . weren't they?

Phil seemed to want to talk about Pamela, and Sally didn't mind listening. She knew that it was cathartic for him to do so. She remembered how, when Martin had been killed, she had felt the need to talk about him. It had seemed, somehow, to alleviate the grief she was feeling.

They sat near the window of the lounge bar of a seafront hotel, looking out across the promenade to the vast expanse of the Irish Sea. The days were lengthening now as it was well past the spring equinox. Dusk was falling and they watched the sun gradually disappear behind the grey-green sea. It was not such a spectacular sunset that evening – the sunsets in Blackpool were sometimes breathtaking in their beauty – but

152

the mass of cloud, tinged faintly with pale orange and pink, was still a lovely sight.

'I'm glad I came to live in Blackpool,' Phil remarked. 'It took me a while to get used to the flatness of the Fylde. Where my parents live, where I was brought up, in a village called Baildon – it's a suburb of Bradford, really – it's surrounded by hills. Factory chimneys as well, of course, although not so many as there used to be, but there's a rugged charm to it despite the dark satanic mills. It's much cleaner and fresher here, but, as I say, I miss the hills and dales.'

'There are hills quite near here,' Sally told him. 'Not much more than half an hour's drive away. There's the Bleasdale Fells and the Trough of Bowland. And the Lake District, of course, further north. I went on a coach trip once, with my parents, to Ambleside on Lake Windermere; that was long before the war.'

'Much easier to explore, though, if you have a car,' said Phil. 'I had a few days in the Lake District last year, with Alan.' That was one of his colleagues from school. 'We did a spot of fell walking. I've never been to those nearer hills, though, the Bleasdales. Perhaps we could go sometime, could we, Sally, just you and me, I mean? Have you ever done any fell walking?'

'No, actually, I haven't,' she replied. 'It's something I've never really thought about. Fiona – you know, the girl who joined the infant staff not long ago – she was telling me that she'd joined a walking club in Blackpool. She seems to be enjoying it.' Sally didn't answer his question about going exploring with him. It would all depend on when, and on how things worked out for her.

'Was it something you and Pamela used to do?' she asked.

'No, not really,' Phil replied. 'We used to go for short walks, but she wasn't really an outdoor sort of girl, even though she was brought up in the country; well, I suppose Baildon's sort of in the country. I think we both realised, in the end, that it wouldn't work out for us. We weren't very much alike – very few shared interests, you see.'

'Was she a teacher?' asked Sally.

'No, she worked in the local library . . .' He had told her earlier that he and Pamela had been in the same class at infant and then junior school, but had gone to different secondary schools. She had still been there, though, waiting, when he had done his two-year teacher training, and when he had returned from his war service. Sally already knew that he had been in the Eighth Army, in the Western Desert with Monty, something of which he was very proud, and he had returned relatively unscathed.

'When I came back from the war – I was one of the lucky ones, although it's something you never forget if you've been through it – I think I knew then that Pam wasn't the right girl for me. But she'd waited so faithfully for me all the time I was away. My mother told me how she used to go round to see them every week, how she looked forward to my letters, and that she never thought of going out dancing and having a good time as a lot of her friends were doing. So I thought how callous it would be to let her down, how devastated she'd be . . . And so we went on with it. We were actually saving up to buy a house; that was why we didn't get married there and then. And for me . . . well . . . it was an excuse, really. But, as I said, in the end we both knew that it would not be right to carry on. She was really more like a sister to me, and that's how I feel now, that I've lost a dearly loved sister.'

'I'm sorry . . .' Sally said again. 'But it will get easier. 'You've got your job – I know how much you enjoy it – and lots of friends around you.'

'Yes . . .' Phil nodded. 'I've told Mr Williams, and Alan and Brian, about Pamela. If anyone mentions that I'm rather subdued, perhaps you could tell them why, Sally. But I will try and pull myself together. I feel I've made a start already, seeing you tonight . . .'

'So, what about you and me, then?' he continued. 'We got off to a bad start, didn't we? I must explain to you about the day we went to the football match. I would have liked to take you out that evening, but it was my flatmate's birthday. He'd asked me, only the night before, if I'd go to the pub with him and a few more of his mates – strictly men only! – and I couldn't very well refuse.'

'No, of course not,' said Sally, thinking that the explanation had been a long time coming.

'So I thought I'd ask you out later on in the week, and then . . . well . . . there was all this awful business with Pamela, and I just couldn't think about anything else.'

'It's all right, Phil, I understand . . .'

'Anyway, I've enjoyed tonight, Sally. It was just what I needed. Thanks for coming and for being such a good listener. But I would like to see you again, and I promise I'll be in a more cheerful mood. What about Saturday evening?' Sally felt her heart sink; she had already had a feeling about what was coming next.

'I remember you telling me that you enjoy those big musicals,' Phil went on. 'Well, they're showing *State Fair* again at the Imperial on Saturday. A few years old now, I know, but it was one of my favourites at the time; Jeanne Crain and Dana Andrews, they were wonderful singers.'

'Yes, and Dick Haymes,' said Sally. 'It was one of my favourites too. But I'm sorry, Phil, I can't manage Saturday. I've already promised to go out with somebody.'

The smile on Phil's face vanished, to be replaced by a look of surprise, then disappointment, even a trace of annoyance. 'With . . . a man, do you mean?' he asked.

It would have been easier, perhaps kinder, to lie, but she knew she couldn't do so. 'Yes, it is . . . actually,' she replied.

'So . . . who is it, then? Anybody I know?'

She was tempted to tell Phil that it was none of his business, but he was already in quite a vulnerable state of mind and she didn't want to hurt him any more. 'No, you don't know him,' she replied. Well, he didn't, not really, except perhaps by sight. 'I've been out with him a couple of times. Nothing serious,' she added. 'But it wouldn't be right . . .'

'No, I can see that,' he said. 'I've left it too late, haven't I? Just my luck! I might've known this would happen.'

'I'll see how things go,' said Sally, feeling rather uncomfortable. Maybe she shouldn't have agreed to come out with Phil this evening after all. 'As I said, it's not as though this is a serious friendship; I've not known him very long . . .'

'It's OK, Sally,' Phil said, a trifle abruptly. 'There's no need to explain; I understand the way things are. Now, drink up, and we'll get away before they throw us out. I don't want to get caught up in the confusion in the car park at closing time.'

Sally drank the last of her gin and lime, and Phil hurriedly finished his half pint. They spoke very little on the way home. She felt uneasy about the situation. What, at first, had seemed a pleasant sort of evening was ending under a cloud.

'Goodnight, Sally,' Phil said, as he pulled up outside her door. 'I'll see you tomorrow.' It was obvious that he didn't want to sit around chatting; there was nothing more to be said.

'Goodnight then, Phil,' she replied. 'And . . . I'm sorry, really I am.'

'Forget it . . .' He shrugged. 'I'll get over it. Cheerio, then . . .' He drove off hastily, scarcely giving her time to close the car door.

Chapter Eleven

Sally had enjoyed her visit to the cinema with Albert, far more than she had anticipated. They had gone to see a rerun of one of the Ealing Studio comedies, *Kind Hearts and Coronets*, which was showing at the Dominion cinema in Bispham. It was a film that neither of them had seen the first time round and they both enjoyed it. Sally was surprised to hear Albert chuckling quite openly at times. At their first meeting she had come to the conclusion that he was something of a sobersides; but she was gradually changing her mind as she came to know him better.

It seemed there was more to Albert Leigh than met the eye. She had also gained the impression, at first, that he may have been a little self-conscious about his lack of formal education, compared with her own. She knew he had left school at fourteen, as had many lads of his age, and had gone to work straight away in his parents' boarding house. His prowess as a chef had been largely due to his own efforts. He had watched his mother, an excellent cook, at work, and he had learnt a lot from recipe books. His army service too, in the catering corps, had added to his experience. By and large, though, he seemed unwilling to speak much about his time in the army. Maybe he felt rather guilty that he had not taken part in any real fighting; but she guessed it was more to do with the fact that his wife had died round about that time.

In other directions, too, he was self-taught. She had imagined that, in his own home, he was very much a pipe and slippers and daily newspaper sort of man, when he was not hard at work in the kitchen, of course. But she learnt that the newspapers were not his only reading matter. His taste in literature was wide-ranging and by no means lightweight. He enjoyed the works of Somerset Maugham, A. J. Cronin and John Steinbeck. Sally mentioned that she had read, quite recently, the two books by Lloyd C. Douglas that had become very popular: *The Big Fisherman* and *The Robe*. Her comment had received a frosty reception.

'Religious, aren't they? I've got no time for 'owt—' he corrected himself hastily, 'for anything like that.'

'They're good stories, though, the sort that anybody might enjoy,' she told him, half apologetically.

'I've no time for any of that mumbo-jumbo,' he went on. 'I've never set foot inside a church since . . . since my wife died. If that's God for you, then you can keep him.'

'Yes, I suppose I understand,' she replied. 'One is tempted to wonder, at times, what it's all about.'

She didn't tell him, as she might have done, that she had wondered why Martin had had to be killed . . . but then thousands of young women must have felt exactly as she did. She had changed the subject quickly. She knew that Kathy went to Sunday school, and Sally had occasionally seen the little girl in church with her aunt. She, Sally, was not a regular attender; she went from time to time with her mother and would, if asked, call herself a Christian.

One thing that had surprised her was when Albert told her that he had, at one time, loved ballroom dancing. She supposed it was something that both he and his wife had enjoyed, and that he had not felt inclined to dance since he had lost her.

She had been somewhat taken aback, therefore, when he had said, following their visit to the cinema, 'Would you like to go dancing on Saturday night, Sally?'

'Well . . . yes, that would be very nice,' she replied. 'Where are you thinking of? The Tower, or the Winter Gardens?'

'I was thinking of the Palace, actually,' he said. 'It's a nice homely ballroom, from what I remember, and they have old-time dancing there as well as the modern sort. I used to dance a pretty nifty veleta.' He smiled; he had smiled more often that evening as they grew more used to one another.

They were sitting at the time in the lounge bar of one of the seafront hotels, to where they had walked after their visit to the cinema. Albert had, once again, ordered a taxi to take them to the cinema and would, no doubt, order one for their journey home.

Sally noticed that Albert was not slow in knocking back a pint. He was already into his second one while she was still sipping at her port and lemon. She guessed that he might be quite a heavy drinker when he was with the darts team at his local, and that he was used to speaking in the vernacular of the ordinary man. She noticed that he moderated his fairly broad Lancashire accent when he was with her and tried to act in a more gentlemanly manner. Not that it mattered greatly to Sally. Her father was pretty much the same sort of man: Lancashire born and bred and proud of it. Bill Roberts had learnt to talk 'posh', as he called it, as befitted his position as manager of a gents' outfitters, but could easily revert back to his more familiar accent and dialect.

Sally told Albert that she would be very pleased to go to the Palace. They decided they would go, first of all, to the first-house variety show, and then follow this with dancing in the ballroom. The Palace building, on Bank Hey Street, with its front entrance opening on to the promenade, was a multi-purpose building. It housed a cinema, a theatre, known as the 'Palace of Varieties', and a ballroom, as well as various bars, seating areas, cloakrooms and kiosks. It was a very popular venue, especially on a Saturday evening. So that was the date that Sally had referred to, the one that had prevented her from accepting Phil's offer.

She was not altogether sure how she felt about that. Disappointed, she supposed, if she was honest with herself. She liked Phil very much; he was nearer her own age, of course, and was more her sort of a person really than was Albert. But a promise was a promise. She had accepted Albert's offer to go dancing and, in a way, she was quite looking forward to it. She hoped that Phil would not sink into a depressive state again. He had had a severe shock with the death of his former fiancée and seemed to be taking a while to recover.

But with regard to that, it soon seemed as though she was flattering herself. When she encountered him at school the following day he was cheerful and friendly and appeared not to bear any ill will that she had refused his offer to take her out. She did not refer to it again; and she could console herself that maybe it had done him good to talk to her, even though they could not take their friendship a step further.

'That fellow of yours must be loaded,' remarked Sally's father as she awaited Albert's arrival in a taxi, again, on Saturday evening. 'Taxis everywhere! I don't know . . .'

'He's not my fellow, Dad,' she replied. 'He's just a friend, and I don't think for one moment that he's all that wealthy. He has a hotel, as you know, and I think it does quite well, but there's a lot of competition in Blackpool. He's only ordered a taxi because, well, I suppose he thinks it might not be very gentlemanly to take me on the bus.'

Sometimes they had famous stars appearing at the Palace Variety theatre, singers such as Anne Shelton or Vera Lynn, or comedians like Arthur Askey or Jimmy Edwards. That night it was the Andrews Sisters who were topping the bill, along with the comedian Frank Randle, who was very popular with Blackpool audiences, and Wilson, Keppel and Betty, a trio dressed as Egyptians – two men wearing red fezzes and a somewhat scantily dressed lady in the centre – who performed a sand dance. They, too, always went down well with audiences. The rest of the acts consisted of a conjuror, a ventriloquist, another lesser known comedian and his stooge, and a soprano and baritone duo who sang love duets.

Sally had seen Frank Randle before and was not impressed

with his portrayal of a drunk, guzzling from a whisky bottle. His catchphrase, 'I'll be glad when I've had enough of this!', had most of the audience in fits of laughter, but Sally could not do with drunkenness in any shape or form. It seemed to her that Albert was not very impressed either.

'He goes down a treat with the hoi polloi,' he whispered to her, 'but I can't say he's a favourite of mine. Sorry about this, Sally, but it's always the luck of the draw at the Varieties.'

Sally enjoyed the chirpy and cheerful Andrews Sisters, though, singing their bright and flirtatious little songs, 'Don't Sit Under the Apple Tree', 'It's Foolish but it's Fun' and 'An Apple for the Teacher', which caused Albert to nudge her elbow and grin. And she was impressed by the duettists, Mervyn and Maria, virtually unknown, but deserving, she thought, of a higher billing. It was obvious that the audience appreciated their performances of 'We'll Gather Lilacs' and 'I Can Give You the Starlight'. Ivor Novello's melodies always brought a lump to Sally's throat, so she was in a mellow, quite sentimental frame of mind when the show came to an end, and Albert took hold of her elbow to lead her upstairs to the ballroom.

The Palace building was remembered by many of the older Blackpool residents as the 'Alhambra'. It had opened with that name, and was also known as 'The People's Popular Palace of Pleasure', in the early part of the twentieth century; but following a financial crisis it had been bought by the Tower Company and renamed simply as the 'Palace'.

The ballroom was smaller than that of the Tower or the Winter Gardens, and had a more intimate and friendly ambience. It was, however, just as opulent as its rivals, the interior of the Palace having been fashioned in the style of the Italian Renaissance. Gilded pillars and curving balconies led the eye up to the frescoed ceiling, with its brilliant chandeliers. The seats were of red plush, and the highly polished parquet dance floor was a geometrical design of wooden blocks of mahogany, oak and walnut. At one end was a stage for the small orchestra that played for the dancing, alternating with the Wurlitzer organ.

Sally had opted to wear a summery dress that evening as the weather was warmer. As they had travelled to the theatre by taxi and would, presumably, be returning in one, there had been no need for her to wear a coat. Such an article of clothing could be rather a nuisance; it involved leaving it in a cloakroom whilst you were dancing, and then queueing up to retrieve it afterwards, and hoping that you could find the little pink cloakroom ticket. Her dress was one of her favourites, a Horrockses cotton with black and white polka dots on a pink background, with a full skirt and the waistline accentuated by a black shiny belt. With it she wore black patent leather shoes with heels that were suitable for dancing – not too high and not too low – and a small matching black bag, that she could sling over her arm and would not be too intrusive whilst she was dancing, completed her ensemble. Over the dress she was wearing a white lacy cardigan in fine wool that her mother had knitted for her.

The old-time dancing was in full swing when they entered the ballroom. They took to the floor for a military two-step followed by a veleta. She discovered that what Albert had told her was true; he was a very nifty dancer, light on his feet and his lead was easy to follow. By the time they had also danced the 'Gay Gordons' and a Saint Bernard's Waltz, Sally was glad to agree with his suggestion that they should adjourn to a nearby bar for a refreshing drink. She was pleased to see that he ordered a shandy for himself, just a small one, rather than his customary pint of bitter, and so she had the same.

'Well now, are you enjoying yourself?' he asked.

'Yes . . . yes, I am, very much,' she replied, smiling at him.

'That's what I like to hear,' said Albert. 'I am too. It's ages since I danced, and I'm pleased to see I've not forgotten any of the steps.'

'I don't think you forget things you learnt in your youth,' said Sally. 'I can't remember when I first learnt to dance; at church hops, I suppose. But they seem ingrained into your memory, like poetry that you learnt at school.'

'Mmm . . . yes . . . "I wandered lonely as a cloud . . ."' quoted Albert. 'I left school when I was fourteen, but I can still recite that poem word for word. And we learnt "the quality of mercy is not strained". I remember struggling with that, though, I don't think I can go much further. Shakespeare, isn't it? Though I'm blessed if I can remember which play.'

'*The Merchant of Venice*,' said Sally. 'Yes, we learnt that as well. It's a favourite passage with English teachers.'

'I must bow to your superior knowledge,' said Albert, slowly bowing his head to her.

'I just stayed at school a few years longer, that's all,' said Sally, with a dismissive shrug, 'and I took English at a higher level to get into training college. Anyway, never mind all that . . . Thank you for suggesting that we came dancing, Albert. It was a jolly good idea.'

She was surprised, indeed, at how much she was enjoying the evening. Albert seemed much more relaxed and at ease with her, as she was beginning to be with him. And the close proximity to him whilst they were dancing hadn't worried her at all. He had, so far, made no move to kiss her goodnight when they parted or even to hold her hand. She was wondering how she would feel about that. Most men were inclined to make a move in that direction sooner rather than later. She didn't think she would mind too much.

So when Albert said, 'We must do this again soon, seeing that we are both enjoying it,' she answered quite readily, 'Yes, I would like that.'

'We'll be getting busier at the hotel very soon,' he went on, 'but, as I've said before, the boss has to be allowed some time to himself, and so has my sister, of course, especially now she's got her gentleman friend.'

He explained that their busiest time of the day, as it was in most hotels and boarding houses, was at lunchtime, usually referred to in the north as midday dinner. It was then that they served the main meal of the day. High tea at five-thirty was a much simpler meal.

'So I can usually get away early evening,' Albert explained. 'We will be engaging girls to help with the washing-up, and we have a very competent lady starting soon as a waitress and general help; at least my sister seems very taken with her. She gave us a hand at Easter time, and she's tackling the bookkeeping as well. You probably know her, come to think of it. Mrs Morris – Sadie, she's called – her little girl is in your class with our Kathy.'

'Yes, of course,' said Sally. She smiled. 'As a matter of fact, I already knew about it. There's not much that I don't hear about what goes on at home! Katherine hasn't said anything to me, though, about you and me . . .' Not that there was much to say yet, she reminded herself. It was early days and she didn't want Albert to think that she was too eager. 'About you winning the raffle prize, I mean,' she said, 'and us having the meal together.'

'I think she feels a bit – oh, I don't know – embarrassed, like, about me going out with her teacher,' said Albert. 'But she'll get used to it in time.' He paused for a moment, looking at her enquiringly. 'We'll still be able to get out and about, dancing or whatever, even during our busy time,' he continued. 'Now, shall we go back to the ballroom if you've finished your drink?'

He was taking a lot for granted, pondered Sally, assuming they would still be friendly come the summertime. This time he tentatively took hold of her hand as they moved back to the dance floor.

The band had now progressed to more modern melodies. The dancers were engaged in a waltz to the tune of 'Faraway Places', which had been a popular song the previous year. As Sally and Albert joined the dancers the music changed to 'I Wonder Who's Kissing Her Now', and finally, 'You're Breaking My Heart'. They stood and clapped, as did all the other couples, as the band finished on a somewhat discordant crescendo.

When the band started again with 'Slow Boat to China',

Sally recognised the rhythm of a slow foxtrot. 'I'm not really very good at this,' she said.

'Oh, come on, let's give it a try,' said Albert. 'Just follow me; it's only walking backwards, really, with one or two twirls.' She found, as she had with the waltz, that she could follow his lead quite easily. He was holding her closer too, and the sensation was not unpleasant. Then the music changed to 'As Time Goes By', a sentimental song from several years ago.

There was a woman vocalist singing about lovers kissing and saying 'I love you', of lovers remaining constant to one another as the years went by, but also of feelings of jealousy and discord. Sally noticed a change come over Albert. She felt his body stiffen and his accurate steps began to stumble. A surreptitious glance at his face, partly turned away from her, showed his mouth set in a grim unsmiling line. She guessed at once that this song must once have meant something to him. Maybe, to him and his wife, it had been 'their song'. She tried to laugh it off.

'I'm not doing very well,' she said. 'I feel as though I've got two left feet. Let's sit this one out, shall we?'

Albert nodded. He took her arm and led her from the floor. They sat in an alcove and he was silent for a few moments. Then, 'I'm sorry, Sally . . .' he said. 'It was that song; it brought back memories.'

'I guessed so,' she answered. 'Songs can be so evocative. I've had that feeling myself . . . I understand.'

He nodded slowly. She wondered if he was about to descend into a black mood of despair. She didn't know him well enough to be aware of his possible highs or lows of temperament. Just as suddenly, though, he glanced across at her and reached for her hand.

'I'm sorry, Sally,' he said again. 'It's been a long time since I heard that song. But, as the words say . . . time goes by. It doesn't do any good to live in the past. I've been learning that lately.' He smiled at her then, a half-rueful smile, but she could see, also, the light of a growing affection in his eyes.

'It's time for me to move on,' he said. 'And I'm so glad I've met you, Sally.'

*C*hapter Twelve

Kathy was feeling very excited. Miss Roberts was coming to the hotel on Saturday night to have a meal that her dad was cooking for them. A special meal, to be eaten when the visitors had all finished their own meal and had gone off to do whatever they wanted to do on a Saturday evening. They were full up with visitors that week, it being the middle of July. Kathy had heard her father and Aunty Win talking about how they were almost fully booked for the rest of the season, and she knew that that was good.

She was now sleeping in one of the attic bedrooms, her favourite room in all the hotel. There were two single beds in the room, which left space for not much else besides: a small wardrobe, an even smaller dressing table, and the washstand with the bowl and jug, not forgetting the pot that Aunty Win called the 'gazunder'.

Another exciting thing was that the grown-ups had

agreed that Shirley could spend the night in the attic room with Kathy occasionally, as a special treat. Mrs Morris had been working at Holmleigh for quite a while now, as a waitress and general help, as well as helping with what Aunty Win called 'the books'. Her times had to be fitted around her husband's shifts. Mr Morris was a bus driver; he drove one of the cream and green Blackpool buses, and did not always work the same hours each day. Shirley had told Kathy that her mum and dad had had quite a few arguments about it.

'He doesn't really like Mum working at your hotel at all,' she said. 'But she's not taking much notice of him. She says she enjoys it, and she likes being able to earn some money of her own again. And so long as me and our Graham and our Brenda aren't being neglected, then she says she's going to carry on doing it. And it'll be great soon, won't it, when it's the summer holidays an' I can come with her?'

'Yes, and your Brenda as well,' Kathy had reminded her.

'Mmm . . . yes. Well, we'll have to look after her, I suppose,' Shirley frowned. 'She can be a bit of a pest, but she's all right, really. She'll have to do as she's told, though; I won't stand for any nonsense!'

All this would be happening in a few weeks' time, but first of all there was the meal to look forward to. It was going to be something of an occasion, or 'a bit of a do', as she had heard her dad say. Aunty Win's new friend was invited as well – Mr Bancroft, the man that her aunty had met at the drama group. He had been to their hotel a few times and Kathy liked him very much. He had said she could call him Jeff, but Aunty Win had decided that 'Uncle Jeff' would be better. Kathy liked that because she didn't have any real uncles. But the best thing was that Miss Roberts was having a proper meal there for the very first time, and she, Kathy, as a special treat, was being allowed to stay up and dine with them.

She knew that her dad and her teacher had been going out together for quite a while now; but Kathy also knew that they didn't really want it to be talked about. Her dad had put a finger to his lips and said 'shhh . . .' in a mysterious sort of way. So she hadn't even told Shirley about it; she would only go and blab it all over the playground. She supposed everybody would soon know, though, if they kept on going out together. Anyway, she wouldn't be in Miss Roberts' class much longer, so it wouldn't matter as much. In September she and Shirley and Timothy and all of them would be moving up into the juniors.

She kept wondering what it would be like if her dad were to marry Miss Roberts. Because that was what people did, didn't they, when they'd been going out together for a while? Then, she pondered, Miss Roberts would be her mum . . . sort of. That was a very strange thought. She liked her teacher ever such a lot; she loved her, she supposed, nearly as much as she loved her daddy and Aunty Win, but it would be a very odd state of affairs.

And what about her Aunty Win and Mr Bancroft, Uncle Jeff? Would they be too old to get married, she wondered? She knew that her aunt was a few years older than her father, and he seemed a lot older than some of her friends' fathers. And where would they all live if such a thing were to happen? Uncle Jeff had a house of his own, and she knew that Miss Roberts lived with her mum and dad.

And another very exciting thing was that her dad was talking about buying a car . . .

Winifred had been surprised at the change in her brother since he had started seeing Sally Roberts. He was happier in himself, much more amicable towards her and Kathy, friendly and unusually jolly with the hotel guests; all in all, much easier to get along with. He seemed to have shed several years. He was no longer a middle-aged man, which was the impression he had once given, but a young – well, youngish – man, enjoying life to the full.

It was his awakened interest in ballroom dancing that had been the main reason for his changed outlook on life, besides, of course, his friendship with Sally Roberts. Winifred remembered how he and Barbara had enjoyed their visits to the Tower and Winter Gardens, and sometimes to the Palace. He had not danced at all since he had lost Barbara, and Winifred had thought that that was something he would never want to do again. He had admitted to her, however – amazingly – that he had been wrong, that life had to go on, and, although he hadn't actually said as much, she guessed that he was hopeful that he had found someone with whom he might share his future life.

But how did Sally feel about it? Winifred wondered. Although she, Winifred, had encouraged him to ask the young lady out in the first place, she had feared afterwards that Sally might well bring the friendship to an end almost as soon as it had started. But this had not happened. Sally appeared to enjoy his company and especially to take pleasure in their visits to the Palace ballroom. They went there once a week – usually, though not always, on a Saturday, following a visit to the cinema or the variety show.

It was ironic, Winifred thought, after all the time that she and Albert had remained in their single status, that they should both, now, have found someone that they cared about. Her own friendship with Jeff Bancroft was progressing steadily. It was widely recognised now, by their friends at the drama group, that Jeff and Winifred were keeping company, or 'courting', to use the old-fashioned phrase.

They met on other occasions as well as the drama rehearsals, although their meetings had to be fitted around the workings of the hotel and now, of course, around the times that Albert wanted to spend with Sally. One thing that she and her brother had agreed was that Kathy had to be given priority. She must never be made to feel that the grown-ups were having to curtail their pleasures to attend to her needs. It was happening quite often now that she and Jeff would stay in on a Saturday night, enjoying a cosy evening listening to the wireless or gramophone records whilst Albert and Sally were out dancing. They would have supper together when they had attended to the visitors' requests. Then, at about eleven o'clock he would kiss her goodnight and depart for his own home.

His kisses had been chaste at first, now they were loving and were gradually becoming more amorous in nature. It felt strange – strange but pleasurable – to Winifred, who had not experienced the love of a man for so long. She wondered, and worried a little at times, how it would be if Jeff should become more ardent.

And how did Kathy feel about all that was going on around her? Winifred wondered. The little girl seemed contented enough, but who could tell what was really going on in that little mind of hers? Winifred noticed she had been a good deal more thoughtful recently. She had taken a liking to Jeff, which pleased Winifred, and he obviously enjoyed being with Kathy. She had been out with them once or twice at weekends. Jeff had driven the car northwards to Cleveleys, or south to St Annes; they had enjoyed a walk on the promenade and eaten ice creams, just like holidaymakers. Jeff had grandchildren of his own, rather younger than Katherine. His son in Canada and his daughter who lived in Exeter each had two children, and it was a great regret to Jeff that he didn't see them more often. There was a baby grandson in Montreal whom he had not yet seen, and a two-year-old granddaughter he had only seen once. So Katherine, it seemed, was something of a compensation to him, and Winifred could foresee no complications should their relationship progress further. She did not, however, allow herself to think too much about what might happen. There was many a slip . . . she told herself.

Albert had told Sally that the meal would be served at about seven o'clock. When she arrived at six-thirty Winifred greeted her with a glass of sherry, then Winifred and her gentleman friend, Jeff, and Sally chatted together at one end of the family living room whilst Albert was busy in the adjoining kitchen.

The family living quarters were rather limited, especially

during the holiday season when the visitors took up nearly the whole of the house. The living room, however, was large, as it had to act as a dining room and sitting room as well. The table was already set at one end of the room, with a snowy-white cloth and gleaming silver cutlery. Albert popped out of the kitchen in his blue and white striped apron to say hello, and then disappeared again.

'He says that he's in complete charge of the meal this evening,' said Winifred, 'and it's my job to do the entertaining. We're very pleased to have you here, Sally. You've met my friend, Jeff Bancroft, haven't you?' They shook hands again, although Sally had met him before, briefly.

Sally was glad she hadn't dressed up too much. It was, after all, only a casual sort of family meal. She was wearing a shirtwaister dress in blue and white candy striped cotton, with a white square collar and white cuffs to the elbow-length sleeves. Winifred, also, was wearing a summery dress in green spotted rayon, and Jeff had taken off his jacket, revealing a blue short-sleeved shirt and a gaily striped tie.

'You look very nice, Miss Roberts,' said Kathy shyly.

'Thank you, Kathy,' said Sally. 'I don't wear this dress at school,' she added confidingly. 'It's one of my best ones.'

'Yes, you might get it all mucked up with paint, mightn't you?' said Kathy.

Sally laughed. 'Yes, that's true . . . You look very nice as well, dear.' The little girl's dress was bright red and she had matching ribbons that went well with her dark hair and eyes. Sally felt a bit awkward at being addressed as Miss Roberts, but she couldn't very well invite the child to call her Sally. It would be better to leave things as they were. Kathy seemed to have the sense to make the distinction between Sally as her teacher and as her father's lady friend – if that was what she was! – and to keep the identities separate.

The meal was Albert's cooking at its best, although he had not served anything too extraordinary. They started with prawn cocktails, and the main course was roast chicken. The large bird provided each person with white breast meat and dark meat from the plump legs. Sally was impressed by the roast potatoes that were crisped and browned to perfection. (Sally's mother was a good cook, but even she did not get them quite so tasty.) Brussel sprouts, diced carrots and garden peas, with sage and onion stuffing and rich gravy complemented the excellent meal. The sweet was a simple one, fresh strawberries with castor sugar and ice cream, mainly for Kathy's benefit.

'I'm so full up I think I might burst!' the little girl exclaimed at the end of the meal. She seemed to have forgotten her previous shyness.

'That's not terribly polite, Kathy,' laughed her aunt, 'but I think we all probably feel much the same way. Thank you, Albert, for such a lovely meal.'

He grinned. 'All in a day's work.'

'You must have been very busy today, though,' remarked Sally, 'with the visitors and everything else.'

'Oh, Saturday's not too bad really, as far as the cooking's concerned,' he answered. 'It's changeover day – you know, one lot of visitors leaving and the next lot arriving – so we don't provide a midday meal, and we try to make the high tea a simple one. We have two women who come in to change the bedding in the morning, and make everything shipshape . . . And as for the washing-up tonight, that's all taken care of. Kathy's going to do it for us!'

The little girl's mouth dropped open with surprise as she stared at Albert. 'I didn't know that, Daddy!'

He laughed. 'I'm only joking, love. That worried you for a minute, didn't it?' Sally wondered if, maybe, Albert didn't joke with his daughter very often. He wasn't really the most jocular of men.

'We'll see to all the washing-up in the morning,' he went on. 'Get up extra early, eh, Winnie?'

'I expect so,' she agreed. 'Now, Sally and Jeff, you go and sit down and my brother and I will clear away, then we'll have some coffee. And you, Kathy love, you'll have to go to bed soon, when your dinner has digested.'

Kathy asked Sally, still rather shyly, if she would read her a bedtime story. 'Aunty Win and me, we're reading *Milly-Molly-Mandy*,' she said. 'Well, I can read most of it myself, but it's nice to read it together.'

'I'd love to,' agreed Sally. So when Kathy was in her pyjamas and in bed they read the book together.

'Thank you . . .' said Kathy when they finished the story; she didn't call her Miss Roberts that time. 'I won't tell any of the others about this . . .' she added in a confidential whisper.

'That's all right, dear,' said Sally. 'I don't suppose it matters, but it can be our secret.'

She felt a tear come into her eye as she kissed the little girl's cheek. 'Goodnight, Kathy love. Sleep tight . . .' She was really getting very fond of the child.

After they had enjoyed a cup of coffee it was decided

that the four of them should play a game of Monopoly. Sally couldn't remember afterwards whose suggestion it had been in the first place. She rather thought it was Albert's, which was ironic considering the way things turned out.

She was soon to see a different side to him, one that she had not hitherto suspected. It soon became clear that Albert liked to win. If things were not going his way, then he could easily become frustrated and peevish. She had often seen children – more particularly boys – in the playground behaving in a similar manner. If they lost control of the football or failed to win a race some were liable to go off in a tizzy. It was excusable in children; it was all part of the growing-up process and they usually grew out of it. But in a man it was really rather reprehensible.

'I'm afraid my brother takes it all too seriously,' Winifred whispered to Sally, when Albert got a 'Go to Jail' card for the second time and had to miss another turn. 'He regards himself as quite an expert at Monopoly.'

'But it's a game of chance, surely?' said Sally. 'It all depends on the fall of the dice, doesn't it?'

'I suppose there's a certain skill involved in buying the property,' said Winifred, 'but I've always regarded it as fun. It's not real money, is it? But the way Albert behaves you'd think he was really going bankrupt!'

'What are you two whispering about?' he asked then, a trifle snappily, although he was trying to smile.

'Nothing,' replied Winifred. 'Come along, it's your turn now, brother dear.'

Things went from bad to worse for Albert. He was cock-ahoop when he managed to buy houses, then hotels, on Park Lane, but was soon to lose all his wealth to Jeff who was gradually sweeping the board.

Albert was the first out of the game and almost threw, rather than handed, his little red hotels and the remainder of his paper money to Jeff.

'Bad luck, Albert,' said Sally, trying to make a joke of it. 'Never mind, you've got a real hotel, haven't you? It's only a game, but you were unlucky.'

'Yes, so unlucky that he can now go and do the washing-up,' said his sister, who was obviously not too pleased at his behaviour.

'Huh! You must be joking!' he retorted. 'I'm going to read the newspaper.'

'All right, suit yourself,' said Winifred. 'Come on, Sally. Let's see if we can get some of Jeff's hotels off him. He's having too much of his own way.'

Jeff grinned good-humouredly. Sally couldn't imagine him ever behaving so childishly as Albert was doing, should the game have gone the other way. He seemed, altogether, a splendid sort of fellow, and just right for Winifred.

Albert seemed to think better of his conduct in a little while. He put down his newspaper and went towards the kitchen. 'I'll see to the washing-up,' he said, 'then we won't have to bother with it in the morning.' He sounded almost apologetic and managed a sheepish smile in Sally's direction.

'Good!' said his sister, quite curtly.

The outcome of the game was a foregone conclusion. Jeff won hands down, just as Albert emerged from the kitchen having completed his chore. It was just turned eleven-thirty. The game had taken more than two hours, which was not really long compared with some marathons; Monopoly could sometimes continue on to the early hours, or even be postponed to the next day.

'I think it's time to call it a day now,' said Jeff. 'I'm thinking of you good people who have to be up to get the visitors' breakfasts.'

'Yes, that's true,' said Winifred, trying to hide a yawn. 'It's been a good evening, hasn't it? It's been lovely having you here, Sally. We must do this again sometime.'

'Yes . . .' said Sally, though not overenthusiastically. 'Thank you very much for the meal . . . and everything. I've enjoyed it.'

'I'll run you home, Sally, if you like,' said Jeff. She lived not too far from his home near Gynn Square. 'Unless . . . ?' He looked enquiringly at Albert.

'Yes . . . thank you, Jeff,' replied Sally hastily. 'It's OK, Albert. I wouldn't expect you to walk back with me when I can go with Jeff. You need your beauty sleep!' she quipped. The truth was that she had seen enough of him for the time being.

'All right, then, if you're sure,' said Albert. He kissed her briefly on the cheek. 'Goodnight, Sally. See you soon . . .'

Jeff kissed Winifred, a little more lovingly, Sally noticed. They didn't say much on the journey home as Jeff was concentrating on the busy road; it was closing time at the pubs.

Sally was thoughtful. If Albert could behave in such a way over a game, then how might he react if things did not go his own way in real life? And there was another consideration. She had enjoyed the evening, but all of them, Albert, Winifred and Jeff, were several years older than herself. She didn't want to grow old before her time. She realised it was mainly her own fault for carrying on seeing Albert for so long. It might be difficult now to make a break.

Chapter Thirteen

School had broken up and five glorious weeks of freedom lay ahead. Even though Sally loved her job she was not sorry to be having a break from both the children and the other teachers.

Her relations with Phil Grantley had remained cordial; but she had been surprised to learn, about a fortnight before the end of term, that Phil had found 'other fish to fry', to coin a phrase. It was her colleague, Joyce, who had told her that he was now seeing Fiona, the newest teacher to join the infant staff about a year ago. Sally remembered telling Phil that Fiona was a member of a local rambling club. Now it appeared that he, too, had joined the group and that the two of them, with the rest of the club, were going on a week's rambling holiday in the Lake District. It hadn't taken him long, Sally mused, to transfer his interest in her to someone else. She had to admit that she felt a little peeved, although she knew she had no reason to feel that way. It was her own admission that she was seeing someone else that had caused Phil to look elsewhere.

As for Sally, she was still seeing Albert, when he was able to be absent from the hotel. She felt that he was getting keener and was regarding her now, quite openly, as his lady friend; whereas she, Sally, was not so sure that she wanted things between them to get too serious. Following his show of peevishness during the game of Monopoly he had tried to be more amenable and not to show himself up again, although he had, of course, not referred to the incident since.

He had now bought a motor car, a Ford Prefect about two years old, so they no longer needed to rely on taxis when they went out together.

'Will you be able to drive it?' Sally had asked. She knew he had never owned a car.

'Yes, of course,' he had replied. 'Actually, I already have a licence and I can soon brush up on my driving skills. I learnt to drive my father's car before I was twenty. You didn't need a licence in those days, but I got one as soon as it became compulsory – in 1935, I think it was.'

It turned out that Albert was a competent driver. Sally enjoyed, most of all, the times when Kathy went out with them. They had driven out into the countryside and picnicked by the banks of the River Wyre at St Michael's, or by the stream at Nicky Nook, a favourite beauty spot not far from Blackpool.

Kathy was more at ease with her now when they were not at school, and she no longer referred to her as Miss Roberts. She didn't actually call her anything on those occasions, but the feeling of affection and warmth between her and the child was growing. Sally wondered if Albert was now regarding her almost as a substitute mother for the little girl. Winifred had formerly assumed that role and was still doing so; but Sally speculated as to what would happen if Winifred should marry her friend, Jeff. This was seeming more and more likely from hints that Albert had dropped.

And Sally had seen for herself how proud Jeff had been of Winifred when they had attended the performance of *The Importance of Being Earnest*, just before the end of the school term. Kathy hadn't understood all the action of the play, but had enjoyed seeing her aunt in such a very different guise. The two young ladies in the cast, Gwendolen and Cecily, were presented with bouquets of flowers by the stage manager; but it was Jeff, in his capacity as ASM, who presented the bouquet to Winifred, Lady Bracknell. He kissed her lovingly, seemingly not caring about who was watching, and his regard and affection for her were clear to everyone as he stood beside her on the stage.

Drama meetings ceased during the month of August, but Jeff and Winifred were still very much together. Sally watched Albert becoming more and more concerned.

'I rely on Winnie so much in the hotel,' he told her. 'We're a good partnership, our Winnie and me. Of course, she's a perfect right to please herself whatever she does, and if she wants to set up house with Jeff Bancroft – if they get wed, of course – then I suppose there's nowt . . . er . . . nothing I can do about it. I know it'd be a wrench to her, though, if she had to leave our little Kathy.'

Sally was relieved that she would be getting away from Blackpool for a week during the school holidays. Following on from her night school class in French conversation, she was joining a group of the students who had decided to test their prowess in the language by spending some time in France; they had booked places on a coach tour to Normandy and Brittany. Joyce, Sally's colleague from school, was going as well. The two of them had become quite friendly recently. Joyce was a few years younger than Sally, but was the nearest one in age to her on the infant staff. She was married, but there were no children as yet, and she had said she would be pleased to accompany Sally, especially as her husband would be away on a fishing trip that week. They would be sharing a room during what looked like being quite a hectic few days of travelling from one resort to another.

'I shall miss you,' Albert told Sally. 'I can't remember the last time I had a holiday.' He sounded a little put out. 'Perhaps we could manage a few days away – just you and me, eh – when it's your next half-term holiday? The Lights will have finished then and all the visitors gone home. What do you reckon to that?'

'I don't really know, Albert,' said Sally rather evasively. 'I shall need to think about it.'

'Well, give it some thought while you're away . . . And don't forget to send us a postcard. Kathy's going to miss you as well, aren't you, love?'

Kathy nodded. 'Yes, I will,' she said. 'But I shall be busy. Shirley's here with her mum, you know, during the holidays, and we're looking after little Brenda, Shirley and me.'

'Oh yes, I remember,' smiled Sally. 'I'll send a postcard for you and Shirley, then, shall I?'

'Yes, that'll be nice,' agreed Kathy.

It was good fun having Shirley with her, and Brenda as well. They spent a good deal of the time in Kathy's room up in the attic, playing games or crayoning, or looking at books. They were allowed to play in the backyard if the weather was fine, skipping or playing with balls or whips and tops. They couldn't play out in the street, not with Brenda, because of the traffic.

The first two weeks were quite fine, then on the third week it started to rain. It was the week that Miss Roberts – or Sally, which was how Kathy now thought of her – was away. She hoped that the weather was nice and sunny in France.

'I'm bored!' said Shirley, when they had played Snakes and Ladders and tiddlywinks, and gone through their pile of comics. 'What can we do, Kathy? You think of something.'

'I don't know,' said Kathy. 'I'm helping Brenda to colour in this picture.'

'Oh, never mind her,' said Shirley. It was something she said quite often, leaving most of the looking after Brenda to Kathy, who really didn't mind at all.

Shirley stood up on the bed that Kathy slept on and started jumping up and down. 'It's dead springy, your mattress,' she said. 'Come on, Kathy; let's see who can jump the highest.'

'No! I'm not supposed to jump on it,' said Kathy. 'It's quite a new one, and Aunty Win says it'll damage the springs.'

''Course it won't!' retorted Shirley. 'Is the other bed the same?' She took a flying leap from one bed to the other –

187

there was a space of about two feet between them – then started to jump on the opposite bed. 'Yes, it's just as springy. Come on, Kathy. Don't be such a baby! I know . . . Let's pretend it's a river and we've got to jump from one bank to the other. Your Aunty Win'll never know. She's busy in the kitchen, isn't she?'

Kathy knew she shouldn't, but her friend was so bossy and she hated being called a baby. Somewhat reluctantly she climbed onto the bed and jumped across to the other one.

'I know . . .' said Shirley. 'You jump one way an' I'll jump the other way, then we'll cross in midstream. Mind you don't fall in or you'll get wet.' Actually, Kathy thought it was a pretty daft sort of game and she hoped her friend would soon get tired of it.

'Let me! Let me!' shouted Brenda. Before Kathy could stop her she had clambered onto the bed.

'No . . . don't!' yelled Kathy, but it was too late. The child took a leap, as she had seen the bigger girls do, landing with a loud bump on the floor between the beds. 'Ow! Ow!' she cried. 'My leg, my leg, it hurts!'

The two friends looked at one another in horror then rushed to her side. She had landed with her leg bent underneath her. She yelled even more when Shirley tried to straighten her leg.

'Stop it! Stop it! You're hurting me. I want my mummy . . .' The child burst into tears.

'You'd better go and get your aunty, and my mum as well, I suppose,' said Shirley in a whisper. 'She's going to be dead mad with me . . . Don't cry, Brenda. It'll be all right.'

Kathy dashed down several flights of stairs and along the

passage to the kitchen. Her father and aunt were both in there. 'Aunty Win,' she called. 'Can you come? Brenda's hurt her leg.'

'Yes, of course,' said her aunt. 'We'd better tell Sadie – Mrs Morris – as well; she's setting the tables. What was Brenda doing, anyway, to hurt her leg?'

'She was jumping,' said Kathy, a little sheepishly. 'She fell off the bed.'

'I see,' said her aunt, looking rather stern. 'Well, we'd better go and get Brenda's mummy, hadn't we?'

Mrs Morris was in the dining room setting the tables with the cutlery needed for the midday meal and tidying up the napkins.

'I'm afraid Brenda's had a little accident,' said Kathy's aunt. At the look of consternation on the woman's face she hurried on to say, 'It's all right; nothing too bad as far as I can make out. Kathy says she's hurt her leg.'

'Oh dear!' Sadie Morris put down the serviette she was folding and followed Kathy and her aunt out of the door and up the stairs. 'I don't know what my husband will say,' Kathy could hear her muttering. 'Well, actually, I do know. He was dead against me bringing her here; he expects me to be watching her every minute of the day.'

Brenda started crying again as soon as she saw her mother. 'Mummy, Mummy! My leg hurts. Make it better!'

She didn't cry out in pain this time as Mrs Morris gently straightened out her leg and felt tentatively at the ankle. 'You're alright, darling,' she said. 'No bones broken as far as I can see. I think you've sprained your ankle.'

'I'll get some cold water and a bandage,' said Winifred,

who had a little first-aid knowledge, as had Mrs Morris. The ankle was bathed and bandaged, and Brenda did not complain too much, although she couldn't put any weight on her foot. There was no word of recrimination at first, then Mrs Morris turned to question her shamefaced daughter.

'Whatever were you doing, Shirley, to let her fall? I told you to look after her.'

'We were jumping off the beds, that's all,' said Shirley, a trifle belligerently. 'It wasn't my fault. Kathy said we could.'

Kathy was shocked at her friend's betrayal, especially as it had been Shirley's idea. 'It wasn't my fault either!' she retorted. 'But I'm very sorry, Mrs Morris.'

'That's all right, dear,' the lady replied. 'It could have been worse.'

'I think you'd better let the doctor have a look at her, just to be on the safe side,' said Aunty Win. 'You can go now if you like.'

'No, thanks . . . I'll stay and finish my shift,' she replied. 'I'll call on my way home. Oh dear! Brenda won't be able to walk, will she?'

'Don't worry – Albert will run you to the doctor's,' said Winifred, 'and then take you home. It's the least we can do. Now, young lady, you'd better sit quietly in a big chair in the living room, seeing as you're a wounded soldier!'

Her mother carried her downstairs, with Kathy and Shirley, rather subdued, following behind. They all had their dinner after the visitors had been served, and when the washing-up was done, Albert took Brenda and her mother to the doctor's surgery.

'She was very worried about what her husband's going to say,' Albert told his sister later that day as they were preparing the salads for the teatime meal. 'From what I gather, things are not too rosy there. I wouldn't be surprised if we lose Sadie before very long. You'll have to be prepared for her giving notice, Winnie.'

'Yes, I can see the way things are,' agreed Winifred. 'Mr Morris'll have even more of an axe to grind now, won't he? I bet it was Shirley at the root of this, though Kathy won't say very much. She's a loyal little soul. She's very upset about it, so I haven't been too cross with her. But I saw the look on her face when Shirley tried to blame her. She's a bit of a minx, that Shirley . . . Mind you, I don't think Sadie's helping matters at home much either. I don't like saying this, but I've noticed she's got rather too friendly with Barry Proctor. He was here at Easter, if you remember, and I thought then that they were getting on very well together. And now he's here again. I was quite surprised, I must admit, when he booked up for another week.'

'Hmm . . . It doesn't take some fellows long to forget, does it?' remarked Albert. Barry Proctor, with his wife, had visited Holmleigh on a few occasions. Then two years ago Barry had written with the sad news that Joan had died following a bad attack of flu, but that he would still be spending his summer holidays at Holmleigh. He enjoyed the seasonal variety shows in Blackpool, and the bracing winds and clean fresh sea air, a far cry from the rather grimy town of Burnley where he was an overseer in a mill.

'His wife's hardly cold in her grave,' Albert went on. 'I thought he was devoted to her, but it just goes to show . . . Mind you, I blame the women for doing the chasing. I'd have thought better of Sadie Morris, though . . .'

'We can't condemn her when we don't know all the facts,' said Winifred. 'Anyway, it isn't our place to act as judge and jury. I hope she's not acting foolishly, though, more for the sake of the children than anything.'

Albert didn't answer. His sister knew he wasn't in the best of humours that week with Sally being away in France.

Mrs Morris arrived the next morning without Brenda. 'My dad says Brenda can't come here anymore,' Shirley told Kathy. 'He was dead mad with my mum, far more mad than he was with me, and they had an awful row. He didn't want mummy to come either, but she said she had to, and he hadn't to try and stop her.'

'So where's Brenda, then?' asked Kathy.

'She's next door with Mrs Murray. She said she'll look after her, because she's got a little girl the same age, so they can play together. I don't think she'll do it every day, though, so I don't know what's going to happen.'

'What shall we play, then?' asked Kathy. 'We mustn't do any more jumping!'

'I know, I know!' snapped Shirley. They started a big jigsaw of circus clowns, and when they tired of that they each read an Enid Blyton book. But Kathy knew they were not getting on as well as they used to do.

Things went from bad to worse. It was on Saturday morning, changeover day, that Sadie arrived in a very agitated state.

'I can't come anymore,' she told Winifred. 'I can't even

work my notice. I'm really sorry to leave you in the lurch like this, but I can't carry on with the waitressing and helping in the hotel. I'll still do the books for you, just for the moment; I don't see how Frank can object to that, but I don't know for how long . . .'

She explained that her son, Graham, had fallen in the sea the previous day and had to be rescued by a holidaymaker. He had been brought home drenched and frightened, and her husband, understandably, had hit the roof. Graham had gone to the beach with his friend Jimmy, with whom he had been spending most of his time. They had been given strict instructions not to go near the sea, but boys would be boys. Graham had protested that they were only paddling, but a big wave had swept him off his feet.

'Oh, goodness me! That's bad news,' said Winifred, 'and for Graham as well, of course. Is he all right now?'

'He's fine,' said Sadie. 'But I've got to stay at home and see to them now. I daren't do anything else under the circumstances. I'm really sorry, Winifred . . .'

Winifred noticed, though, that she went to find Barry Proctor before he started on his journey home to Burnley.

Chapter Fourteen

Sally was enjoying herself in France. Whether or not her French conversation was improving was beside the point – they spoke so fast that it was hard to understand them, let alone converse with them! – but it was turning out to be a jolly good holiday. They travelled by coach, then by the Channel ferry. Their first stopping place was Dieppe. From there they visited the Normandy beaches, renowned, not all that long ago, for the D-Day landings, and the picturesque old town of Rouen where Joan of Arc was martyred. Then they moved on to Brittany to stay two nights in the fishing port of St Malo, and lastly in the medieval town of Dinan. They were enchanted by this quaint place with its stone ramparts and wood-fronted houses leaning crazily towards one another across the narrow streets.

They were enjoying the different sights and sounds and

smells – a mixture of Gauloises cigarettes and fragrant coffee – of a foreign country. Although it was so near to England, it seemed so very far away. Possibly, above all, they were savouring the tastes of France. The country seemed to have recovered from the restrictions of wartime. They dined on pancakes – crêpes – served as a savoury dish with scrambled egg, ham and cheese or meat, or as a dessert with fruit, ice cream or chocolate; the fish and seafood – monkfish, red mullet or John Dory – fish they had never encountered at home; or the speciality of Brittany, the *plateau de fruits de mer*, an assortment of exotic sea creatures served on a bed of seaweed. This last creation they only looked at in shop windows, but were not brave – or rich – enough to try. The sweets were their downfall, though; eclairs topped with coffee cream, chocolate gateaux, and featherlight sponges flavoured with Grand Marnier and served with almonds, fruit and cream.

Sally and Joyce had grown closer to one another that week, away from the strictures of the classroom. On their last evening they sat at a pavement café on the long street that led down to the quayside, enjoying the rich dark coffee they had grown accustomed to, and a bottle of Muscadet, the favourite drink of Bretons.

'It's been a good week,' said Sally. 'Thank you for coming with me, Joyce; I've enjoyed your company.'

'Likewise,' answered Joyce. 'There's not much time at school, is there, to socialise? I didn't realise until now that you and me . . . well, that we could be such good friends. I mean, you're older than me and . . .'

'Don't rub it in!' laughed Sally. 'Yes, I do know what you

mean, but age shouldn't really make a great deal of difference. Anyway, here's to us . . .' She raised her glass. 'And to our new-found friendship.' They clinked glasses and smiled at one another. 'I expect your husband will be glad to see you home again, though, won't he?'

'Yes, he will,' agreed Joyce. 'It'll be nice to see Roger again, I must admit. Although it doesn't do any harm to have some time apart now and again. It helps to stimulate the relationship. I expect Albert will be missing you too, won't he?'

Word had gradually got round the staffroom that Sally was seeing Mr Leigh, the father of one of the girls in her class, but, to her surprise, little had been said about it, in her hearing at least. Sally sighed.

'Yes, I daresay he'll be missing me . . . I'm not sure that I can really say the same myself, though.' She decided that she would like to confide in Joyce; she had not, so far, talked about Albert to anyone.

Her parents had met him and appeared to like him, but they had kept their own counsel, probably thinking that she was old enough and wise enough to know her own mind. But did she? That was the problem. She liked Albert; they got on well together for the most part. She knew he could be moody at times and liked things his own way, but she told herself that nobody was perfect. She guessed that since he had met her he had, in a sense, recaptured some of his youth; she was thinking in particular of the ballroom dancing. But she predicted that, should they embark on a more permanent relationship, he might revert to being set in his ways, to being as intransigent and unbending as she guessed he had been in the past. Winifred had remarked to her that there had been a big change in her brother since the two of them had been friendly. But, she reminded herself, he was eleven years older than she was . . .

'Why?' asked Joyce, in answer to Sally's remark. 'Don't you get on well with him? I met Mr Leigh when Kathy was in my class, and I can't help wondering . . . I mean, he seemed such a morose sort of chap. No, that's very unfair of me.' She shook her head. 'I don't really know him, do I? You don't need to tell me anything if you don't want to. It's none of my business, is it?'

'But I'd like to tell you,' said Sally. 'Yes, we're OK together; he's not really such a sobersides when you get to know him. I've got on with him much better than I expected to. I didn't mean it to carry on so long but . . . well . . . it has done. And now, you see, he's getting keener, wanting to see me more often and . . . everything. And I don't really think that's what I want.'

'Then you'll have to tell him, won't you?' replied Joyce. 'Before he "pops the question", as they used to say.'

'Mmm . . . I suspect that might be in his mind, even though I've only known him for – what? – about five months. And I can't help thinking that he may well be wanting a mother figure for Kathy. Her aunt's always been like a mother to her, and she still is. Winifred's a wonderful person; I like her very much. But I think it's quite likely that she'll be getting married herself, so she may no longer be there to see to Kathy. I don't know, of course, but it's looking as though it might happen. I'm very fond of little Kathy; I always was, and she's grown closer to me since I've been seeing her dad.'

'Yes, she's a lovely little girl,' agreed Joyce. 'She was in my class, as you know, before she moved up to you. I never felt she was any worse off, not having a mother; far happier, in fact, than she might have been in some of the homes I can think of. Is she still friendly with Shirley Morris?'

'Oh yes, they're bosom pals. Shirley's inclined to be bossy, as you probably know, but I think Kathy's learning to hold her own . . . Yes, I think you're right, Joyce. I shall have to tell Albert that there's not much point in us going on seeing one another. I don't mind being friendly with him, but I don't want it to go any further. I would like to get married one day, I suppose. Maybe have children of my own, if I don't leave it too late. That's another issue; I doubt that Albert would want any more children . . .' She was silent for a moment, deep in thought.

'I lost my fiancé, Martin, during the Battle of Britain,' she went on, 'and there's never really been anyone else since then that I could feel the same way about. I know that I don't love Albert, so it wouldn't be right, would it, for either of us?'

'No, it wouldn't, if you want my honest opinion,' said Joyce. 'I had heard that you lost someone during the war; I'm sorry about that . . . Weren't you getting friendly with Phil Grantley, not so long ago? I know some of the staff thought so – you know how they can gossip at times – and then he started seeing Fiona Wilson.'

'Yes, we were friendly; in fact, I thought at one time that it was really going somewhere. To be quite honest, I think I was on the way to falling in love with him, then it all seemed to go wrong. I suppose I went on seeing Albert on the rebound.

The first time Phil asked me to go out on what you might call a proper date, I had already promised to go out with Albert, so that was that. Then, as you say, he started seeing Fiona . . .'

'Never mind, Sally,' said Joyce. 'There's more fish in the sea.'

'That's what I keep telling myself,' replied Sally. 'But why won't a prize catch swim my way?' She laughed. 'Thanks for listening to me. I know now what I have to do. I can't let it drag on any longer . . . I suppose we'd better be heading back, hadn't we? We've a long journey ahead of us tomorrow.'

It was hard to tell whether Albert had anticipated Sally's news that she didn't want to go on seeing him.

He had phoned her at home soon after she had arrived back and she had agreed to go out with him the following evening; but just for a quiet drink, she had said, not to the cinema or to go dancing. He had kissed her eagerly when she got into the car, but she could not respond to his ardour.

She told him almost as soon as they had ordered their drinks and sat down in the lounge bar of the Cliffs Hotel.

'I like you very much, Albert,' she told him, 'and I've enjoyed our times together, but it wouldn't be fair to go on seeing you.' She explained that, although she had grown fond of him, she didn't love him, and that rather than get more involved with him – which she felt was what he wanted – it would be better for them to part.

'But I think I love you, Sally,' he protested. She noticed

that he had said only that he thought he loved her. 'And I've never loved anyone else, not since I lost Barbara. I really thought we might have something good.' He looked so disappointed and dejected that she felt sorry for him. 'But I suppose it was too much to hope for. I'm too old for you, Sally. That's the problem, isn't it? You want somebody more lively and go-ahead, not an old stick-in-the-mud like me.'

'But you're not like that,' she insisted. 'It's not the age difference, not really. I just feel that – in the end – it wouldn't work.'

'Fair enough,' he mumbled. 'I suppose I should have seen it coming. Kathy's going to be disappointed, I know that. She's got used to you coming round. She thinks the world of you, you know.'

'Yes, I suppose so, but I've told you how young children get attached to their infant teachers. I'm very fond of Kathy too. But I shall still see her at school, even though she won't be in my class.'

'Poor Kathy!' Albert shook his head. 'She's got another shock coming as well. She's about to lose her best friend, Shirley.'

'Why? Whatever has happened?' asked Sally. 'Shirley's not ill, is she?'

'On no, it's nothing like that. You know that Sadie Morris has been helping us at the hotel, and Shirley and her little sister were coming along to play with Kathy?' Sally nodded. 'Well, there was a bit of trouble; the little girl had an accident – nothing serious – but the father was furious. And then, to make matters worse, the next day the boy, Graham, fell in the sea.'

'Oh, goodness me! Is he all right?'

'Yes, he's fine. But Mr Morris hit the roof, understandably, I suppose. He had never wanted his wife to work for us in the first place. So the upshot of it is that he's forbidden Sadie to come anymore. Kathy knows about that, but what she doesn't know yet is that Mrs Morris is leaving her husband and taking the children to live with her parents in Southport.'

'Good gracious! That's a drastic step,' said Sally. 'Is it for good, or have they just had a tiff?'

'Rather more than a tiff. Sadie came round to tell Winnie about it this morning. She and her husband have had no end of a bust-up; apparently things have not been too good for a while. So she's off at the end of the week, to Southport. I think she's hoping to get a job there, and her mother will look after the children.'

'That's bad news,' said Sally. 'Poor Shirley . . . and her brother and sister as well, of course. I hope they manage to sort things out and get back together.'

'Well, that remains to be seen,' said Albert. 'I'm afraid Sadie has got rather too friendly with one of our visitors – a man, I obviously don't need to add. So that won't have helped matters. She hasn't admitted as much, but Winnie's very astute and she got a fair idea of what's going on.'

'Good gracious!' said Sally again. 'I'm stunned, really I am. I would never have thought that about Mr and Mrs Morris.'

'It just goes to show,' said Albert grimly. 'You can never tell what's going on in a woman's mind. "*La donna è mobile*" . . . Didn't you tell me that it meant "woman is fickle"?'

'Yes, that's right; so it does.' Albert was looking at her quizzically. 'You mustn't think . . . There's no one else involved, for me, I mean,' she tried to explain.

'I didn't think that, Sally,' he replied. He looked very sad for a moment and she felt sorry if she had hurt him so much. 'I didn't mean you. I was just speaking generally. Some women can be very fickle.' He gave a sad smile. 'I'm sorry . . . about you and me. It was good while it lasted. I suppose that's all I can say. I'll take you back home when you're ready. There's not much point in staying on here, is there?'

He downed his half pint almost in one gulp. She was glad it wasn't a full pint as he had to drive home and she knew he would be preoccupied about recent happenings.

He kissed her on the cheek as they said goodbye outside her house. 'I'll see you around, no doubt, Sally,' he said. 'Take care of yourself . . . and good luck.' He nodded unsmilingly as he got out of the car to open the door for her.

'Goodbye, Albert,' she said. 'You take care of yourself as well.' She hurried up the path without a backward glance.

It was Winifred who told Kathy, one night just after the little girl had got into bed, firstly, that her father was not seeing Sally Roberts anymore, and then that Shirley had gone with her mum and her brother and sister to live in Southport with her grandparents. Kathy, understandably, was puzzled about both issues.

'Why?' she asked, regarding her father and Sally. 'Have they had a row?'

'I don't think so, not exactly a row,' Winifred replied. 'They've decided that maybe they're not right for one another. Your daddy is a few years older than Sally – Miss Roberts – and people have to be very sure, if they're thinking of staying together, that they're always going to get on well with one another.'

'Did he want to marry Miss Roberts, then?' asked Kathy.

Winifred smiled. 'I think he might have done, but it wasn't to be.'

'I like Miss Roberts,' said Kathy. 'Well, I always liked her, but we've got more friendly – you know, as though she's not just a teacher – since she's been going out with Daddy.'

'Well, you'll still see her at school, won't you? And I'm sure she'll be just as friendly, even though it didn't work out for her and your daddy.'

'Are you going to marry Uncle Jeff?' Kathy asked, surprising Winifred by the suddenness of the question.

'I think that might be . . . quite likely,' said Winifred cautiously. 'But a lady has to wait until she's asked, you know. So don't go saying that to Jeff, will you, or to anybody else?'

'No, I won't,' said Kathy. 'But would you like to marry him?'

'You're a nosey parker!' Winifred laughed. 'Jeff and I get on very well together. I like him very much and I think he likes me. But, as I said, you have to be very sure. Now, I don't think I want to say any more about that at the moment, young lady!'

'No, that's all right,' said Kathy. 'But why is Shirley's mum going to live somewhere else? Don't Mr and Mrs Morris love one another anymore? I thought he was nice, real good fun; he made me laugh.'

'You can't always tell what people are really like,' said her aunt. 'Sometimes they can be quite different with their own families.'

Kathy nodded. 'Yes, Shirley used to tell me about her mum and dad having rows. And I know he was real mad about Brenda getting hurt, and then Graham falling in the sea.'

'That's what caused the big fall-out,' said Winifred. 'Mr Morris wants to be sure that his children are being looked after properly, just like your daddy cares about you. And he thought Mrs Morris was neglecting them by coming to work here.'

'But she wasn't, was she?' Kathy frowned. 'I mean . . . it was Shirley's fault – and mine as well – that Brenda got hurt. We'd been told to look after her. And Graham wasn't doing as he was told either, was he? He'd been told not to go near the sea.'

'Yes, it was all very unfortunate,' said Winifred. 'But you mustn't worry your head about it anymore, Kathy love. Maybe when Mrs Morris has had time to think about it she'll be sorry she's moved away. And perhaps Mr Morris will be sorry for all the things he said. It's what happens sometimes with married people. I know you'll miss Shirley, but you've got lots more friends at school, haven't you?'

'Oh yes, there's Maureen and Dorothy . . . and Timothy. Actually, Aunty Win, Shirley was a bit bossy. I liked her, though.'

Winifred laughed. 'It'll all sort out, I'm sure.' She kissed her cheek. 'Now, you snuggle down and go to sleep. Goodnight, darling; God bless . . .'

Kathy settled down well in her new class. Her teacher was called Mrs Culshaw, whom the children soon decided was good fun but could be strict as well when the need arose. They still sat in tables of four, not at desks yet, like the older classes in the junior school. Kathy was pleased to be put on a table with Maureen who, after Shirley, was her next-best friend. It seemed as though Mrs Culshaw had been warned to separate Timothy Fielding and his sparring partner, Stanley Weston. To Kathy's disappointment, although she didn't admit it to anyone, Timothy was not on their table, but was seated at the other side of the room. Sitting opposite her and Maureen were Stanley, whom she knew and didn't mind too much, and a boy called Neville who was quiet, well behaved and clever.

She encountered Timothy, though, in the playground the first day. 'Hi, Kathy,' he greeted her. 'Would you like a pear drop?'

'Ooh yes, thank you.' She popped the pink and yellow sweet in her mouth.

'I've got another joke for you,' he said. 'What did the caterpillar say when he fell off the leaf?'

'I don't know,' she replied dutifully. 'What did he say?'

'Earwigo . . . !' He fell about laughing. 'D'you get it? Here – we – go. Eer – wig – o!'

'Yes, of course I get it,' she said a little impatiently. 'It's . . . quite funny.'

205

'I can't hear you laughing,' he said. 'I 'spect you're upset about Shirley going, aren't you? My mum found out about it and she told me. I 'spect they'll be getting a divorce, Shirley's mum and dad.' Kathy wasn't sure what that meant but she didn't admit it.

'Oh . . . I don't know,' she said. 'My aunty thinks they might come back when Shirley's mum's thought about it.'

'I don't think so,' said Timothy. 'My mum says if they get a divorce they'll be able to get married to somebody else.'

'Oh . . .' said Kathy, feeling even more confused. 'Look, I'll have to go, Tim. Maureen's waiting for me to turn the other end of the skipping rope. See you . . .'

'Aunty Win,' said Kathy that night as she was getting undressed ready to go to bed. 'What's a divorce?'

Winifred was startled. 'Why?' she enquired. 'Why do you want to know?'

'Because Timothy Fielding says that that's what Shirley's mum and dad are going to do, get a divorce. And I don't know what it means.'

'I think that your friend Timothy Fielding says a great deal too much,' Winifred replied.

'It was what his mum said . . .'

'Well, I'm sure she doesn't know,' said Winifred indignantly, 'and she shouldn't be spreading rumours like that.'

'But what does it mean?' Kathy persisted.

'Well, a divorce is what happens when a husband and wife decide that they don't want to live together any longer. So the judge grants them a divorce . . . so that they're not married anymore.'

'And then they can get married to somebody else?'

'Well, yes . . . Is that something else that Timothy said?'

'Yes, he did . . .'

Winifred sighed. 'I don't think for one moment that Mr and Mrs Morris are going to get a divorce, or marry somebody else . . . so you just forget about it, love. I've told you, sometimes grown-up people fall out, but very often they make it up again. You mustn't talk about Shirley's mum and dad. You won't, will you? And don't take any notice of what people are saying.'

'No, of course I won't.' Kathy shook her head. 'Aunty Win . . . the Illuminations are on now. D'you think we could go and see them?'

'Yes, I'm sure we could,' said Winifred, glad about the change of subject. 'That will be something nice to look forward to, won't it?'

'That's a good idea,' said Albert, when Winifred told him about Kathy wanting to see the Illuminations. 'Why don't we all go? You and Jeff, and Kathy and me. We could go in my car. An evening during the week would be better than the weekend; it gets very busy on the promenade. Then perhaps we could go and have a fish and chip supper afterwards. That'll be a treat for Kathy, seeing that it's something we hardly ever do.'

'Aren't you forgetting something?' said Winifred. 'Somebody will need to stay here to see to the visitors' suppers. I don't see how we can all go, although I must admit I'd like to see the Lights as much as anyone.'

'Yes, that's a thought,' agreed Albert. 'We haven't got all

that many folks in, though, next week. Perhaps Betty could come in for the evening, just for once; we'd pay her extra, of course.'

Sadie Morris's departure had meant that they had to employ another waitress-cum-general help. Betty Jarvis, a member of the church that Winifred attended, had been pleased to step into the breach. She had no children to worry about as they were both married, her husband had no objection to her working – in fact, he had welcomed the idea – and she seemed to be fitting in very well. It was the bookkeeping, though, that was the problem. Winifred had got used to having someone else to cope with it, and now, for the moment, she was once again doing it herself.

She was pleased that Albert was so enthusiastic about the visit to the Illuminations. He had been very downcast after the ending of his friendship with Sally, and she had feared that he would revert to being as miserable and uncommunicative as he had been when he lost Barbara.

'I shall never try again,' he had moaned. 'What's the use? I really thought Sally and I were getting on well. It just goes to show . . .' What it showed, Winifred was not quite sure. 'Anyroad, that's it for me as far as women are concerned.'

'Don't say that, Albert,' she had tried to console him. 'You never know, do you? I didn't think I would ever meet anyone; it was really unexpected the way I met Jeff. Try not to be downhearted.'

'Well, at least I've got Kathy, haven't I?' he said. 'She's a bit upset an' all about Sally, and about Shirley, though she was a little madam, if you ask me! I'll have to try and make it up to her.'

And the visit to the Illuminations was one way of doing so. The Lights had recommenced the previous year after the years of darkness during and following the war. They were a great boost to Blackpool's economy, especially to the boarding house and hotel trade.

Betty agreed to come in to see to the suppers on the Monday evening at the start of the last week in September. Albert drove along the backstreets to the southern end of the promenade; the customary route for the traffic to take was from south to north. Kathy sat at the front with her dad, with Jeff and Winifred in the rear seats.

The Lights really were a fantastic spectacle, living up to the proud boast that they were 'the greatest show on earth'. All along the several miles of the promenade they sparkled like diamonds, rubies, emeralds and sapphires – a long, long necklace of jewels. Here and there were dazzling arrays of shooting stars, crescent moons and shining rainbows. There were juggling clowns and acrobats, colourful fishes and tropical sea creatures, and nursery rhyme characters, all dancing and darting about against the night sky. Now and again an illuminated tram passed by on the tram track on their left-hand side, transformed into a gondola, a paddle steamer or a rocket.

On the cliffs at North Shore were the tableaux, huge illuminated boards depicting jungle animals, fairy tales and circus scenes. One tableau, called 'The Rejuvenating Machine', showed a group of old men and women going into a strange-looking engine, and coming out at the other end as youthful boys and girls; such was the life-enhancing benefit to be found by taking a holiday in Blackpool.

Winifred was touched to see Kathy's delight at the new experience. She had 'oohed' and 'aahed' at first, then grew silent as her eyes took in one amazing vista after another.

'That was terrific!' she pronounced when they came to the end of the tableaux and turned off the promenade into the comparative darkness of Red Bank Road.

There was a fish and chip shop about halfway along that served meals to eat out or to eat on the premises. Albert parked the car on a side street and they went into the dining area at the rear of the shop. They sat at a table for four, covered with a red and white checked tablecloth, on top of which were large canisters of salt and pepper and a giant-sized vinegar bottle.

The fish and chips were delicious; the fish was white and flaky and covered in crispy batter, and the chips were hot and steaming and a perfect golden brown. At the side of each plate was a small carton of mushy peas. Even Albert declared that he couldn't have cooked it any better himself! They hadn't had a meal that night, after serving the visitors' high tea, and so between them they demolished the pile of bread and butter that accompanied the meal, and drank the huge teapot dry.

'Well, it's home time now, I suppose,' said Albert. It's been a grand evening, it has that!'

They got into the car and Albert set off driving, as carefully as he always did, back towards the sea. He would turn off soon and make their way home through the quiet back streets of the town.

Winifred could never say exactly what happened next. All she saw was a motorbike heading towards them, on the wrong side of the road as it tried to overtake a car.

'Look out, Albert!' she cried, but it was too late. There was a deafening crash as the motorbike plunged into the front of their car, and then a piercing cry as Kathy was thrown forward towards the windscreen.

Chapter Fifteen

'It wasn't your fault, Albert. How many times do I have to tell you? That thing was coming straight towards us. There was no way you could have avoided it.' Winifred had told Albert the same thing umpteen times, but he was still in need of reassurance. She knew how guilt-ridden he was feeling, and would continue to be so until he knew that Kathy was going to be all right. And how Winifred was praying that the little girl would open her eyes. She had been unconscious now for two days . . .

It had all happened so quickly, and even now it was still largely a blur of confusion in Winifred's mind. The almighty bang; the motorbike skidding away out of control and the rider lying motionless in the middle of the road; Kathy's cry of anguish, and then her silence; and Albert cursing as she had never heard him do before. In the back of the car she and Jeff clung to one another. They were, miraculously, unhurt, just suffering from the inevitable shock and a few minor bumps and bruises. A police car and an ambulance, then a second ambulance, arrived – she could not have said how long it had taken – called, no doubt, by a bystander. It seemed as though Albert might have a broken arm and a dislocated shoulder, and bumps and bruises, of course, but little else. It was Katherine who had borne the brunt of the collision, and Albert was still finding it hard to forgive himself for that.

They had all been taken off to hospital. Winifred and Jeff were treated for shock and then discharged, although they stayed behind for a while for news of Albert and Kathy. As they had guessed, Albert's arm was broken and he would need to stay in hospital overnight. Kathy, too, had a broken arm and the bang to her head had resulted in concussion.

They had waited anxiously for news. Then, at midnight, a doctor had informed them that the little girl was still unconscious, but not too seriously injured, as far as they could tell, apart from the broken arm, which had already been set. Winifred and Jeff went home as there was nothing else they could do.

They had phoned Betty Jarvis at the hotel, explaining that they would be delayed; they could not say for how long. She was shocked to hear of the accident, but assured them that she would wait there, no matter how long it might be before they returned. It was, in fact, one o'clock in the morning when the taxi dropped Winifred and Jeff off at Holmleigh. Jeff insisted on staying the night there, and Mrs Jarvis went home – only a few streets away – promising to be back in a few hours to help with the visitors' breakfasts. Fortunately there were only six guests booked in that week. Albert would be incapacitated with his broken arm; but Winifred, who was almost as good a cook as her brother, declared that she would be able to manage, with help from Betty and the part-time staff who came in for a few hours each day.

Their main concern, though, was for Kathy. Albert was discharged on the Tuesday morning, and he and Winifred went to the hospital whenever they were able to do so, after the visitors' requirements had been dealt with.

They sat at her bedside on Tuesday evening, then again on Wednesday afternoon, but there was no change in her condition. The doctor assured them, however, that there was no real cause for alarm; it was just a matter of time whilst her body recovered from the shock. Kathy looked very peaceful, but very small and helpless in the large bed, with her broken arm – fortunately her left one – encased in plaster.

'Poor little lass,' said Albert as they sat there on the Wednesday evening. 'I've not been much of a father to her, have I?'

'Albert, you must never say that!' Winifred remonstrated with him. 'You love her very much. She knows that, and she loves you too. We are all a victim of our own personality, and losing Barbara . . . well, that had a great effect on you, didn't it? But I don't think Kathy has suffered from not having a mother.'

'And that is thanks to you, Winnie. You've been wonderful. You've loved her just as much as any mother could have done.' Albert was not often moved to utter such words of praise. She had felt, at times, that he took her largely for granted; but she could see the remorse in his eyes now, and

214

the trace of a tear. 'But I'll be different,' he went on. 'If she comes round . . . I'll make it all up to her.'

'Albert, there's no "if" about it,' said Winifred. 'She will get better; the doctor has said so. Now, you must be positive about this; she's going to be all right.'

Albert nodded. He continued to look at the motionless figure in the bed. Suddenly, her hand moved, grasping at the sheet.

'There, what did I tell you?' said Winifred, in a hushed voice.

They hardly dared to breathe as they watched the little girl's head begin to move, slowly, from side to side. Then she opened her eyes. She blinked, then her eyes wandered around the room, as if to familiarise herself with her strange surroundings.

'Thank God . . .' whispered Winifred. 'Oh, Albert . . . I can scarcely believe it. I tried to believe, but . . . Oh, thank you, thank you, God.' She buried her head in her hands, unable to stem the tears of relief.

'Yes, indeed . . . thank God,' muttered Albert.

Kathy was looking at them now. 'Daddy . . . Aunty Win . . .' she said, in such a tiny voice. 'Where am I?' She raised her head a fraction and tried to look around. 'I feel a bit funny,' she said. 'What's happened?'

'You had an accident, darling,' said Winifred. 'You hurt your arm and your head. You're in hospital.'

'Oh . . .' Kathy glanced down at her arm encased in plaster. 'My arm, yes . . . Is it broken?'

'It was,' said her aunt. 'But the doctors have mended it. And you're going to be fine. Now, just lie still and I'll go and fetch the nurse. She'll be so pleased that you've opened your eyes.'

'Have I been asleep, then,' asked Kathy, 'for a long time?'

'Yes . . . for quite a little while.'

'Like Sleeping Beauty,' smiled Kathy.

'Well, not quite as long as that, love,' chuckled Albert. 'Not a hundred years. But quite long enough for your aunty and me to have to wait. See, your old dad's got a broken arm an' all. A couple of old crocks, aren't we?'

Kathy smiled at them, and there were tears in Albert's eyes as well as Winifred's as he and his sister looked at one another, almost too choked to speak.

'I'll go and get the nurse . . .' murmured Winifred.

Kathy, of course, needed to stay in hospital for a while longer. But they knew now that she was out of danger. It was fortunate that she had suffered only from a broken arm and concussion. It could, indeed, have been much worse. Albert knew that they could all have been seriously injured or even killed. They were pleased to hear, also, that the motorcyclist was out of danger. His injuries were more severe, but he was recovering. What was more, he knew he had to take full responsibility for the accident; but that would all be sorted out in the not-too-distant future.

Winifred knew that she must ask Albert about the comment he had made when Kathy opened her eyes. 'You said "thank God"' she told him, but not in words of recrimination. He had sounded as though he really meant it. 'I thought . . . well, you always refused to believe in him.'

Albert nodded. 'That's true; "thank God" . . . that's what I

216

said, and I meant it. I prayed, Winnie, when our Kathy was unconscious. I told myself that if God doesn't exist, then it would make no difference. But if he really was . . . somewhere up there, listening to us, then maybe he might answer our prayers. I knew you would be praying as well, you see, and that he would most likely take more notice of you than he would of me.'

'Don't say that, Albert,' whispered Winifred. 'I believe that he listens to everyone. We don't always get the answer that we want, but this time . . . we did.'

'Yes, thank God, we did,' echoed Albert.

'I'm glad you've changed your mind about God.' Winifred smiled at her brother. 'He can make such a difference to life.'

'Well, I shall certainly give him a try now,' replied Albert. 'What have I to lose? I nearly lost the most precious thing in my life. But I shall be different now, Winnie, you'll see. I'm going to be a father that Kathy can be proud of . . .'

Chapter Sixteen

Kathy had no memory at all of what had happened. The last thing she remembered was sitting next to her dad as he drove along Red Bank Road . . . and then she had woken up in hospital with a broken arm and a fuzzy head. Aunty Win told her that there had been an accident with a motorbike, and that she had been asleep for two whole days. They had all been very worried about her, but her dad and aunty assured her that she was going to be fine. Her broken arm would heal, and so would the few bumps and bruises caused by the accident. She would need to stay in hospital for a while and then stay at home until she was fit to go back to school.

She cried a little bit that night when her dad and aunty said goodbye. But the nurses and the doctor were very kind to her and after a day or two she started almost to enjoy being in hospital.

She had quite a few visitors – not all at once because the nurses were very strict about not having too many people round the bed – and that cheered her up a lot. Mrs Culshaw, her teacher, came to see her and brought her some flowers and chocolates and an Enid Blyton book, as well as letters and cards from all the children in the class. She had laughed at the one from Timothy Fielding. He had done a little drawing of himself with his sticky-up hair and a sad downturned mouth because Kathy was poorly. And Maureen, her best friend now that Shirley wasn't there, had sent a pretty card she had made herself with a pattern of flowers and butterflies.

And there was even more of a surprise the next day when Miss Roberts – Sally – came to see her. Kathy had been so disappointed when Sally had stopped seeing her dad. She, Kathy, had even been hoping that the two of them might get married and then Sally would come and live with them. And then, suddenly, it had all come to an end. She hadn't seen her favourite teacher nearly so much as she had hoped she would since moving into the juniors. But now, here she was!

Sally hugged her and kissed her cheek, and Kathy was almost too overcome to speak.

'All the teachers send their love,' said Sally. 'We were all sorry to hear about your accident, but you're looking quite bright-eyed and bushy-tailed, aren't you, dear?' Kathy had a broad smile on her face and her cheeks were pink with excitement. 'And here's a little present from me,' Sally went on. She opened her bag and took out a box of jelly babies and a book, quite a large green one. 'This is a book I enjoyed when I was a little girl,' she said. 'It's called *The Green Book of Fairy Tales*, and I'd like to give it to you now, Kathy.'

'Gosh, thank you!' said Kathy. 'I'll look forward to reading it. I'm feeling a lot better now. Daddy and Aunty Win, and sometimes Uncle Jeff, come to see me every day, and I might be going home next week. Daddy broke his arm as well. Did you know that . . . Miss Roberts?'

'Yes, I called to see him and your aunty,' said Sally. 'He seems to be managing all right. He's more concerned about you, Kathy, about you getting well again . . . Your daddy loves you very much, you know.'

'Yes, I know,' replied Kathy. 'He's been . . . sort of . . . kinder, you know, while I've been in here. He used to be a bit grumpy sometimes. I was ever so sorry, Miss Roberts, when you and daddy stopped seeing one another.'

'Yes, I know, dear,' said Sally. 'But you mustn't worry about it anymore. Grown-ups know, you see, when something isn't going to work out. And we didn't think it would. But you and me, we'll always be friends, won't we?'

Kathy nodded. 'Yes, I hope so.'

'I'll let you into a little secret,' said Sally, leaning closer to her. 'You remember Mr Grantley? Phil – that's what he's called.' Kathy nodded again.

'Yes, I know Mr Grantley. He teaches one of the top classes and takes PE and Games.'

'Well, we've started going out together again, Phil and I. We were quite good friends, you see, and then your dad asked me to go out with him – to the restaurant, you remember, when he won that raffle prize? And so Phil and I drifted apart; it was all rather a mix-up, really. But we're friendly again now, and I'm very pleased about that.' Sally smiled and she looked really happy.

'Oh . . . that's nice,' said Kathy, quite pleased that Miss Roberts had confided in her, just as though she was a real grown-up friend. 'I like Mr Grantley. He looks as though he's good fun . . . Are you going to marry him, then?'

Sally laughed out loud. 'Oh, goodness me! It's early days to be thinking about that, Kathy love. Anyway, a lady has to wait until she's asked, you know.'

'Yes, that's what Aunty Win said when I asked her if she was going to marry Uncle Jeff,' replied Kathy. 'But I think they will get married, you know,' she added confidingly. 'They're quite old, really, but I don't suppose that matters, does it?'

Sally chuckled again. 'I don't suppose it matters at all. But what they are all concerned about at the moment is you getting well again.'

They chatted for a little while about what was going on in the hospital. Kathy said that the food was quite nice and that she liked all the nurses and the doctor who was in charge of her. And Sally told her about her new class of top infants.

She stayed for about half an hour, and Kathy breathed a sigh of contentment as she left. It had been really lovely to see her. With her good arm she opened the book. It was quite an old-fashioned one with lovely coloured pictures on shiny paper. Kathy knew she would enjoy reading the stories of fairy tale princesses, wizards, witches and dragons. And how nice it was to have a book that had belonged to Miss Roberts. 'Sally . . .' she whispered quietly to herself.

Sally was on top of the world at the moment. It had been a dreadful shock to hear, in the staffroom, about the accident that had put Kathy Leigh in hospital and caused injuries to

Albert as well. It was Mrs Culshaw – Mavis – who, as Kathy's class teacher, had been given the news. At that time the little girl was still unconscious, and Sally had found it hard to concentrate on her work for the next day or two until the news came that she was recovering.

She was surprised, but pleased, to see Phil Grantley coming into her classroom after lessons had finished that day.

'It's good news about Kathy, isn't it?' he began, leaning casually against the teaching desk where Sally was sitting. 'I know how worried you must have been about her. You grew very fond of her, didn't you, whilst you and her father were friendly? I don't know her very well, but she seems a dear little girl.'

'Yes, so she is,' agreed Sally. 'I shall go and see her soon. I'll ask her Aunty Win first to make sure it's OK for me to go.' She hesitated, then she went on. 'It was never really serious between Albert Leigh and me, you know. At least . . . I think he wanted it to be, and that was when I decided to call it a day. It would never have worked out, although he's quite a nice chap when you get to know him. But not right for me.'

'Yes, I see . . .' replied Phil. 'That's the main reason I've come to see you, Sally, apart from saying that I'm pleased to hear about Kathy. You and me . . . it all went wrong somewhere along the way, didn't it?'

Sally gave a rueful smile. 'Yes, so it did. Bad timing, you might say, and things happening that were out of our control.' They looked steadily at one another, and Sally knew that the stirrings of love that she had started to feel for him a few months ago were still there.

He reached out a hand to her across the desk. 'Could we

try again, Sally?' he said. 'I really have missed you, and we've wasted such a lot of time.'

'What about Fiona?' she asked. 'You went on holiday together, didn't you?'

'With a crowd of others,' he replied. 'No, that has come to an end. Fiona and I had nothing much in common, really, only that we are both teachers, and are both quite keen on walking. But it's not enough. We know we're not right for one another. How do you feel, Sally? Would you come out with me . . . tonight?'

'I'd love to, Phil,' she said simply as she squeezed his hand. She stood up, and he put his arms around her, kissing her gently on the lips.

'Come along,' he said. 'I'll run you home now, then I'll call for you tonight. Seven-thirty OK?'

'Very much OK,' she smiled.

He kissed her far more ardently as they said goodnight that evening, after a quiet drink at a seafront hotel. 'How about a meal and then the pictures on Saturday night?' he said. 'We'll paint the town red!'

They didn't exactly do that. They were both, deep down, quite reserved people, not given to extremes. But they both knew that they were at the start – though somewhat delayed – of something good.

Plans were afoot, too, at Holmleigh. Jeff Bancroft had asked Winifred if she would marry him and she had quietly agreed that of course she would. They had both known that it was inevitable.

He had proposed to her on the evening that Kathy had

regained consciousness. They sat together in the family living room, Albert having tactfully left them alone for a while, as if he knew what was about to happen.

'I know you're concerned about Kathy,' said Jeff, 'especially now, after the accident. And I know you won't want to move away from here and leave her.'

'That's true,' she replied. 'I'm not saying that Albert wouldn't look after her well, but he's always left a great deal of her bringing up to me, and I know she would miss me. I did think he might get married again, but I feel now that that isn't likely to happen.'

'Well, I'd like to suggest that I sell my bungalow and come to live here,' said Jeff. He smiled. 'That is, if you and Albert will have me?'

Winifred smiled. 'I think that's a splendid idea. I'd thought of it, I must admit, but I didn't like to suggest it myself. After all, it's your home that you're going to sell, isn't it? Besides, I had to wait until you popped the question!'

Jeff kissed her lovingly. 'My home is anywhere that you are, my dear,' he said. 'But I don't want to wait too long. There's no point in waiting, is there?'

They agreed on a quiet wedding just before Christmas. They hoped that, by that time, Jeff's house would be sold and they would then settle in their own private rooms at Holmleigh.

'Come on, let's go and tell Albert,' said Jeff.

Albert was quietly pleased to hear their news, although it was not his way to enthuse too much. 'I can't say I'm surprised,' he remarked. 'You two are made for one another. By Jove, this calls for a celebration. Your good news, and our

Kathy getting better.' He took out a bottle of rich dark sherry from the kitchen cupboard and poured it into three glasses.

He raised his own glass. 'Here's to the pair of you. I wish you all the happiness you deserve. And to our dear little Kathy, God bless her . . .'

Winifred noticed that her brother's eyes were moist with tears.

They had been told that Kathy would need to stay in hospital for at least another week just to make sure that all was well. As Winifred was getting ready to go to church on the following Sunday morning she was feeling that she did, indeed, have a great deal to be thankful for that day. Jeff, who had also started attending the morning service, would be calling for her shortly. To her surprise Albert joined her, dressed in his best suit with a clean white shirt and a colourful tie.

'I'll come along with you, if you don't mind,' he said, just a trifle sheepishly. 'I reckon I've a lot to thank him up there for an' all, don't you?' He grinned as he gestured towards the ceiling.

'You have indeed,' said his sister. 'And I'm so pleased that you realise it, Albert.' There was a ring at the doorbell.

'There's Jeff,' she said. 'Come along; let's go.'

PART TWO

Chapter Seventeen

1961

Kathy stood by one of the large pillars that surrounded the Empress ballroom. She was trying to look nonchalant as she watched the dancers drifting by, as though she was not a wallflower or at all eager that someone – anyone – should ask her to dance.

She had come with her friend, Marcia, whom she had met at night school. Her father approved of Marcia; he thought she was a decent, well-brought-up girl as, indeed, she was. But there was another side to Marcia that Albert Leigh knew nothing about. She could be very silly and giggly when she had had a drop too much to drink; and it didn't take much – only a couple of shandies – to make Marcia lose her inhibitions, although, to be honest, Kathy thought that she put it on a bit. And, besides that, she was a dreadful flirt. Kathy watched her now as she jigged past with the RAF lad who had asked her to dance, laughing up into his face and behaving in what both Kathy's father and her aunt would consider to be a most indecorous manner.

Marcia was a blonde, a very attractive, vivacious, blue-eyed blonde, although she could appear sweet and demure when she wanted to. It seemed that the old adage that men preferred blondes was true, because Marcia was always the first to be asked to dance.

But it didn't worry Kathy all that much. She knew that after the dance Marcia would come back to her. The RAF lad would most likely be only a bit of fun, easily forgotten, and the two girls would go home together at the end of the evening. Marcia, in fact, was engaged to a young man who was doing his national service in Germany. She was twenty years of age, two years older than Kathy, but she saw no reason, she said, to stay at home being miserable whilst Eric was overseas.

Kathy enjoyed her company and she liked to think that, maybe, she was a steadying influence on Marcia, there to prevent her going completely off the rails. It was only quite recently that Kathy's father had agreed to her going to the local dance halls. He drew the line at the Tower, which he considered for some reason to be 'common'; but he had set his seal of approval on the Winter Gardens – the Empress ballroom – or the Palace which, Kathy gathered, held certain memories for him. But he was not one to give too much of himself away. She seemed to remember that he used to go dancing at the Palace with Sally Roberts before that friendship had come to an abrupt end. That was round about the time of the accident. And it was following that occurrence that her father had started taking a good deal more interest in her, Kathy.

The dance was coming to an end, the couples applauding as the band stopped playing, as they always did. Marcia would be back with her soon. But before she saw her friend she heard a voice at the side of her.

'Kathy? It is you, isn't it? Kathy Leigh . . .' She turned to look at the young man in the khaki uniform of a soldier who was addressing her. A thickset young man, not very tall, with a shock of fair hair that stood up on end, a pair of bright blue eyes and a wide smiling mouth.

'Tim!' she cried. 'Timothy Fielding! Well, fancy that! I haven't seen you for ages. Where have you been?'

He laughed. 'Well, that's pretty bloomin' obvious, isn't it? I'm in the army!'

'National Service?' enquired Kathy.

'No, the regulars,' replied Tim. 'I joined the REME when I was seventeen and a half – as soon as they would take me! I signed on for three years.'

'REME?' queried Kathy.

'Royal Electrical and Mechanical Engineers,' said Tim. 'I would have just missed National Service, you see – it finished last year – and I didn't want to miss out on the experience. Call me daft, if you like!' he laughed. 'Actually, it was to give me a good grounding in my career, which I find it is doing. I'm training to be an electrician. I'm stationed up at Catterick Camp, and I've just got a spot of leave. It's great to see you again, Kathy. Come and have a drink with me, will you? Or . . . are you with someone?'

Marcia was coming back, on the arm of the RAF lad.

'Yes, I am, actually,' she replied. 'I came with my friend, but I'm sure she won't mind. Marcia, this is Tim, an old friend of mine from schooldays.' The two nodded at one another and mumbled, 'How do you do?'

'We're going to have a drink and catch up on old times,' said Kathy. 'Is that OK with you?'

'Sure it is,' replied Marcia. 'This is Simon; he's taking me for a drink as well, but we won't play gooseberry.' She winked at Kathy. 'I'll meet you later, then, shall I? In the usual place at eleven o'clock?' They usually met in the Floral Hall, at the top of the steps that led down to the cloakroom, when the dance was coming to an end.

Kathy nodded. 'Yes, see you later.' She drew her friend to one side. 'Watch what you're doing now,' she said in a whisper. 'Don't forget about Eric!'

'It's all right.' Marcia grinned. 'Simon's a good laugh, that's all. I've already told him I'm spoken for. So is he, actually. He's from Birmingham and he's got a fiancée there. Cheerio, then. Don't do anything I wouldn't do!'

Marcia's new friend was one of the myriad RAF men, mainly the last intake of National Service recruits, who were to be seen in the streets of Blackpool and in the local dance halls and cinemas. They were stationed at the nearby camps at Weeton and Warton.

Timothy led Kathy to a quiet corner of a bar near to the ballroom. 'Now, what are you drinking?' he asked. 'A pint of best bitter, or something more ladylike?'

She laughed. 'A shandy, please; just a small one, with ginger beer, not lemonade.'

'Okey doke . . .' He was back in a few minutes with a

brimming pint glass for himself and a smaller one for her.

'Cheers,' he said, raising his glass. 'It really is the most wonderful thing, bumping into you. I must say, you're looking stunning! You always liked red, didn't you? I remember your red jumpers at school and the red ribbons in your hair.' He was smiling at her with the fondness of their remembered friendship.

'Yes, I run pretty true to form, don't I?' she replied, smiling back at him.

She knew that the dress suited her. It was a pinkish shade of red, like crushed strawberries – a simple sleeveless shift style in the new terylene material, with a knee-length skirt, a rounded neckline, and a neat black bow at the low waistline. Her Aunt Winifred often helped her to make her own clothes, but she had bought this one from her favourite dress shop, Sally Mae's.

'It's great to see you again, Tim,' she told him. 'It's been years, hasn't it? I'm surprised you recognised me.'

'You haven't changed at all,' he said, looking at her admiringly.

'No, neither have you,' she answered.

She had lost touch with him when they had both left junior school as they had gone to different secondary schools; most schools in Blackpool were single-sex ones anyway. Tim had attended a secondary modern school – he was a bright boy but one who did not apply himself as well as he might – whereas she, Kathy, had attended the only commercial school in the town.

She had almost – but never entirely – forgotten about him. She had seen him occasionally at church dances, which were the only dances her father would let her attend when she was in her early teens. Tim had never asked her to go out with him; it was doubtful, anyway, that she would have been allowed to go out with a boy before she was sixteen. And Tim, at that time, had been far more interested in knocking around with his mates, although he had always seemed pleased to see her and have a chat with her. Then, a few years ago, he had seemed to disappear off the scene completely. She asked him about that now.

'Do you still live in Blackpool – I mean, when you're not away doing your army service?' she asked. 'I don't think I've seen you for – what? – it must be three or four years.'

'Yes, my parents still live here, and my younger brother and sister,' he replied. 'You didn't see me because I was working away. When I left school I started an apprenticeship with a firm of electricians, and I was sent away on a lot of jobs out of town – Preston, Wigan, Blackburn, some as far away as Yorkshire – so I wasn't in Blackpool very much. Then I decided to join up.'

'How long have you been in the army?'

'Since a year last March.' It was now September. 'So I've another eighteen months to do. I'm on leave till Tuesday, so it's a nice long weekend. I came here with a mate tonight, though I have to confess I'm not much of a dancer. He lives in Blackpool, South Shore, though, so I didn't know him until we joined up at the same time. I daresay he's got himself fixed up for the evening.' He laughed. 'He can charm the birds off the trees, can Jerry. But the bird rarely stays around for more than one date.' He paused, looking at her fondly, and she thought how lovely it was to see him again. And he was just as garrulous as ever!

'What about you?' he went on. 'When I asked if you were on your own I wasn't referring to your friend. I meant . . . is there a boyfriend on the scene?'

'No,' she smiled. 'Not at all.'

'Phew! That's a relief!' He gave an exaggerated sigh. 'Maybe we could meet again, then, before I go back on Tuesday?'

'Yes, I'd love to,' she replied without hesitation.

'Tell me what you've been doing, then, Kathy.' He leant forward eagerly.

'Well, I'm working at our hotel,' she began, 'as I've been doing ever since I left school. It was more or less taken for granted that I would, so I didn't have much choice in the matter, with it being a family business.'

'So what do you do exactly? Are you training to be a chef, like your dad?'

'Oh no. Dad and my aunt are in charge of that side of things. You remember Aunty Win? She's still living at the hotel. She married her gentleman friend, though, Jeff Bancroft, and they have their own rooms at Holmleigh. I'm in charge of the accounts and bookkeeping and all that side of things. You remember I went to the commercial school on Palatine Road? It was ideal for what I was going to do: shorthand and typing lessons, and accountancy. Then I took a further course at night school, so I'm quite well qualified.'

'And you're not hankering to do something else? I seem to recall that you wanted to be a writer – like Enid Blyton!'

She laughed. 'That was a childhood fantasy. Although I do write short stories, after a fashion, in my spare time.

There's not always too much of that, though, especially in the summer. We're kept pretty busy at the hotel. Don't ask if I'm published, because I'm not! Perhaps one day, though; I live in hope!'

Timothy nodded. 'Yes, you were always top of the class at composition, weren't you?'

'I might have been,' she replied dismissively, 'at junior school at any rate. I missed quite a lot, though, after the accident I had.'

'Yes, I remember that,' he replied. 'We had just gone up into the juniors, and we were all real worried about you. You broke your arm, didn't you, and weren't you unconscious for a while?'

'Yes . . . and when I woke up I remembered nothing about the accident. Then Mrs Culshaw came to see me and brought me some flowers and chocolates, and a new Enid Blyton book! And letters and cards from all the children in the class. I remember yours especially, Tim,' she smiled. 'Sally Roberts came as well; I was so thrilled when she came to see me.'

'Yes, we all liked her, didn't we? Mrs Grantley, of course, as she is now. Wasn't she friendly with your father at one time, before she married Phil Grantley?'

'Yes, my dad and Sally had been going out together for a little while, then it came to an end just before we had the accident. My dad was like a bear with a sore head when they finished, and I remember I was very disappointed as well. Of course, I'd just lost my best friend, Shirley, when she moved to Southport with her mother. You remember Shirley Morris, don't you?'

'Yes; what a bossy knickers she was! She and I never got

on very well. You had some other friends, though, didn't you, after she left?'

'Yes, but it was quite traumatic for me at the time – Shirley going, and then my dad and Sally splitting up, then the accident on top of it all. That was why my aunt and Jeff stayed at Holmleigh. I'd always been very close to Aunty Win – she was like a mother to me – and they didn't want to upset me by moving away. So Jeff sold his bungalow and moved in with Aunty Win – after they were married, of course!'

'Of course!' smiled Timothy.

'Jeff's a freelance artist,' Kathy went on. 'He's always done very well, but they seem content to stay where they are, especially with my aunt still working at the hotel.'

'And what about your father? Did he never get married again?'

'Oh no . . . After my mother died – I don't remember her, of course – he was very bitter for ages. That's what my aunt has told me, and there was never anyone who could match up to her, in his eyes. I think Sally Roberts might have done, but I think it was Sally who finished their friendship, not my dad. I wish I'd known my mother . . .' she added wistfully. 'I used to feel . . . not exactly envious, but I used to wish, sometimes, that I had the sort of family life that Shirley had – a nice friendly mum and dad, and a brother and sister. But then . . . well, it all went wrong for Mr and Mrs Morris, didn't it?'

'Yes, Shirley never came back, did she?'

'No, her mum got married again to a man called Barry Proctor. Apparently she met him at our hotel, and she'd already got rather too friendly with him before she moved to Southport. My aunt said she felt terrible about it, with them getting friendly under her roof! I didn't know anything about it at the time, of course, and I've never seen Shirley again. I've seen her brother, though, Graham. He came back to Blackpool to live with his dad, and Mr Morris got married again as well.' She shrugged. 'So much for the family life I was so envious about!'

'It's not always like that, though, is it?' said Tim. 'My parents are still very happy together. And what about Sally Roberts – Sally Grantley – and Phil? Do you hear anything of them?'

'Oh yes, Sally and I are very friendly. Funny that, isn't it, with her being our teacher? She kept in touch with me after I had the accident, and then she asked me to be a bridesmaid at their wedding; that was the following summer.'

'Oh yes – I seem to remember that now,' said Tim. 'You were always quite a favourite of hers, though, weren't you?'

'I think it was because I didn't have a mum,' said Kathy. 'I was a bit worried about the bridesmaid thing, in case some of the others said I was a "teacher's pet". But Sally said not to bother about it. I wasn't in her class anymore. Anyway, she'd become quite friendly with my Aunty Win and that was one of the reasons that she asked me. We still see her and Phil and their children, and my dad's come to terms with it all. Actually, my dad's quite a changed man now.'

'Mr and Mrs Grantley have a family, then?' enquired Tim.

'Yes, Lucy's eight and Daniel's six. I babysit for them sometimes. They're smashing little kids.'

'And . . . what were you saying about your father? That he's changed quite a lot?'

'Yes, he really has. So I suppose, in a way, some good came out of the accident. From what my aunt says he was out of his mind with worry and guilt when I was injured. Then when I recovered, he saw it as an answer to prayer. He'd always said he didn't believe in God; he'd stopped going to church after my mother died. But now, well, he's never away from the place. He started going with my aunt and Jeff, then he became a sidesman, and now he's a churchwarden! He still plays darts, though, and has the occasional pint – and, of course, he still goes to football matches. But he's so much happier in himself.'

'So you and your dad are happier together as well?'

'Yes, we are,' she smiled. 'He was never very affectionate before, although I always knew, deep down, that he loved me. Now, though, he can't do enough for me. It has its downside, though. He always wants to know where I'm going and who I'm with. Especially if there's a lad involved!'

'And have there been . . . some boyfriends?'

'Only a couple of lads from church. Nothing to write home about, as they say!'

'And what do you think your father will say about me?' Tim smiled at her, with his head on one side. 'Because I'm going to see you again, Kathy. There's no doubt about that, is there?'

'No, none at all, Tim,' she replied. He reached out his hand across the table and she took hold of it. They smiled into one another's eyes, knowing already that this was what they both wanted so very much.

Chapter Eighteen

Kathy and Tim agreed to meet again the following day, which was Sunday. It was mid September and the hotel was fairly busy, although not completely full, with visitors who had come to see the Illuminations.

Kathy would be busy during part of the day as she helped out doing a spot of waitressing, but she agreed that she would see Tim in the afternoon after the midday meal was finished, and again in the evening.

She decided to put her cards on the table, so to speak, right at the start, so she asked Tim to come and call for her. Her dad would want to know where she was going and who she was with anyway, so it would be best to be up front about it. She had already confided in her aunt that she had met Timothy Fielding the previous night at the Winter Gardens, and that she was seeing him again that afternoon.

'How exciting!' said her aunt, looking quite delighted.

'You always liked him, didn't you?' she added roguishly. 'I remember when you were in Sally's class you were forever talking about him.'

'Was I?' said Kathy, laughing. 'Yes, I suppose I was, but it's a long time ago. He hasn't changed much, though. He still chatters as much as ever. I've asked him to come here, then he can meet my dad, and you of course, Aunty Win.'

'Yes, that would be best,' said Winifred. 'You know what your dad's like. He likes to keep an eye on you and what you're up to. It isn't that he doesn't trust you, but I suppose he still sees you as his little girl. I keep trying to tell him that you're grown up now.'

'He's not such a bad old fellow, though, as dads go,' said Kathy affectionately.

'Not so much of the old!' teased her aunt. 'I'm five years older than Albert, and I don't consider that I'm old, not by a long chalk!'

'No, of course you're not, Aunty,' laughed Kathy. 'Neither is Uncle Jeff. You two don't seem any older than on the day you got married.'

Winifred smiled. 'That's because we're so happy together,' she replied, her cheeks turning a little pink.

When Tim arrived at half past two Kathy took him into the living room where her father was taking his ease for a little while with his pipe and the Sunday paper.

'Dad,' she called. 'There's somebody here that I think you might remember. It's Timothy Fielding – we were at school together – and I met him again last night.'

Albert took off his reading glasses and looked at the young man, seeming a little puzzled. Then he said, 'By Jove, yes! I do remember you. Our Kathy used to talk about you quite a lot. And I remember watching you at sports days and suchlike. You were a bit of a scallywag weren't you, when you were a youngster?'

'Dad, honestly!' said Kathy reprovingly.

Tim laughed. 'Yes, you're quite right, Mr Leigh. I think I gave the teachers a run for their money. But I never got into serious trouble. My mum and dad made sure of that.'

'So you're in the army now, lad,' said Albert. Tim was wearing his uniform, as many soldiers did when they were home on leave. 'Enjoying it, are you?'

'Yes, I am,' said Tim. 'I joined the regulars – the REME – to help in my career. I'm an apprentice electrician, you see. And my job's still here for me when I'm demobbed. I'm up at Catterick Camp, and I must admit I'm quite enjoying it, really.'

Albert nodded. 'Aye, that's where I was an' all, during the war, in the catering corps. So, I suppose you're off out now, you two?'

'Yes, I think we'll have a walk on the prom,' said Tim. 'Catch up on old times.'

'I'll be back to help with the teas, though, Dad,' said Kathy.

'Oh, that's all right,' said Albert. 'We're not full up this week. Winnie and I'll manage. Off you go and enjoy yourselves. Good to see you again, Timothy.'

'Thank you, Mr Leigh,' said Tim. 'It's good to see you as well.'

'Cheerio then, Dad,' said Kathy, thinking to herself that

her father was in a remarkably good mood. And he seemed to have taken to Tim at once.

She took him to say hello to her aunt and Jeff and they were very nice to him as well.

'How lovely that you two have met up again,' said Winifred. 'I remember you very well, Tim. I used to hear such a lot about you. Kathy was forever talking about you and telling me jokes that you'd told her. Quite the class comedian, weren't you?'

'Aunty!' said Kathy, a mite embarrassed as she had been at her dad's remarks. But it was clear that Tim was already making a good impression.

Tim laughed. 'Yes, I liked to think I was,' he replied in answer to Winifred's remark. 'I must have been a real cheeky little brat. I've calmed down a lot . . . er . . . Mrs Bancroft. That's your name now, isn't it?'

'Yes, it has been for quite some time now, Tim,' said Winifred, as she and Jeff exchanged fond glances. 'It's getting on for eleven years now.'

'Good grief!' said Tim. 'How time flies, as my mum is always saying. Anyway, as I was telling you, I don't think I'm as cocky and such a damned nuisance as I used to be. And it's great meeting Kathy again.' Their happiness was clear to see as they smiled at one another.

'Off you go, then, and enjoy yourselves,' said Winifred, just as Kathy's father had already said. 'I hope we'll see you again, Tim.'

'Oh, I don't think there's much doubt about that,' replied Tim, putting an arm gently and caringly around Kathy's shoulders as they went out of the door.

'Well, that wasn't too bad, was it?' he remarked as they set off down the street, heading towards the promenade. He took hold of Kathy's hand. 'I think I've managed to convince them I'm OK and not the obnoxious little squirt I used to be.'

Kathy laughed. 'You were never that. As you said to my dad, you never got into any serious trouble, did you? I think you've made a really good first impression.'

They walked hand in hand along the promenade, northwards towards Bispham. There were several people, most likely visitors in the main – residents did not often take advantage of their resort's attractions – strolling along the prom, hand in hand, or arm in arm, and children bounding along ahead of their parents. It was a pleasant early autumn afternoon with the sun shining in a blue sky patterned with fluffy white clouds. There was a nip in the air, though, that gave a hint of the coming change in the season.

'Let's stop and have an ice cream,' said Tim, and they found a little café just off Gynn Square. They indulged themselves with vanilla and strawberry ices topped with chocolate flakes and nuts, covered with a gooey pink sauce.

'I really should be watching my weight,' said Kathy. 'I don't often spoil myself like this. I shall have to cut down on the cakes for a while to make up for this.'

'There's no need, is there?' smiled Tim. 'You look all right to me. In fact, you look pretty damned amazing . . .' He was regarding her with a look almost of wonder in his eyes. He recalled that she had been a pretty little girl, but now she was a good deal more than just pretty. Her dark curly hair was almost shoulder length, framing a rounded fresh-complexioned face, out of which shone a pair of lovely luminous brown eyes. She was not dressed in her favourite red today, but the bright-yellow jacket with the stand-away collar suited her colouring just as well. She looked, he mused, like a ray of sunshine. Tim knew at that moment that he had fallen in love with Katherine Leigh, and how he hoped and prayed that she might feel the same way about him. He vowed that he must do nothing to mar this budding relationship.

Kathy lowered her eyes, a little fazed by Tim's adoring glance. She already knew, though, that she was so very glad that they had met again, and she felt sure that their friendship would blossom and go from strength to strength.

'No, I really do need to watch what I eat,' she said now, quite definitely. 'I wear size twelve in dresses now, and I mustn't get any bigger.'

'Well, I don't know what that means,' said Tim. 'But it sounds OK to me. Come on, then, if you're ready. We'll go and walk it off.'

North of Gynn Square there were large tableaux on the cliffs, stretching as far as Bispham, depicting fairy tales and colourful scenes of all kinds. In a few hours' time they would be lit up, forming one of the main attractions of Blackpool's famous Illuminations.

'No point in looking at them now,' said Tim. 'Shall we come and see them tonight? We could take a tram up to the end and then walk back. What d'you think, Kathy?'

'That would be great,' she replied. 'I haven't seen the Lights for ages. Funny, isn't it, that when you live here you never bother about them. I used to like them, though, when

I was a little girl. That was when we had the accident, of course, after we'd been to see the Lights . . .'

'Well, you're going to be quite safe tonight,' said Tim, putting an arm around her and drawing her close. 'I shall take care of you, Kathy . . . always.' She noticed his remark with a feeling of warmth and delight, but she did not comment on it.

Tim called for her again that evening at seven o'clock. 'So where are you off to now?' asked Winifred. She and Jeff were watching a variety show on the television, and Albert had gone to church. He went twice every Sunday now, apart from the times when the hotel was extra busy, to fulfil his duties as churchwarden.

'We're going to see the Lights, like a couple of day trippers,' laughed Kathy. 'It's ages since I saw them last.'

'That's nice,' said her aunt. 'I thought you might have been going to the pictures. It doesn't matter so much to me, but I know that your dad doesn't approve of the cinema on a Sunday. It's the way we were brought up, you know. And, of course, your dad's been much keener on Sunday observance since he started going to church regularly. But he won't object to you going to see the Lights.'

'We wouldn't want to do anything to upset him,' said Kathy. 'But in some ways he's much easier to get on with now, isn't he?'

'That's true.' Winifred nodded. 'Have a good time, then. We'll perhaps see you the next time you're home on leave, then, Tim?'

'Sure thing!' he replied with a broad smile. 'It's been good meeting you again.'

'And you, Tim,' added Jeff. 'Take care of yourself now.'

'What a grand couple they are,' said Tim, as they made their way once again to the promenade.

'Yes, Jeff's a great guy,' replied Kathy. 'He's made Aunty Win so happy. I don't think my dad imagined she would ever get married. And I'm sure my dad won't, not now. He's not taken much interest in women since that brief episode with Sally. He's happier in himself, though. He used to be such a grumpy old so-and-so at times.'

Tim laughed. 'Well, I seem to have got off on the right foot anyhow. I hope I can keep it that way.'

They boarded a tram near to North Pier. It took them along the prom to Bispham where the tableaux and the garlands of overhead lights came to an end. It was completely dark by now and the myriad multicoloured lights shone out brilliantly against the midnight-blue sky.

When they alighted from the tram they crossed the road to get a better view of the tableaux across the wide promenade. The scenes were a spectacular display of man's ingenuity and creativity, and it was often remarked that they got better each year. They had been shining in Blackpool since the early years of the century, apart from the duration of the two world wars.

Kathy recognised many familiar scenes – a circus scene with jugglers, clowns and acrobats; jungle animals and creatures from under the sea; favourite characters from nursery rhymes and fairy tales – and overhead, strung across the promenade and decorating the lamp standards, there were Chinese lanterns, shooting stars and arching rainbows. It was a wonderland of colour and fantasy that brought out the child in everyone who was drawn into its spell. No more so than Kathy. She was filled with awe and delight, not only at the scene around her but at her closeness to Tim as they strolled along with his arm around her.

When they had walked a mile or so back towards the town centre they crossed the road and the tram track and made their way to the lower promenade. It was dark and quiet there away from the brilliant lights and the noise of the crowds and the clanging trams. There were a few other couples, who, like themselves, were seeking solitude. They had not kissed properly yet, apart from a peck on her cheek that Tim had given her as they walked along.

But it was all the better for the waiting. He drew her into a secluded corner in the shadow of the sea wall, and there they exchanged their first real kiss. It was tender and loving, filled with memories for both of them of their childhood friendship. There were still vestiges of the old Tim in his cheeky grin and his cheerful chatter that led him effortlessly from one thing to another. But he was grown-up now, and so was Kathy. Their next kiss was more passionate, holding promise of an awakening love of which they were both aware.

They drew apart after a few moments. He had not sought to do any more than kiss her. Nor did he tell her, yet, that he loved her. It was too soon; but the affection had been there long ago when they were children, and they both knew now that it would grow stronger. All he said, in a whisper, was, 'I'm so glad that I've met you again, Kathy.'

'So am I, Tim,' she whispered back.

'Come along; I'd best take you home,' he said. 'I must

keep on the right side of your dad. Anyway, I'd better spend a bit of time with my parents.'

It was not yet ten o'clock but Kathy understood what he was saying. 'I'll see you again tomorrow, though, won't I?' he asked. 'D'you think your dad would let you off to come to tea at our house? I told my mum and dad how we met, and they'd love to see you again. Then we can go out tomorrow night.'

'I am allowed a little time to myself!' said Kathy. 'So I'm sure it will be OK with my dad and Aunty Win. I shall look forward to meeting your parents. I remember your mum, but not your dad.'

He kissed her again as they stood at the gate, then smiled and winked in the irrepressible way that she remembered, before walking off, with his soldier's gait, along the street.

He called for her the following day at five o'clock. The Fielding family lived only ten minutes' walk away, in a semi near to the school that Kathy and Tim had attended.

She was made most welcome and felt at home straight away. Tim's mother was quite young – not yet fifty – and pretty, with a rounded face and a plumpish figure.

'Oh, I remember you very well, dear,' she said. 'You've hardly changed at all.'

'I must be rather bigger,' smiled Kathy. 'It's lovely to see you again, Mrs Fielding.'

Tim had a younger sister, Linda, who was fifteen, and a thirteen-year-old brother, Bobby. She remembered seeing him in his pram, but she didn't say so. Kathy could hardly remember Mr Fielding at all. She had known that he worked as an electrician for the local council, a job he was still doing.

Tim had followed the same trade but for a different firm.

When he came home from work at six o'clock he, also, greeted her in a most friendly manner. Then they all sat down to a meal of steak-and-kidney pie and chips, followed by apple crumble with fresh cream. They finished off with a 'nice cup of tea', without which no northern meal was complete. Mrs Fielding had been hard at work in the kitchen for the latter part of the afternoon preparing the meal, as she did each day. She was, as she said herself, 'a full-time housewife and mum, and proud of it.' Like the majority of her generation she had not gone out to work after her marriage, nor had she ever wanted to.

'Times are changing, though, I realise that,' she remarked. 'I daresay you will want to go on working, Kathy, after you get married . . . Not just yet, though,' she added in the rather awkward silence that followed. Kathy felt herself blushing a little; was Tim's mother already thinking of her as a future daughter-in-law? But it seemed that she was just speaking in general terms. 'I mean, that's what today's young women seem to be doing, to help with the mortgage and everything, till the children come along.'

'Let 'em have a bit of freedom first, eh, Elsie?' joked her husband. 'Although there's nowt wrong with getting wed young if you're sure it's what you want.' Kathy wondered if he, too, was looking at her with an eye to the future.

She and Tim went out soon after the meal to catch the start of the film, *I'm All Right, Jack*, which was showing at a local cinema not far from both their homes. It was a rerun from a couple of years back that neither of them had seen the first time round. They laughed out loud with the rest of the audience at the antics of Ian Carmichael, as a graduate, trying to find his niche in industry, and the superb performance of Peter Sellers as the shop steward.

Tim bought her an ice cream in a little tub at the interval, and they held hands all the time, like a real 'courting couple', which she knew they almost were already.

They walked back to Kathy's home through the dark streets, both a little sad because it would soon be time to say goodbye, at least for the moment. They kissed several times as they stood by the gate, marvelling again at how wonderful it was that they had found one another again.

'You will write to me, won't you?' asked Tim.

'Of course I will, all the time,' she assured him. 'But you'll write as well, won't you?' She knew that a lot of young men were not great at correspondence.

'I'm not the world's best letter writer,' he confessed. 'My mother complains about it, but for you . . . yes, I promise I'll write every week, at least. But I'll see you again very soon, I hope, in a few weeks' time if I can wangle it.'

After another tender kiss and a fond backward glance he was gone. But Kathy could not feel too sad at their parting. She knew that what they had found was 'for keeps'.

Their courtship followed the pattern of many of their peer group, where the young man was completing his national service. Tim still had a year and a half to do. He managed to get leave, though, every couple of months and they spent most of the time together. Their love for one another grew stronger and deeper. They had both uttered the 'three little words' that meant such a lot quite soon in their courtship, both of them knowing that 'I love you' meant for now and for ever.

It was not until the Christmas of 1962, though, that Tim asked Kathy to marry him, knowing that she would say yes. Holmleigh was open for four days over the Christmas period, so the two of them had not been able to spend as much time together as they could have wished; Kathy wanted to make sure that she pulled her weight at what was a very busy time. Tim had given her a ring that he had chosen himself, a sapphire surrounded by tiny diamonds which she loved.

They agreed, though, that it would be better to approach Kathy's father – to ask for his consent, in the old-fashioned way – when he was not quite so fraught with his hotel duties.

Kathy and Tim said goodbye at North Station the day after Boxing Day, hoping that it would not be very long before he was home again. Tim intended to wangle a forty-eight-hour pass at the end of January, then he would ask her father if he would agree to them being officially engaged.

Chapter Nineteen

Kathy and Tim had decided that she should broach the subject in advance. She guessed, although he didn't admit it, that Tim was a tiny bit nervous about approaching her father. She brought up the subject one morning over the breakfast table. Albert would not be running true to form, however, if he did not have something contrary to say.

'You want to get engaged?' He stared in astonishment at his daughter. 'But you've only known the lad five minutes!' Kathy could see, though, that there was a twinkle in her father's eye, and she knew he was not as surprised as he was pretending to be.

'Now, that's not true at all, Dad,' she replied, 'as you know very well. I was at school with Tim; we've known each other since we were five years old. I should think that's quite long enough for us to know what we want.'

'Aye, but you were only kids then, weren't you? What I

mean is . . . you've not been together all that much recently, with him being in the army. You've not had a chance to get to know him properly.'

Kathy smiled. 'Tim and I are very sure about what we want, Dad. Anyway, he's coming home on leave this weekend, and he's coming to see you. I know it might seem a bit old-fashioned, but he wants to do things properly, to ask your permission to marry me. I'm just paving the way, like, because I think he's a bit nervous.'

'It's not old-fashioned at all,' retorted Albert. 'You're only nineteen . . . well, twenty in June, and he's not much older, is he? Anyroad, I'm pleased he's going to do things correctly. You'll not be wanting to get wed just yet, though, will you?'

'I'm not sure.' said Kathy evasively. She and Tim were planning to have a short engagement with a wedding later that summer. It was now January, 1963, and Tim was due to be demobbed in March. His job with Fothergill's electricians, an old-established local firm, was there for him to return to. They could see no point in waiting any longer as they were both sure of their feelings for one another, and had been so ever since they had met at the Winter Gardens, some sixteen months previously. They had both seen it as fate that they had met again, and felt sure that if they hadn't met at that time, then they would have done so at a later date.

'Well, he's a nice enough lad, I must say,' said Albert. 'Aye, you could have done far worse, Kathy. But I want you to be very sure, both of you. It's too late once you've tied the knot. We don't want any divorces in the family, like that Sadie Morris. She was a flibbertigibbet if ever there was one! But she had us all fooled. I'd never have believed it.'

'But that's ages ago, Dad,' said Kathy. He did tend to harp on so about things that had happened in the past. 'Don't start on about divorce when we're not even married yet. Anyway, that's not going to happen, I can assure you, with Tim and me.'

'You can never be too sure,' said her father, shaking his head in a mournful way.

'Dad, for goodness' sake!' Kathy was starting to get cross with her father, but she could see the funny side of it as well. 'Don't be so bloomin' pessimistic!'

Albert smiled. 'No, you're right. I'm being silly, aren't I? But you know how I feel, Kathy love, don't you? I want the very best of everything for you. I want it all to be just right.'

'I know, Dad,' she replied. Indeed, she did know. He had been so caring and loving – overprotective at times – ever since she had had her accident and he had feared that he might lose her. She couldn't say, though, that he had ever been domineering or dictatorial with her; besides, her aunt and Jeff had always been there to stick up for her if he had ever been too intractable.

They were taking their ease at the breakfast table. There would be no more visitors until the week before Easter, unless some of their regulars asked to come and stay for a few days. They were always willing to oblige their clients, and that was why the hotel had a deservedly good reputation.

Kathy's aunt spoke up now. 'Well, I think this is very good news, and I'm not surprised at all. You've only to look at our Kathy and Tim to see that they're made for one another.' Her eyes twinkled. 'And I've a feeling that Kathy thought so when she was only seven years old!'

Kathy laughed. 'Yes, I always had a soft spot for Tim.'

'I'm sure you'll be very happy together,' said Winifred. 'So let's not have any negative thoughts about it, eh, Albert? You should be looking forward to your only daughter getting married, and then some grandchildren coming along!'

'Well . . . yes, so I am,' Albert admitted, looking affectionately at his daughter.

'I must love you and leave you now,' said Kathy, putting her pots together and getting up from the table. 'I'm sorry – I've left it a bit late to help with the washing-up, Aunty Win.'

'Don't worry, dear; I'll have it done in a jiffy,' said Winifred. 'Then I'm going to have a day of leisure before we make a start on the attic bedrooms tomorrow.'

Kathy had a part-time job during the winter months when the hotel was quiet. She did the accounts for a nearby newsagent's shop all the year round, but during the winter she served at the counter as well, to give the newsagent's wife a well-earned rest. Albert and Winifred still caught up with decorating and general maintenance of the hotel during the off-season, with help from Jeff in between his commissions for book illustrations and greetings cards.

The four of them were a contented little family group. Winifred and Jeff had found happiness that they had not anticipated so late in life. Kathy was looking forward to marrying the man whom folk were referring to as her childhood sweetheart. She hoped that they would be married sooner rather than later, if her father could be persuaded to give permission for her to marry before she officially came of age at twenty-one. And as for Albert, he seemed to have come to terms with his situation. He was no longer bitter about the death of his young wife, the event that had altered his view of life for so long. Nor did he resent his daughter's friendship with Sally and Phil and their young family. He could see that the young woman with whom he had – almost – fallen in love was happy with a man of her own age, one who was far more suited to her than he, Albert, would have been. The only women in his life now were his beloved daughter and his sister. And, along with his devotion to them, his commitment to his church and his rediscovered faith were a great solace to him.

Albert did not take much persuading to allow his daughter to marry before she was twenty-one. The wedding took place at the church that Albert now thought of as 'his' church, on a glorious sunny Saturday in mid August. What did it matter that it was the height of the holiday season? This was Kathy's day and she must have priority for once over the needs of the visitors. It was Tim's day as well, of course, although the bridegroom usually found himself overshadowed, and Tim was no exception to the rule.

Kathy had insisted, however, that she did not want a huge fuss, just a simple buffet meal after the wedding ceremony, with family members and friends. There were very few relatives on Kathy's side of the family, only her father and her aunt and Jeff; her grandparents had died a couple of years previously. But Tim's family made up for the sparsity; there were grandparents still living, as well as aunts, uncles and cousins.

Her wedding dress was a simple style: white silken satin with a boat-shaped neckline and an ankle-length bell-shaped skirt. Her short silk-tulle veil flowed from a neat pillbox hat decorated with seed pearls. Her bridesmaids were her friend, Marcia, Tim's sixteen-year-old sister, Linda, and Sally and Phil's ten-year-old daughter, Lucy. Their dresses, too, were simple, in keeping with the fashions of the day – sky-blue silken rayon in the now very popular shift style. Their matching pillbox hats complemented that of the bride, and they all, bride and bridesmaids, carried small posies of white and cream flowers: roses, sweet peas, lily of the valley and stephanotis.

The wedding breakfast – although it was at midday – was at Holmleigh, prepared in advance by Albert and Winifred and then laid out ready for their return from church by a team of hired helpers who would, later, see to the clearing away and washing-up. Kathy's father and her aunt wanted to be entirely free that day, and so guests who would normally have arrived on the Saturday had been asked to delay their arrival until the Sunday.

It was a joyful occasion, with the toast to the happy couple drunk in champagne.

'To Kathy and Tim . . .' The chorus of good wishes echoed around the room, and tears welled up in Albert's eyes – a rare sight – as he gazed lovingly at the daughter who meant so much to him.

The couple departed for their honeymoon in Scarborough, a train journey from coast to coast as they, as yet, had no motor car. Tim had a driving licence, as he drove his firm's van, but they knew they would have to wait a little while before they could afford a vehicle of their own.

It was Kathy's first visit to the Yorkshire seaside resort, although Tim had been a couple of times with his parents when he was a child and he assured Kathy that she would love the place.

And so she did. In some ways it was like Blackpool – busy and bustling at this time of the year, and it also had its fair share of amusement arcades, ice cream and hot dog kiosks and 'Kiss me quick' hats. She had to admit, though, that Scarborough had a beauty of its own that Blackpool lacked.

They stayed at a small hotel near to the Spa Bridge. Kathy was captivated by the view from the bridge, across the wide expanse of the bay to the busy harbour. There the fishing boats were unloaded, and beyond was the huddle of fishermen's cottages on the steep slope of Castle Hill. And on the horizon the ruins of the old castle were silhouetted against the blue of the summer sky.

Kathy would have loved the place wherever it happened to be, because she was with Tim, who was now her beloved husband. She had felt a little apprehensive about the honeymoon and all that it entailed. Their love had not yet reached its fulfilment, partly because the opportunity had not arisen. They were both a teeny bit old-fashioned about such things. The time and the place had to be right; besides, they knew that their respective parents would not have approved of them anticipating the wedding date.

She soon realised that Tim was as concerned as she was about the matter. They were good friends and companions, though, as well as being very much in love, and they knew that all would be well. Very soon they discovered that they were as attuned physically as they were in every other way.

After a gloriously happy week it was time to go back and settle into their new little home. They knew that they were very fortunate. They were getting off to a very good start, far better than that of many young couples embarking on married life. They had saved up themselves for a deposit on a terraced house, and both sets of relatives – Tim's parents and Kathy's father, aunt and uncle – had contributed as well. The house was quite small, but it had a little garden at the front and also at the rear. It was only five minutes' walk away from Holmleigh, and not too far, either, from Tim's place of work.

Kathy intended to carry on working at the hotel, with Tim's wholehearted agreement. The majority of young wives went out to work now, as well as running the home, but Tim had promised to help his wife as much as he could. Kathy, remembering his efforts at school, reminded him that he was not much good at handiwork! Between them, though, they had made quite a good job of wallpapering their bedroom and the living room.

It was an ideally happy marriage with scarcely a wrong word to mar their contentment. As a young married couple Kathy and Tim were a part of what soon was to be called 'the Swinging Sixties'. As a popular song of the era said, the times were a-changing. The Fifties had started off with a period of austerity, when food was still rationed. But by the end of the decade Britain was again finding its way in the world and it was regarded by many as 'the best of times'.

The Sixties came in with an explosion of colour, sound and vitality. Kathy knew she must buy a miniskirt to be in the fashion. The new tights, too, instead of nylon stockings, were essential to wear with the short skirts. And a maxi-coat, almost floor length, and knee-high boots to compensate in winter for the cold around one's thighs. She had her hair cut shorter, and tried to make it less curly with backcombing and lacquer, whilst Tim grew his hair longer . . .

They listened to the Beatles, the Rolling Stones and Bob Dylan on records and on the radio and television. And they actually saw the Beatles live at a performance they gave at Blackpool's ABC Theatre.

They watched *Six–Five Special*, *Juke Box Jury*, *Steptoe and Son* and *Morecambe and Wise* on the television; and went to the cinema to see kitchen sink dramas such as *Alfie*, *A Taste of Honey* and *Saturday Night and Sunday Morning*.

They both wanted to start a family, though, to complete their happiness. They were delighted when their first child, Sarah, was born in 1965, followed in 1967 by Christopher; and so were the doting grandparents. Winifred was, in fact, a great-aunt, but as near as could be to a grandparent. She had always regarded Kathy as the daughter she had never had.

Kathy stopped working at the hotel when the children came along; that was to say, she no longer went in each day, as had been her custom, to help out wherever she could with the waitressing or general duties. She continued to help with the bookkeeping, although she could foresee a time in the not-too-distant future when her father and aunt might decide to retire.

The hotel and boarding house trade was gradually changing; it was necessary to keep up with modern trends to run a successful establishment. There were some regular visitors who still came year after year, but many had dropped away. Holidays abroad were now very tempting and, in many cases, just as affordable as staying in Britain. In this way, too, the Sixties was a time of change.

It was in the early spring of 1970 that Winifred told Kathy of their intentions.

'Your dad and I have decided it's time to sell up,' she said. 'Guests are wanting so much more these days. A bar, for instance, because they would like to be able to order drinks – alcoholic ones, I mean – with their meals. It's not that your dad and I are against that, but it would mean applying for a licence, and then paying extra bar staff. And there's another thing . . . A lot of the hotels now have gone over to what they call "en suite" facilities.' Kathy knew what that meant: a private bathroom or shower – or both – and a toilet attached to the bedroom.

Winifred shook her head. 'That would be no end of an upheaval for us, but if we stayed much longer we would have to do it. Times have certainly changed, Kathy. In the old days it was a jug and bowl in each room. Mind you, that was jolly hard work carrying water up the stairs every day . . .'

'And a "gazunder" underneath the bed,' laughed Kathy. 'I remember that up in the attic rooms.'

Winifred smiled. 'Yes, but it wasn't often that we had guests sleeping up there. We put in the required number of toilets, one on each landing, and a bathroom on each landing too, and washbasins in every room. It used to be quite acceptable – the norm, in fact – but folks seem to want a bath every day now instead of once a week.'

Kathy nodded. 'Yes, that's true . . .' So did she and Tim and the children, but she guessed her aunt still stuck to the tradition of bath night on a Friday. Winifred was always very clean and tidy, though, and still quite modern in her outlook in many ways.

'Anyway, we've decided to put Holmleigh up for sale,' Winifred went on. 'It would be best to let the new owners do any renovations they want in their own way.'

'And they'll be getting a place with a very good reputation,' said Kathy loyally.

'Yes, I must admit that's true,' said Winifred. 'And it's time for us to have a change – and a rest. I'm seventy now, so is Jeff, and your dad is sixty-five. It'll be a big upheaval for us and no doubt it'll take some getting used to. Do you know, I have lived in this house all my life, and so has Albert, apart from his time in the army, of course, and you were born here, Kathy . . .' Her aunt looked pensive for a moment.

'So . . . where will you retire to?' asked Kathy. 'You'll want to stay in Blackpool, I suppose?'

'Of course,' said Winifred. 'I'm a true "sand-grown 'un". I don't think I could live anywhere else now. Jeff and I rather fancy living in Bispham. We're going to look for a semi-detached house, not too far away from the sea. We'll have time to walk on the cliffs and ride on the trams! Things we never have time to do now. And your dad will be coming with us. We've talked it over with him and he agrees it's the best thing to do. We get along very well, the three of us. And if we get a large enough house he can have his own rooms. A sitting room as well as a bedroom, I mean; then he can be private when he wants to be.'

They did not have much difficulty in selling the property. A youngish couple from Blackburn, who seemed to be 'not without a bit of brass' as Albert put it, bought Holmleigh. They said they would carry on as usual with the visitors who were booked in for that summer, then start the alterations they required when the season came to an end. Albert, Winifred and Jeff found a house that suited them all on an avenue leading off the promenade, in the area known as Little Bispham.

In 1971 Kathy and Tim and their two children moved to a larger house, a semi-detached, not too far – but not too near – to that of their relatives. Tim was doing well at work and had been made a partner in the firm. On the strength of this they had bought their first motor car, a second-hand Morris that was roomy enough for a family of four. Sarah, aged six, was now at school, and Christopher would very soon be starting; he already went to a playgroup a few mornings a week.

Kathy now had more time to herself. She had continued with her story writing and was determined not to give up despite the inevitable rejections. Sally, whose friendship still meant a great deal to her, had insisted that she must keep on trying. It was a great day when, in the autumn of 1971, her first children's story was published by the magazine *People's Friend*. That was only the beginning. By the summer of 1972 her stories, both for adults and for children, were to be found in several of the women's magazines.

'I knew you would do it!' Sally told her delightedly. 'I knew when you were in my class that you had a talent for storytelling.' And Kathy knew that it was thanks to Sally and to teachers who came later for fostering her love of literature, without which she would not have been able to express herself so well.

And no one was more proud of Kathy than her father when her first serial story was published. 'That's my girl,' he said. 'I always knew you were a clever lass. My goodness! An authoress in the family. Just wait till I tell them all at the club and at church!'

Kathy was touched at her father's pride in her. She had seldom known him to be so excited about anything. The father and daughter were good friends now, something that at one time she could never have imagined. They all settled down to what seemed to be a period of stability, all of them well contented with the lives they were leading.

Chapter Twenty

It was in 1972 that Albert's health started to fail. He had two minor heart attacks and was warned to take things easy.

'I've done nowt else but take it easy ever since I retired,' he grumbled, showing a little of the tetchiness that at one time had been typical of him. 'I don't see how I can do much less than I'm doing now.'

Albert had not settled too well into retirement, although he had thought it was what he wanted. He still rose early every morning from force of habit. Then he bought a newspaper from the local shop, and after reading it he took a leisurely walk along the cliff top, if the weather was fine. He found then, for the rest of the day, that he had too much time on his hands. He still played darts, he watched Blackpool's football team – now, sadly, relegated – on a Saturday afternoon, and carried on with his church duties each Sunday.

His grandchildren were a source of delight to him. He had to admit, though, to a feeling of self-reproach as he realised that he was finding much more pleasure in their company than he had in that of his daughter at a similar age. He knew that this had been entirely his own fault, and he hoped that he had made it up to Kathy in later years. Indeed, he and his daughter were closer now than they had been at any time.

There was still a void in his life, though, after so many years in the cut and thrust of hotel life. Kathy discussed her fears about him with her aunt one afternoon when she called to see her. Winifred was on her own as Albert had gone to the bowling green. He didn't play himself but he liked to watch the team from his 'local'.

'Dad's not himself,' she said. 'At least, he's not the same person that we've all come to know and love. You remember we said how much he had improved? And I've been getting on with him much better than I did when I was a little girl.'

'Yes, it's since you had your accident, dear,' said Winifred. 'He realised then how much he loved you. He always did, you know, but he found it difficult to show it.'

'I was so pleased about the change in him,' Kathy went on. 'But now it seems to me as though he's going back to how he used to be. You know – those bouts of moodiness and silence. Sometimes I think he has something on his mind.'

Kathy thought then that her aunt gave her an odd look, as though there was something that she knew, but wasn't divulging it. 'Oh, I think he just gets a bit fed up sometimes,' Winifred replied. 'Retirement has not been quite what he expected. He's been so active all his life that he can't adjust to all this freedom. And those heart attacks he had scared him quite a lot.'

'He appears to have recovered from them, though,' said Kathy. 'He looks quite well in himself . . . but I still have the feeling that there's something troubling him.'

'He's probably just concerned about his health,' replied Winifred, a trifle too quickly. 'We are inclined to be, you know, as we get older and we find we can't do everything that we used to do.'

'Well, I've really come to invite you all to come to tea on Sunday,' said Kathy. 'You and Jeff and my dad. That might cheer him up a bit. I know how much he likes to see the children . . .'

But the tea party did not take place. It was on the Thursday prior to the planned event that Albert had another heart attack. Winifred knew at once that this one was much more severe. It was now September, 1973, over a year since the two minor ones he had suffered. She called an ambulance and he was taken to hospital without any delay. Kathy and Tim were informed and they, too, rushed to the hospital. All the family spent an anxious evening awaiting news of him. Eventually they went home to rest, knowing there was nothing else they could do but leave him in the capable hands of the doctor and nurses.

He had recovered a little by the following day when Winifred and Jeff went to see him again in his private room. He stretched out his hand towards Winifred and she took hold of it. He looked imploringly at her and he began to speak in an urgent manner.

'When's our Kathy coming?' he asked. 'I want to see her . . .' It was clearly an effort to speak. He was short of breath and his voice was husky and weak. 'There's summat . . . summat I've got to say to her . . .'

'Kathy will be here very soon,' his sister told him. 'But . . . leave it be, Albert. It's too late now.' She had a good idea what it was that Albert might want to tell his daughter. Kathy had been quite right when she had said that her father appeared to have something on his mind. She, Winifred, had noticed it as well. 'Just concentrate on getting better, there's a good lad,' she told him. 'Things are best left as they are.'

Albert shook his head regretfully. 'I'm done for, Winnie. I know that, and I know I've not been fair to the lass . . . I should've told her.'

'Leave it, Albert,' she said again. 'It would be for the best.' She stooped to kiss his pale cheek and he closed his eyes. It was obvious that he was exhausted and he said nothing more. He appeared to be sleeping, so they decided after a while that there was no point in them staying any longer.

'We're going now, Albert,' said Winifred, just in case he could hear her. 'We'll see you tomorrow, Jeff and me. Goodbye, dear. God bless . . .'

'He's not good at all, is he?' she whispered to Jeff as they made their way out of the hospital.

'No, I'm afraid not, my dear,' said Jeff, 'but he's in good hands. All we can do is trust, and say our prayers.'

'I'm worried about Kathy,' said Winifred. 'I'm bothered, Jeff, about what he might say.'

'I think he's too weak to say much at all,' replied Jeff. He kissed her cheek. 'Don't worry, darling. He probably wants to tell Kathy that he loves her, that's all.'

Kathy and Tim went to see her father later that afternoon. He was awake again but looked very frail and ill. He reached out a hand to his daughter. 'Kathy . . . Kathy love, come here . . . I want to tell you summat.'

She moved closer and took hold of his hand. 'What is it, Dad?'

'I've not been a good dad to you . . . I should have told you . . . I know I should . . . but I couldn't do it. But I always loved you, Kathy . . . I loved you, so much . . .'

'I know that, Dad,' she replied. 'I always knew. You're worried that you didn't tell me so, aren't you? But I always knew that you loved me.' She leant over to kiss his papery cheek. At that moment his head lolled sideways and his hand dropped away from hers. She knew that he had gone.

'Tim, Tim . . . call the nurse!' she cried. 'But I think it's too late. Oh dear! I think my dad has . . . gone!'

Kathy was filled with a deep sadness at the death of her father. She could not have said, truthfully, that she was heartbroken. She reflected that she might well have been more grief-stricken if it had been her aunt who had died. She had always felt much closer to Winifred, who had been everything to her that a mother might have been. However, this was her father, and she knew he had done his best, according to his lights, especially of late. She recalled how, when she was a child, he had seemed remote at times and uninterested in her, but she knew he had been coping with his resentment and bitterness at the death of her mother. Following her accident, however, he had been much more approachable and caring, and this had awakened in her a strong affection for him. She had had a premonition, though, that he would not 'make old bones' as the saying went, so his death had not been too much of a shock to her.

He had died on a Friday, and the funeral was arranged for the middle of the following week; a service at the church followed by the burial at Layton Cemetery. Kathy went round to her aunt's home on the Saturday morning to help to sort out certain matters. Sarah and Christopher stayed at home with Tim, who worked a five-day week.

'We'll have to find your dad's will,' said Winifred. 'There should be a copy in his bureau, and the original one is with our solicitor. It's pretty straightforward, though.'

Kathy knew that the house belonged jointly to her father, Winifred and Jeff. It had been bought with the proceeds from the sale of the hotel plus a contribution from Jeff. The house would now belong to her aunt and uncle, and after their deaths would be willed to Kathy. Also, the remainder of Albert's share of the profit from the hotel and any other monies he had accrued in his lifetime would now go to his daughter.

'I'll have a look in his bureau, shall I?' said Kathy. 'Although I must admit I shall feel rather guilty, as though I'm prying. He was always very secretive about the contents of that bureau, wasn't he? I know it's always kept locked, and once, when I was a little girl, I tried to open it and he was furious with me.'

'Well . . . yes,' replied her aunt, evasively. 'There were certain things that your dad was secretive about. Never mind about it now, Kathy love. I'll see to it later. I'm not quite sure where the key is anyway.' Winifred looked flustered and ill at ease.

'It'll be on that jug on his chest of drawers where he keeps – sorry, kept – his odds and ends,' said Kathy. 'I know his spare door key is in there and his football season ticket.'

'Yes, perhaps so,' said Winifred. 'Go on, then, you're his daughter. I daresay you've more right than anyone to look at his private papers.' She looked doubtful, though, and more than a little anxious.

'I won't, if you really don't want me to,' said Kathy.

'No, you carry on, dear,' said her aunt. 'It'll happen be for the best.'

As Kathy had thought, the key to the bureau was in the pottery jug on her father's chest of drawers, along with other odds and ends: pencils and biros, books of stamps, a screwdriver, a penknife, and his season ticket for Bloomfield Road, the home of his beloved football team. He had only used it a few times that season, and Kathy pondered that it would be a shame for it to go to waste. Jeff didn't attend the matches regularly, and neither did Tim, who preferred to spend his free afternoons with the children and herself. Kathy decided, if her aunt approved, that she would give it to Phil Grantley, whom she knew was still an ardent supporter.

But there were other more important issues to be dealt with at that moment. The bureau, a solid-looking piece of furniture made from mahogany, was in her father's sitting room. It had a pull-down front that served as a writing desk.

The key turned easily in the lock, and Kathy looked inside for the very first time. Everything seemed to be very neat and tidy.

The first thing that caught her eye was what appeared to be several photographs in stiff cardboard covers. She pulled them out, then looked in amazement at what she recognised at once was the wedding photograph of her father and the mother she had never known. She gasped as she gazed at the young woman in the photograph, knowing that she might almost be looking at a picture of herself. The bride had the same dark hair that fell in natural waves, framing a rounded face, the same mouth and nose, and she guessed that the eyes, like her own, would have been brown. Kathy realised then that she had never before seen a photograph of her mother, and what was more strange was the fact that she had never even asked if she might see one; for the life of her, now, she could not imagine why she had been so lacking in curiosity.

The young woman was wearing a dress that was obviously a wedding dress, but not a conventional long one with a veil. It was impossible to tell the colour from the black and white image; it could have been a white dress, or possibly pale pink or blue. It had padded shoulders and a sweetheart neckline, a yoke trimmed with lace, puffed sleeves and a knee-length skirt. The small hat was trimmed at the side with a posy of flowers, and she was carrying a small bouquet of what looked like roses in bud. The bridegroom – Kathy's father – was dressed in the uniform of a soldier; the three stripes on his arm denoted that he was a sergeant. What year had it been, she wondered? She was born in 1943, so it would be 1941 or 1942, she guessed. The war had been going on since 1939,

273

and she knew it had been a period of quite severe austerity in Britain, hence the less-than-formal wedding dress.

Another photograph showed a wedding group. There were the bride and groom, a much younger Aunt Winifred, and another young man and woman whom she did not know – the bridesmaid and the best man, she supposed. She recognised her Grandma and Grandad Leigh who had died a few years ago, and there was another middle-aged couple whom she did not know. Her other grandparents? she pondered, the parents of her mother. Then why had she never met them or heard anything about them? Kathy realised now that a whole chapter from the past had been closed to her. When she thought again about her lack of curiosity, she recalled that she had never been encouraged to ask questions about her mother. Her father had always been evasive or short-tempered on the few occasions she had dared to broach the subject, and even her aunt had been unwilling to say very much. She supposed that eventually she must have understood that it was a closed book, and so she had stopped worrying about it.

There were two more photographs. In one of them her father and the woman she had now gathered was her mother were seated, and the woman was holding a baby, a very young one, wrapped in a shawl. The baby's chubby face was crowned with a cap of dark curls, and the dark eyes seemed to be looking up at the mother, who was gazing at the child with a look of wonderment and love. Myself as a baby, thought Kathy, looking at the photo in bewilderment. The second one showed the same couple with the baby. In this one the woman was smiling straight into the camera, with the same look of joy and contentment in her eyes. Behind the couple, standing, were Aunt Winifred and, again, the couple whom Kathy had assumed were the bridesmaid and best man at the wedding, two people whom she had never met, at least not as far as she could remember. These, then, must have been her godparents, because these obviously were christening photographs. Curiouser and curiouser, thought Kathy, shaking her head in amazement.

She laid the photos to one side and took out a pile of foolscap envelopes from the next cubbyhole. She opened them one by one, no longer feeling that she was prying, but that she was gradually uncovering a mystery that had been hidden from her, but which she felt she had a right to know about.

The first envelope contained the marriage certificate of her mother and father. The marriage had taken place at the church the family still attended, on 27th June, 1942. She, Kathy, had been born in the June of the following year. So there was no question of it being what they called a 'shotgun wedding', she pondered. There was the name of her grandfather – Albert's father – with his occupation, given as hotel proprietor. And for the first time she knew the full name of her mother. She had heard her referred to as Barbara, but here was her name in full: Barbara Jane White. Instead of her father's name there was the name of a man referred to as her guardian, Benjamin White, presumably an uncle or a grandfather.

Opening the remaining envelopes she came across her own birth certificate; a baptism card, given as a memento to every child that was christened at the church – a custom they still followed; and the death certificate of her grandparents, Alice and William – Alice had died in 1960 and William the following year. She still hadn't come across the will that she was supposed to be looking for.

She opened the next envelope and drew out another certificate covered in the black spidery writing that seemed to be the typical handwriting on all of them. Then she gasped, first in astonishment, then in gradually dawning shock and horror, as her mind tried to make sense of what her eyes were seeing. For this was a certificate of divorce – the divorce of her parents, Albert Leigh and Barbara Jane Leigh, in the July of 1945. And there was the name of a co-respondent . . . Nathaniel Castillo. Kathy knew little of such matters, but she thought that the co-respondent was the person named as having committed adultery with the respondent. But this was not what really mattered to her. The amazing – awful – truth that was now being revealed to her was that her mother had not died, as she had always been told. Her parents were divorced, something that Kathy had been brought up to believe was a shameful thing. Her mother, in fact, might still be alive!

Her hands were trembling as she drew out another sheet of paper that was in the envelope. It was a letter from her mother to her father. It was dated January 1945, a few months before the divorce. Kathy could hardly read what was written there because her eyes were blinded with tears. She gathered, however, that Barbara, her mother, was agreeing to leave baby Katherine with Albert and was promising never to contact any of the Leigh family again.

She snatched up the letter and the certificate and fled

from her father's room, downstairs to the living room used by Winifred and Jeff. Her aunt was sitting motionless in an armchair. She looked up, her eyes full of apprehension, as her niece stormed into the room.

'Aunty Win . . .' she shouted. 'What can you tell me about all this?' She waved the offending papers at Winifred. 'You *were* going to tell me, weren't you? I should hope you were! Don't you think it's time I knew about it?'

'Oh . . . Kathy love, I'm so sorry,' her aunt began. 'I guessed it would all come to light now, although I didn't really know if your dad had hung on to . . . everything. I wasn't able to tell you. It was a promise I made, so long ago . . .' Her aunt's eyes, too, were moist with tears, but it made no difference to Kathy, her anger was so great.

'But my mother wasn't dead!' she cried. 'She might still be alive. Most probably she is . . .'

'That's something we don't know, dear,' said Winifred. 'But I'm sorry, so dreadfully sorry.'

'It's too late to be sorry now,' said Kathy, in a tone of voice she had never before used to her aunt. She couldn't remember ever having a real quarrel with Aunt Winifred, but this was unforgivable. 'You deceived me, Aunty Win,' she yelled. 'All these years, you've known about my mother and you never let on. I shall never forgive you.'

Scarcely knowing what she was saying or doing, Kathy grabbed her coat from the back of a chair where she had left it and fled out of the room, out of the front door. She leant against the garden wall, brushing the tears away from her eyes and trying to steady her breath. Her aunt had not followed her. She discovered she was still holding the papers and she shoved them into her handbag.

What should she do now? She had walked to her aunt's house, although she was able to drive the car – she had recently passed her driving test. Perhaps by the time she had walked home she would be feeling slightly more composed. She would start crying again, though, when she saw Tim, and the children would be upset.

She decided to go and see Sally. Her former teacher had been a good friend to her over the years. Despite the difference in their ages – Sally, and Phil too, now must be in their fifties – they had a lot in common and were able to talk about all manner of things. Sally and Phil also lived in Bispham, but it was a fair distance away. Kathy decided she would take a bus, but before that it might be as well to let Sally know that she was coming. She popped into the nearest phone box.

'Kathy, how nice to hear you,' said Sally. Kathy had rung her the previous day, of course, to tell her of Albert's death. 'Yes . . . of course you can come round; I'll get some coffee ready . . . No, I'm on my own; well, Phil's out in the garden, taking out all the dead flowers ready for autumn, and the kids are out, as usual.' Lucy and Daniel were now in their teens and were usually pursuing their own interests. 'Are you all right, Kathy? You sound a little upset . . . Well, I suppose you're sure to be, about your father . . . That was a daft thing to say.'

'Actually, I am upset,' replied Kathy. 'Not just about Dad; it's something else. That's why I want to talk to you . . . Yes, see you in a little while . . .'

* * *

'Come along in and tell me all about it.' Sally ushered Kathy into the comfortable living room.

Sally Grantley had not changed much over the years. She was still a most attractive woman. Her silvery-blonde hair had kept its colour; it was a shade that turned to grey very becomingly. It was always beautifully styled. Kathy guessed that her friend could afford some little luxuries. She was now the headteacher of a nearby infant school, not the one that Kathy had attended. And Phil had moved on too, to become the head of department for English at a comprehensive school, where he also taught games and PE.

'The coffee's all ready,' said Sally. 'Go in and make yourself at home.' Sally went to the kitchen and Kathy made herself comfortable in an armchair in the homely room. It was never over-tidy; evidences of Sally's and Phil's occupation were to be seen on the sideboard and in corners, mixed up with the usual teenage possessions: a pile of books waiting to be marked; football boots; an orange and white scarf; library books; and an assortment of long-playing records on top of the radiogram.

'Now, what's it all about?' asked Sally, handing Kathy a mug of hot coffee and a plate. 'You don't mind a mug, do you?' she said, offering her a biscuit, which Kathy refused.

'No . . . thanks, and a mug is just fine. It's what we always use . . . I don't know where to begin, Sally, I really don't,' she started. She placed her mug on a mat on the small table next to her. 'Well, perhaps it might be better if I showed you these, then you'll understand . . . Not that I really understand any of it myself,' she added. She unzipped her bag and handed the papers to Sally.

Her friend perused them. 'Good gracious!' she muttered, after a few moments. 'I don't wonder you're upset. Have a drink of your coffee, love. It'll do you good. This has knocked you for six, hasn't it?'

Kathy sipped at her coffee, feeling the warmth flow through her. She had felt cold all over, although it was quite a pleasant autumn day. 'It's unbelievable,' she said in a small voice. 'You know that I was always told she was dead. She might still be alive.'

'And your aunt never said anything, never even hinted?'

'Not a word. I'm afraid I've fallen out with her, the first time ever. I stormed out . . . and came here. Tim doesn't know yet.'

'I'm glad you came,' said Sally. 'It's a shock to me as well.'

'When you were friendly with my dad . . . you didn't have any idea then?' asked Kathy. 'You didn't suspect that his wife might not be dead?'

'No, never,' said Sally. 'I must admit I found it rather odd, though, that he would never talk about her. I mean . . . a lot of men lose their wives, don't they? But they get over it in time. I remember, though, when we were dancing at the Palace, soon after I'd met Albert, he got quite upset when they were playing . . . now, what was it? "As Time Goes By"; I think that was the song.' She began, softly, to sing the first line . . . 'Yes, that was it. I wondered if it might have been "their song"; you know what I mean. He said something about it bringing back memories.'

'I can't understand why I never asked any questions,' said Kathy. 'But I suppose, as a child, you accept what you are told. My mother was dead, or so I'd been led to believe, and they as good as told me not to ask any more about it. My aunt always assured me, though, that my mother had loved me very much.' She was thoughtful for a moment. 'But she deserted me, didn't she? It looks as though there was someone else involved. This . . . Nathaniel Castillo. What am I to make of that? He sounds like an Italian to me . . .'

'More likely to be American,' said Sally. 'The Americans entered the war in 1941.'

'Yes, of course,' said Kathy. 'Then she . . . my mother . . . she committed adultery. Maybe . . . maybe she was a "bit of a flibbertigibbet", as my father used to say about some women! All the same, she was my mother.'

'We can't conjecture,' said Sally. 'We don't know all the facts. I'll say one thing, though, Kathy . . . Your father wouldn't have been the easiest person to live with, would he? If you'll forgive me for saying so.'

Kathy gave a wry laugh. 'You can say that again! Although, in all fairness, he did improve a lot as the years went by . . . and I shall miss him,' she added wistfully.

'Of course you will,' Sally smiled at her. 'But now, I really think you should go and sort things out with your aunt. I know you're angry with her, and you have every reason to be. But Winifred's a remarkable person, you know, Kathy. And I'm sure she believed she was acting in your best interests.'

'Yes . . .' agreed Kathy, meekly. 'I'm sorry now. She's been like a mother to me. That's how I always thought of her, and I know she'll be feeling dreadfully upset.'

'She'll be able to explain everything to you,' said Sally. 'I daresay she's wanted to do so for a long time . . . Oh, here's

Phil.' Her husband had just come in from the garden; he had not seen Kathy arrive.

'Hello there, Kathy,' he greeted her. 'I was sorry to hear about your father. Sally and I will be there, at the funeral. Is that what you've come to tell us about?'

'Partly . . .' began Kathy. 'But there was something else. Sally will tell you about it . . .'

'Yes, Kathy's had a shock,' said Sally. She told her husband, very briefly, about what had happened. 'And I think, Phil, that Kathy needs to go back now to sort things out with her aunt. You'll take her back in the car, won't you?'

'Of course,' said Phil. 'Right away. Oh dear, Kathy. I'm so sorry.' He shook his head, as bewildered as the rest of them. 'You never know, though. Good may come out of this.'

'I certainly hope so,' agreed Kathy. 'It feels like a dream at the moment, but whether it's a good one or a bad one, I'm not sure.'

Sally gave her a hug as she put her coat on. 'Chin up, love. And remember, we're always here if you need us.'

Winifred rushed to greet her when she came in through the back door, which was always left open during the day. 'Oh, Kathy love, I've been so worried. Where were you? I rang your number, but Tim said you weren't there. So now he's concerned as well.'

'Oh dear, I'm sorry, Aunty Win,' said Kathy. 'I was at Sally's.' She put her arms round her. 'I shouldn't have said all those awful things, but it was such a shock.' They clung together for several moments, each finding solace in the embrace.

'Of course it was a shock,' said Winifred. 'And I'm more sorry than I can say. Now, you give Tim a ring and tell him you're here. You can explain everything to him later. Then we'll sit down and I'll tell you everything that you ought to have known long ago . . .'

PART THREE

Chapter Twenty-One

1942

'Aunty Myrtle . . . Albert asked me to marry him last night, and I've said that I will.' Myrtle White turned to smile at her niece. Barbara, too, was smiling and she looked quite pleased, but Myrtle could not have said in honesty that the girl looked ecstatic at the news she was telling.

Myrtle put her arms around her and kissed her cheek. 'Well, that's wonderful news, my dear. Albert's a grand young man; I've always thought so, and I'm sure he'll make you a very good husband.'

'Yes . . . I think so too,' replied Barbara, sitting down at the breakfast table in the large kitchen. 'We don't want a long engagement. We're going to choose the ring this afternoon and we plan to get married in the summer; June, we think. Albert should be due for another spot of leave by then.'

Albert Leigh was home on leave at the moment. He was in the army catering corps, stationed up in the north of

England, and there didn't seem to be any likelihood of him being sent overseas. He was now thirty-seven, considered rather too old for active service. Besides, all troops were at their various camps in Britain now, in this spring of 1942 – apart from those fighting in the desert areas in the Middle East – and had been ever since the debacle of Dunkirk.

Albert lived next door in the boarding house that was run by his mother and father and his sister, Winifred. He had worked there ever since he had left school, until he joined the army. They were a lovely family, on very good terms with Myrtle and Ben White who ran a similar boarding house next door.

Albert was a quiet man, but Myrtle was sure he was a good reliable one. She sometimes wondered why he had never married, but she had guessed he had been sweet on her niece, Barbara, ever since the girl was seventeen or so. But it was only quite recently that they had started going out together. Barbara was twenty-two, and her aunt thought that marriage to Albert would be a very good thing.

She glanced at her now, tucking into the plate of porridge that her aunt had placed in front of her. She enjoyed her food, did Barbara, and didn't seem to mind that she was a wee bit plumper than some girls of her age. She was a most attractive girl, with dark-brown hair that had a natural curl, warm brown eyes and a flawless pink and white complexion. Myrtle was not surprised that Albert had been attracted to her, and there had been one or two others who had been smitten. But since she had lost Mike, two years ago, Barbara had quietened down considerably. She had a lovely disposition too, very kind and thoughtful, and that was what was important, really, far more so than a beautiful appearance.

Myrtle was very proud of this young woman, her niece by marriage; she loved her as though she were her own daughter. She and her husband, Benjamin, had had custody of her ever since Barbara's parents, Thomas and Lilian, had been killed in a car crash when the little girl was eighteen months old. Benjamin was Thomas's elder brother; there had been just the two of them, eight years apart. Ben and Myrtle had not been blessed with children, although they had been married for ten years and were extremely happy. And so they had brought Barbara up as lovingly as they would have done with any child of their own. They had decided, though, that she must know the truth when she was old enough. It would have been quite easy to pretend they were her real parents, but Barbara had been well aware that Ben and Myrtle White were her aunt and uncle, and therefore they shared the same surname.

'See you later then, Aunty,' said Barbara, finishing her toast and tea and getting up from the table. 'Must go or I'll miss the bus.' She gave her aunt a quick kiss. 'It's my half day, though, as you know. Albert's meeting me from work, then we're going to choose the ring.'

'How exciting!' said Myrtle. 'Perhaps we could all get together tonight – your uncle and me, and Albert's parents and Winifred, and you two, of course, and have a drink of sherry to celebrate.'

'Good idea,' said Barbara, smiling, as she departed.

She worked as a telephonist at the GPO in Blackpool, as she had done since leaving school, helping out in the boarding house as well when required. Benjamin White was a postman and had left much earlier that morning to start his duty at 5 a.m. An ungodly time of day but he was used to it. He finished work, however, at lunchtime and then he was free – after he had had a quick nap – to help his wife in the boarding house.

At the present time they had RAF recruits billeted with them. It had been so since early 1940, one batch of young men following another. The Leighs' house next door was also an RAF billet, as were the majority of boarding houses in this area of North Shore, Blackpool, and also in the centre and south of the town. It was the largest RAF training centre in Britain.

When the first lot of recruits had arrived at the Whites' boarding house in 1940, the young woman, Barbara, who was assumed by the men to be the daughter of the house, had attracted a goodly number of admiring looks and wolf whistles, as well as invitations to go out to the pictures or dancing.

But Barbara White was quite indifferent to the fact that Blackpool was now a veritable sea of air force blue. These young men were everywhere: drilling in the streets; practising manoeuvres on the sands; and in their spare time, walking in twos along the pavements; frequenting the cinemas, dance halls and shops. Barbara, aged twenty, was already engaged to her soldier sweetheart, Mike Thompson. He was stationed in the south of England and she did not see him very often. They corresponded regularly, though, and planned to marry quite soon, depending on the progress of the war and the availability of leave.

But Mike did not return from Dunkirk with the thousands of other retreating soldiers. He was shot by gunfire from an enemy aeroplane. Barbara was devastated at his death, and it was little consolation to her that she was only one of many girls to have lost a loved one in similar circumstances. She did accept invitations, later that year and in 1941, from some of the RAF lads, but there was still a deep sadness at the heart of her.

She had known for a long time that Albert Leigh from next door carried a torch for her. She liked him very much, but he was fifteen years older than herself, and at times seemed like a different generation. He was kind, though, so very kind, and well mannered towards her. His manner of speech betrayed his Lancashire origins, but she, Barbara, was a Lancashire lass too, and proud of it, and she didn't hold with snobbery or pretentiousness. Before he joined the army, Albert had spent a lot of his time, when he was not busy working in the hotel, with his mates at the local pub, where he played in the darts team, and she knew that he was an ardent supporter of Blackpool's football team. A man's man, one might say.

She had wondered, over the years, why he had never married. She could not be so vain as to think that he was waiting, hopefully, for her to smile encouragingly at him. He must have seen her in the company of lads when she was growing up, and then there had been Mike . . . Albert had told her how sorry he was on hearing of her fiancé's death.

But then, during the autumn of 1941, when he was home on leave, he had plucked up courage to ask her to go out with him. He had told her then how much he had always admired her, had loved her from afar, and how it would make him so happy if she would go out with him when he was home on leave, and write to him whilst he was away.

And he was so kind and thoughtful, so gentle and loving in his conduct towards her, that she had agreed readily. She had discovered that he was not so serious as she had once thought. He was able to make her laugh – not frequently, but often enough – and pull her round from the bouts of sadness that still came over her from time to time. She noticed, too, that he was not a bad-looking fellow. He looked much younger when he smiled, and his blue eyes sparkled with merriment, in between his far more sober moods.

When he asked her to marry him she did not hesitate before agreeing that she would do so. He had kissed her passionately then, as they stood on the promenade looking out across the dark sea.

'You have made me the happiest man in the world,' he told her. 'I shall look after you, and love you always, my lovely Barbara. I shall never let you down.'

'I know that, Albert,' she replied meekly, quite overcome that someone should love her so devotedly. Mike had loved her, as she had loved him, but theirs had been a happy, carefree relationship, not so serious and ardent as this was showing signs of being. All the same, she felt that she was doing the right thing. Her aunt and uncle were good to her and she knew that they loved her dearly. She was contented living with them; after all, it had always been her home and she had never known any different. But she could not say that she was always entirely happy or completely satisfied with her lot. Aunty Myrtle was inclined to fuss and be overprotective of her at times. Barbara knew that it was because of her love for her niece, and that she was being true to the promise that she and Uncle Ben had made to look after her. She felt, though, that marriage to Albert would give her more independence. She would be more of a person in her own right, and to be married was, of course, something of a status symbol. It was all to the good that her aunt and uncle approved wholeheartedly of her engagement to Albert.

He met her out of work that day in February and they went to Beaverbrooks, the jewellers, in Blackpool, to choose a ring. Barbara, with Albert's approval, chose a sapphire with a diamond at either side, and it fitted her perfectly. He placed it on her finger there and then, in the shop. He kissed her, though not quite so ardently this time, in front of other people, and told her again that he was the happiest man in the world. The shop assistants looked on with smiles of approval, although they had probably seen it all before; but Barbara felt a mite embarrassed.

The wedding, after an engagement of only four months, was a somewhat quieter affair than it would have been in peacetime. Barbara did not choose to wear a traditional white dress, which would cost an extravagant amount of money and clothing coupons. She opted for a pale-blue dress that she might be able to wear again, and a small hat that would not look out of place at church on a Sunday morning. Her friend, Dorothy, whom she had known since she was at school, was her bridesmaid, and likewise Dennis, an old school friend of Albert's, acted as best man.

Just a few friends and family members met together at the

293

Whites' boarding house after the church service. The buffet lunch, consisting of various sandwiches, meat pies, sausage rolls, fancy cakes, and trifles – topped, inevitably with synthetic cream, as fresh cream was by now an unobtainable luxury – had been prepared beforehand by Myrtle White and Alice and Winifred Leigh. Not a lavish spread, because of the rationing and because people believed it was their patriotic duty to be prudent. There was, however, tinned red salmon on the sandwiches, as well as a wedding cake that was quite rich with fruit. Both Mr and Mrs White and Mr and Mrs Leigh were not averse to a discreet amount of what was known as 'hoarding'. And so, between them, they had been able to provide tinned salmon, and tinned pears and peaches, as well as a fair amount of dried fruit, ground almonds for the almond paste, and icing sugar, to make a really acceptable wedding cake. It had been baked by Alice Leigh and iced by Myrtle White.

At many wartime weddings a large white cardboard structure, shaped like a cake and known as a 'whited sepulchre', was displayed, with a tiny fruit cake hidden inside. But that was not the case at this wedding reception. Although it was only of medium size, the cake for these newly-weds was the real thing, and was duly cut by the bride and groom whilst their health was drunk in brown sherry.

The honeymoon was spent in the seaside resort of Southport, often regarded as a rival to its near neighbour, Blackpool. Southport could be seen clearly across the Ribble estuary as one stood on the promenade of nearby Lytham St Annes, but could only be reached by a roundabout route by road or rail.

'Is Your Journey Really Necessary?' the propaganda posters enquired of civilians, but Albert considered, as a serviceman, that he and his new wife were entitled to travel away on honeymoon, be it only for a long weekend.

Barbara knew that her new husband was blissfully happy. He was more cheerful and amusing to be with that weekend than she had ever known him to be. He told her time and time again how much he loved her.

'I'll never let you down, Barbara, my darling,' he told her once again. 'I'll always be there for you. I'll love you for ever.'

It was flattering, if a little discomfiting, to know that she evoked such feelings in Albert, especially as she knew he was not a sentimental sort of fellow. At least, that was the impression he gave to others. As for Barbara, she told him that she loved him too. It would have been churlish not to do so; besides, she was very fond of him already and she felt sure she would grow to love him in time.

Although Barbara had had a few boyfriends before she met Mike, she was still a virgin when she married Albert. She had been brought up to believe that it was right to save oneself for marriage. She had, therefore, been a little apprehensive about the wedding night, but she had found that there was no need to be. Albert proved to be a sensitive and considerate lover, and although the experience was not what she could call earth-shattering, she knew she need no longer worry about it. Anyway, she knew it was a part of married life, something her husband would expect of her. She did not know whether or not it was the first time for Albert. She guessed that it might not have been, but it was something she would never know.

Albert went back to his camp a couple of days after they returned to Blackpool. Barbara continued to live with her aunt and uncle. It seemed pointless to move next door to the Leighs' boarding house to the room that Albert slept in, seeing that her husband was not there. They hadn't really discussed the future very much, but the idea was that they would save up and buy a home of their own when the war was over.

Barbara continued with her job as a telephonist. She stayed at home most evenings, writing letters to Albert in answer to the long loving letters she received from him, or listening with her aunt and uncle to their favourite programmes on the wireless: *Monday Night at Eight*, *In Town Tonight* (broadcast on a Saturday), *Happidrome*, *Garrison Theatre*, and *ITMA*, with the irrepressible Tommy Handley, the comedy show above all others that managed to keep the people's spirits up in those depressing wartime days.

Occasionally she went to the cinema with a friend from work. She enjoyed *Gone with the Wind*, and the light-hearted Hollywood musicals, starring such glamorous female stars as Betty Grable, Veronica Lake and Alice Faye, as well as the movies put on for propaganda purposes to boost the morale of a population becoming more and more war weary: *Mrs Miniver* and *In Which We Serve*. She could not be persuaded, however, to go out dancing. Albert, to her surprise, was a very good dancer and she looked forward to stepping out on the ballroom floor with him the next time he came home on leave.

That was in September, when he was granted a whole

week's leave. They went dancing a few times that week, to the Tower, and to the Empress ballroom in the Winter Gardens. But their favourite venue was the smaller Palace ballroom, a more intimate place, but just as splendid in its own way as its larger counterparts. The superb ballroom floor was perfect for the thousands of dancing feet that trod it each evening.

They danced to an old-time medley; the veleta, the military two-step and the St Bernard's Waltz, as well as the quickstep, the modern waltz and the foxtrot. Albert confessed that he had been to lessons in ballroom dancing some years ago, and he was certainly a very accomplished dancer. Barbara had never been able to master the slow foxtrot, but under Albert's patient guidance she found she was now able to do so, following the expert lead that he gave.

Barbara sang softly beneath her breath to the music of 'As Time Goes By', a sentimental song that captured exactly the mood that they and hundreds of other young couples were feeling that night; a tale of moonlight and kisses and sighs, and of love that would last for a lifetime.

'I'll always love you, my darling,' Albert whispered to her. 'No matter how the time goes by . . . you will always be the only girl for me.'

Barbara felt, almost, as though she might be falling in love with her husband. One thing she was certain about was that their child was conceived later that same night.

Baby Katherine Louise was born on 30th June, 1943.

Chapter Twenty-Two

As 1943 dawned there was hope, at long last, that the tide was turning. It seemed that victory – hopefully in the not-too-distant future – was now a possibility; some, indeed, believed that it was assured. Civilians and servicemen alike were now starting to look towards the long-term future and to think about what sort of a world would emerge after the war-torn years.

A significant event had been when the Russian armies defeated the Germans. Hitler's greatest mistake had been, undoubtedly, his belief that Russia could be conquered along with the rest of the Western nations. He had not reckoned with the severity of a Russian winter, which proved to be the undoing of the German armies. The last of the German troops at Stalingrad surrendered on 2nd February, 1943.

The surrender of Italy followed a few months later. The North Africa campaign had ended in total victory for the

Allied forces, and that army was now freed to take part in the planned invasion of Europe, which was being known as the 'Second Front'. The ongoing Battle of the Atlantic in May was another turning point. Forty German U-boats were destroyed and the transatlantic supply line was secure once again.

On 17th May came the news that nineteen Lancaster bombers had successfully breached the two largest dams in the manufacturing district of the Ruhr Valley, by means of what was known as the 'bouncing bomb'. The devastation and loss of life was tremendous, giving way to the thought in many thousands of minds that the majority of the casualties must have been innocent civilians. It had been reported in the newspapers that four thousand Germans had lost their lives in the flooding, and one hundred and twenty thousand had lost their homes.

The loss of life in Great Britain had been equally catastrophic in the blitz of the major cities – London, Liverpool, Manchester, Plymouth, Coventry – in the earlier years of the war, and still there was continuing loss of life amongst the soldiers, sailors and airmen who were fighting and believing in an ultimate victory. Indeed, it was reported that several of the bombers that had taken part in the breaching of the Ruhr dams had not returned.

At the time that baby Katherine was born on the last day of June, a mood of optimism was prevalent in the majority of households, none more so than in the homes of the Leigh and White families.

It was a straightforward, comparatively easy birth.

Barbara stayed at home for the confinement, and the baby was born in the bedroom that had always been hers and in which she and Albert sometimes slept when he was home on leave.

All babies are beautiful, at least to their parents and close members of the family, but Barbara believed that her baby was, truly, the most beautiful baby she had ever seen. Her head was already covered with a mass of dark hair, clinging to her scalp in damp curly tendrils. Her cheeks were a rosy pink and her eyes, when she opened them, were a sort of inky grey. Barbara knew that babies couldn't focus properly, not so soon after the birth, but they seemed to be staring right into those of her mother, who already adored her. Tentatively, Barbara reached out a finger, placing it in the tiny palm of the baby, and the minute fingers, like a little pink starfish, closed around her own. She felt a deep thrill, unlike anything she had experienced before, and a feeling of wonder that she should be entrusted with the care of this tiny child.

'She looks just like you,' her aunt and uncle, and Albert's parents, told her.

'And I think she'll have your brown eyes when she's a few weeks older,' said Aunt Myrtle. 'Babies' eyes change, you know. They always look a sort of muddy grey at first.'

Albert was granted a forty-eight-hour compassionate leave, and he was delighted with his new daughter. 'I didn't believe I could ever be any happier than I was when you said you would marry me,' he told Barbara, 'but now I know that I am even happier. I'm the happiest man in the world. Thank you, my darling. She's . . . just perfect.'

Between them they chose the names Katherine Louise, just because they liked them. But before long the little girl became known as Kathy.

She was a good baby, waking only once in the night for a feed, and by the end of September, when she was three months old, she was sleeping right through the night.

'You're lucky,' Albert's mother told her. 'I had endless trouble with both of mine. I forgot what a good night's sleep was like until they were more than twelve months old, especially with our Albert. He was on a bottle by that time, mind you, so I made sure that Bill took his turn . . .'

Albert, of course, could not take his turn at feeding the baby because he was not there, but Barbara was pleased that he did his share whenever he was home on leave. By the time baby Katherine was four months old she was being bottle-fed. In spite of Barbara's somewhat shapely figure – she could not be called plump, but she was certainly not skinny and had a bust that might be the envy of many girls – she found that her supply of milk soon dried up. She had no regrets about this and Kathy took to the bottle without any problems.

Albert came home on leave for the Christmas of 1943, but only on a forty-eight-hour pass. Barbara was sad to see him return to his camp, although, in a way, it was nice to have the baby all to herself again. He had, in fact, seemed at times to be more interested in the baby than he was in her, or had she been imagining it, she wondered? He was certainly taking his duties as a father very seriously. He watched her continually to make sure she was doing everything correctly – that the bath water was not too hot or too cold, the same with the bottle of milk, and that the nappies and little vests were well aired before the baby wore them.

'How do you think I manage when you're not here?' Barbara asked him jokingly.

'I'm sure you manage perfectly,' he replied, kissing the end of her nose. 'You're a wonderful mother, but I like to do my share. I'm hoping it won't be too long before I'm home for good, once we've got the better of old Hitler, then we can see about getting a little place of our own. Just you and me and little Kathy . . .'

Yes, it would be nice to have their own place, thought Barbara, although her aunt and uncle, and Albert's parents too, were very good to her. She had, of course, finished work well before the baby was born and there was no talk of her going back. Besides, mothers with young children were exempt from war work.

Despite having the baby to care for, time began to hang rather heavy for Barbara and she was even feeling a little depressed, an unusual state for her. She had enjoyed her job as a telephonist and the camaraderie of the other girls. Her aunt persuaded her to go to the pictures now and again with a girlfriend; Dorothy was the young woman who had been her bridesmaid. She was unmarried, although she had a fiancé serving in the merchant navy. She was now working at a munitions factory in Blackpool.

'Go out and enjoy yourself,' said Barbara's aunt, 'and don't worry about little Kathy. You know she'll be quite all right with me and your uncle Ben.'

And so Barbara and Dorothy started to go to the cinema once a week, very occasionally twice, and Barbara knew that her baby was in safe hands. She liked to get home by ten-thirty if possible, as her aunt and uncle did not keep late hours. She had her own door key, of course, but she did not want them to think she was taking advantage of their kindness. Her friend had been trying – though unsuccessfully at first – to persuade her to go dancing, to the Tower Ballroom, which was a favourite haunt of Dorothy's.

'No, I don't think so,' said Barbara. 'It wouldn't really be fair, would it? I mean, with Albert away. I don't think he would like the idea of me dancing with . . . well, with other men.' She knew, in fact, that Albert would hate it.

'You have to wait to be asked!' joked Dorothy. 'You'd be surprised how many girls you see dancing together. Although I must admit there's no shortage of male partners, especially now the Yanks are here. I'll dance with you. I can do a pretty nifty quickstep, and Albert can't object to that, can he?'

'What does your Raymond think about you going dancing whilst he's away on the high seas?' asked Barbara.

'I don't know, because I don't tell him,' answered Dorothy, laughing. 'He wouldn't mind, though. He knows I don't intend to stay at home knitting. I write to him every week, but I don't see why I shouldn't go out and have a good time. Life can be pretty grim, and boring too, you must admit, in spite of them saying that victory's just round the corner. Please say you'll come with me, Barbara, just for once and see how you like it.'

And so Barbara agreed, although she was very unsure about it, to accompany her friend to the Tower Ballroom the following Saturday, the first Saturday in the February of 1944.

'Good for you,' said her aunt. 'Off you go and enjoy yourself. And don't worry about what Albert would say.' In Myrtle White's opinion, although she liked Albert very much, she had realised after spending more time in his company that he was something of a fusspot. He was clearly devoted to Barbara, and to the baby, but she had a feeling he might turn out to be rather critical and possessive, once the euphoria of marrying the girl of his dreams had worn off. 'There's an old saying, you know,' her aunt went on. 'What the eye doesn't see, the heart doesn't grieve at. And it isn't as if you're doing anything wrong. Lots of girls go dancing, even those whose husbands are away. I know how much you used to enjoy going dancing at the Palace.'

'That was with Albert,' replied Barbara. 'It was Albert, really, who taught me how to dance properly. I wasn't much good until he took me in hand.'

'Well, there you are, then,' said Myrtle. 'Go and trip the light fantastic and you'll feel better for it. And take your key. I know how you always try to get back early, but there's no need. It isn't as if you're still a fifteen-year-old, is it? You're a married woman now, and your uncle and I understand that.'

'I shouldn't be all that late, anyway,' agreed Barbara. 'I think the dance halls all close round about eleven o'clock. And I'll be walking home with Dorothy, so we'll be quite all right.'

'Well, don't forget to take your torch . . .'

'No, I won't forget,' smiled Barbara, 'and my gas mask. Although folks don't seem to be bothering quite so much now. The danger seems to be past . . . thank God,' she added.

The blackout was still in force, though, but everyone had grown quite used to going out in the dark, armed with a torch, and finding their way by means of the white edgings on kerbs and road crossings.

'I'm ever so glad you decided to come with me,' said Dorothy, squeezing her friend's arm as they stood at the bus stop, waiting for the bus that would take them to the Central Station stop, near to the Tower. 'You'll enjoy it, I know you will. It's been ever such fun since the Yanks came to Blackpool.'

There were two American bases where the GIs were stationed, at the outlying villages of Weeton and Warton, a few miles distant from Blackpool.

'You hear a lot of tales about them,' Dorothy continued, 'but they're real nice guys, the ones I've met at any rate. And you should see them do the jitterbug! They're not supposed to do it on the ballroom floor, because it's a bit dangerous, all that prancing about and throwing the girls around. But they usually find a spot away from the ballroom where they don't get in the way of the more . . . what shall I say? . . . more prim and proper dancers.'

'And can you do it?' asked Barbara, smiling. 'This jitterbugging?'

'I've not tried yet,' said Dorothy. 'I've not been asked. But you never know, do you? Oh see, here's our bus. We're going to have a whale of a time, Barbara, I know we are.'

Chapter Twenty-Three

America had entered the war two years previously. It had been on 7th December, 1941, that the war had entered upon a new and significant phase. The Americans, led by President Roosevelt, had delayed entering the conflict, believing it to be a solely European war and, therefore, of no real concern to them. However, the Japanese attack on the US naval base at Pearl Harbour, Hawaii, forced them to change their outlook. The neutrality and isolationist policy of the American people was at an end, and when the USA eventually did enter the war they did so with determination.

The arrival of the American servicemen – known as GIs – had, so far, had little impact on Barbara or on her family and that of Albert's family next door. At the time of their marriage both the Whites' and the Leighs' boarding houses were still being used as billets for the RAF personnel, one group of men following upon another as their initial training came to an end.

Barbara had seen the GIs, of course, strolling around the streets of Blackpool. Their smart uniforms – a sort of brownish green and made of a fine cloth – contrasted greatly with the coarse material of the RAF and army uniforms of the British troops. Those had been designed for practicality and hard wear, not to enhance the figure! 'And not to attract the birds, either,' Barbara had overheard one of the RAF lads saying to his mate. The higher ranks in the British services wore uniforms of a finer material, but all ranks of American servicemen, both privates and officers, were dressed in the same impeccable manner.

Barbara had also heard the phrase 'overpaid, oversexed and over here' on the lips of some of the RAF lads who were billeted at the boarding house; it was a phrase that was being bandied about both by servicemen and civilians. In some instances it could be seen as a question of 'sour grapes'. It could not be denied that the American troops were overpaid, at least by British standards. They were paid five times as much as their British counterparts. The wages of an ordinary soldier in the US army was, in some cases, as high as those of a British officer.

As well as that, the GIs had access to what was known as the PX (Post Exchange), a sort of NAAFI, where all kinds of luxury goods were available, goods such as had not been seen in Britain for years. Chewing gum, sweets (which they called candies), oranges, butter, spirits, cigarettes, razor blades, and sweet-smelling soap – a contrast to the hard carbolic soap being used in the British households, and even that was rationed. Ice cream had been banned for the duration in the September of 1942, but it was available on the American bases.

Barbara's friend, Dorothy, had even managed to acquire a pair of the newly invented nylon stockings, which no British girl had ever seen before. She had been given them by her friend, Mavis, a girl who worked with her at the munitions factory. Mavis was keeping company – for the time being, at least – with a GI from Maryland whose name was Hank. It seemed that a goodly number of them were called Hank.

'Honestly, they're so fine you can't tell you're wearing them,' Dorothy had told Barbara. 'Except for the seam up the back, of course. They're just like gossamer, not that I'm really sure what gossamer is,' she laughed. 'I'll have to be real careful not to ladder them; they're so sheer, though, that a ladder might not even show. She's had chocolates from this Hank as well, my friend Mavis, and tinned peaches. And he got her dad a carton of Camel cigarettes. I didn't ask her what she had to do to get them, mind you, if you know what I mean.' Dorothy winked and sniggered.

'Dorothy, really!' exclaimed Barbara. 'You don't think, surely . . . ?'

'Well, she's footloose and fancy free, is Mavis. She's not got a husband or fiancé, like you and me. And I must admit she's done the rounds; she's had a go with most of 'em. Our own RAF lads, Poles, Aussies, Free French, and now the Yanks. You've heard the expression about the Yanks?'

'You mean, overpaid . . . and all that?'

'Yes, that's it. Of course, I don't really know about the "oversexed" bit. Mavis plays her cards very close to her chest.

It may well be that she just likes to have a good time with no strings attached. She's a stunning-looking girl, I must admit; it's no wonder that the blokes all go for her. She might be there on Saturday night, at the Tower. If she is I'll introduce you to her. She told me that Hank is teaching her to jitterbug . . .'

It was not without a certain amount of trepidation that Barbara made her way to the Tower Ballroom on that Saturday night. The last time she had been dancing had been with Albert, and that had been long before baby Katherine was born. It had been the Palace Ballroom, rather than the Tower or the Winter Gardens, that Albert had favoured, and so Barbara had come to prefer that smaller and, she believed, much friendlier venue.

She had been to the Tower a few times, before Albert had come on the scene. She had danced there with her fiancé, Mike, who had been killed at Dunkirk. She had always felt that the Tower was somewhat brash and noisy, the place where the good-time girls hung out to 'click with a feller'. And there were plenty of those around at the moment, to be sure. But she told herself not to be stupid. She was a married woman now, mature and self-confident and well able to look after herself. She was going along solely to enjoy the music and gaiety, to have a change from the day-to-day routine and to forget the gloom and the deprivations that were a result of the ongoing war.

It was hard to believe that Britain had now been at war for more than four years. Admittedly there was no longer the despondency and fear for the future that there had been in the early years. Some believed that victory was assured and that it could even be brought about before the end of the year. All Barbara knew was that one had to go on hoping and praying . . .

The Tower Ballroom had been the dream, brought to life, of John Bickerstaffe – later Sir John – the first chairman of the Blackpool Tower Company. It had been his ambition to create a ballroom to equal, or preferably better, the Empress Ballroom in the Winter Gardens. To achieve this aim Mr Bickerstaffe had engaged the noted architect, Frank Matcham, to transform the room that was at first known as the Grand Pavilion. Frank Matcham was already well known and revered in the town, having designed Blackpool's Grand Theatre in 1894.

The ballroom was decorated in the French renaissance style and when it was completed in 1899 it was believed to be one of the three finest in the country; it had even been described as the finest in the whole of Europe. It was said that up to seven thousand people could be seated comfortably in the two tiers of balconies, supported by massive gilded pillars. At one end of the room was a large ornate stage with a quotation inscribed above it in gold lettering. 'Bid me discourse, I will enchant thine ear' it read, a quotation from Shakespeare's *Venus and Adonis*. Large classical paintings adorned the ceilings and the surrounding walls, depicting idyllic scenes of nymphs, shepherds and shepherdesses, Grecian gods, and heroes taken from ancient legends; gilded motifs, too, bearing the names of famous composers, Bach, Beethoven, Mozart, Chopin . . .

Two large and elaborate chandeliers were flanked by

a series of smaller ones, casting a radiance of electric light down onto the ballroom floor; this form of lighting was in its infancy at the end of the nineteenth century. The floor was a marvel in itself, comprising thousands of blocks of mahogany, oak, walnut and maple woods arranged in an intricate geometric design.

The Tower and the buildings underneath were now playing their part in the war effort, and not only by providing entertainment for the troops billeted in Blackpool and the holidaymakers – the many folk who were still visiting the town for a brief respite from the gloom and, in later years, the boredom of the war. The Tower top had been taken over by the RAF as an emergency radar station. A forty-foot section of the spire was replaced by a wooden structure bearing the receiving aerials, and a number of steel cantilevers were inserted into the iron girders of the Tower to carry the transmitting aerials.

The Tower top was also used as a lookout by the men of the National Fire Service and the Home Guard, and the buildings below were used by the RAF and the Royal Artillery for training purposes. The ballroom and the circus became the venues for training sessions and lectures; and in the evenings they both reverted to their normal roles.

Barbara and Dorothy joined the queue of young women to deposit their coats in the cloakroom. When they had been handed the little pink cloakroom tickets they joined dozens of other girls at the mirrors in the washroom, titivating their hair, and applying a dusting of powder or a smear of lipstick before moving on to the ballroom.

Barbara renewed her lipstick. It was a brighter red than the paler shades she usually favoured, but it had been the only colour that was available at the local chemist's shop; all types of make-up had been in short supply since the outbreak of war. Anyway, it matched her dress much better than a paler pink or coral shade would have done. She pressed her lips together, then, on second thoughts, wiped some of it off again; she hated to think that she might look tarty.

Her dress was a couple of years old, but it was one that she liked and thought suited her; new dresses were a luxury anyway, and considered an extravagance. She had toyed with the idea of wearing her wedding dress. She had chosen it believing, at the time, that it was one that she might wear again, but she had decided it was too pale and 'weddingy-looking' for a winter evening. The one she was wearing that night was of a silky rayon. It had a red background patterned with a bold design of black and white daisies; it was knee-length and had the fashionable padded shoulders.

'You look stunning in that dress,' Dorothy told her. 'It really suits you, with your dark hair and eyes and everything. You'll have the fellers queuing up asking you to dance.'

'Thank you . . . but that's not really the idea,' replied Barbara; she was feeling, again, for a brief moment, that she shouldn't be there. 'You look very nice as well.'

Barbara and Dorothy were complete opposites as far as looks were concerned. Dorothy was blonde and petite. She had let her hair grow and it fell in a pageboy style almost to her shoulders; she had trained it to fall over one eye, in the style made popular by the film star, Veronica Lake. Her blue and white candy-striped dress with the puffed sleeves and sweetheart neckline enhanced her fair prettiness. She looked angelic, but she was a high-spirited lass, and Barbara looked to Dorothy to give her the confidence she needed to face the crowds in the ballroom.

It was, indeed, crowded, the girls two or three deep in some places at the edge of the ballroom floor. The dance floor itself was a rainbow of bright colours: red, blue, orange, green, pink, yellow, on the flowered, striped, and spotted dresses worn by the girls and some older women. They were a vivid contrast to the darker uniforms of the men: air force blue, khaki, the navy blue of the Royal Navy, and the brownish green of the Yanks' uniforms; there was scarcely a civilian man to be seen amongst the hundreds of couples circling round the dance floor. Many girls were dancing together, as Dorothy had said they would.

'Come on, let's give it a whirl,' Dorothy said to her friend, taking her hand and pulling her towards the ballroom floor. 'Can you lead, though? You're a few inches taller than me.'

'Yes, I think so,' said Barbara. 'It's a quickstep rhythm, so I should be able to manage that.' They stepped out to the music of 'Don't Sit Under the Apple Tree', the song that had been made famous by the Andrews Sisters.

The organist on the mighty Wurlitzer organ was the talented lady, Ena Baga. She had replaced Reginald Dixon, whose name had become synonymous with Blackpool, when he joined the RAF in 1940. His signature tune, 'Oh, I Do Like to be Beside the Seaside', had come to typify the jollity and the carefree mood of a holiday in Blackpool. Now, however, Ena Baga's signature tune, 'Smoke Gets in Your

Eyes', was becoming almost as familiar to the dancers as that of her predecessor.

When the dance came to an end they moved off the ballroom floor. 'I don't know about you,' said Dorothy, 'but I don't fancy standing around with all these wallflowers.'

'No, neither do I,' agreed Barbara.

'Let's have a saunter around, then, and see if there's anybody we know, shall we? And in a little while we could go and have a coffee, or something stronger if you like.'

'No, coffee's OK for me, or tea,' said Barbara. 'Not just yet, though. We've not been here very long.'

She had been brought up with the belief that nice girls didn't go into bars on their own, or even in the company of another girl. She had learnt, though, that Dorothy had no such inhibitions. She, Barbara, and her fiancé, Mike, had not frequented pubs and bars very much either. They had both been very young, only nineteen years old, when the war had started. Albert had enjoyed a drink, though, and probably still did, in the company of his fellow soldiers. Barbara had begun to feel more at ease in a bar when she was with Albert, but it was rather different now. She hoped that Dorothy would not consider her too much of a killjoy.

They made their way round the edge of the ballroom floor, pushing their way, as politely as they could, between the crowds of girls and servicemen. After a few moments Ena Baga struck up with the music of the 'American Patrol', a tune made popular by the Glenn Miller Orchestra and one which was being played more and more often in dance halls up and down the country.

As Dorothy had already told her friend, there was some

jitterbugging going on in a space away from the ballroom floor where the music could still be heard, loud and clear. The couples on the dance floor were dancing a normal quickstep or, in some cases, a milder form of jitterbugging. Here, however, there were two couples who were really letting it rip.

'Hey, that's my friend, Mavis!' exclaimed Dorothy. 'You know, the one I was telling you about.'

'You mean the one who gave you the nylon stockings?'

'Yes, that's right. I'll introduce you to her when they've finished the dance. And I suppose that must be the famous Hank who's with her.'

Barbara's first impression of the girl, Mavis, was that she was the word 'glamorous' brought to life. 'Glamour' was a word much used with regard to the stars of the silver screen: Betty Grable, Vivien Leigh, Rita Hayworth, Ginger Rogers and countless others. This Mavis, to Barbara, was a Rita Hayworth sort of girl. Her bright-ginger hair, worn in a pageboy style, bounced around her shoulders as she danced. She was very pretty, and small, but curvaceous in the right places. Her tight-fitting emerald-green dress accentuated the swell of her bustline, and clung alluringly around her hips as she jigged and jumped about to the rhythm of the music, affording a frequent glimpse of shapely knees and thighs. Hank, if that was who it was, swung her around in an uninhibited way, pushing her away from him, then grabbing her and whirling her around in a frenzy. Barbara found herself gasping as the American lifted her off her feet then flung her over his shoulder, giving the onlookers a momentary glimpse of her stocking tops and frilly pink panties. The next minute she was back on the floor and upright again, seeming not a jot embarrassed.

The couple next to them were dancing in an equally reckless manner, and quite a crowd was gathering to watch the fun.

'D'you fancy a try?' said a voice at Barbara's side. She turned to see a pair of humorous grey eyes smiling down at her. A GI, of course; she could tell by his accent at first, and then by his uniform. She knew in that instant, though, that he was not aiming at a 'pickup'; he was just trying to be friendly.

'No, not me!' she laughed. 'Fun to watch, but . . . no thanks! Not my scene at all.'

'Nor mine,' he smiled. 'But I wanted to see Hank doing his stuff. I've heard such a lot about it.'

'You know him, then?' she enquired.

'Yes, we're in the same unit, stationed at Warton. And the other chap, that's Marvin. Quite a lively pair, as you can imagine. And I'm Nat, by the way.' He held out his hand towards her. 'Nat Castillo. I'm pleased to make your acquaintance . . .' His eyes twinkled. 'Whoever you are?'

She didn't hesitate to shake his hand. He seemed such a nice fellow, or 'guy', which was what the Yanks said. 'Oh . . . I'm Barbara,' she said. 'Barbara Leigh. I've come with my friend, Dorothy.' As she glanced around she could see that her friend, too, was talking to another of the GIs. 'I'm . . . I'm pleased to meet you too.'

'You don't mind me talking to you, do you?' he continued. 'I know we Yanks have got a reputation for being brash and too familiar. Some of us are, or at least that's the impression we give, I guess. But me . . . I'm quite shy, really.' He grinned as he gave a little shrug. 'I'm just wanting to be friendly, that's all . . .'

And that was how it all started. In that instant Barbara's life was completely turned around, although she wasn't aware of it at first. She was aware, though, of the immediate attraction between herself and the American soldier.

Looking back on how it had begun, a long time afterwards, she recalled a sermon she had once heard about temptation, and how one could either give in to it or turn away. She recalled the preacher's words . . . 'Maybe you can't help yourself at the first look, but you can avoid the next look, and all the subsequent ones . . .'

What, then, should she and Nat have done? Should she have refused to go for a drink with him, which was the next thing that happened? They had been in the company of others, though, and it would have been impolite to refuse. And after that, although it had begun so slowly and innocently, it was as if they both had known that it was inevitable; there had been no stopping the attraction they felt for one another.

She had known very soon that she and Nat were what was known as 'kindred spirits'. When she was in her early teens, Barbara's favourite book had been *Anne of Green Gables*. It was in that book that she had first come across the term. Anne Shirley, the heroine, with whom Barbara felt a great affinity, had gone on at length about how she and her friend, Diana, were kindred spirits. They thought and felt the same about everything, like the two halves of a complete whole; they were truly compatible.

Barbara was not sure that she had met anyone before, of either sex, to whom the term could apply. But now she had. She and Nat Castillo were, without doubt, 'kindred spirits'. And very soon they knew, come what may, that they belonged together.

Chapter Twenty-Four

When introductions had been made, the group of GIs and young women made their way to the nearest refreshment place, not far from the ballroom. It seemed perfectly natural for them all to gravitate there. The couples who had been jitterbugging were ready for some sustenance, as well as being too hot and dishevelled for comfort. Mavis and her friend Hilda, the other dancer, went off to the ladies' cloakroom to repair the damage done to their hair and apparel. They rejoined the party a few minutes later looking spruce and composed again.

'Over here, you guys,' shouted the fellow called Marvin, standing up and waving. 'We've already got yours in.' Barbara was to learn that everyone was referred to, in the American parlance, as a 'guy', whether they were male or female.

'Gee, thanks, Marvin,' replied Hilda. She had obviously

picked up some of their vernacular already. 'Ginger beer shandy, for both of us? That's just hunky-dory!'

There were eight of them, and it seemed inevitable that they should pair off. Mavis and Hank, and Hilda and Marvin, already seemed to know one another rather well. Dorothy had struck up an acquaintance with Howard who was Nat's closest friend, or 'best buddy', as he called him. And so Barbara found herself with Nat . . .

Barbara had gone along with the rest of the girls and agreed that she would have a shandy, lemonade ones for herself and Dorothy. She and Nat were sitting side by side on a red velvet bench that ran along the side of the bar room, with Dorothy and Howard on stools opposite them. They were sharing a glass-topped table, and the other four were seated near to them.

Nat lifted his tankard – a pint of bitter – saying 'cheers', and so Barbara did the same with her smaller glass. They clinked them together, then smiled a little shyly and uncertainly at one another.

'So . . . Barbara Leigh, are you enjoying yourself?' he asked.

'Yes, I am, very much,' she replied. 'I wasn't sure that I wanted to come here tonight, but Dorothy persuaded me. It's the first time I've been here for . . . ooh, for ages.'

'The first time for me too,' agreed Nat. 'And I must admit I'm real impressed with your Tower Ballroom. I haven't seen anything like this back home.'

'Really?' said Barbara. 'I'm surprised. I thought everything in America was bigger than what we have over here.' She had been going to say 'bigger and better', but realised it might sound rather rude.

Nat laughed. 'Yeah . . . I know that's how some of us Yanks like to talk. When we say bigger, we are sometimes implying that it's better as well, but it ain't always so. There are always guys who like to boast that everything's giant-sized in the good old US of A, but it all depends on where you come from.'

'And . . . where is that?' asked Barbara.

'Me? I come from a village called Stowe – well, a small town, really – in the state of Vermont. The loveliest little old place in the world to me, but we ain't got nothing like this.' He waved his arm around in the direction of the ballroom.

'Oh, I see,' replied Barbara politely. She sounded, and was aware that she probably looked, rather vague. She didn't think she had ever heard of Vermont, although she had heard of lots of places in the USA: New York, and Chicago, and Tennessee . . .

Nat smiled. 'Vermont is one of the New England states. You know . . . the Pilgrim Fathers sailed from England in the *Mayflower* and landed in Plymouth?'

'Yes, I know a little about that,' replied Barbara. 'We learnt about it at school, but the facts are rather hazy to me; and so is my geography of the United States . . . I'm sorry.'

'Nothing to apologise for,' said Nat. 'It can't be as bad as my scanty knowledge of your little country, and that goes for most of us Yanks . . . Anyhow, the settlers called the area New England, to remind them, I guess, of the old England they had left behind. That's why we have a lot of towns with the same names as yours. We have a Plymouth, of course, and a Portsmouth, Manchester, Boston, London, Norwich, Windsor . . . Dozens of them, I guess.'

'You must be missing your hometown,' said Barbara. 'Stowe, did you say? I should imagine it's nothing like Blackpool.'

He laughed. 'You can say that again! Nothing at all. Except that we depend a lot on tourists, as you do here. It sure is a lovely place where I live, surrounded by mountains, and in the winter we get hordes of skiers staying there; we have some of the best ski slopes in the whole of the USA. And in summer there's lots to do as well – rock climbing, fishing, canoeing, or just enjoying the scenery.'

Barbara smiled at him sympathetically. He surely must be homesick for that lovely place, although he was cheerful and bright, clearly determined to make the best of his exile in what must seem a very strange and different sort of land. 'And . . . what do you do there, Nat?' she asked. 'Your job, I mean?'

'Like scores of others, my family run a hotel,' he replied. 'We're busy all year round with guests. I help out wherever I can, like the rest of the family, my parents and my aunt and uncle. I'm studying to be a chef, though, so that I can take over from my father, eventually . . . God willing,' he added. 'And in the winter I'm a part-time ski instructor. We all learn to ski, from an early age.'

'That's quite a coincidence,' said Barbara, 'about the hotel, I mean, because that's where I was brought up as well, in a hotel. We call them boarding houses here, though, unless they're bigger and have more amenities, then they're called hotels. And . . . my husband had a similar boarding house background. Actually, his family's boarding house is just next door to ours, and he helps with the cooking and everything else, like you do. At least he does when he's here. At the moment he's in the army, stationed up in the north of England . . .' She found her voice petering out as Nat looked at her thoughtfully.

'Yes, I noticed you were married,' he remarked. She was wearing her wedding ring, of course, which she never took off.

'We were married in 1942,' Barbara told him. 'We have a baby girl, Katherine. She's eight months old,' she said, trying to smile brightly.

'Gee, that's swell!' commented Nat. 'I can understand why you were hesitant about coming here tonight. You must miss her.'

'Well, yes, but I know she's being well looked after, by my aunt and uncle. They brought me up, you see, after my parents died when I was quite small. And I'm still living there, because it just makes sense to do so. When Albert – my husband – comes back, no doubt we'll move into a place of our own.' Why am I telling him all this? she asked herself. She had only just met him, but already it seemed as though they had known one another for ages.

'And . . . what about you, Nat?' she asked; she knew she had to ask. 'Have you a wife, at home in the USA?'

'No, not me.' He smiled a little ruefully. 'I guess I never met the right girl . . . not yet.' He paused, and they looked at one another steadily for a few moments, Barbara's brown eyes mesmerised by the intense regard in his silvery-grey ones. She knew then, as she often told herself later, that this was probably the point at which she should have said to herself, 'No! No more; turn away now before it's too late.'

But, of course, she didn't turn away and neither did Nat.

He smiled then, and gave a little shrug. 'I guess I was always too busy working in the hotel, all the hours God sends . . . No, to be fair, that's not strictly true. I found time for leisure in between. I ski, as I told you, although that can be classed as work as well. I play baseball, though not very well; I canoe and I've done a little rock climbing. At least I did, until Adolf Hitler – and, of course, our own Franklin D. Roosevelt – thought otherwise, and now I've found myself over here.' He grinned. 'Yes, I know what they're saying about us – overpaid, oversexed, and over here!'

Barbara smiled at him. 'I believe you always have to speak as you find.' Then she added, rather daringly, 'You seem a nice normal sort of fellow to me.'

'Thank you kindly, ma'am!' He touched an imaginary forelock. 'You know, we were all given strict instructions as to how we must behave while we're over here in your country. In fact, we were all issued with a little booklet with a list of dos and don'ts. The worst thing we can say, apparently, is to tell a Britisher that, "We came over here and won the last one – and now we're here to see that you win this one."'

'It's true, though,' replied Barbara. 'We've stood alone for a long time, since 1940, when our allies were forced to surrender. None of us believed it would go on for so long.'

'Ye-eh, that's what it says in our little book, that the Brits are weary of it all. How the houses might look shabby because they haven't been painted for years; the factories are making planes now, not paint. And that British trains are cold because the power is being used for industry, not for heating. And how the rationing of food is affecting you all.

That sure must be hitting you hard, being restricted to – what is it? – two ounces of butter a week, four ounces of bacon?'

'Something like that,' Barbara nodded. 'We manage. We've got used to it and I haven't heard of anybody starving. Actually, some people regard it as being fair shares for all.'

'You sure are a tough breed of people, and I take my hat off to all of you,' said Nat. 'That goes for most of us guys, I guess.'

Barbara didn't know how to answer that. She knew they all put up with the hardships and inconveniences because there was nothing else they could do. But they all did their share of grumbling from time to time, which was only human nature. It was probably true, however, that on the whole they had rallied round as a nation and supported one another, more than they had been inclined to do in peacetime.

'I notice you're a sergeant,' said Barbara, to bring a new topic to the conversation.

'Sure,' Nat replied, 'and so is my pal, Howard. We were both made up recently. And we're the genuine article, I can assure you. No badges of rank that we're not entitled to.'

'What do you mean?' asked Barbara.

'Oh, some of these corporals and sergeants that you might see around are real phoneys. They're privates in disguise. Artificial stripes that are taken off when they leave the dance hall, or if they're in danger of being seen by an NCO or an officer who knows them. Stripes put on to attract the girls, don't you know? Medals as well, sometimes; they're known as "Spam" medals.'

'Well, fancy that!' said Barbara. 'That's something I didn't know. Mind you, I've heard of some of our lads pretending to be something they're not. RAF lads telling stories of how many German planes they've shot down, when they're really ground crew . . . My husband's a sergeant as well,' she went on, feeling somehow that she ought to make some reference to him. 'Probably because of his age and maturity – he's fifteen years older than me – and he's in charge of the meals at the officers' mess. He's doing pretty much the same thing as he did at home.'

'So . . . how long has he been in the army?'

'He joined up almost straight away, in 1939. He's never been sent abroad – he escaped Dunkirk – and there's not much likelihood of him having to go now. What about you, Nat?'

'Who can tell?' Nat shook his head. 'One never knows. We all know there are preparations going on for a second front later this year. That's why we're here. I sure would like to have a bash at old Hitler but, like your hubby, I'm in charge of catering. Coincidence, eh?'

Barbara nodded. 'Well, I'm sure it's as important a job as any other. I've been relieved that it's kept Albert away from the battle zone.'

'That's exactly what my parents say,' agreed Nat. 'But some think, of course, that we've got a cushy number. At least I'm seeing the world, aren't I? Or a part of it at any rate. I hope to see some more of your little old country before I'm through. Blackpool sure is a swell place.' He smiled and nodded appreciatively. 'I've walked along your prom a time or two, and been drenched when those mighty waves came crashing over the sea wall. Gee, what a sight! It puts me in mind of the coast of Maine. That's the furthest I'd ever been from home, apart from a week in New York.'

'I've never been very far from Blackpool either,' said Barbara. 'I spent a week in London with my aunt and uncle just before the war, and I've been up to the Lake District. But since the war started we've been encouraged to stay at home. Tell me, I know I may sound terribly ignorant but . . . what does GI stand for?'

'General infantryman,' replied Nat. 'It's as simple as that.'

Barbara nodded. 'Well, I'm sure glad to know that,' she smiled. 'Another thing – I'm being real nosey, aren't I? Did you say your last name was . . . Castillo?'

'Yes, that's correct. Nat – short for Nathaniel – Castillo.'

'It sounds Italian . . .'

'That's because, way back, my forefathers must have come from Italy. We're a cosmopolitan nation, you see. Folks from all over Europe came to settle in America: Italians, French, Spaniards, Germans, and the British, of course. We've got our fair share of Smiths, Browns and Robinsons, same as you have over here. But I suppose my great-great – I don't know how many greats – grandad must have been Italian. I can't speak the language, though. Eventually, you see, we all ended up speaking English.'

'Or your version of it,' smiled Barbara.

'Ye-eh, point taken.' Nat laughed. 'Some quite amusing differences, aren't there? I know that when we talk about a "bum" we mean someone who's lazy, but it has rather a different meaning to you, hasn't it? We have to be careful or we might be thought indelicate. Although, I asked where the restroom was, in one of your big stores, and the girl looked at me as though I was crazy. Apparently you have no qualms about calling it a toilet or a lavatory? Goodness knows why we Yanks have to be so discreet about it. On the whole, though, we're united by a common language, aren't we? And I've sure been glad of that. It would have been quite a problem to struggle with a new language as well as everything else.'

The band had now taken over from Ena Baga, and the music of 'Moonlight Serenade' was being played. Glenn Miller's captivating tunes had become very popular in Britain, especially since the arrival of the Americans. 'In the Mood', 'American Patrol', 'Pennsylvania, 6-5000', 'String of Pearls'; these tunes were heard on the wireless and in dance halls all over the country, but none was more popular than the haunting melody, 'Moonlight Serenade'.

Nat looked questioningly at Barbara. 'Would you care to dance?' he asked.

'Yes . . . yes, I would . . . thank you,' she replied.

They walked hand in hand to the ballroom floor. Barbara was aware of Dorothy's eyes on her, and she smiled at her friend. Dorothy winked; she, too, seemed to be getting along very well with Nat's friend, Howard.

It was a slow foxtrot rhythm, the most difficult of all the dances to Barbara; but Albert had taught her well and she was able to follow Nat's lead quite easily. She wasn't thinking of Albert, however, at that moment. Nat was not tall, about half a head taller than Barbara, that was all. His hair was neither dark nor fair, just an in-between shade, cut short as regulations required, but it was quite abundant and had a natural wave. His silver-grey eyes were the first thing she had noticed about him; she had known at once that he was a kind and thoughtful sort of person.

He placed his hand in the small of her back and drew her a little closer, and she glanced up at him. His wide mouth curved in a tender smile, and she could not avoid the sudden indrawn breath that she took as their eyes met. The look they exchanged was one of perfect understanding. Barbara knew that was the moment when she started to fall in love with Nat Castillo.

Chapter Twenty-Five

Barbara and Nat were still dancing together as the last waltz was played, the evocative melody 'Who's Taking You Home Tonight?' They danced with their heads close together, scarcely moving, just taking small steps and swaying gently in time to the rhythm. Dorothy and Howard were near to them as the band ended the tune on a poignant diminuendo. The dancers all applauded, a tribute to the band and to Ena Baga, then the four of them together walked off the ballroom floor.

It was Howard who made the suggestion. 'May we have the pleasure of escorting you two ladies home tonight?'

'I don't see why not,' answered Dorothy cheerily. 'What do you say, Barbara? Shall we let them?'

'Yes . . . that would be very nice,' said Barbara with a shy glance at Nat. He did not speak, just nodded his head and winked.

'We'll see you at the top of the stairs, then, near the front entrance,' said Dorothy. 'Come on, Barbara; let's go and get our coats.'

'Nice fellow, that Howard,' Dorothy went on, as they stood in the queue for their coats. 'Good company; great to talk to and have a laugh with. I put him in the picture straight away, though. I told him about Raymond; I thought it was best to tell him. But it appears that he's married; he's got a wife and a kiddy – a two-year-old boy – back in the USA. His home's in Texas. What about you? You seemed to be getting on quite well with Nat. Did you tell him about Albert?'

'Of course I did!' replied Barbara, rather edgily. 'And about Katherine as well. He knew I was married, though, because of my wedding ring.'

'So that's all right, then,' said Dorothy. 'It's best to be above board, then we all know where we stand. Is Nat married too?'

'No, actually he isn't,' replied Barbara, as nonchalantly as she was able.

'Well, it doesn't matter, so long as he knows that you're spoken for. I don't see any harm in them walking back with us tonight. It's obvious that they're both very polite, well-brought-up young men. They probably think it's the right thing to do.'

They left the Tower building at the promenade entrance, turning right towards Talbot Square. Dorothy and Howard were leading the way, with Barbara and Nat close behind as they walked up Talbot Road, then turned left along Dickson Road. At Nat's invitation Barbara linked her arm through his.

'It's good of you to see us home,' she told him. 'The blackout can be rather scary sometimes.' It was a dark night with only a dim crescent moon. 'Although we've all got used to it by now. What about you? How will you get back to your camp?'

'No problem,' answered Nat. 'There's transport laid on for us from the centre of Blackpool, in about half an hour.'

'Known as the passion wagons,' called out Howard, who had overheard the conversation. 'At least, that's what some of the guys call them. Those who've been up to no good.'

'Ye-eh . . .' Nat laughed. 'We've heard tales of some of your RAF lads taking revenge on the GIs and misdirecting them when they've missed their transport back to Warton. Some have found themselves on a tramcar bound for Bispham when they should've been going the other way, to Squires Gate.'

'Oh dear!' said Barbara. 'Well, it's not very far now to where we live.'

Dorothy lived slightly nearer to the centre of the town than did Barbara, so she was the first one to leave the foursome.

'What do you say that we do this again?' suggested Howard, as they stood together at Dorothy's front gate. 'Same time, same place, next Saturday? Is that OK with you girls?'

Dorothy looked at Barbara. 'What do you think? Is that all right with you? I've enjoyed it tonight.'

'Yes, so have I,' agreed Barbara in a quiet voice. 'Yes, that would be very nice.' She smiled shyly at Nat. 'Thank you, both of you, for seeing us home.'

It was Howard who answered. 'It was a real pleasure, ma'am.'

'Cheerio, then,' said Dorothy, walking up her path. 'See you next week. I'll be in touch with you, Barbara.'

Nat and Howard walked one on each side of Barbara, along the street and round the next corner to her aunt's boarding house. She was relieved that the house was in darkness. Her aunt and uncle had no doubt retired for the night, and probably all the RAF recruits, too, who were still stationed there. They were allowed a key if they knew they were going to be late back. The dark street was silent and the three of them found themselves whispering their goodnights.

'Thank you again,' said Barbara. 'See you next Saturday, then.' They had agreed to meet inside, near to the cloakroom, at seven-thirty.

'Goodnight, Barbara,' said Nat. She noticed the note of tenderness in his voice.

'So long, Barbara,' said Howard. 'It's been swell meeting the two of you. See you soon.'

Barbara and Nat exchanged a telling glance as Howard turned to walk away; then Nat followed him.

What have I done? What on earth was I thinking about? Barbara was to ask herself these same questions time and again over the next few days. She even tried to persuade herself that she must have imagined the intensity of feeling she had experienced on meeting Nat, and had only imagined, too, that it was the same for him. At one point she decided that she would not go on Saturday. This thing, whatever it was, must be nipped in the bud before it was too late. And yet she knew, deep down, that she would be there.

'I'm glad you're getting out and about a bit,' her Aunt

Myrtle said to her, when she asked if she and her uncle would look after Katherine again on Saturday. 'Don't look so worried about it, dear. Kathy will be perfectly all right with us; she was as good as gold. And you're not doing anything wrong, going to a dance hall. Did you meet anybody else you knew?'

'Yes, we met some friends of Dorothy's,' said Barbara. 'They were dancing the jitterbug with some Yanks, and then a few of us got talking. It was rather good fun.' She didn't say, however, that they had agreed to meet up again.

Dorothy was unaware of the turmoil going on in her friend's mind, and Barbara intended to keep it that way.

They met again the following Saturday as they had arranged. Barbara felt dreadful lying to her aunt and uncle. Although it was not really a lie; it was what might be called a half-truth, a lie of omission. She was letting them think that she was just meeting Dorothy as she had done the previous week. The guilt she experienced made her feel that she was doing wrong, but she was to find that as the weeks, then the months, went by, her sense of guilt lessened. By that time she and Nat had fallen so deeply in love that all other considerations were of minor importance.

Excepting for the matter of her dear little daughter, Katherine. She loved her baby girl so very much. She was at the interesting stage now, sitting up and smiling at everyone; she was such a happy little girl. At ten months old she was even trying to talk. She repeated the sounds of 'ma-ma' and Barbara convinced herself, as all mothers did, that she was trying to talk to her mummy.

The sounds of 'da-da' did not, as yet, feature in her infant utterances. Albert was able to get a forty-eight-hour pass only occasionally, not long enough for his little daughter to form any lasting memory of him. He was clearly delighted with her; he made a tremendous fuss of her every time he came home, and the little girl would smile winningly at him as she did at most people. It was then that Barbara's guilt would surface, as she wondered what would be the outcome of this problem. She entered into lovemaking with Albert as she knew she must. She did not think he noticed any reluctance on her part. She was still fond of him and he was always gentle and considerate towards her at such times.

For the first few months the love that was gradually developing between herself and Nat did not reach its fulfilment. They both knew that the consummation was inevitable, but Nat was, deep down, an honourable man. Barbara knew that he was trying to show her that he loved her in every way, and not just in the physical sense; and she knew that she loved him in the same way. They were truly soulmates.

The relationship had begun quite slowly. She greeted Nat in a casual manner the second Saturday evening, the same way that Dorothy greeted Howard. They made their way to the ballroom first of all, where Ena Baga was already well into her stride, playing 'Deep in the Heart of Texas'.

'Gee whizz! She's playing my song!' exclaimed Howard. He sounded pensive for a moment, although he was still smiling. 'Come on, Dorothy, we must dance this one.' He took her arm and led her towards the dance floor.

'That's his state, Texas,' remarked Nat. 'I guess it means

as much to him as Vermont means to me. He sure talks a lot about it.'

'But you've never been there?' asked Barbara.

'Gosh, no! It's about as far away as you can imagine from where I live, thousands of miles. And as different as you can imagine as well. Vermont's one of the smallest states in the USA, right up near the Canadian border, and Texas is one of the largest, way down in the deep south, bordering on Mexico. We get snow, and they get tropical sunshine and hurricanes. We get along great, though, Howard and me. We enlisted at the same time and we've stuck together ever since . . . Care to dance, Barbara?'

They moved easily together to the quickstep rhythm. Barbara had a feeling of rightness and familiarity with Nat's arms around her, although he was not holding her too closely. He sang softly along to the tune of 'Deep in the Heart of Texas', about the bright stars and the prairie sky and the perfume of the sage in bloom, and she joined in as well. The song had become very familiar since the Yanks had come to Britain. The organist moved on easily from that melody to the rhythm of the 'American Patrol'. This was the signal for some of the more enthusiastic couples to start their jitterbugging.

Barbara and Nat danced carefully around them, avoiding a collision. The more energetic couples would, no doubt, be asked to move off before long, or would of their own accord continue their gymnastics away from the ballroom floor. When the sequence of dances ended the four of them met up again in the spot where they had all congregated the previous week.

'What do you say we have a little refreshment?' suggested Howard. 'I was thinking of tea and cakes actually, at the moment, rather than beer. That's one of your English specialities, isn't it?'

'That's true,' replied Dorothy. 'Usually in the afternoon, though; it's called "afternoon tea".'

'I thought you Americans preferred coffee,' remarked Barbara.

'Sorry to say it, but your coffee is undrinkable,' said Howard, laughing. 'Isn't that so, Nat?'

''Fraid so,' said Nat with a rueful grin. 'But I guess it's not your fault; another inconvenience caused by old Adolf, eh?'

'I don't think we were ever really coffee drinkers,' said Barbara. 'We used to drink Nescafé, but we can't get that now. We have to make do with that Camp coffee that comes in a bottle. I must admit, it's pretty awful.'

'Well then, we'll have a nice cup of tea,' smiled Nat. 'That's what you Brits say, isn't it? A nice cup of tea. And I must say it's a mighty fine beverage, the way you make it.'

'Let's go to that posh place upstairs,' said Dorothy. 'There's a lot more to our Tower than just the ballroom, you know.'

She led the way to a refreshment room on the next floor up, where ferns and greenery, even a palm tree, added to the pleasant ambience of the place, a contrast to the rowdier downstairs bars and tea rooms. They sat at a table for four where a waitress served them with tea in a silver pot and a selection of cakes on a cake stand. The cream in the eclairs was 'mock' and, most probably, so was the filling in the 'almond' tarts, but they all agreed that they

337

were as good as any you could get at the present time.

'It's rather more select up here, isn't it?' remarked Nat, 'away from the noise and the crowds.'

'I've told you, there's far more to the Tower than you see at a first glance,' said Dorothy. 'When we've finished our tea we could go and look at the animals.'

'Animals?' queried Nat.

'Oh, didn't you know? There's a zoo just over there. Or a menagerie, some people still call it. It's been there since the Tower opened, that's about seventy years ago, though no doubt the animals have changed.'

'Not much of a zoo by your standards, I don't suppose,' said Barbara, as the four of them, a little while later, sat on the raised seating in the centre of the room watching, from a distance, the animals in their cages.

'A quaint idea, though,' said Nat. 'I guess the children like to come and see the monkeys.'

A few braver folk, including children with their parents, were pushing nuts through the bars of the cages, encouraging the monkeys to perform their tricks. But Barbara and Dorothy preferred to keep their distance, away from the lion and the rather fierce-looking bear.

'Is that the lion that the poem was written about?' asked Nat. 'Wallace, the one that had the "'orse's 'ead 'andle" poked in his ear?'

Barbara laughed. 'I'm not sure if it's the same one that swallowed Albert.' She felt a momentary spasm of guilt as she said the name that was also the name of her husband. 'I didn't think you Americans would know about that.'

'Oh yes, we've heard all about *Albert and the Lion* and

Stanley Holloway since we came to Blackpool,' said Howard. 'Did he write the poem?'

'No, it was a man called Marriott Edgar,' said Dorothy. 'He's the man who writes the monologues for Stanley Holloway. I know because I recite it sometimes at church concerts, don't I, Barbara?'

'Yes, you do indeed,' answered her friend. 'And it always goes down well with the audience. Are you going to recite it for us now?'

'No, I'd rather not,' laughed Dorothy. 'Some other time, maybe. I say, it pongs in here, doesn't it? Shall we move on?'

'Yes, it is a bit niffy,' agreed Howard. 'And I can't say I really approve of animals in cages, although they look contented enough.'

'There's an aquarium as well on the ground floor,' said Barbara, as they left the menagerie. 'And an aviary with exotic birds up near the top of the Tower. And in peacetime you could go up to the top of the Tower. Not now, though, of course; there's a radar station up there and a lookout post.'

The other two were a few steps in front as they all headed towards the ballroom again. They sat on one of the red plush seats in an alcove from where they could see the ballroom floor. If they vacated their seats, though, to dance or to seek refreshment, they were almost sure to lose them. The place was always crowded on a Saturday evening and that night was no exception.

'Have you been up to the top of the Tower?' asked Nat.

'Yes, once, when I was a little girl,' replied Barbara. 'I was with my aunt and uncle. I must admit it was a bit scary until I got used to it. Then I stopped being frightened and just enjoyed the wonderful views. You can see right across to Southport and the Welsh hills on a clear day, which it was at the time.' She smiled. 'We learnt at school that Blackpool Tower is five hundred and eighteen feet high. Not as tall as your Empire State Building, though!'

Nat's eyes twinkled with amusement as they met hers. 'No, I guess not. The Empire State is twice as high. Sorry about that, Barbara! Three hundred and eighty-one metres, so we're told; I guess that must be well over one thousand feet.'

'And have you been to the top?'

'Yes, so I have, on my one and only visit to New York. We went as a family when I was in my teens. We did all the sights: the Statue of Liberty, Central Park, Fifth Avenue, Broadway . . . It's a mighty fine city.'

'I'm sure it must be. I've only been to London once, ages ago,' Barbara said wistfully.

'I'm sure you will, one of these days,' said Nat, smiling understandingly at her.

'When the war is over . . .' mused Barbara. 'That's what we all keep saying, don't we?'

'Yes. All we can do is take a day at a time,' said Nat. 'None of us knows what's in the future. But we can try to make the most of every day, can't we? Every day, every hour . . . ?' His voice was hushed so that no one but Barbara could hear. The other two, anyway, were engrossed in their own conversation.

Nat took hold of her hand, gazing at her intently. 'You know what I'm saying, don't you, Barbara?'

'Yes, Nat . . . I guess I do,' she replied as they exchanged a look of total empathy.

'Shall we go and take a look at the aquarium?' he suggested. 'It'll be nice and peaceful there, won't it?'

'I'm sure it will,' said Barbara. 'It's ages since I was down there. It's a strange place; at least I thought so when I was a little girl – all green and mysterious.'

Dorothy and Howard had gone onto the ballroom floor again, and Barbara could see them jigging about happily to the tune of the 'Woodchopper's Ball'. They seemed to be getting on very well, she pondered, but she doubted that there was the intensity of feeling that had developed between herself and Nat. Again a tiny voice at the back of her mind tried to tell her that she was playing with fire . . . but it was already too late.

They wandered downstairs, hand in hand, to the dimly lit, greenish gloom of the aquarium. It resembled a cave with limestone pillars, where exotic fish from all over the world swam around in glass tanks. They strolled about, taking a brief look at the fish, but Barbara knew that what Nat wanted was a place where they could be on their own for a little while. There were just a few people, like themselves, gazing at the fish, but also enjoying the solitude of the surroundings.

They stopped near to one of the stone pillars. Nat put his arms around Barbara and drew her towards him. He leant forward and, very gently, kissed her on the lips. It was no more than that the first time, a very gentle, loving kiss. 'Barbara . . .' he murmured. 'You know what has happened, don't you? I've fallen in love with you. Tell me,

341

please . . . I have to know. Is it . . . is it the same for you?'

She nodded. 'Yes, Nat, it is. I've only known you for a week, but I feel as though I've known you for ages. Yes, Nat . . . I love you.' Her voice was the faintest whisper. 'I don't know what we're going to do. I've tried to tell myself that it's wrong, that I mustn't . . . but it's no use. I feel as though we were meant to be together . . . Is that dreadful of me?'

'No . . . no, it isn't!' he answered, quite vehemently, although he was still speaking quietly. 'I know that some might think so, that they will certainly think so. But I knew, almost the first moment I met you. I've never felt like this before, about anyone. God help me, I love you, Barbara!'

'I have a husband and a little girl,' said Barbara, although neither of them needed reminding of that fact. 'I told you so, last week. I knew I had to tell you . . . and I do love Kathy, so very much.'

'And . . . your husband?'

Barbara sadly shook her head. 'I'm fond of him. Albert was good to me, and I knew he'd take care of me. I wanted the security, but I know now that it was wrong of me. I should never have married him, not for that reason. I think I knew it at the time. Oh Nat . . . what are we going to do?'

He smiled at her, then he tenderly kissed her again. 'For the moment, we're not going to be miserable. As I said before, we have to take each day as it comes. We'd better go back now, hadn't we, or the other two will wonder where we are.'

Dorothy and Howard were standing at the edge of the dance floor, as they had lost their seats. Barbara fancied that her friend gave her an odd look, but she, Barbara, smiled

342

nonchalantly. 'We've been to look at the fishes,' she said brightly.

They danced again, then had a drink in the bar, and at ten-thirty they headed for home.

'How about a change of venue next week?' suggested Howard. 'I'd sure like to take a look at your Winter Gardens; that is if you girls still want to see us?'

They agreed that they did, and that they would go to the Winter Gardens, rather than the Tower. Howard hung back as Nat said goodnight to Barbara.

'Here . . .' she said, stopping at a shop doorway, a little distance away from the boarding house. 'My aunt and uncle might still be around. I'm sorry, Nat . . .'

He kissed her again, a little more ardently. 'Don't worry,' he whispered. 'I love you; just remember that. It'll all sort itself out in the end, I'm sure.'

Chapter Twenty-Six

'What you're doing is wrong,' Dorothy told her friend. 'You're playing with fire; surely you must see that? For heaven's sake, Barbara, put an end to it before it's too late.'

The two friends were walking along the promenade near to the North Pier; Barbara was pushing little Katherine, fast asleep in her pram. Dorothy had phoned her asking if they could meet for a chat. They had decided on Wednesday afternoon, which was Dorothy's half day off from the munitions factory where she worked. Barbara had already guessed that her friend might have some strong words to say to her. She knew now that she had not been mistaken about the odd looks – searching, knowing looks – that Dorothy had cast her way on Saturday night.

She had been surprised that Dorothy had agreed to go along with the Americans' suggestion that they should go to the Winter Gardens the following Saturday. But to refuse, of course, would have been to put an end to the fun that Dorothy was having with Howard – light-hearted, innocent fun, Barbara was sure. She knew that Dorothy was a far more easy-going person than herself. She seemed more able to take life as it came, in a much less serious way. Barbara did not think that her friend felt too intensely about anything, not even about her engagement to her fiancé, Raymond. All the same, she had made it clear that she would not cheat on him, and that her friendship with Howard was enjoyable, but of no consequence.

Barbara listened to her, as she knew she must. 'I understand what you are saying,' she replied, 'and only a few weeks ago I would have agreed with you. I would have thought it was dreadful that a married woman, such as I am, could even think of carrying on with someone else. But you must see, Dorothy, that we're not "carrying on". Nothing has happened between us; you must understand that. When we met, Nat and me, there was an immediate attraction, a magnetism between us; we were both aware of it. And now . . . well, I'm afraid it's already too late. I love him, and he loves me.'

'But you've only known him for two weeks! You've only met him twice. You can't really be sure that you love him, not in such a short time. And what about your husband, and your little girl, bless her! Just look at her, Barbara, what a little treasure she is!'

'Do you think I haven't said the same thing to myself, time and time again? Yes, I know it's wrong, Dorothy. Not that we've done anything really wrong as yet. And I wouldn't do that anyway. You know what I mean; I would never sleep with him, have an affair, whatever you want to call it, as though it didn't matter. It isn't like that; I know that Nat respects me too much for that. It isn't what either of us want . . . but we do love one another.'

Dorothy glanced across at her in what looked like a pitying way. She shook her head. 'But that's what it will lead to; you must know that, Barbara. Yes, I know he seems like a very nice bloke. They both are, Nat and Howard. But we don't really know all that much about them, do we? If I were you I would put an end to it, now, before it goes any further. Look . . . why don't I meet them on my own on Saturday night, and tell him that you've decided not to come? Believe me, Barbara, it'd be the best thing to do. It might hurt at first, but you're going to get in too deep if it goes on any longer.'

Barbara shook her head. 'You say "if you were me". But how can you say that? You're not me, are you? You can't possibly know how I feel, or what you would do if it had happened to you. I know you're concerned about me. You're probably annoyed with me, and I suppose you have every reason to be . . . but there's nothing you can say that will make any difference.' She glanced into the pram. Katherine was just opening her eyes and Barbara leant over to touch her downy cheek.

'Yes, I love my little daughter more than I can say. It's the one good thing that has come out of my marriage to Albert. Because I know now, Dorothy, that I should never have married him. I did so for all the wrong reasons. I don't love him, not the way I should, and I know now that I never did. But there's Kathy; that's the awful part about it, and that's what hurts, so very much. It's agonising when I think how much Kathy means to me. And Albert thinks the world of her too. She doesn't really know him yet, not in the way she knows me, because he's not here very often. But I know it would hurt him if he ever had to part with her.'

She was silent for a few moments and her friend made no comment. But she could sense Dorothy's disapproval, waves of reproach drifting across to her.

'I'm so happy when I'm with Nat,' she continued. 'Yes, I know it's been only a short time, but when I'm with him I feel like a different person. I've never felt like this before about anyone; not even when I was engaged to Mike, although I was so sure that I loved him. And that's what Nat said to me, that he's never felt like this before. Oh, Dorothy, whatever are we going to do?' She looked imploringly at her friend. But Dorothy's reply was far from sympathetic.

'I've told you what to do, Barbara. It's the only way. You'll have to put an end to it, straight away. You'd get over it . . .'

Barbara could see that Dorothy was getting exasperated, and the last thing she wanted to do was to quarrel with her friend. Heaven knows, she might need a friend who understood before long.

'Please don't be angry,' she said, almost crying. 'I didn't ask for this to happen . . . the way I feel about Nat. It's been totally unexpected, and I can't just finish it, in spite of what you say. And I wouldn't get over it, not so easily . . .'

'Thousands of girls have had to get over far worse things, when their husbands and fiancés have been killed, just as you had to get over losing Mike. It's wartime, Barbara. You don't know what might happen to Nat. You and Nat, Howard and me, we're what you might call ships that pass in the night.'

Barbara didn't answer, and Dorothy was beginning to realise that nothing she could say was going to make any difference. And she, too, did not want to lose her friend. 'I'm sorry,' she said. 'I don't want to quarrel with you, but I wouldn't be a very good friend if I didn't tell you how I feel. I'm concerned for you, Barbara, but maybe I can't understand what you're feeling. Maybe it hasn't happened to me. I love Raymond, but it's a pretty uncomplicated sort of relationship. Perhaps I'm better at compartmentalising my life than you are. Gosh! That's a big word, isn't it?' She laughed. 'Do you know what I mean, though? My time with Howard is separate from my feelings for Raymond. Howard and I will say goodbye at the end of the war or maybe sooner – whenever he's sent elsewhere, who knows? – and we'll have no regrets. But I can see, I suppose, that your involvement with Nat is rather different.'

Kathy was stirring now and making little cooing sounds as though she was singing to herself. Barbara stopped and sat her up against the pillow at the back of the pram. She was warmly dressed in a bright-pink jacket, bonnet and mittens. The colour suited her dark curls, peeping out from under the fur-trimmed bonnet. She smiled appealingly at both her mummy and Dorothy – she was not a shy child – reaching out her arms and saying something that sounded like 'ma-ma', followed by 'ba-ba-ba'.

Dorothy laughed. 'Isn't she delightful? Is she trying to say Barbara?'

'I don't think so,' smiled Barbara. 'She says it all the time. It's one of the easiest sounds to say.'

The feeling of tension between them was over as Barbara turned the pram round and they headed towards home. No more was said about the situation until they stopped to say goodbye at the end of the street where Dorothy lived.

'Saturday evening, then?' said Dorothy. 'I suppose I can take it you'll be going?'

Barbara nodded. 'We agreed to meet them outside the Winter Gardens at half past seven, didn't we? Shall I see you at the bus stop, then, at about ten past seven?'

'That's OK with me,' said Dorothy. 'Er . . . if you change your mind, just let me know.'

'That's not going to happen,' replied Barbara without smiling. 'Just leave it, Dorothy, OK? I won't change my mind. See you on Saturday . . .'

Barbara was aware of a feeling of foreboding for the next day or two. At first, little niggling doubts crept into her mind as she recalled all that her friend had said. Two weeks was such a short space of time, so how could she feel so sure? Was it just physical attraction, or the novelty of meeting someone so completely different from anyone she had known before? Did Nat really mean everything that he said? And what about the future, the time when Albert would have to be told, as he surely must? She knew, though, despite her confusion and the misgivings that Dorothy's words had given rise to, that she would be there again on Saturday night.

And, sure enough, all the negative feelings were put to one side when she met Nat again, at least for the time that they spent together. They danced and they had a drink at one of the several bars, the four of them chatting easily together.

The men agreed that they were impressed with the glories of the Winter Gardens building. It was sumptuous throughout, comparing very favourably with the Tower. A flight of stairs from the Indian Lounge, which was lavishly decorated in an oriental style, led up to the equally splendid Empress Ballroom.

There were quiet walkways too, adorned with palm trees, ferns and lush foliage, where Barbara and Nat were able to be alone for a little while. They sat in a quiet alcove, looking at one another without speaking for several moments, but experiencing again the feelings and the attraction that had first drawn them together. Nat put his arms around her; he kissed her gently and tenderly, then again, more ardently.

Then he stopped. It was not the time nor the place, and both of them knew that. They did not want to make an exhibition of themselves, as very many couples were doing in wartime Blackpool. On promenade benches; on the sands or the grass in the park, if the weather was clement; on the back row of the cinema; or under the pier . . . they were to be seen all over the place, girls with soldiers, sailors, airmen and GIs, and who could tell whether it was a one-night stand, a passing fancy, or something that would stand the test of time? Barbara and Nat knew that the feelings they had for one another were private and precious, and that they would have to wait.

They spoke very little of the future, not then or at further meetings. They both knew, though, that it would ultimately have to be faced; there would be a day of reckoning.

Nat told her about his life back in his hometown in Vermont, about his parents and his brother and sister. They were both older than he was and married with families. His brother, Lawrence, was thirty-five; unlike his brother he had not joined the army. Neither was he part of the family business as Nat was. Lawrence had shown no inclination for it; he was a bank manager in Montpelier, which was the capital city of Vermont. His sister, Nancy, was thirty and married to the owner of a sports emporium in Stowe, not far from the family hotel. Nat, at twenty-seven, was the baby of the family.

Barbara told Nat about her family background, how her parents had been killed when she was very young, and her upbringing with her aunt and uncle. She told him, too, about her engagement to Mike, who had not returned from Dunkirk.

She felt honour-bound to mention Albert from time to time. Nat didn't say, 'Never mind about him,' or words to that effect. Her husband was there as an undeniable fact, as was her baby daughter, and they could not be ignored.

'Albert is a good man,' she told Nat. 'I've known him . . . well . . . for ever, really, because he lived next door. He was literally "the boy next door", although he is fifteen years older than I am. He never seemed to be all that interested in girls; I don't remember ever seeing him with one. He's more of a man's man, really, if you know what I mean. He loves his football and darts, and a pint at the pub now and again. He's been good to me, kind and thoughtful.' She did not say how Albert had spoken of his undying love for her and how he had said he would always be there for her, come what may. She tried to push memories such as those to the back of her mind.

And Albert likes his own way, she also thought to herself. He could be dogmatic and unbending, and when she forced herself to think about the future she could foresee trouble ahead.

'Let's take a day at a time,' Nat always told her when she became too introspective. 'When it's time to face up to it all, I shall be with you every step of the way.'

There was a weekend when Dorothy's fiancé was home on leave, but Howard came along with Nat – to the Tower on that particular Saturday – and he found plenty of partners to dance with. Barbara was sure he knew of the situation between herself and Nat, and he was extremely tactful and understanding. Whether he approved or not she was unable to tell.

Another time it was Barbara herself who was not there because Albert was home on leave. There were two such occasions during the time that Nat was stationed at Warton. On the first occasion she and Albert made love, though not without a sense of guilt on Barbara's part. On the next occasion, some six weeks later, Barbara was relieved when the onset of her monthly period prevented this from happening.

Occasionally she was able to meet Nat during the week. Almost every afternoon, if the weather was not too cold or rainy, she took Katherine out for a walk in her pram. It seemed that the life at the American camp was pretty free and easy because Nat was able to get time off to be with her. She met him near to the North Pier and she wheeled the pram down the slope to the lower prom. It was far more secluded than the upper promenade, where the RAF recruits who were stationed in the town were often to be seen walking along in small groups, and where the tramcars clanged and clattered by, bound for Squires Gate or Cleveleys.

They sat on a bench, Nat's arm around her, relishing their brief time together. They could hear the sound of the waves beating against the sea wall and the cry of the seagulls as they exchanged kisses of love and longing. They knew, though, that that was all they could do, that now was not the time nor the place.

Nat was enchanted with Kathy, who cooed and laughed and held out her arms to him. She had learnt to wave 'bye-bye', one of the first things learnt by all babies. She waved dutifully as they parted by North Pier where Nat boarded a tram to take him towards Squires Gate. In fact, Kathy then continued to wave to imaginary people all the way home, and was still doing it when they entered the house and saw Aunt Myrtle.

'Who is she waving to?' laughed Myrtle.

'Oh, she's been doing it ever since she woke up,' answered Barbara. 'It's a new trick she's learnt. She's waving "hello" to Aunty Myrtle, aren't you, darling?'

Barbara reflected that it was fortunate that Kathy had not yet learnt to talk. Aunt Myrtle was still unaware of the secret life her niece was leading.

Chapter Twenty-Seven

By the end of May everyone, civilians as well as the fighting forces, was aware of the tension in the air. It was common knowledge that D-Day, the start of the liberation of occupied Europe, was imminent.

'Barbara, could you meet me this week, on your own?' asked Nat. 'You know how I love to see your little daughter; but we do need to be alone for a little while. Could you possibly leave her with your aunt one afternoon?'

'Er . . . yes; I'll manage it somehow,' replied Barbara, although she hated the subterfuge and the lies. She had not really told any out-and-out-lies, but she had failed to tell the whole truth. This time, though, it might be necessary to lie to her aunt.

'I could say that I have a dental appointment on Wednesday afternoon,' she suggested tentatively. 'I really do need to go before long. And the dentist will no doubt want to see me again – they always do – so I could make the actual appointment for the following week. My dentist is in the centre of Blackpool, and my aunt is sure to tell me to take as long as I like, and have a look round the shops.'

'Don't look so worried, darling,' said Nat. 'I know you hate telling lies, and that's one of the reasons I love you so much. You're such a good honest person, Barbara.'

She shook her head. 'How can I be, the way I'm behaving?'

'I know . . . I know what you mean.' He drew her closer to him on their seat in the Floral Hall of the Winter Gardens. 'But you really are – good and honest and thoughtful. I know you don't want to hurt anyone, but we can't let anything come between us, to spoil what we have. You know that, don't you, Barbara?'

'Yes, I know that . . . I'll meet you on Wednesday, then, shall I? Two o'clock at the usual place?' That was near to the North Pier entrance.

Her Aunt Myrtle fell in readily with the story of her supposed dental appointment. 'I'll have Kathy for as long as you like,' she said. 'Go and have a look at the shops while you're in town; and why don't you treat yourself to tea and cakes at Robinson's café? Unless you've had a bad time at the dentist's, of course.'

'No, it'll just be a check-up the first time,' said Barbara. 'Thank you, Aunty. You're very good to me.'

'No more than you deserve,' said Aunt Myrtle, which caused Barbara a severe stab of guilt.

They met as arranged by the North Pier entrance on the following Wednesday afternoon. Nat kissed her on the cheek, smiling broadly. 'Hi, good to see you. Glad you could make it. No problems, then?'

'No, not so far,' she replied. 'Nat . . . you do love me, don't you?' Once again the enormity of what she was doing became very real to her. She knew that the time had arrived when she and Nat would bring their love for one another to its inevitable climax. 'I mean . . . this is for ever, not just for now?' she whispered. 'You are very sure . . . about us?'

'I've never been more sure about anything,' he answered. 'I love you, Barbara, more than I can say, and I always will.' They were talking in hushed voices, but no one was paying any heed to them. Couples such as themselves were to be seen all over the town.

'Come along . . .' He took hold of her hand and they hurried to the tram stop. They boarded a tram bound for Squire's Gate.

'But you've already come from there,' said Barbara.

'No matter,' said Nat smiling. 'It's a good deal quieter down there, and I didn't want you to travel so far on your own.'

She laughed. 'Why ever not? I'm a big girl now, you know. I'm not likely to get lost, not in Blackpool.'

'But I'm here to take care of you, aren't I?' He reached for her hand.

They did not speak very much throughout the journey along the stretch of Blackpool promenade. They sat hand in hand, looking out at the crowds of both civilians and servicemen thronging the promenade, and at the expanse of golden sand, and beyond it the vast stretch of sea.

It was a glorious May day. The sun shone from a cloudless

sky, glinting like silver coins on the bluey-grey ocean. The sea at Blackpool was ever changing, taking its colour from the heavens – often dark grey and stormy, but today as still and as blue as Barbara had ever known it to be.

They alighted from the tram at the stop known as Starr Gate and walked towards the sandhills, as Barbara had already guessed they might do. The sandhills stretched southwards from Squires Gate to St Annes – hillocks of fine, pale, golden sand, interspersed with the clumps of star grass that helped the dunes to keep their shape. The sea never came so far inland, but could be seen in the distance beyond the stretch of coarser sand that was covered daily by the incoming tide.

This was a favourite spot for courting couples. Barbara and Nat clambered across the dunes, their feet sinking into the soft sand. It crept through the straps of Barbara's sandals and between her toes. She was not wearing stockings, an economy measure that many women were adopting, especially when the weather was warm. She pondered that every trace of sand would need to be removed before she went home.

They found a secluded hollow where the sandhills rose above them on all sides. Nat took off his jacket and laid it on the ground. They sat on it together, looking at one another speechlessly for several moments. Then he drew her into his arms and kissed her passionately, in the way they had both been yearning for and anticipating for so long.

'Barbara . . . I love you,' he murmured, and it did not seem at all sordid or wrong as they made love for the very first time. She felt tears of pent-up emotion and sublime happiness misting her eyes as their love reached its fulfilment.

'I love you too, Nat,' she whispered. 'Whatever happens

– and God alone knows what is going to happen – I love you, so very much.' She knew now that there was no turning back, but there was so much that was unknown, so much that they must face, together. 'Oh, Nat . . . what are we going to do?'

She looked around, feeling a shade guilty, and worried lest there was anyone near enough to see or hear them. It was not the sort of thing she had ever done before. She had always thought that making love out of doors as they had just done was something rather shameful, not at all the sort of thing that a 'nice' girl would do. She adjusted her clothing feeling, now, a little embarrassed, and Nat did the same.

He clearly understood how she felt. 'I know, my darling,' he said. 'This . . .' He gestured with his hand towards the sandhills. 'It is not ideal. But you do know, don't you, that this was inevitable? And some day, Barbara, we will be together for always. You must try to cling on to that, just as I will, because . . .' He took a deep breath. 'I had to see you today, to show you how much I love you, but also because there is something I have to tell you. The first draft of men from our camp has already left for the south of England, in preparation for D-Day. And it's almost certain that I will be going with the next draft, in a couple of weeks' time. And Howard as well.'

'But I thought you were needed here. You said, didn't you, that you had an important job in charge of the catering? Oh, Nat, this is dreadful news.' Tears welled up again in her eyes, but she brushed them away. She knew that to weep and wail about this would only make things worse for Nat. She was not surprised at his next words.

'It's war, my darling, and it's far more important than cooking meals and looking after the officers. And we have to obey orders. We didn't join up just to have a cushy number and keep out of danger.'

'But how will I know where you are?' she asked. 'How will we be able to keep in touch?'

'I don't really know at the moment. But there will be an address – a sort of address – you can write to once the assault is under way. I'm sorry to have to leave you, Barbara. I'm more than sorry; I'm torn apart. I was planning to be with you, for us to be together when we tell your husband about . . . you and me.'

'No, I don't really think that would have been a good idea, Nat.' She shook her head. She knew that Albert could be aggressive when he was roused and she shuddered to think of his reaction. No – it was far better that she should face him on her own, although she was already quaking at the thought. 'I will tell him,' she said. 'I'm not sure when, but I will, I promise. Will I see you again before you go?'

'Yes, on Saturday, I hope. We arranged, didn't we, the four of us, that we should visit the Tower again?'

She nodded numbly. The sun had gone behind a cloud – a few clouds had now appeared in the formerly clear blue sky – and she shivered, although not just with the cold. 'I must go, Nat,' she said. 'Aunt Myrtle said I could take as long as I wanted, but I'd better be getting back. Don't come back with me on the tram. It would be a waste of your time, and I'm all right, honestly.' She needed a little time on her own to compose herself and to adjust to Nat's news before she joined her family again.

'OK, if you're sure, darling . . .'

They walked to the tram stop where they said goodbye. Their parting was far less joyful than their meeting a couple of hours ago had been.

At nine-thirty in the morning of Tuesday, 6th June, the sombre voice of John Snagge told the nation over the radio that, 'D-Day has come. Early this morning the Allies began the assault on the north-western face of Hitler's European fortress . . .' The news had been long awaited and the majority of Britons had felt sure that 'Operation Overlord', as the attack was called, would be successful. It was reported that before nightfall on 6th June, one hundred and fifty-six thousand men had been put ashore on the coast of Normandy. There were heavy losses, mostly among the RAF and in the American assault area known as Omaha.

Nat was not part of that first offensive but, as he had told Barbara, he was posted soon afterwards with the next draft, to somewhere in Devon. It was to be a long time before he and Barbara were in contact. She knew, though, very soon after he had departed for the south coast, that she was expecting his child.

At first she was shocked and frightened, then she realised that this was inevitable, just as their one and only act of love had been. Perhaps it was meant to be; at all events it forced the issue and compelled her to admit, first of all to her aunt, what had been going on in her life for the past few months.

She decided to talk to her aunt on her own, and she chose an evening when her uncle had gone to have a drink and a game of dominoes, as he did from time to time, with his mates at the local pub. She had put Kathy to bed, and she and her aunt sat one on each side of the fire in the family living room.

'Aunty . . . I've something to tell you,' Barbara began. She did not hesitate before she said, 'I'm having another baby.'

'Oh!' her aunt gasped, then she beamed with pleasure. 'That's wonderful news. It's rather soon after Kathy, but I'm sure you're very pleased. Does Albert know?'

'No, not yet,' Barbara replied. 'Actually, Aunty Myrtle, there's something else I have to tell you. You see . . . it isn't Albert's baby.'

Her aunt's expression changed from one of delight to one of horror. 'Barbara! Whatever are you saying?'

Barbara explained how she had met Nat Castillo and how their friendship had developed over the months. 'We love one another,' she said, 'in a way that I have never loved Albert. I know what you will think about me. I know what you will say – that I have behaved disgracefully and that I can't be sure that I love Nat . . . but I do love him; I'm very sure, and so is he.'

Her aunt's face had blanched and she was grasping hold of the chair arms to stop herself from trembling. Barbara felt dreadful at the effect her news was having. Myrtle did not weep, or shout at Barbara. After a few moments, during which she was trying to compose herself, she said, 'That's *exactly* what I'm going to say, Barbara. You've been a silly girl. You've behaved very badly, but I suppose I can understand that you might have had your head turned by this young man. A Yank . . . yes!' She shook her head despairingly. 'They're a long way from home, and who can blame them if they find girls who are willing?'

'But it isn't like that,' Barbara protested. 'I know the reputation they have, but Nat isn't like that. He's a good honest man . . . and we fell in love.'

'You couldn't help yourselves, I suppose?' Myrtle smiled a little cynically, and Barbara couldn't blame her.

'Well, yes . . . I mean . . . no. We couldn't help – can't help – how we feel about one another.'

Her aunt sighed. 'You've been very foolish and I can't condone what you've done. Nor have we ever encouraged you to tell lies, but there is a way round this. Albert need never know, not if you let him think that the baby is his. I know it's wrong, but there's nothing else you can do under the circumstances.'

Barbara shook her head. 'I'm afraid I can't do that. The last time Albert came home on leave I was having a period, and so we didn't . . . you know. Anyway, I couldn't deceive him like that. When he comes home the next time I couldn't trick him into . . . doing that, then pretending the baby was his. You see, Nat and I, we want to be together, when he comes back, when it's all over.'

'And when is he due home again – Albert, I mean?'

'In just over two weeks. I shall have to tell him, Aunty Myrtle. It's not going to be easy, but I know I must.'

'And what about . . . the other one, Nat? Does he know about the baby?'

'No, I only found out after he'd gone. He's somewhere down south now. I don't know when I shall see him again.'

'Isn't it possible that you might be mistaken,' said Myrtle, 'about being pregnant?'

'No, not at all. 'I'm always so regular, you see. And anyway . . . I just know.' Barbara felt instinctively at her breasts, which were already a little tender.

'I can't pretend I'm not shocked,' said Myrtle, 'especially at you, Barbara. It's the last thing I could ever have imagined you would do. But I shall stand by you. I'll help you in any way I can, and I know your uncle will too. I shall have to tell him, of course. We love you, Barbara. We've tried to make up to you for you losing your parents, and we'll do whatever we need to do now, you can be sure of that.'

'Thank you, Aunty Myrtle,' said Barbara in a subdued voice. 'You've always been so good to me, and I hate to upset you like this.'

Myrtle thought to herself at that moment, and during the following weeks, that she would not like to be in Barbara's shoes when she broke the news to Albert. And, despite her disappointment and her annoyance at what her niece had done, she reflected that Barbara's marriage was by no means the perfect one. Myrtle had come to the conclusion, over the last couple of years, that Albert was not really the right man for Barbara.

The scene with Albert, inevitably, was a bitter one, but poignant and distressing as well. Barbara had never seen Albert so angry or, on the other hand, so dejected and bewildered as he was at first. She had deliberated and agonised as to how to tell him. She decided that the bold approach, telling him straight away that she was pregnant, was not the right one to adopt with Albert. Instead she began in a regretful way, telling him that whilst he had been away she had met someone else and that they had fallen in love.

Whilst he stared at her, open-mouthed with disbelief, she went on to say that she was sorry to hurt him, but she knew now that she had been wrong to marry him, that what she felt for him was affection but not real love.

'What are you saying, Barbara?' he cried. 'That you want to leave me? You want to go off with this other fellow, whoever he is? That you want . . . a divorce?' He shook his head decisively. 'Oh no, Barbara; I shall never let you go. A divorce is out of the question.' Then, as her aunt had done, he said, 'You've had your head turned by some fancy words, I daresay. A Yank, is he?' He had guessed correctly, but it might just as well have been an RAF man. There were hundreds of them in the town, even billeted in the same house.

'Forget him, Barbara. You belong to me; I'm your husband and I love you. Maybe I'm not as glamorous or as young, eh? Is that it? But I love you far more than he ever could.'

She knew then that she had to pluck up the courage to tell him the truth. 'There's something else,' she said. 'Yes, you're right; he is an American GI . . . and I'm expecting his child.'

It was then that Albert lost control of himself. He did not strike out at her physically, but she had never heard such a tirade of abuse as he flung at her, nor had she believed he could use such words.

'You're a whore, a trollop!' he yelled, as he turned white with rage. 'I said I loved you, and yes, I do – heaven help me – and I suppose I always will. But I despise you, Barbara.

At this moment I almost hate you! How could you do this? I don't know what you are trying to tell me, what it is you want; but if you're expecting me ever to accept this child that you're having as mine, then let me tell you that I never will. Go to him, then, your Yank, if that's what you want. But you are not taking Katherine. She is my child and she stays with me.'

There was a lot more in the same vein before Albert left her alone that night. He went to sleep in an attic room, leaving her alone in the bedroom they shared when he was home on leave, in the Leighs' boarding house.

She tossed and turned in the bed, lying awake for hours and only falling into a fitful sleep as dawn was breaking. An hour or two later she dressed herself and Kathy and crept out of the house before anyone else was stirring, back to her home next door with her aunt and uncle.

She was left in no doubt about Albert's feelings. He would never accept the child she was carrying as his, nor did she want him to; this was Nat's child. But if she and Nat, sometime in the future, were to be together, which was what they both wanted so much, then Albert would force her to leave Katherine behind. And however could she bear to part with her precious little daughter?

Chapter Twenty-Eight

1973

'So my mother went away and left me, then?' said Kathy. 'She deserted me and married this American fellow? At least I'm assuming she married him?'

'Yes, she did marry him, eventually,' said Winifred. 'It sounds dreadful, Kathy, to say that she deserted you; it's not a word she would have wanted to use. But she really had little choice in the matter; in fact, she had no choice at all.'

Her aunt was trying to explain to Kathy about the circumstances that had led to her father and her mother parting, all those years ago in 1944.

'There was a dreadful scene when Barbara – your mother – told your father that she was expecting someone else's child. I wasn't there, of course, but Albert told us about it the following morning, myself and my mother and father. We were horrified, as you can imagine, and Albert was so very bitter. But I'd always liked Barbara – she was such a pleasant and thoughtful girl – and I couldn't believe that she would behave like that, have an affair with another man, without it really meaning something. And I guessed she must be feeling terrible herself about everything. She was such a nice girl, she really was. Anyway, I went next door to see her, and she told me about how she had met this American soldier – GIs, they were called – and how they had fallen in love. She was already expecting his child, you see, my dear, and he'd been sent away from Blackpool, down to the south of England.'

'So . . . what happened? Did she go off and join him?'

'No, how could she? He'd been posted down there in preparation for D-Day. He took part in that offensive, although he wasn't part of the first landings. Barbara didn't know when she would see him again. Anyway, she stayed with her aunt and uncle, next door, until nearly the end of the year – it was 1944. Myrtle White – she was Barbara's aunt – had a sister who lived Manchester way, and Barbara went to stay with her until after the baby was born.'

'And . . . she left me here?'

'Like I said, she had no choice. It must have broken her heart to leave you; in fact, I know that it did. But your father wouldn't let her take you. And even if she had stayed here, Albert had made it very clear that he would never accept the child she was carrying as his. Yes, she left Blackpool in the December of 1944 . . . and I never saw her again. You were about eighteen months old, Kathy love, and you stayed with your Grandma and Grandad Leigh, and with me, of course. Your father was in the army until peace was declared the following year, so we looked after you.

'Albert had told her that she must never contact any of our

family ever again, and she must certainly not think of trying to get in touch with her daughter – I mean you, Kathy, dear. And eventually he divorced her; they'd been married long enough for a divorce to be possible, and there were grounds for it with her expecting a child by this . . . Nat Castillo.'

'You never met him, then?'

'No, I never met him. I knew they got married, possibly in 1945. I didn't know all the details, of course; I just put two and two together. I presume that Nat came to find her, wherever she was in Manchester, after the war was over, or he may have been given leave before the end of the war; I'm not sure. The baby would have been born by then. They would have to be married before she went off to join him in the USA. There were strict regulations about that, from what I remember. A lot of girls became what were known as GI brides, but the men had to have married them before they set sail for America. In case the fellow changed his mind, you see, and decided he didn't want to go through with it after all.

'As a matter of fact, Barbara wrote to me, just once. She wasn't supposed to, of course, and I could never let on to Albert that I'd heard from her. He'd have gone mad! She told me that the baby was a little girl, and that she and Nat and the baby were living with his parents in a town called Stowe, in the state of Vermont. I looked it up in the atlas, and it's in New England, up near the Canadian border. Whether she is still there or not I have no idea; it's quite a long time ago.'

'Then . . . she could still be alive? She probably is. She was younger than my father, wasn't she? Do you mean to say, Aunty Win, that you've known all this time that my mother might still be alive? You even knew her address, but you never told me?'

'It was the promise I'd made to your father, love. In his eyes, she was as good as dead to him, and that's what everyone else believed – what we were forced to tell them – that she'd died. I know it was dreadful, and many's the time I've wanted to break that promise, but I knew that I couldn't. It would have opened a whole can of worms, as they say. Except . . . I must confess that I told Jeff, after we were married. There's nothing that I won't tell Jeff.'

'And what did he think about it?' asked Kathy.

'He thought it was one of the most dreadful things he'd ever heard, that the poor girl had been forced to leave her baby behind; and he felt so sorry for you, that you'd been told lies about your mother. But he had to try and act normally with Albert – I know he found it hard at times, especially as they weren't very much alike. I'm sorry, my dear; I can't tell you how sorry I am. Jeff and I knew that it would probably all come to light now.

'But there's one thing you must be very sure of, Kathy, and that is that your mother loved you very much. I always told you that, didn't I? I made a point of telling you that from when you were a tiny girl. It really must have torn her apart to leave you.'

'But she had another baby girl, you say?' Kathy couldn't help feeling resentful and she knew it was obvious in her tone of voice. 'She probably has lots more children by now. She'll have forgotten all about me.'

'The Barbara I knew would never forget you, my dear,' said her aunt. She smiled reminiscently. 'I wish I could make you understand what a lovely girl she was. Yes, I know she did wrong, that she behaved very badly – so did hundreds of other girls in that dreadful war – but I believe that she really must have loved this Nat.'

'And . . . she didn't love my father?'

'Probably not in the way she should have done when she married him. Your father was a good deal older than she was, quite set in his ways when they got married. You must remember that, Kathy. He could be difficult. But he really did love her – he adored her – which made it so much worse when he found out what she'd done. I never thought, to be honest, that they were just right for one another. They might have found that they didn't get on so well had they ever lived together. They never had the chance to have their own home because your father was in the army when they married. Barbara stayed with her aunt and uncle whilst Albert was away, and then she usually came to stay here when he was home on leave.

'And then when you were born he was over the moon! He loved you so very much. In fact, I was amazed at the way he fussed over you when you were a tiny baby. That's why he refused to part with you. The mother is usually given custody when it comes to divorce but . . . well, I suppose the judge decided that she was the one at fault. So perhaps you can understand now, Kathy love, why your father behaved the way he did when you were a little girl. He was rather moody and awkward and he didn't find it easy to show you how much he cared for you. He was still grieving over Barbara.'

Kathy shook her head. 'I'm finding it hard to forgive him for the lies he told me, and her – my mother – for leaving me. It was really you who brought me up, wasn't it, Aunty Win, not my dad? He always seemed so withdrawn, so unapproachable.'

'So he was, especially at first. I really wished he would get married again and try to forget how badly he'd been hurt.'

'He nearly did, didn't he, to Sally Roberts?'

'Well, that was as near as he ever came to it. But it wasn't to be. He was upset about that as well for a while. He always had a lot to say about unfaithful women. Not that I'm saying Sally was like that; she could probably see that it wouldn't have worked out with your father. No, I'm thinking about Sadie Morris. You remember her, of course, your friend Shirley's mum? Your dad had a lot to say about that, what a flibbertigibbet she was. I think that was the word he used. She met a fellow who was staying here on holiday and went off with him. It brought it all back to your dad, you see, and his friendship with Sally was coming to an end at about the same time.'

Kathy was silent for a few moments, deep in thought about all she had heard. 'So . . . my mother was brought up by her aunt, like I was?'

'Yes, her aunt and uncle. Both her parents had been killed when she was a baby. Ben and Myrtle White; they were really good to her and I know they loved her, just as her real parents would have done.'

'And what happened to them?'

'They moved away from their boarding house next door to ours just after the war ended. They gave up the business and went to live in Marton. We lost touch with them because of all that had happened. We didn't hear any more about them. It was a pity, really; my parents had always been friendly with Myrtle and Ben, but it made it all rather difficult for the friendship to continue. I doubt that they're still alive now.'

'They were my – what would they be? – my great-aunt and – uncle, then, weren't they? And you never saw them again, you say, after they left the boarding house? So they never saw me again either? Didn't they want to know how I was getting on as I was growing up? I must have lived in the same house as them when I was a baby.'

'I'm sure they would have liked to keep in touch, my dear, but as I say, it really caused quite an upheaval. No doubt they thought it was the best policy to keep their distance. Your father was so cut up about Barbara, very angry, and deeply hurt as well. And as it was their niece who was the cause of it all I suppose they didn't want to encounter Albert again. But I'm very sure they must have thought about you a lot.'

Kathy was slowly coming round to grasping the significance of all her aunt had told her. She was filled with a mass of conflicting emotions. Disbelief at first, then shock, anger, sadness, bewilderment . . . But one thought stood out from the rest.

'How old would my mother be now?' she asked.

'Barbara would be – let me see – she'd be fifty-three. She was fifteen years younger than your father.'

'But that's no age at all,' said Kathy. 'It's more than likely that she's still alive, isn't it?'

Winifred sighed. 'Most probably she is, Kathy love . . . I'm so terribly sorry. I'm wishing now that I'd told you, years ago, but you know what your father was like, and I'd made a promise, you see. I suppose I convinced myself that what you'd never had you'd never miss; and I did try so hard to make it up to you for not having your mother with you all the time you were growing up.'

'I know, Aunty Win,' said Kathy. 'I'm finding it hard to believe that you could keep it to yourself all that time, but I'm trying to understand why you did it . . . But it's not too late, is it? It might be possible for me to find her again?'

Winifred had feared – almost dreaded – that this was what Kathy might say. 'Oh, I don't know, love,' she replied. 'I'm not sure that it would be a good idea. It's a long time ago. I doubt that they're still living in the same place, Barbara and Nat, and they'll probably have some children, grown up of course, though, now . . . She'll have made a whole new life over in the USA. It's such a long way away, and such a long time ago. Maybe it's best left alone.'

'You told me, though, didn't you, how much she loved me?' Kathy insisted. 'And that she would never forget about me? It's no use, Aunty Win; I've got to try and find her. It might not be possible . . . but at least I've got to try. It's what I want to do, what I must do, can't you see?'

'Yes, I suppose I can,' said Winifred. 'No doubt I would feel the same if I were in your shoes. But wait a little while, Kathy. Wait until after the funeral at least. And then, if you're still in the same mind, we'll try and make some enquiries. It might not be so easy; it's not as though it's the same country . . .' And Barbara might not want to be found, Winifred thought to herself, but she could not burst her niece's bubble of hope. She had already hurt and disappointed her far too much.

* * *

The church was more than half full for Albert's funeral service. He had been a popular and respected member of the congregation and the church council, and was well known generally as a former hotel owner, and a member of the darts team at his 'local'. The vicar spoke kindly of him, praising his work for the church and community.

'Albert was a quiet, unassuming man,' he said. 'A little reserved until you got to know him, but his heart was in the right place, and he had a deep affection for his family.'

An appropriate cliché, thought Kathy, a trifle cynically. There was a good deal that the vicar and countless others did not know about her father; but she was trying not to let bitter thoughts spoil the reverence of the occasion. And there were many things in her father's life for which she knew she must be thankful. She knew, deep down, that he had always loved her and he had tried to do his best for her according to his beliefs.

Tim had been almost as shocked as Kathy on hearing the revelations about Albert's secret past. After he had got over his initial reaction – disbelief at first, and then amazement that Albert could have been so deceitful for so long – he came to the same conclusion as Kathy, that her mother, Barbara Castillo as she was called, would most probably be still living. And he agreed wholeheartedly with Kathy that she must try to find her.

They sat discussing it the night after the funeral. Sarah and Christopher had been in bed for ages; Kathy and Tim enjoyed their quiet time together in the evening on their own. They were still as compatible and as happy as they had been when they were first married.

'I get the impression that Aunty Win is not entirely in favour of me trying to trace my mother,' said Kathy. 'She thinks I should "let sleeping dogs lie" as they say. On the other hand she won't try to discourage me; she knows she has caused me enough distress already. I still find it hard to believe it of Aunty Win that she could have lied to me for all these years.'

'I don't suppose it's been easy for her,' said Tim. 'They all made a promise to keep up the pretence, didn't they? And you found that letter that your mother wrote, saying she would never contact your family again. It must have been dreadful for her as well, Kathy love. And I'm quite sure what your aunt says is true, that Barbara really loved you very much.'

'Yes . . . that's what I'm trying to believe,' said Kathy. 'We know she had another little girl, and she may well have more children by now, grandchildren as well. She'll have made a whole new life over there in America.' She was deep in thought for a few moments. 'It's quite possible that she and her husband have kept the past hidden from their children. They might not know anything about me, just as I've been kept in the dark about my parents' divorce and everything. It might come as a tremendous shock to them; I'm saying 'them' although I don't know how many children there might be, my half-sisters and –brothers . . .' She shook her head bemusedly.

'All the same, I've got to try, Tim, no matter what the consequences might be. You do agree with me, don't you, love?'

'I shall be with you every step of the way, my darling,' he told her.

Kathy was unsure how to go about starting the search for her mother, and it was Tim who sorted things out for her. It turned out to be much simpler than they could have believed. Winifred had the address that was on Barbara's letter, written all those years ago, but there was no telephone number. However, a long-distance call to the telephone exchange in the town of Stowe in the state of Vermont proved fruitful. Kathy and Tim were amazed to discover that a family called Castillo were still living at the same address. And now they had the telephone number.

Kathy's hands were trembling so much that she could scarcely hold the receiver when she decided, late one night in mid October, to make the all-important call to the USA. She knew that the time in America would be different, some five or six hours behind the time in Britain, so it would be early evening over there. Who would answer the phone? she wondered. Her mother, Barbara? The thought of that filled her with wonder, but also with fear. Or might it be Nat Castillo? She had tried to conjure up a picture in her mind of what he might look like, but of course, she had no idea. And what on earth should she say? She had tried to compose a few opening remarks in her head, to ease her way into the situation. She knew that she must not say straight away that she was Katherine, Barbara's long lost daughter.

It was a woman's voice that answered the phone, giving the number and saying that it was the home of the Castillo family.

Kathy took a deep breath. 'Hello . . . Could you tell me who it is I'm speaking to, please?'

'I'm Beverley Hanson . . . Who is it you wish to speak to?' The voice, with the typical accent of a north American, sounded puzzled.

'Well, I'm wondering if that is the home of . . . Mr Nat Castillo?' asked Kathy hesitantly.

'Yes, it sure is. He's my father. I was Beverley Castillo before I married. I'm just visiting. Look . . . who are you? Where are you speaking from?'

'From a town called Blackpool in England. My name is Katherine Fielding. I was Katherine Leigh before I was married. And I have reason to believe that your father was in Blackpool during the war . . .' Kathy was finding it hard to keep her voice steady '. . . and I believe he knew some of the members of my family. It's really important that I should speak to Mr Castillo, if you don't mind.'

There was silence for a moment, then she heard the voice again. 'My father is not too well just now, but I guess he'd sure like to speak to you when he's feeling more himself again. I've heard him say that Blackpool was the place where he met our mom.' Kathy's heart gave a jolt, but she could not pluck up the courage to ask to speak to this woman's 'mom'. 'Listen . . . give me your address and your telephone number and I'll ask my dad to get back to you. Tell me again, what did you say your name is? . . . Katherine Fielding, and you used to be Katherine Leigh . . . Yes, I promise I'll tell him. Just a minute and I'll get some paper and a pen . . . Yes, I've got all that. I'll tell him to contact you as soon as he's feeling better . . . Bye for now, Katherine.'

Kathy's legs as well as her hands were trembling as she replaced the receiver. She collapsed into the nearest armchair.

'Well?' asked Tim. 'Any joy? Who was that you were speaking to?'

'She's called Beverley,' replied Kathy in a hushed voice. 'She must be my half-sister . . . She says her father will get back to me. Oh, Tim . . . whatever have I done?'

PART FOUR

Chapter Twenty-Nine

1945

Barbara was fascinated by her new home and touched by the welcome she received from Nat's parents and the rest of his family: his brother Larry and his wife, Shirley; his sister Nancy and her husband, Frank; and their children, six in all, ranging in age from five to fifteen. The warmth of their greeting and their continuing care and concern for her helped a great deal to ease the heartache she had been feeling ever since she had been forced to part with her beloved little daughter. She knew that she would never forget Katherine; there would always be a special place in her heart and mind for her firstborn child.

She often cried about her, but always in secret. She knew that she, Barbara, was in the place where she must be, with the man she loved and who loved her, and with their own little daughter, Beverley.

* * *

It had been a traumatic time for Barbara in the December of 1944, when she had left Blackpool and had gone to stay with her Aunt Myrtle's sister, Muriel, in her Manchester home. Muriel and her husband, Jack, had been very kind and understanding. They had been made aware of the circumstances and she had met with no reproach or condemnation, only sympathy and friendliness. Muriel's commonsensical approach helped Barbara to look forward, not only to the birth of her baby, but to her future life with the man who loved her.

Beverley was born in the February of 1945. Barbara was pleased that she had given birth to another baby girl, not to be a replacement for Kathy – no child could ever be that – but to give her, Barbara, the chance to start again and to be an even better mother this time. She knew that she had failed Katherine. She did not try to convince herself that she was not responsible for what had happened. She knew that both she and Nat had been guilty of wrongdoing in the eyes of many people . . . but was it wrong to fall so deeply in love? She had paid the price for it – a bitter, agonising price – but good must be allowed to come out of it. She would do her utmost to be an ideal wife and mother.

Baby Beverley did not resemble Katherine in any way, and Barbara was glad of that. Whereas Kathy was dark with Barbara's brown eyes, this baby was fair, with Nat's colouring. The little hair she had was like the fluffy down on a newborn chick and Barbara guessed she would be blonde-haired, and probably grey-eyed too, like her father, although it was hard to tell at first.

The war was drawing to a close by the time Barbara's baby

was born. 'Operation Overlord' had proved to be a victory for the Allies, although not without a few setbacks and severe loss of life. Barbara had heard intermittently from Nat and thanked God that he was still safe. The German troops were in retreat; Paris had been liberated, followed by Brussels, in the late summer of 1944. In the following March the US forces had seized a bridgehead on the Rhine and British troops were now occupying the Ruhr Valley.

Probably because the conflict was in its last stages, Nat was given compassionate leave to be with Barbara and their baby daughter in the month of April. Her divorce was now absolute, and she and Nat were married quietly at the nearest register office, with Muriel and Jack, who had proved to be true friends, as the only witnesses. Unfortunately Nat had to return to Germany to await his demobilisation, leaving Barbara behind once again. She was, however, feeling much more optimistic by now, making arrangements to join him in the USA as soon as it was possible.

She sailed from Liverpool in early October. Her Aunt Myrtle and Uncle Ben, as well as her good friends, Muriel and Jack, were at the quayside to wave goodbye as the ship sailed away. Nat had been demobbed from the US army a couple of months earlier, and the letters they exchanged told of their love and their longing to see one another again. Despite her heartache over Kathy, which was still very intense, Barbara knew she must try to look forward to her new life and, first of all, to the journey.

It was, of course, the longest journey she had ever taken, and the same was true for the many GI brides who were making the voyage along with her. It was a completely new experience for all of them, and as they exchanged stories of how they had met their husbands and about where they were going to live in the USA, the time passed quite quickly. Some of the women had young babies with them. Barbara felt very proud and pleased that she had her lovely nine-month-old Beverley with her. She did not say a word to anyone, however, about the other precious little girl whom she had been forced to leave behind.

The ship docked in New York harbour. It seemed like an impossible dream to Barbara as she caught sight, for the first time, of the Statue of Liberty and the skyscrapers of New York. They were far taller than she could ever have imagined. She remembered joking with Nat about the height of Blackpool Tower. It was true, it seemed, that everything over here was so much bigger and bolder.

Her meeting with Nat, when at last they found one another amidst the milling throng of people, was a rapturous one. Their kiss was full of the delight of seeing one another again and the pent-up longing of the last few months; there was the promise, too, of the joy and contentment of a happy life together.

Baby Beverley, held by her mother, was wide awake and staring around, especially at the smiling stranger who, of course, she could not remember. She had been only two months old when her father had seen her for the first and only time. She had been nearly squashed by their embrace, but now Nat took her from her mother as they made their way to the customs hall to deal with all the rigmarole of disembarkation and entry to a new country.

Finally, they were aboard a long-distance bus, setting off on the long journey to the state of Vermont. They headed north from the state of New York to Connecticut, Massachusetts and, finally, to Vermont.

Barbara was tired and she dozed a little at first, but as they drove through the landscape of hills and valleys, streams and woodlands, she became too enraptured by the scenery to do anything but stay awake. Never had she seen such a kaleidoscope of colour, opening up on either side and in front of her, as far as the eye could see. Vibrant colours such as she had never imagined, ranging from palest yellow through the whole spectrum – gold, orange, scarlet, vermilion, russet – to the deepest brown, as the leaves of the vast variety of deciduous trees changed from their summer green to the varying hues of autumn.

'This is fantastic!' she breathed, after she had gazed at the view in awe for mile upon mile, with Nat watching her with pleasure and pride in his country, and in some amusement as well.

'You ain't seen nothing yet!' he joked. 'Just wait till we get to Vermont. All the New England states are a sight to behold in the fall, but our little state beats the lot. It's known as the Green Mountain State in the summer but it's even lovelier in the fall.'

'Look at the deep crimson,' remarked Barbara. 'I've never seen such a vivid colour.'

'Those are maple trees,' Nat told her. 'The maple leaf is the symbol of Canada, but it's one of the most common trees in New England as well. You've heard of maple syrup?' She nodded. 'Well, our state is one of its chief producers. It's one of our specialities, pancakes with maple syrup. You sure have some treats to look forward to, Barbara . . . And not just maple syrup either,' he smiled as he leant across and kissed her.

'I'm quite overwhelmed already,' she said. 'It's just . . . so beautiful.' She really was at a loss for words.

'We're fully booked with visitors at the moment,' Nat told her. 'We are very busy for most of the year, but in the fall we get a lot of what we call "leaf peepers", folks from the South or Midwest, staying maybe for only a couple of nights and then moving on to the rest of the New England states to enjoy the scenery.'

'I'm looking forward to meeting your family,' said Barbara. 'I had a lovely letter from your mother.'

'And they're sure looking forward to meeting you too,' replied Nat. 'We'll have our own quarters, you know, at the hotel, and Mom and Pop will leave us alone when we want our privacy. It won't be like living with your in-laws, I promise you. It's just that it makes sense, with me helping with the running of the hotel. And Pop has sure made me work since I came home. He may well think of retiring in a few years' time, although I could never see him giving up altogether, nor Mom.'

Barbara was reminded of her own aunt and uncle, Myrtle and Ben, still running their Blackpool boarding house, although they were talking of selling up soon. And of Albert and Winifred next door, working along with their parents in the family business. She pushed the thoughts away, though, as she always tried to do whenever they recurred. She had been instructed, and had promised, that she would have no further contact with them. She must look to the future, the future that had now become the present.

It was good to be part of a large family after being brought up as an only child, and an orphan as well, although Barbara had never had cause to doubt the love that her aunt and uncle showed towards her. Larry and Nancy, Nat's brother and sister, soon made her feel as though she was a welcome addition to the Castillo family, and their children, all six of them, were delighted with their new little cousin.

Then there were Martha and Jacob, known as Jake, whom Nat called Mom and Pop; and Uncle Elmer and Aunt Carrie who lived nearby and helped in the hotel when they were needed.

The hotel was vastly different from anything Barbara had known before. It was a wooden building, as were the majority of houses, a very large white chalet with a wide veranda where the guests could take their ease. The family, too, if and when they had time to do so, because Barbara soon realised that they were busy almost all the year round.

The little town of Stowe, and the surrounding countryside, was as beautiful as Nat had described it to be, ringed by mountains and surrounded by woods and pastureland. The highest peak in the area, Mount Mansfield, could be seen from Barbara and Nat's bedroom window. She never tired of the view: the verdant green of the spring and summertime, the glorious tints of autumn, and the pristine white of the winter snow.

Winter began early in Vermont, as it did in all the New

England states. There was a decided nip in the air when Barbara arrived in mid October. By November it was considerably colder, and in the middle of that month the first snow began to fall. When they awoke in the morning it was to a very different scene. The rooftops and church spires, pavements, trees and bushes were now clothed in a mantle of silvery white, glistening in the early-morning sun, virgin white in the places where no feet had trodden.

Barbara soon learnt that the New Englanders adjusted quickly to the change in the weather. Houses were centrally heated, so there was no huddling round a coal fire, then feeling frozen as soon as you moved away, as was the case in England. The snowploughs were soon at work to clear the roads, and people took the weather in their stride, equipped with boots, fleece-lined coats and fur hats.

The snow remained all winter, fresh falls arriving throughout the succeeding months. There was none of the slushy brown mess left behind when a thaw came, as there was back home.

Nat was busy, not only with his duties at the hotel, but also as a ski instructor. He persuaded Barbara that she must learn to ski as most people did in Vermont. She promised she would do so, but not that year. Or the next as it happened . . .

Winter continued until the end of March, and by that time Barbara knew she was pregnant again. Their son, Carl, was born in the November of 1946, on Thanksgiving Day, to the delight of all the family members.

Another daughter, Anne-Marie, was born in the summer of 1949. Barbara and Nat decided then that their family was complete.

She did learn to ski, but not until several years later when the children were old enough to accompany their parents on a skiing holiday to the Green Mountain range.

They enjoyed many holidays, as a family, to some of the other New England states. To the city of Boston, where they walked the Freedom Trail, visited the State House of Massachusetts and climbed to the top of Beacon Hill; to the lake district and the mountains of New Hampshire; to Portland and the rocky coast of Maine; and to the beaches and quaint colonial villages of Cape Cod.

Their holiday times were precious to them, a time for relaxing together as a family and following new pursuits. They were a happy family, and although there were, inevitably, minor disagreements as the children entered their teens, there was never any serious discord.

Holidays were taken when it was convenient to Martha and Jake. Nat's father, although he had been saying for ages that he would retire, did not do so for many years, not until 1960, when he was seventy-five years of age. He and Martha then went to live in a smaller house on the outskirts of Stowe, leaving the hotel in Nat's capable hands.

Barbara had helped there too, over the years, with various kinds of work. She became responsible for the office work and bookkeeping when Nat took control of the business. Their three children were still at school. Their parents had no wish to persuade them to take part in the family business unless they wanted to do so. Barbara and Nat had high hopes for them all, that they would go on to college and do well in their chosen professions.

*　*　*

What was Katherine doing now? Barbara sometimes wondered about her, although the heartache had eased considerably over the years. Her firstborn child was there in her mind, though, as a poignant memory. She thought of her especially on her birthday each year, the last day of June. Now she would be eleven, eighteen, twenty-three . . . She might even be married.

Nat had agreed with her that it would be better if their three children, Beverley, Carl and Anne-Marie, were never told of their half-sister back in England. Barbara had begun a whole new chapter in her life when she had come to live in Vermont. To tell the children about Kathy would only cause complications and give rise to endless questions.

There were times – although only occasionally, and she never mentioned them to Nat – when Barbara felt a deep longing to know how Kathy was faring. Had she been happy with Albert and his parents, and with his sister, Winifred? Perhaps Albert had married again, in which case Kathy would have a stepmother. She felt, though, intuitively, that Winifred would have had a lot to do with the little girl's upbringing. Barbara had always been fond of Winifred, and she felt sure she would have done her very best for the little girl entrusted to her charge.

These times of anguish, fortunately, were of short duration. Barbara continued with her new life, keeping herself busy and forever seeking new interests. On the whole she was happy and contented, and she knew that Nat loved her as much as he had always done, just as she loved him.

* * *

It was in the early spring of 1971 when Barbara discovered a lump in her right breast. She made an appointment to see a doctor – something she rarely needed to do as she was normally in very good health – and within a week she was admitted to hospital for an exploratory operation.

Nat, as always, was a great support and comfort to her and did all he could to encourage her to be optimisitic about the outcome. 'Now, don't start getting all worked up about it, darling,' he said. 'It's more than likely that it'll turn out to be benign, and you'll be fine once it's been removed. You're strong and healthy, and young as well.'

She smiled. 'Not all that young, Nat.'

'You'll always be young to me,' he told her, with the same loving smile that had not diminished with the passing years. 'Still the same lovely girl I met at the Tower Ballroom.'

Barbara knew, though, that to be young – or comparatively so – was not always a good thing if what she was secretly dreading was diagnosed. The older you were, the slower the disease spread, or so she had heard.

'We won't tell the children just yet,' she said. 'Let's wait until I've had the first op, then we'll know the worst . . . or the best,' she added, trying to be optimistic.

The children by now were grown-up and no longer living at home. Beverley, who had trained to be a teacher, had married young and now had a two-year-old son. Carl, who was an accountant, had also married at an early age and he and his wife were expecting their first child. Anne-Marie, aged twenty-two, was still single and enjoying herself too much to marry and settle down just yet. She had taken after her father with her interest in all kinds of sports. She was a qualified swimming instructor, and in the winter, as her father had used to do, she taught skiing to the locals and the many visitors who came to the town. She was sharing an apartment with a girl she had met at college. And so Barbara and Nat had found themselves alone, apart from the few live-in staff that they had appointed when Nat's parents had retired.

Barbara seemed to recover well from the operation and they waited in some trepidation for the results in a few days' time. Then came the news that Barbara, secretly, had been dreading all along. The cancer – for that was what it was – had spread further than had been anticipated. A mastectomy of the right breast was deemed necessary and it was imperative that it should be done quickly.

By the autumn of 1971 it seemed that she was well on the road to recovery. She had adjusted well to her incapacity and she was hopeful that the treatment she was receiving would make sure that the dreaded disease did not recur. She had started dealing with the hotel office work again, and she and Nat were planning a trip to New York in the late spring of 1972. She had wanted to see the city for a long time, but with their commitments at the hotel and with their family, it was a visit they had never got round to taking.

She found New York to be fascinating, wonderful, awesome . . . and all so unbelievably big and bold, just as she and Nat had joked about when they first met. She loved it all: Macy's and Bloomingdale's, the huge department stores; the shows on Broadway; Central Park and Fifth Avenue; Manhattan Island; the Statue of Liberty (which she had seen, briefly, on her arrival twenty-seven years ago); the blaring horns of the taxicabs; the gigantic steaks and beefburgers; and the pancakes with maple syrup and ice cream. She was no stranger to that delicacy, but here it seemed even more tempting and delicious. It was all like a dream coming true, the other face of America that she had long imagined, so different from the quiet beauty of Vermont.

She did not tell Nat that she was feeling tired, more so than she knew she should, although it was truly an exhausting holiday. She had started to feel pains in her back and abdomen, and she thought – or had she only imagined? – that there was a small lump in her left breast. She knew that it was not likely to disappear and that she must not delay to do something about it as soon as they returned home. The pains in the other parts of her body, that she hoped might be due to tiredness, did not improve either.

Nat was devastated when she told him, the day after they had flown home. She could tell how concerned he was by the look of horror on his face, which he quickly tried to hide with a show of optimism.

The operation was done quickly, a partial mastectomy, but Barbara knew, this time, that there was no point in trying to convince herself that it was not serious. All the members of her family knew too, although they tried to hide their deepest fears with brave attempts at cheerfulness.

By the autumn of 1972 she was spending more and more time resting – she was often too weary to do much else – although she was not confined to bed. She remembered how her Aunt Myrtle had used to say, when she was feeling not too well, 'I'm not going to bed! You die in bed!' Barbara's illness, of course, was much more serious, but she was determined to keep going and remain cheerful – at least from outward appearances – as long as she was able.

Thoughts of the little daughter she had left behind in England started to loom large in her mind. How old would Kathy be now? Twenty-nine years old, probably married by now with children of her own. And what of Albert? Barbara calculated that he would be sixty-seven, not a great age at all. Surely by now he would not be as bitter as he had been about what she had done? Surely he would understand if she tried, at long last, to contact her daughter?

She sat in an armchair near the window of their bedroom, one afternoon in late autumn, looking out at the view of which she never tired. The distant mountains were already capped with white after the first snowfall, and, nearer to the house, the trees that lined the road glowed with the glorious tints of the fall: russet, scarlet, orange, gold and amber. A thick carpet of leaves covered the ground, and two boys were scuffling through them, crunching the leaves underfoot and sending them scurrying away in little flurries.

She experienced a sudden feeling of joy and contentment amidst the sadness and the fear that she sometimes felt at what she knew was inevitable. Nat was wonderful, though, at helping her to keep her spirits up. She was alone, though, at the moment, and knew that there was something she must do.

She opened the drawer of her bedside cabinet and took out a notepad and pen. The urge to write to her firstborn child was so great that it could not be ignored.

'My dear Katherine,' she began. 'I have no idea how much or how little you have been told about me . . .' She went on to explain what had happened and how she had been compelled to leave her behind. As she wrote of how she had loved Kathy and had never forgotten her, Barbara's eyes began to mist with tears. She felt overwhelmingly sad and so very tired.

She closed the pad and put it back in the drawer underneath her private documents and photograph albums. She would finish the letter another time . . .

Chapter Thirty

1973

Beverley hurried away to find her father. He was not very ill, just suffering from a bad cold which threatened to turn to bronchitis if he didn't take care. He was not in bed, just resting in his favourite armchair in the bedroom, looking out at his favourite view, now at its best, resplendent with all the glowing colours of the fall. Beverley remembered how her mother had used to sit there drinking in the beauty of the scenery, almost to the very end.

He looked round as she entered the room. He was reading, one of his favourite Jane Austen novels. Her mother, Barbara, had stimulated his interest in this very English authoress, who had long been a favourite of her own. No doubt it brought back memories now of the wife he had loved so very much.

'Dad, I've just had an intriguing phone call,' she began, 'from England. From a young woman who lives in Blackpool. That's where you met Mom, isn't it?'

'It sure is,' replied her father. 'Who was it? What did she say?' His voice was a little hesitant; he sounded almost nervous.

'She's called Katherine Leigh; at least, that was what she was called before she was married. She's called Katherine Fielding now. She said that she knew you'd been in Blackpool during the war and that you knew some members of her family. She said she would like to speak to you, Dad – to Mr Castillo, she said – but I explained that you're not too well at the moment.'

Her father's face, already pale, had blanched. 'So . . . what did you tell her?' His voice sounded husky with emotion. 'Did you say I'd get in touch with her? You've got her address, I suppose?'

'Yes, and her telephone number . . . Who is she, Dad? Did you know her? She sounded very sure of her facts.'

Nat sighed, such a deep sigh that seemed to come from the very depths of his being. 'Yes . . . I knew her. At least, I met her when she was just a tiny girl. They called her Kathy. It's a long story, Beverley. A very sad story that perhaps your mother and I should have told you. But we decided it was best not to.'

'Who is she, then, this Kathy?' Beverley asked again. She was perplexed, and concerned too, at the shock that this had clearly been to her father.

'Your mother's name was Leigh before she married me,' he replied. 'I don't think you ever knew that.' He shook his head. 'We didn't tell you, any of you, that Barbara had been married before.' He paused and took a deep breath; then, 'Kathy Leigh is your half-sister . . .' he said.

'What!' To say that Beverley was surprised would be a vast understatement. 'You mean . . . Mom had another child, back in England? But why . . . how . . . ? I don't understand. Why didn't we know about it?'

'Because it was too painful for your mother ever to talk about it.' Beverley could see that her father was very distressed and close to tears. 'Look, Beverley . . . this has come as a great shock. But it's only right, now that it's happened, that you should all know about it. Let the others know, will you, honey? Tell them I'd like to see them; I mean Carl and Anne-Marie. Come here tomorrow night, all of you. I'll probably have recovered a bit by then. As I say, it's been a shock. Then I'll tell you all about what happened; I know it's what Barbara would want.' He nodded slowly, seeming to have aged a few years in those last moments.

'OK, Dad,' she said. She kissed his cheek. 'I'll phone them right away. I won't say what it's about, just that you want to talk to us all. Now, you'll be all right, will you? I must get along because Freddie will be due home from nursery school.'

'Sure, don't worry about me.' Nat smiled. 'I've been spoilt rotten these last few days, Sam and Ellie waiting on me hand and foot. They're worth their weight in gold in the kitchen, those two. We haven't many folks in at the moment, fortunately, but I hope to be up and doing in a day or two.' He nodded, seeming now a little more composed. 'I'm OK, honey, honestly I am. See you all tomorrow.'

It had certainly been a bombshell, though, Katherine phoning like that, out of the blue. Dear little Kathy . . . What an enchanting child she had been. The image of her mother, with the same dark curls and lovely warm brown eyes. He and Barbara had not spoken of her very much as it would have been upsetting for his beloved wife; but he knew that the little girl had always been in her thoughts. He knew the times when she had been thinking particularly about her, so well attuned had he been to her various highs and lows.

He had wondered what to do ever since he had found Barbara's half-written letter to Katherine in her bedside drawer, soon after his wife's death. He had realised then how she must have longed to contact her firstborn child when she knew that her life was drawing to a close, although she had not told him, Nat, what she wanted to do. Had she changed her mind, he wondered, or had she become too poorly to complete the letter? He would never know. He had done nothing about it partly because there was no address and, also, it was unlikely that the Leigh family would still be at the same place after all these years. Maybe it was best, he had told himself, to leave well alone. He had no idea what Katherine, as a child, would have been told about her mother; there would be no point in contacting her now that her mother had died.

He was aware now, though, that he could not leave the matter unresolved for any longer. Katherine, too, must have had a desire to find her mother, although it was he, Nat Castillo, that she had asked to speak to. But why now, after all these years? Maybe she had only just found out . . . It was no use speculating. He knew he must get in touch with Katherine, either by letter or by phone. First of all, though, he had to speak to his family.

Beverley, Carl and Anne-Marie all came round the following evening, the elder two having left their spouses and children at home. Anne-Marie was still single, but was now engaged to a fellow swimming instructor. They planned to marry the following summer.

The other two were stunned, as Beverley had been, to hear the news, but their reactions were somewhat varied.

'Gee! That's great!' said Carl, always the most outspoken of the three, forever optimistic and ready to see the best in all situations. 'A long-lost sister over in little old England! It's like a fairy story, Dad. When can we meet her?'

But Anne-Marie's response was rather different. She was always more cautious, which was probably the reason she had not married at a very early age as the other two had done. She was also a very sympathetic sort of girl.

'That poor little girl!' she said. 'Just imagine how sad it must have been for her, her mother disappearing like that and leaving her all alone. Honestly, Dad, I'm very surprised at our mom. How could she have done it?'

Nat had already tried to explain that Barbara had had no choice; her first husband had been such an intransigent sort of fellow. Also, he admitted, a little embarrassedly, that she had already been expecting a baby – Beverley. He told them how he and Barbara had been so very much in love, and that he was due to be sent overseas for the final assault on Europe. It had been a traumatic time for both of them.

'I have no idea what little Kathy was told,' he said. 'I know, though, that she would have been very well looked after by her father, and particularly, I guess, by her aunt. I never met Winifred, but Barbara always spoke very highly of her.'

Beverley had had time to think about the situation. 'You must contact her, Dad, as soon as possible,' she said. 'I have a feeling, somehow, that she's just found out where her mother might be and she wants to get in touch with her. It'll be a shock to find that she's . . . no longer with us.' It was a euphemism, she knew, but the word 'dead' sounded so harsh and final. 'After all, Mom was young, wasn't she? Katherine would expect her to be still living. Perhaps you should write to her first of all, Dad, and then speak to her later on the phone? But it's down to you, of course. How do you feel about it?'

'Yes, that's the best idea,' he agreed. 'I've been stunned by this, as you all have. And many, many times I've agonised about my own share of guilt in all this. I didn't like to talk too much to your mother about little Kathy; it was so painful for her. But now, maybe there's a way of putting things right. As I told you, she was such a cute, lovable little kid. If she's grown up in the same way, and I've a feeling she will have done, then I know we'd all like to meet her.'

'Kathy, there's a letter here for you from America,' Tim called out to his wife one morning in mid November. He took it into the living room where Kathy was making sure that the children – Sarah, aged eight, and Chris, aged six – had all they needed before departing for school: PE kit; recorder and music book; last night's homework; and their dinner money, as it was a Monday morning.

Her face lit up with pleasure. 'Gosh, that's great!' she exclaimed. 'I'll read it when these two have gone,' she added in a quieter voice.

'I'm dying to know what it says as well,' said Tim, who had been just as excited as she had been after she had made contact with America. She had been a little worried at first, wondering what she had done. Would they really be pleased to hear from her? By now she had convinced herself that they would. That young woman, Beverley, had sounded very nice, if you could tell from a voice, and had promised that she would ask her father to get in touch.

'Listen,' Tim went on. 'I'll just drop these two off at school, then I'll come back and we'll read it together, OK? There's no rush to get to work now I'm one of the bosses!' Kathy knew, though, that he was joking and that he worked just as hard as any of the employees.

'All right; I'll wash up while I'm waiting,' she said.

Tim was back in less than fifteen minutes and they sat together on the settee as Kathy tore open the flimsy blue and red envelope. 'I'll read it out to you,' she said.

'*My dear Katherine,*' the letter began. '*My daughter, Beverley, told me that you had phoned. You won't remember me. I am Nathaniel – known as Nat – Castillo, and I met you in Blackpool when you were a tiny girl, just about one year old. I can only guess that you are trying to find out about your mother, Barbara, the dear girl whom I married in 1945. Kathy, my dear, I am not sure how much or how little you know, but I must tell you that Barbara and I had almost twenty-eight very happy years together. I am sorry to have to give you the sad news, though, that my dear wife . . . died . . . in the January of this year . . .*' Kathy's voice faltered as she read the last sentence, then she burst into tears.

'Oh Tim! How dreadful! I thought I'd found her.

I made myself believe I was going to meet her, and now . . . this!'

He put his arm round her and she leant her head against his shoulder. 'I never knew her,' she murmured, her voice husky with tears, 'but this is so very sad. Why didn't my father tell me about her? If only he had told me . . . even a year ago, then I could have gone to meet her. And now it's too late. I'm finding it very hard to forgive what he did to me, telling me all those lies. I tried to understand, and I thought maybe we could make things right, my mother and me. But she's . . . she's gone!' She was not crying now, just shaking her head sadly and unbelievingly.

'I'll read the rest of it to you, shall I?' said Tim gently. Kathy nodded.

'*I am truly sorry to have to impart such sad news,*' Tim read. '*My dear wife had cancer, so you will understand how tragic it has been for us. But I do know that she, too, wanted to get in touch with you, Kathy. I found a half-written letter to you that I can only assume she became too poorly to finish.*

'*I won't say any more now, but I would very much like to speak with you over the phone. I have your telephone number, so how would it be if I phone you on the last day of November – it's a Friday – at 8pm, your time? That will be early afternoon for us over here. We can have a chat and exchange news about our families. I expect you have children, Kathy? Barbara and I had three children – two daughters and a son – and now they have learnt about you they are all longing to meet you.*

'*With my kindest regards, Nat Castillo.*'

Kathy was more composed by the time Tim had finished

reading. 'Well, I think that's a splendid letter,' he said. 'I'm really sorry about your mother, darling, but this Nat seems a real nice sort of fellow. And he remembered you, didn't he?'

'So it seems,' said Kathy. She smiled sadly. 'I know they say that what you never have you never miss. And I never knew her, did I? Barbara, my mother . . . But I can't help feeling there's a great emptiness . . . here.' She touched the region of her heart. 'How I used to wish, when I was a little girl, that I had brothers and sisters, like my friends had. Shirley, in particular – you remember, Tim? I was so envious of her having a little sister and an older brother. And now I find I've got two sisters and a brother at the other side of the world. Ironic, isn't it?'

'Not really the other side of the world, love,' said Tim. 'Australia's the other side of the world. America isn't all that far away, comparatively speaking. And Nat says they all want to meet you. Just think about that!'

'Let's wait and see what he has to say when he phones,' said Kathy. 'My head's in a whirl, Tim. It's all happened so quickly, I can scarcely take it in.'

Nat Castillo phoned, as he had promised, at the appointed time. His voice, though so far away, came over loud and clear, and Kathy felt at once the warmth and sincerity of this man who had been married to her mother. They spoke for half an hour or so; he said not to worry about the cost – they had a lot of catching up to do. Kathy learnt of her half-sisters, Beverley and Anne-Marie, and her half-brother, Carl; and also a half-nephew and half-niece, Freddie and Patsy-Lou

– they would be half-cousins to her Sarah and Chris? she pondered.

Nat told her how he and her mother had met at the Tower Ballroom and had very quickly fallen in love. 'I knew she was married,' he said, 'but I guess it made no difference to the way we felt. I just hope you can understand and forgive us, Kathy. It was heartbreaking for your mother. She had no choice, though, but to do what she did. I'm only sorry that you haven't had the chance to meet her. She was a wonderful lady . . .' His voice faltered as it did more than once as he spoke of her. 'I'll write again,' he promised, 'and send some snapshots.'

Another letter with the photos arrived in a few weeks' time, after Kathy had replied to the first letter. She had told Nat of her disappointment and sorrow that she was too late to meet her mother, but of how delighted she was to hear of her three step-siblings.

Kathy gasped, and so did Tim, when they looked at the photos that Nat had sent.

'Wow! She looks just like you,' he said. 'You could be twin sisters.'

The image he was referring to was that of her mother, Barbara. One was a family group – Barbara and Nat, whom they agreed appeared to be a nice, friendly sort of guy, and the three children, taken several years ago, Nat explained, before the eldest two had married. Beverley resembled her father more than her mother, and so did the son, Carl. They had the same fairish mid-brown hair and wide smiling mouths. The younger girl, Anne-Marie, looked more like her mother. She was dark-haired and petite, although a little on the plump side.

So was Barbara, Kathy noticed. She had a full face and a nicely rounded figure, dark curling hair, and the expression in her brown eyes was the very same that Kathy saw when she looked in the mirror. Barbara looked relaxed and happy; and Kathy felt, again, a momentary sadness. Why did it have to happen like this, only a year too late?

Chapter Thirty-One

Over in Vermont the Castillo family agreed that the wrong that had been done to Katherine all those years ago must be put right, or as right as they could possibly make it. Anne-Marie was to be married in early August. What a splendid idea it would be if Katherine and her husband and children were to be there as well.

The invitation arrived in the February of 1974, and Kathy and Tim wasted no time in making all the necessary arrangements. Sarah and Chris were thrilled at the prospect of flying in an aeroplane all the way to America, but no more so than their parents; it would be their first flight as well.

There was all the excitement of getting passports, visas, and buying new clothes and suitcases, before they boarded the aeroplane at Manchester airport one early afternoon in August. They touched down in Boston some seven hours later. It was evening now by their reckoning, but it was still afternoon in the USA. It was certainly going to be a long day ahead of them!

No one was sleepy, though, with the myriad sounds and sights and impressions that followed one another in quick succession. They had no difficulty in finding Nat or, rather, he found them. He hugged Kathy, making her feel at home right away, and shook hands with Tim and the children. Then they were all bundled into his Cadillac and were soon on their way along the wide straight highways leading north.

They travelled at a speed they had never experienced before, but were not scared because the roads, though busy, did not appear so, and the traffic was well controlled. Back home in England the motorways were starting to be congested at busy times, with aggravating hold-ups and traffic jams. But there was so much more space over here, Kathy mused, as they travelled mile after mile through scenery that became more beautiful – with mountains, river valleys, and great stretches of verdant trees and pasture land – as they went northwards.

The Castillo family home, where only Nat resided now, along with his live-in employees, was a comfortable, homely hotel, now partially converted to a motel. It was very different from Holmleigh, the hotel-cum-boarding house where Kathy had lived as a child. There was plenty of room for the Fielding family, especially as Nat had restricted the number of guests staying there in the weeks leading up to and following Anne-Marie's wedding.

The following day Kathy and her family had the pleasure of meeting some of the members of Nat's large family –

his brother and sister, and just a few of their six sons and daughters; and there were numerous grandchildren who would all be present at the wedding. Nat's mother and father – Mom and Pop – now well into their eighties but still spry both in body and in mind. They told Kathy how much they had loved Barbara and how her death had saddened them.

'But now you're here with us, my dear,' said the old man. 'We couldn't be more delighted to see you and your family. Gee! It's almost like having Barbara back with us, isn't it, Martha?'

The dear, old, rosy-cheeked lady nodded and smiled. She hugged Kathy. 'Yes, it sure is wonderful,' she said. 'And you've brought a smile back to our Nat's face, honey!'

Then there were her half-siblings: Beverley, her husband Greg and their five-year-old son, Freddie. Beverley was the young woman whom Kathy had spoken to on the phone – they had conversed again since that first call – and she proved to be just as friendly and welcoming as her voice had suggested she would be. It was Beverley who spoke out loud what was in all their minds.

'You're more like Mom than any of us,' she said, 'and we sure are glad to meet you at last.' The two half-sisters, less than two years apart in age, hugged one another without any restraint, just a real feeling of sisterhood. They knew at once that the two of them, possibly even more so than the rest of the family, would become firm friends.

There was Carl too, with his wife Donna, and their cute little two-year-old Patsy-Lou; and Anne-Marie with her ruggedly handsome fiancé, Bruce, who would be married in a few days' time.

The wedding took place at a typical New England church, a white wooden building with a tall spire, on top of a hill and surrounded by maple trees. The church was almost full with the many wedding guests – countless numbers of relatives of both the bride and groom as well as numerous friends – and other well-wishers too, who had come along to share in the joy of the popular young couple.

The reception afterwards was held at the family hotel, an informal affair where Kathy and Tim and their children had the pleasure of meeting their many new relatives, and friends of the family too, who had heard of the daughter back in England.

Anne-Marie and Bruce had planned a honeymoon in San Francisco, far away on the west coast of the USA. They were to set off on the long journey later that evening; but before that, as Anne-Marie told Kathy, there was something that she wanted to do.

They left their children behind in the care of the many relatives, then Nat and his three children and their spouses, with Kathy and Tim, made their way, in two cars, back to the same church on the hill.

Barbara's grave was in a secluded spot at the edge of the cemetery, beneath an overhanging willow tree. There were flowers in the glowing colours of late summer – red roses, yellow and orange dahlias and early flowering chrysanths – in a large earthenware vase. They looked fresh and vibrant, and Kathy guessed that Nat renewed them frequently.

The family group stood in silence as Anne-Marie placed her wedding bouquet of white roses next to the vase of flowers. 'God bless you, Mom,' she said quietly. It was Anne-

Marie's day and she wanted her beloved mother to be a part of it.

Kathy read the gold lettering on the black marble headstone.

'Barbara Jane Castillo, 1920–1973. Beloved wife of Nat and dearest mother of Beverley, Carl and Anne-Marie.' And below, in brighter letters that must have been added fairly recently, 'And mother of Katherine, in England.'

Kathy's eyes misted with tears. 'Thank you, thank you . . .' she whispered. 'That is . . . so lovely.' Beverley, standing next to her, took hold of her hand and they smiled at one another.

Kathy's heart was too full for words. She felt very close to the mother she had never known. She knew that not meeting Barbara was something she would always regret. But now she had found two sisters and a brother . . . and England and the USA were not all that far apart.

Author's Note

The question I am most frequently asked as a novelist is 'Where do you get your ideas?' It is not easy to answer. Sometimes they just happen, but more often they arise from an incident in my own life or in that of a member of my family or a friend. In this novel it was an incident in the life of my sister-in-law, Linda, that gave me the initial idea, and I thank her for that.

The story, however, is a work of fiction, and all the characters and happenings therein exist only in my mind.

I decided to set this book in my hometown of Blackpool, as I did with my earlier books. The setting of Blackpool is, of course, real, and the boarding house where the Leigh family live resembles the one in North Shore where I was born and lived as a child.

The childhood memories are mine, as are the recollections of the day to day life of a primary school, experienced during my time as a teacher of infant and junior school children.